W9-BCN-244

PATPONG SISTERS

Hi Gerry
สวัสดี เจริ

— Cleo
คลีโอ

PATPONG SISTERS

*An American Woman's View
of the Bangkok Sex World*

Cleo Odzer

 Blue Moon Books • *New York*

ARCADE PUBLISHING • NEW YORK

With special thanks to Barney Rosset for his advice, editorial guidance and friendly support in seeing this book through from manuscript to publication. We shared an experience—my love for Thailand and his—very fortunately for me because it has not been a short trip but rather a long and arduous journey.

Copyright © 1994 by Cleo Odzer

All rights reserved. No part of this book may be reproduced in any form or by any electronic or mechanical means, including information storage and retrieval systems, without permission in writing from the publisher, except by a reviewer who may quote brief passages in a review.

FIRST EDITION 1994

Library of Congress Cataloging-in-Publication Data

Odzer, Cleo
    Patpong sisters : an American woman's view of the Bangkok sex world /
by Cleo Odzer.   — 1st ed.
        p.   cm.
    ISBN 1-55970-281-8
    1. Prostitution—Thailand—Bangkok. 2. Child prostitution—Thailand—
Bangkok. 3. Teenage prostitution—Thailand—Bangkok. 4. Sexually transmitted
diseases—Thailand—Bangkok. I. Title.
HQ242.55.B3038 1994
306.74'5'09593—dc20   94-15551

Published in the United States by Arcade Publishing, Inc., New York,
and Blue Moon Books, Inc., New York
Distributed by Little, Brown and Company

10 9 8 7 6 5 4 3 2 1

PRINTED IN THE UNITED STATES OF AMERICA

Introduction

Some things on Patpong have remained the same since the 1970s: bars, sex shows, women for sale, men shopping for women, venereal disease. Some things have changed. There are now more bars and different types of bars; a new generation of women and more of them; a greater variety of sex shows; and another type of sexually transmitted disease—AIDS.

This account of Patpong took place between 1988 and 1990. Only in the past few years has Thailand acknowledged having an AIDS problem. Since most of the country's foreign income comes from tourism, the government had previously tried to hide the extent of its infection. The first AIDS case was diagnosed in 1984, but with so little mention of AIDS in the newspapers, Patpong and the Thai populace considered themselves safe from it until very late. In 1988, most bar girls had never heard of it.

Buying sex is common for Thai males at every level of society, and as of 1993, they've hardly slowed the practice. *"Kwai"* prostitutes, similar to battlefield camp followers, are women who travel with the *kwai*, the water buffalo that are hired to plow the ground for crops. The majority of Thailand's population is rural and lives off the land. A poor farmer with no *kwai* of his own must hire one and, while doing so, he engages the services of the prostitutes. The *kwai* and the women then travel to the next farmer. Not only are many *kwai* prostitutes HIV positive, but an alarming number of the farmers' wives are also turning up infected. The men contract the virus, pass it to their wives, who then pass it to their unborn children.

From *kwai* prostitutes to high-priced movie-star call girls, the virus is spreading through Thailand. The government is now encouraging the use of condoms, but beyond that, only fundamental alterations in perceiving gender roles will change Thai men's sexual behavior patterns. The Thai Population and Community Development estimates that 5.3 million Thais will be infected with the AIDS virus by the year 2000.

The major difference between present-day Patpong and the time of this story is the fear of AIDS. But the girls are still there. The sex shows are still there. And the customers are still there.

Diagram of Patpong Area

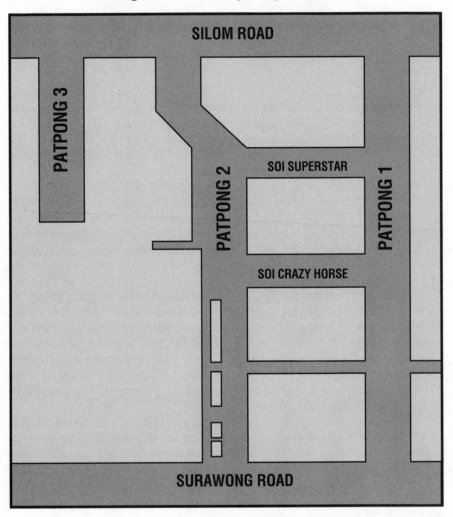

1.

June 1988

Narrator: If life can be chosen, who would want to stand here. But since we are here, all we ask for is understanding . . . and a chance to live the hope that one day we can walk away. We are life, we are part of society. We have to struggle for a better life. There are many roads leading to it, and the one we are walking on is called Patpong.

Music: "Part-time Lover"

—From the Patpong musical presented by Empower, 1987

At night, the streets of Patpong, a red-light district in Bangkok, Thailand, teemed with Thai men attempting to hustle customers into bars. As I turned the corner onto Patpong 2, one fell into step beside me. My being a female did not discourage him. He noted only the blond hair and blue eyes, which marked me a foreigner and therefore a potential source of revenue. Or, he may have just wanted to meet me, or if not, then to annoy me. Western women were still rare on Patpong at that time.

"Want see Pussy Show? Pussy Smoke Cigarette. Pussy Open Bottle. Pussy Ping Pong Ball Show."

"*Mai ow* (Don't want)," I said without looking at him. I hoped speaking Thai would impress him into not thinking of me as a tourist. Maybe he'd go away. He didn't. He continued to walk with me and held a plastic card in front of my face. In English, German, and Japanese, it listed the sex shows performed in his bar. In case I didn't want to read, he cited them for me aloud: "Pussy Write Letter. Snake Show. Eggplant Show. Banana, you see already?"

"*Du leeow* (Have seen already)," I lied. I hadn't seen a show yet. I supposed I'd have to sooner or later. I aimed a half smile at the tout; I'd probably have to befriend all these characters too. They were part of my research into Patpong prostitution. I'd have to know everything that went on in the area, which included three parallel streets: Patpong 1 and Patpong 2, plus the short *Soi* Jaruwan, also known as Patpong 3 or *Soi Katoey*, Homosexual Street.

Though I'd passed through Patpong many times, I'd not yet begun the research. The professors on my dissertation committee had advised me to take time to learn the language first. However, they'd suggested I do this for only the

1

first three months. So far it had already been a year. I had to start studying Patpong soon, but I needed an inspired burst of courage to launch me into it.

Patpong was a tourist strip with bars next to, and on top of, one another. The women working in the bars were prostitutes. Bar work was only half the job. The real money came from selling sex. Polygamy and prostitution have long been a privilege of Thai men, but during the Vietnam War Thailand became proficient in serving up its women to foreigners. American military personnel flocked to the country for R&R, rest and recreation, which they called I&I, intoxication and intercourse.

The name *Patpong* came from the Patpong family, which owned a strip of the land that lay between the roads Silom and Surawong. Those roads made up the heart of Bangkok's business district. Contrasting the tall modern buildings surrounding it, the Patpong streets held dumpy two-story structures.

Though the Vietnam War may have boosted Patpong into the entertainment industry, Thailand's reputation as a sex paradise took off on its own at the war's end. Germany arranged cheap charter flights. Holland organized sex tours. As Taiwan and Japan grew prosperous, their males flew in too. Many Americans from the war chose not to go home. The saying was that there were no MIAs in Vietnam; in reality they were all MIBs—Mischiefing In Bangkok.

The Children's Rights Protection Center estimated that two million females in Thailand earned their living from prostitution, including 800,000 children under sixteen. During the year of my study, 1988, men poured into Thailand from all parts of the world. Some ethnic groups had their own areas, so the women specialized in certain people. Those working in the Arab sections learned to speak Arabic. Others focused on French or Japanese or, if they worked the cargo dock, perhaps Burmese. In Bangkok, two main areas targeted Westerners, *Soi* Cowboy and Patpong. Thais called Westerners—Americans, Europeans, Australians, Israelis, etc.—*farangs*.

Many male *farangs* who resided in Thailand were there because of the bar girl scene and because of the way they were treated as royalty. They viewed Thailand as a paradise for foreign men. One morning in my apartment building, while reading the English language newspaper that the building kept in the lounge downstairs, I overheard two journalist neighbors—one Australian, one English, both male—tell a joke.

"This *farang* dies and goes to heaven," said the English neighbor with the sports section resting on his knee. "He arrives at the pearly gates and Saint Peter is there checking the book. 'My, my, you've led an exemplary life' says Saint Peter. 'And because you've been so good, we're going to grant you all the wishes you want. What do you fancy?' 'I have only one wish,' the *farang* answers. 'Send me back to Thailand. I want to live in Thailand forever.' 'Very well,' Saint Peter says. And presto! the man gets his wish. He's back in Thailand. But guess what! He is reincarnated as a Thai man!"

"A THAI! Bloody hell!" The two *farangs* laughed and made agony faces. "Poor sod!" Ho ho ho.

I pretended to be absorbed in my newspaper. I couldn't join their merriment, for as a Western female I'd been excluded. They didn't regard me with any more esteem than they had for Thai men. Western men often used the notion of Thailand as a foreign male's sexual utopia to needle Western women. The number of female *farangs* living in Thailand was far smaller than that of males, and *farang* men treated them as outsiders who didn't belong. "What are YOU doing here?" was the men's attitude to me, whether spoken with a chuckle or implied; it served to perpetuate the idea of Thailand as "For Men Only."

"Pussy Write Letter Show? You want see? I take you," the tout offered again. He'd followed me the entire length of the block.

Well, why not? I thought. I'd have to do this eventually. Why not take the first step? Here was the opportunity to set forth on my task. Studying Patpong could also be a way to retaliate against Western men. By becoming an expert on Patpong, I'd be invading their privileged territory. If I could know everything about prostitution on Patpong, I could make it mine too.

"Okay," I said to the tout with determination. I'd found the well of motivation I needed to start the research, only it wasn't fueled so much by courage as by pique. "Show me."

He led me to *Soi* Crazy Horse, a short street that connected Patpongs 1 and 2, and up a staircase into Winner's, a long and narrow bar. A naked Thai woman soaping herself in a shower caught my eye first. Then I flashed on the two stages on either side of her. On one stage, a naked woman danced with a Coke bottle in her hand. Fair-haired heads of Western men sitting at tables speckled the dark areas against the walls. All looked toward the other stage, where another naked woman squatted over her Coke bottle. I noted that the neck of the bottle was inside her vagina as a few of the men turned to notice me. Oh dear, how could I make my face look nonchalant? The tout bequeathed me to a hostess who directed me to a table on a raised platform along the wall. Applause followed a loud popping sound, signaling that the woman onstage had opened the bottle successfully.

Immediately after I sat down, someone in see-through lace slid next to me and offered her hand stiffly, as if about to make a karate chop. Shaking hands was not a Thai custom but Patpong men and women did it, thinking it was the *farang* greeting for all occasions.

"Hello. What you name?" she said.

"Cleo, and you?"

She let me shake her passive hand, then she laid her index finger along the length of her nose and said, "Pong."

By this time I knew that laying one's finger along the nose signified "me"; I would have done it by pointing to my chest. At the beginning I'd had no idea why people were touching their noses and misinterpreted it as meaning either they were thinking about something or indicating a bad smell.

"Drink," said Pong. I ordered her one as I knew I was supposed to. A "drink" meant a cola or an orange juice. Alcohol was one of the pleasures Thai culture reserved for men. Though some Thai women did drink, they berated themselves for doing it. When I asked for club soda, Pong approved. "Cleo no drink whiskey, very good."

Pong had puffy, shoulder-length hair and a long, skinny body. Bright purple lips punctuated her sharp-angled face. We smiled at each other. Here was my first informant.

In Thai, I asked her, "How old are you?"

"Twenty-eight," she answered in an English no better than my Thai.

"Are you from Bangkok?" I asked in Thai.

"No, come from North," she said in English. Most Patpong women came from outside Bangkok, from the impoverished countryside. Their work often supported dozens of relatives back home.

Pong scooted over close to me. The see-through lace barely reached her crotch, leaving her legs bare as they pressed against mine. Between Pong and the women on stage, I felt overwhelmed by naked female flesh.

Somehow we managed to exchange morsels of information in the wrong languages. As facts piled up, I realized I had to write them down or they'd crowd each other out of my brain. "Where's the toilet?" I asked in perfect Thai grammar. That phrase was practiced often in the language class at A.U.A. (American University Alumni), where I went for lessons during the day.

Pong took my arm to escort me but detoured to the dressing room first to show me her shiny red dress. "Is pretty or not?" she asked, clearly finding it beautiful. She held it out. "Cleo try on."

"Oh no, no. That's alright. Thank you, Pong."

"PONG," she corrected me. I'd used the wrong *p* and the wrong tone. Thai was a tonal language, so saying the right word with the wrong tone could result in calling someone bad luck (*suey*, midtone) when you meant to say she was beautiful (*suey*, rising tone). "My friend," she said next, motioning to a naked person there.

The friend shook my hand. Female? Male? I couldn't decide. Completely naked in the dressing room, she was obviously a go-go girl on a break, but something in me said this was a male. Whatever she was, she was charming and modeled her own microminiskirt for me.

"Cleo try?" she also offered.

"No, no. Thank you."

She was shorter and thinner than my five foot three, one hundred and six pounds. She had a pixie haircut and small bare breasts above the skirt. But I still read "male." Very disorienting. It almost made me dizzy.

As Pong led me out of the dressing room, she whispered, "*Katoey*. Ladyboy," meaning a male who's had a sex change operation.

When we returned to the table, Pong had to leave for the stage. Following the pattern I'd noticed with previous performers, she danced one song nude and then prepared for a trick show. I hid my face behind a glass of club soda and glanced around. Not too many people were watching me watch Pong. I wondered if they thought I was gay. Onstage Pong wrapped a Magic Marker in toilet paper before inserting it in her vagina. Then she poised herself over a sheet of paper. One leg crossed over the other; her arms supported her as she swung her hips to and fro. She wrote, "Good Luck to America." Pong had told me she'd had only one year of school. I knew she couldn't read or write more than her name in Thai. She had to be even less knowledgeable of English. The fluency of her "Good Luck to America" must have attested to years of those shows.

Back at my table, she handed me the paper. She'd written it for me. It also contained her name and number, 22. A government regulation required employees to wear number badges. The girls wore them on their lace coverings, making it easy for men to pick someone and order her a drink. I thanked Pong for the gift and folded it for safe keeping—my first artifact. I felt thrilled to have found myself a contact and envisioned a long-term close relationship with Pong, an anthropologist with her informant. I'd achieved a foothold in the project—now how to follow through?

"Next week, you want to go to dinner with me?" I asked her in Thai. "I'll pay the bar." Everyone in Bangkok knew how prostitution on Patpong worked. Every Saturday, a column in the English newspaper explained the routine. First, you paid the bar to take the girl off work. Then you made arrangements with the girl herself for sex, thereby profiting both the girl and the bar. Though I had no intention of buying sex or paying Pong for anything, I figured she'd be happy to get out for a night and we could become acquainted. I didn't know when or how to tell her I wanted to interview her. I'd have to wait till we established a rapport.

"Thank you," she said in English. She leaned her arm on my leg. Did she think I wanted her for sex? Well, it didn't matter what she thought at this point. We were going to be best buddies, I just knew it.

"Friday, I'll come back and we'll go out and have fun," I promised. "Now I must leave."

She yelled "CHECK BIN" to the hostess. Instead of asking for a check or a bill, Thais said "check bill," which they pronounced "check bin."

A wide man in a gold lamé gown with matching gold high heels delivered the "check bin." As I looked it over, I spotted the 250 *baht* ($10) charge "for the show," a small fortune in Thailand. The tout had sworn there'd be no cover charge. I realized Winner's was a "ripoff bar." It was one of the eight bars in Patpong that overcharged customers and resorted to violence to collect. I knew the door would be locked until I paid. Tourist magazines advised what to do if you found yourself in this situation—PAY. Then go to the tourist police and complain. After a hassle, the money would be refunded. But I couldn't go to the police. I'd finally found myself an informant; I didn't want to lose her now.

Pong's face set into a stony shape as she gazed at the stage, pretending not to notice anything was amiss. She probably had to sit through this ordeal several times a night. Beneath his sparkly eye shadow, the man's eyes glared as if daring me to protest. Would he hurt me if I made a fuss? His muscular form did not match a female shape, despite the ruffles on his hem. Clipped in rhinestones, his long hair swooped to the side of his brow. I paid.

Outside, I felt relief at having escaped a ripoff bar unharmed. No wonder the touts were so eager to muster clients. They must have received a commission for each person brought to the bar.

What about my promise to buy out Pong Friday night? Should I find myself someone from an honest bar instead? What if I lacked the gumption to go through all that again? If I didn't ride this out, it might be another year until I met someone else.

A Thai appeared beside me. "Hello," he said. "You want a man?"

A man? What was he asking? Was he offering himself for sale? Or was he offering to sell me to someone? Whichever it was, here was another contact for me. I gave him a friendly smile and said, "Who are you?" I found his baby face attractive. His Thai eyes held a glimmer of humor.

He stopped and shook my hand. "Jek. What's your name?"

I told him and said I lived a block away off Silom Road—and what kind of man did he mean? I didn't want to say outright I didn't know what he was talking about. I hoped I'd figure it out as he went on.

"What kind of man you like? Big one?"

"Oh no, I hate big ones. I don't like too tall or too muscular."

"How you like then? What type you think is handsome?"

"Well, like you. You're perfect," I said honestly.

"Oooh-aaah!" he said in a drawn out exclamation. He looked away with an ecstatic face. "Where you go now?"

"I'm going home."

"I come with you?"

"NO! I'll go alone." I started walking and he walked with me. "You work here?" I asked him.

"Over there. Patpong 3. *Soi Katoey*. Many gay bar."

"Are you gay?"

He looked horrified. "Only work there. My job."

His pronunciation was atrocious, so we spoke half in my scrambled Thai and half in his scrambled English. In this manner, I found out that Jek was a "bringer." He brought lovers to people. He said he'd been working in Patpong for five months and had graduated from Chulalongkorn University, majoring in business administration.

"Do you take people to ripoff bars?" I asked.

He laughed. "How you know?"

I didn't want to admit I'd just been to one. "How much commission do you make?"

"One hundred *baht* each customer, five hundred *baht* for group of four. You go hotel with me?"

"Uh . . . well, no, not tonight, thank you." Was he selling himself? Or, now that I'd proven friendly, did he view me as available for sex? While *farang* men thought all Thai women were up for sale, Thai men thought all *farang* women gave it away free to anyone.

6

"Have short-time hotel, very nice, very clean."

I laughed. "Maybe next time," I said in a tone of voice a *farang* man would know meant "Never!"

When we reached the place where I had to turn off the avenue, I said goodbye and he shook my hand again. He had a great smile.

As I continued home, I laughed to myself, thinking I should buy a little cutie for an hour of sex to get an angle on the other side of prostitution, the customer's side. Wouldn't that be what they called "participant observation"? Jokingly, I composed a letter in my mind to my professor: Dear Dr. Rapp, I've assessed the situation and found a need for a slight change in research design. In addition to studying Thai prostitutes, I will investigate the psychological consequences to the customer. To this end, I have found myself an adorable Thai man . . .

THE SHOW PROGRAME FOR THIS NIGHT
PUSSY PINGPONGBALL PUSSY SHOOT BANANA
PUSSY SMOKECIGARETTES. PUSSY WRITELETER.
LESBIAN SHOW. BOY AND GIRL FUCKING SHOW.
BEER BOTTLEPOKER PUSSYOPENBEER BOT TLE.
PUSSY PICK THE DESERT WITH CHOPSTICKS
BIGDILDO SHOW. FISH PUSH IN SIDEHER.
EGG PUSH IN TOHERCUNT. CAN DLE SHOW.
ORAL SEX AND SEX 69 SHOW.
LONG-EGGPLANT PUSH INTO HER CUNT.
PUSSY DRINK WATER BOTTLE SHOW.
BLUE MOVIES FILM TOO GIRL AND SNAKE
SEXY DANCE.

STRIPTEASE.
BANANEN STECKT INDIE SCHEIDE UND WIRFTAUS
ZIGARETTEN MIT DIE SCHEIDE,
BRIEFE SCHREIBEN MIT SCHEIDE.
GUMMI-SCHWANZ STECKT INDIE SCHEIDE
FLASCHEN STECKT INDIE SCHEIDE.
EIER STECKT IN DIE SCHEIDE.
PINGPONG BALLE.STECKT INDIE SCHEIDE-
UND WIRFT AUS.
FISCH STECKT IN DIE SCHEIDE.
LESBISCH SHOW (FRAU UND FRAU)
MANN UND FRAU-GESCHLECHTSAKT.

Tout's Card

2.

June 1988

Karnjanauksorn (1987) believes 200,000 Thai women work as prostitutes in Europe. The Thai Development Newsletter (1986: 13) reports 50,000 Thai prostitutes in Japan. In 1988, Skrobanek (Rattanawannatip: 18) stated that "15 to 25 per cent of all Thai women between the ages of 15-30 are prostitutes." During a debate over the British documentary Foreign Bodies, about prostitution in Thailand, no one argued when Skrobanek (from the Women's Information Center) said, "We are turning into a SIC—sex industry country—not a NIC [newly industrializing country]" (Usher, 1988: 31).

I grew up in a New York City apartment overlooking Central Park and experienced my teens during the 1960s. While I was espousing the wildness of that decade—picketing, smoking pot, rock-and-rolling—my father developed Parkinson's disease and died. By the time I turned twenty-one, my family's money had run out, leaving me with the values of the Love Generation but little else—no money, no skills, no sense of responsibility or allegiance to the work ethic, no goal in life. Disgruntled and empty, I gave my Yorkshire terrier to my mother and escaped the city that seemed to have no place for me.

First I spent two years roaming Europe, supporting myself with occasional modeling jobs. Then, hearing of a Freak community on a beach in India, I headed there. Six years later, after the death of a close friend and with my own life in ruin, I landed back in New York needing a new philosophy and purpose.

How to pull myself together and move in a different direction? The horizon seemed to hold nothing but shadows of things I'd lost.

I enrolled in school.

Feeling like an alien in my home culture, I drifted toward anthropology and the study of foreign lifestyles. I loved it. Learning about the development of my species, from caves to skyscrapers, drove me to do the same for myself—from beach bum to computer whiz. Mastering theories raptured my brain as well as any psychotropic drug I'd taken. Knowledge was on par with LSD. I could have studied forever, but the student loans guaranteed by the government would only carry me as far as a Ph.D.

I had a few years of financial aid left to fund the field work required for the doctorate degree. I still longed for Asia, but now I wanted to return there in a manner that had meaning. I needed a mission.

Charged with dedication and commitment, I decided to do something magnificent for the prostitutes of Patpong. My friend who'd died in India had once married one. Exactly what I would do for them, I didn't know yet.

When I first arrived in Thailand, I applied to its National Research Council for permission to study Patpong. They rejected the topic and told me to change it if I wanted to stay in the country. Prostitution was illegal in Thailand. It was, nonetheless, a major source of foreign income, a situation the government didn't like to admit. They didn't want someone snooping around and calling attention to it.

My Australian neighbor advised, "You better change your topic, kiddo. How 'bout silk factories? They'd like you to write about that. Might bring in business."

After mulling it over, I resolved not to change objectives. My concern lay with the women of Patpong, whom I felt were unjustly condemned as abominations of society and disgraces to womanhood. From my studies in preparation for the trip, I knew that Thailand considered these women to be bad human beings. In reality, they supported entire families and even communities. I wanted to spotlight what the Thai government wished to hide. It accepted the money generated by prostitutes but called them loathsome at the same time. My topic had become a cause I believed in. And I needed to do something worthwhile to make up for the years I frittered away in hippydom. Besides, silkworms didn't rouse me.

After growing up in the '60s, rebelling against authority was second nature to me. It never entered my mind to notify my professors of the National Research Council's decision. I doubted the Council had an enforcement branch. So far, no one had knocked on my door demanding to know my new topic. I did have to be careful not to be noticeable, though. Since the Council had rejected my proposal, they also had refused me a research visa. I lived in Thailand on Double-Entry Non-Immigrant visas and had to cross the border every three months. I didn't want to find myself blacklisted next time I faced Immigration.

Patpong Go-Go

Patpong 1

Three days after I met Pong, I headed back to Winner's to buy her out of bar work for the night. I looked for Jek as I passed the corner of Patpong 3 and Silom Road. He was there, sitting on someone's parked motorbike. He jumped down and shook my hand.

"Oah, we meet again. Where you go now?" he asked. When Thais greeted each other they didn't say, "How are you" the way Westerners do. They said "Where are you going?" One was not supposed to answer with geographic details any more than English speakers were supposed to give health particulars. The Thai equivalent of "Fine, thanks" was to make a directional motion with the chin and go on to another subject. As someone who hadn't been raised with this custom, I found it hard not to say where I was going.

"To *Soi* Crazy Horse."

"What you doing?"

I didn't think I should tell him about the research so I covered by saying, "I was looking for you."

"Oah!"

Before he could get the wrong idea, I added, "I just wanted to say hello and see if you were here."

"I always here. Never have day off. We go hotel?"

I still didn't know if he was selling himself or not, so I probed: "Is the hotel expensive?"

"Short-time not expensive. We go now? I pay hotel."

Well, at least it was flattering to know he didn't view me as a customer wanting to buy his time. "Not today," I said. "Maybe next month." I started to walk away.

He stopped me to shake my hand goodbye. "Okay, then. I wait you pass again."

"Uh, sure thing."

I walked on thinking I had to watch what I said to that one, because he was too dangerously good-looking to play around with. He might think I was serious. Or worse—what if I took him up on it?

Winner's Bar, at the early hour of 8 p.m., was devoid of customers. Seven girls danced naked. About thirty more sat at tables against the wall. Pong looked surprised to see me. She and the lady-boy *katoey* waved from the stage, then Pong rushed to hug me without bothering to cover herself first. I gave her the 500 *baht* ($20) to buy her out for the night, and she went to pay the bar and dress. As she passed the stage, she waggled the money at the other girls. I wondered again if I wouldn't be better off having an informant whose place of employment didn't specialize in swindling foreigners.

We taxied to the Brown Sugar jazz club near the A.U.A. language school, the only restaurant I could think of. I hoped I wouldn't run into fellow students. I hadn't told Pong about the research yet and I worried someone would say something offensive to her.

Menu in hand, I watched to see how she'd order without being able to read the selection. She frowned at it, then asked the waiter if he had sandwiches. We settled in to await our food.

Pong said, "Cleo give money buy cigarette, okay?"

I gave her the money. When she left the table, I hurriedly wrote in my book: "Asked for money easily, expecting people to give her whatever she desired."

She returned with a pack of cigarettes and lit one. Now I had to make us friends. I wanted her to trust me so she'd tell me her life story. I told her, "I used to be a hippy. I lived on a beach in India." I thought that would ingratiate me as a fellow renegade, but she merely nodded and looked around at the other diners. "I came to Thailand during that time and fell in love with it," I continued. "Eventually I had to give up my home in India. Drugs and parties nearly did me in. I had to change my way of life. Now I'm a serious student seeking knowledge to make the world a better place." Pong seemed disinterested, but I went on anyway. "Well, maybe I can't change the world, but I'd like to do something for women."

Here was the opening to tell her about the research, about how I'd previously noted the strength of Patpong women and wanted to portray them as heroines rather than the monsters Thai society believed them to be.

Pong didn't appear to be listening, though. Her attention was focused across the room on a table of businessmen. So I asked her in Thai, "Are you married?" which is actually asked "are you married yet?" In Thailand, it was unthinkable for someone to go through life without a spouse.

"Husband. Have," she replied in English.

"Where is he?" I asked in Thai.

"Work bar," she said. "Husband, Islam man." She touched her nose. "Pong, Buddhist. Before, have husband from Iran."

In Thai, I confirmed, "Your husband works at Winner's?" She nodded. I didn't ask how he felt about her working there because that would imply I thought he had reason to disapprove. I had to be careful in Patpong conversations never to appear critical.

I learned that Pong came from Northern Thailand. She hadn't been able to go to school because of her family's poverty. "Papa die. Mama and younger sister, no money. Last month, younger brother have accident." She laid a finger on her nose. "Pong sick," and described her illness—heart disease.

At this I suspected she was engaging in a hustle. A hustle, even if true, could be discerned by the string of misfortunes and the manner in which they were presented, as if recited often.

"Do you send your family money?"

"If I no send, they no eat. Send money for aunt and uncle too. Nephew need pencil for school."

Newspapers often reported the destitution found in rural Thailand, and Patpong women were adept at using the well-known facts to stir compassion and generosity in foreigners. Men had told me the depths of altruism the bar girls inspired in them and the large sums it cost. I figured Pong's rundown of her family's plight might be followed by a plea for charity. To change the subject, I asked in Thai if she'd travelled anywhere.

"Pong go *Ko* Samui," she told me in English. Samui Island in southern Thailand was a tourist resort where foreign men sometimes took bar girls for a few days.

"Alone?" I asked knowing otherwise.

"With German man. He pay bar for one week." She laughed, knocked my shoulder, and raised two fingers. "Only two time make love. Other time, Pong tell him no feel good. Sick. Cannot."

I laughed with her. "Do you have children?"

"Boy and girl."

"Have any pictures of them?"

She did and other pictures too. One was of her in a hotel room. "Not pretty," she said. "Too skinny." Thais generally found skinniness ugly because of its association with poverty. I saw pictures of a Japanese boyfriend and an American one. She displayed the American's address and said she had many, many addresses.

After dinner she wanted to go back to her bar. She said she'd introduce me to her husband. She seemed keen on returning to Patpong, suggesting a variety of Patpong places we could visit if I didn't want to stay at Winner's. She didn't really want to go anywhere except Patpong and any place on Patpong would do, though her bar or someplace close to it was best. We settled on the SuperStar Discotheque across the hallway from Winner's. Since it was still early, we'd wait in the bar till disco time.

"Okay, but I don't have to pay for the show again, right?"

"No more. Cleo friend now."

So we returned to Patpong. We left the taxi on the avenue and went by foot through the crowded street, packed with touts, tourists, and vendors whose stalls prevented anyone from walking in a straight line. Occasionally Pong stopped to chat with friends. We entered the club by the Patpong 2 entrance, which shared a hallway with SuperStar. At the inner door stood a young man wearing an earring and a modern punkish haircut.

She introduced him as her husband. "Ong," she said. Ong was twenty-two, six years younger than Pong. In Thai, the names Pong and Ong didn't rhyme, one being a "falling tone," the other a "rising tone" that sounded like a question—"Ong?"

Inside the club, she scanned the room before pulling me to sit next to a blond man she knew. She placed her hand on the *farang's* knee and devoted herself exclusively to him for the next half hour. Once or twice she turned to me with a "just a minute" gesture. When a hostess came by, I had to order a drink. I ordered one for Pong too, hoping it would remind her of me. She lifted it in salute and gave me another "just a minute" sign.

I resigned myself to watching the girl onstage shoot a dart from her vagina. Lying on her back, she contracted her stomach muscles, aiming the protruding blow gun at a balloon. I marveled that the men nearby were unafraid a badly aimed dart might go their way.

Pong caught hold of the manager as he passed and introduced him to me.

In his early twenties, Hong Kong Chinese, the manager took hold of my elbow and led me to a private corner before I had time to object. Hey! I wasn't interested in him! I didn't want to separate from Pong. I'd bought her for the night; she wasn't supposed to be working!

Sitting by the disk jockey booth, between a pillar and the manager, I couldn't even see Pong, I had hoped at least to observe her actions. Wait a minute, this was not how it was supposed to go! Pong was preoccupied with a *farang* and here was this man taking possession of me. He took hold of my hand and gave me a drink on the house. He invited me for a movie. He asked for my phone number. He made the personal inquiries of polite Thai chitchat, one of which was—contrary to Western courtesy—how old are you? I told him.

"Thirty-eight! No, never," he said. People generally took me for younger than my age. "You must not tell anybody thirty-eight. Say twenty-one. And you should cut your hair," he advised.

Cut my hair? I'd never had it other than long, straight, and stringy. How had I trapped myself with the manager of a ripoff bar? I wanted my hand back, but every time I pried it from him, excusing the move by taking a sip of my drink, he retrieved it as soon as it was free. When I decided to keep hold of the glass, he seized my other hand. How had I lost control of the situation? Well, hopefully Pong and I would leave soon for the disco.

I paid little attention to the manager's conversation. Instead, I considered whether I should lie about my age next time someone asked. When I'd told Pong, she too had gone into shock. In Thailand, a female was over the hill at twenty-five. And an unmarried one without children? Inconceivable. Revealing my age had made both the manager and Pong look at me as if I were an extraterrestrial. On the other hand, it didn't seem to have dampened the guy's ardor much. My palm, imprisoned in his, was growing clammy.

Finally disco time; I left the manager, collected Pong, and we went across the hall, where I paid our entrance fees into SuperStar Discotheque. We sat at the bar and I soon gave up trying to yell questions at her over the blaring music. Her husband joined us for a minute, then went back to his post. The manager came next, pressing against me as he squeezed between my bar stool and Pong's. Fortunately, he didn't stay long either.

"Boss love Cleo," Pong said when he left.

"*Mai ow* (Don't want)," I told her, rolling my eyes and grimacing.

"Ong and Pong, go Cleo tonight," she said in English.

"Where?" I asked in Thai.

"Cleo."

I pointed to my chest. "Me?" She nodded as if pleased it was settled. "Who?"

"Ong. Pong."

"Go where?"

"Yes."

Not understanding what I'd agreed to, I finally said, "No, it's late. I have to go home soon. I'm tired."

She patted my knee.

"I don't understand," I said in English.

In Thai, she explained, "My husband and I will sleep at your house tonight."

"NO, no, no. *Pen pai mai dai.* Not possible," I said quickly, aghast at the thought.

Her chin puckered in disappointment. Or was it confusion? I felt confused too. I couldn't bring myself to ask what she had in mind for the three of us. Besides, I suddenly felt defeated by my limitations with the Thai language and my lack of control over events. She said no more about it.

Meanwhile, the manager had instructed Pong to bring me back to the bar, and I followed her as she convinced me she had to return to Winner's to get something. She led me straight to him, and he found us a corner (without Pong) where he again took custody of my hand. Patpong seemed to run along two currents only—money and sex. How would I get by without being swept away by either? I left shortly after.

At home, I tallied the night's expenses—the bar fee, the restaurant, the taxis, SuperStar—$50. Very expensive for someone living in a foreign country on a student loan. I couldn't afford many more of those nights. Had I learned much? Not terribly. At that rate, I'd never write the dissertation. And had I really found myself an informant? No, I had to admit. I'd have to find a better strategy for collecting data. But what?

The population of Western men who lived permanently in Thailand was quite huge. Statistics on actual numbers weren't available because most of them were not legal residents. They stayed in the country (some already ten, twenty years or more) on Double-Entry Non-Immigrant visas and had to cross the border every three months the way I did. They stayed because of the Thai women. Though initially men paid outright for sex, prostitution in Thailand differed from the West in the way the women used poverty and the Third World conditions of Thailand to turn the customer/prostitute relationship into a savior/damsel-in-distress relationship. It was hard for men to leave the country where they played the role of hero so completely.

Though some men had been there since Vietnam, having found Thailand more hospitable than America, new ones came as tourists or travellers, military or business men, and often got stuck there, unwilling to go home, where no one viewed them as equally special. In Thailand, women gave them worshiping looks when they set foot in a bar or a store, or walked down the street. Where poverty was rampant, Western boyfriends were treasures. Many men eventually married the women they met in a Patpong bar.

The purpose of the A.U.A. language school, where I studied Thai, was to teach English to Thais, not Thai to foreigners, and many *farang* residents worked there as English teachers. Resident men rarely went there to learn Thai. Most resident *farang* men, no matter how long they'd been living in Thailand, never learned more than a few common phrases. This situation, in which the subordinate one in the relationship had to learn the dominant one's language, resulted in an alienation for those living in Thailand unable to speak Thai. Most resident *farang* women, on the other hand, did learn Thai.

One day, in A.U.A.'s cafeteria, I met Seymour, one of the English teachers. "You should talk to my wife, Tik," he said when I told him my reason for studying the language. It was a regular occurrence for resident men to offer me their ex-Patpong wives or girlfriends as informants without first consulting them.

"Oh?" I debated accepting his offer. Now that I'd officially started the research, I had to keep going before I became discouraged by lack of progress. Already a year in Thailand, and so far I'd had only one private encounter with a Patpong person—an expensive and unfruitful one at that. When I learned that Seymour's wife had been away from prostitution six years, meeting her sounded like a good idea. "Okay," I told him. "Thanks."

Seymour, from the American Midwest, with a beard and longish blond hair, told me he'd first come to Thailand as a soldier during the Vietnam War. To support himself, Tik, and their two daughters, he taught English ten hours a day and hated it.

When Seymour picked up his lunch tray and left, another teacher at the table said, "Don't tell Seymour I told you, but he's AWOL from the war."

An AWOL! Seymour and Tik's story was sounding better and better. Maybe I'd get a handle on the research after all.

The next weekend, Seymour arranged for me and his wife to meet for lunch at a coffee shop. Short and chubby, Tik had tied her long black hair behind her. Thai women were generally tiny and very thin. Many Patpong women wore their hair long and loose, which made them irresistibly sexy to Western men. When bar girls lived a while with *farangs*, though, they sometimes gained weight and lost their striking beauty. Chunky Tik, with her hair tied unattractively behind her, was no longer a treat for the eyes.

Right off she told me, "It too dangerous for you go Patpong. Someone maybe want you dead, uh." She leaned in closer. "On Patpong, many gangster. Kill easy, uh. They no like *farang* ask question about prostitute."

Tik suggested I hire her to do interviews for me.

After the fiasco with Pong, this sounded peachy. "Great," I said encouragingly.

Tik had already planned it out. "I have many Patpong girlfriend. I go see them and they tell me their story. I hide tape recorder in my bag. You have tape recorder?"

"No, but I can buy one."

"See-mon will translate for you in English."

"Seymour speaks Thai?"

"No. I tell to him. He write in English, make good. Then later I introduce you to my friend so you can interview for yourself. You no go Patpong alone.

16

Too much danger, uh."

I wondered how those people would feel when they found out Tik had been secretly taping their conversations. But I didn't believe she really found Patpong a danger. It sounded like a hustle to get me to hire her. I didn't challenge her on it. Hiring her was just what I wanted to do. I needed help, and I didn't want her to feel mistrusted.

"I'll pay you 500 *baht* a week plus expenses. How's that?" I offered. Since $100 a month would be considered a good full-time salary for a college graduate (which she wasn't), 500 *baht* a week ($20) was a good deal. I didn't expect her to work anywhere near full-time.

She looked down for a second with a sly smile and said, "I see how is. I tell you soon if okay."

We then chatted. "My father, he open first go-go bar on *Soi* Cowboy," she told me. "He also have go-go bar in Udon Thani, my home town in Isan. When I small, American army in Udon. My family, they rent bungalow to GI. I wash shirt. Make good money, 150 *baht* a month from each GI, uh. I was eleven year old. Thai men no like GI because wife leave to go with GI, never come back. Girl make too much money there. Have ten, twenty GI send money every month."

As Tik spoke, I tried to figure out what was true and what were invented tidbits to portray Tik as the ideal informant. I found it hard to believe her father just happened to be the founder of the go-go business. Washing shirts, on the other hand, sounded plausible.

Tik made a gesture toward the nearby window that gave onto a commercial street. "Father, he own building back there. Nine floor, uh. My family very rich. One time I meet Mr. Patpong through my family. Next year when I am thirty, I inherit too much money."

At this, I wondered if she'd fabricated everything she'd said so far. I saw the glint of con artistry in her eye. After each outrageous statement, she'd pause to scan me, as if assessing my gullibility. I made an effort to show no disbelief and thought I detected a pinch in her lip as she rated my gullibility as high.

Though Tik had been a "housewife" for six years, she retained that hard-line hustle so mandatory for life on Patpong. Competition in the bars being fierce, aggressiveness and the ability to connive were vital characteristics for survival. Where resources were scarce and the seizure of opportunity crucial, daring to exaggerate and lie could make the difference between living well or not.

After we parted company, with her promising to get right to work, I felt half elated that the project wasn't hopeless after all, and half in dread that either Tik would give me nothing but farfetched tales or the plan, with tape recorder and third-party interviews, would prove unrealistic.

When a week went by with no word from her, I told myself I had to come up with another approach. Even if she did fulfill her improbable promises, I knew deep inside that I had to be the one out there on the front line. Hiring someone to do interviews for me was another form of avoiding the battle. So much for Pong and Tik, Plans A and B. I groaned at the thought of Plan C—Empower, an

17

organization for Patpong bar girls.

I'd known about Empower since before coming to Thailand. I knew they used Western volunteers to teach English. Since Patpong dealt with tourists, the girls' ability to speak English was conducive to everyone's prosperity, so employers didn't mind their attendance. If I could work for Empower, I'd meet lots of Patpong people, and it seemed a perfect strategy for finding out about them. But the thought of sacrificing hours of time to give English lessons depressed me. I didn't have much choice, though. My options were running out.

Thailand had few women's organizations, and they made little headway in bettering women's lives. The country held rigid views about women's inferiority, granting them fewer legal and social rights than men. Thailand exalted males and reared females to deference.

A Buddhist country, Thailand's belief about women's place was codified by the Buddhist religion and its ideas about reincarnation. A person's life was viewed as a link in a chain of lives, each conditioned by acts committed in previous existences. The aim was to be free from the eternal cycle of rebirth and to attain Nirvana. People achieved this by making "merit." Karma was the sum of actions and thoughts from previous lives and determined one's present status. Karma also determined sex. To be born a woman meant one had an inadequate store of merit from past lives. Thai women, therefore, had fewer privileges than Thai men because that's what they deserved.

Thai women's groups often rallied round the subject of prostitution. Because Thais adhered to the double standard of sexuality where males had the right to sexual freedom but females had to restrict themselves to one male, they considered prostitution an evil that ruined women for life (evil only for the women, not for the men who were their customers). I, on the other hand, thought Thai culture was ruinous to women and applauded the sex industry for at least offering them the opportunity to escape their historic role of powerlessness. Having read Empower's literature, I knew they regarded bar girls as helpless victims, and I had warned myself to keep my opinions in check when I got there.

One day I put on my immigration dress, a conservative outfit I wore when I had to deal with government officials, and set out for Empower. Even after years as a hard-working college student, I didn't look much different from the old hippy days. Fashioning myself into a no-nonsense appearance still took an effort.

My apartment was only seven minutes from Patpong, and Empower was another three farther down Silom Road. Finding an address in Thailand was no easy thing. House numbers didn't always run consecutively, and I'd have never found Empower had I not been able to read the Thai sign at the mouth of an alley. Lucky for me I'd studied reading and writing Thai to justify my procrastination in starting the research. My professors had originally told me not to bother with the written language.

I entered the building into an empty area and climbed to the second floor, where I found the office. A Thai woman sat at a desk, and a Western woman with wavy, light-brown hair stood by a file cabinet.

"Hi," I said. "Are you looking for volunteers?"

"Hello," said the *farang*. "I'm Etaine. Do you know what we do here?"

"Only that you teach English to Patpong bar girls."

"Come, I'll show you around."

She led me to the stairs and explained the organization. "Empower's been in operation since 1986. Besides free English lessons, we also offer Thai lessons for women unable to read and write Thai. Many upcountry people have no more than second- and third-grade educations. They're too poor to go to school."

"How long have you been working here?" I asked.

"Two years. I was recruited from New Zealand—that's where I'm from—to help run the place." We climbed to the third floor. "This is the classroom."

A group of women sat on floor mats by the window. Seven Thais surrounded the *farang* who led the lesson. Ready to start work in an hour's time, the Thai women's eyelids glittered with bright colors. Tomato red lips and cheeks glowed in the dimness against the brightness of the summer sky outside. Jewelry jingled every time someone made a gesture. Etaine and I tiptoed close and stood to the side.

The teacher pointed to a girl looking no older than fifteen, wearing a low-cut blouse and a miniskirt that revealed a sliver of pink panties as she sat with her legs folded to the side. The girl uttered an incomprehensible string of words.

Etaine explained she'd recently arrived from the Northeast. "Girls begin working in Patpong without one word of English. But they learn fast."

The *farang* told her to slow down and try again. This time I could make out, "Welcome, please come in, sit down, what you name, what you want drink?"

"And what else you want, baby?" another asked. The Thais covered their mouths, bent their heads, and giggled.

Etaine whispered, "Our English conversation lessons are geared around bar behavior because that's most relevant."

"Now let's practice the passing again," said the *farang*. "I'll start. May I have the ashtray, please?"

"Here you are," said a Thai with a Betty Boop bow in her hair.

"Thank you."

"You welcome."

Assorted props lay strewn around, and the girls took turns pointing to things and passing them to each other. "Please pass the coaster. Thank you." "You welcome. Would you like a condom?" "Yes, please." "Here you are." "Thank you." "May I have ice cube, please?" "Here you are. And I take condom too. You welcome."

Etaine explained that many women had never heard of condoms before coming to Empower. To instill AIDS awareness, the lessons brought up the subject as often as possible. I wanted to ask more about AIDS but not in front of the class.

When we tiptoed back out, I told her I wanted to teach.

"We do need people for the next term, which begins Monday. We're actually between terms now, but some girls come in anyway. We never discourage them.

Terms are six weeks, and then there's a two-week break when we put out our newsletter. It's called *Patpong* and serves to build a communication network for the girls. It's about them and for them. Our goal at Empower is to give them a sense of self-esteem. Have you seen the newsletter?"

When I shook my head, she gave me a back issue from April. The four glossy pages contained pictures and stories of a few bar girls, their hometowns and their activities. She said I could keep it—my second artifact. I noted the cartoon. Featuring a bar scene, it pictures a Western man with his arm around a bikinied Thai who has a faraway look in her eye. He is asking her, "What are you thinking about?" The balloon representing her thoughts shows images of April's *Songkran* festival as she fantasizes celebrating it with her family upcountry, instead of in Patpong, where she has to work.

"We're expecting the printer to deliver the next issue tomorrow," said Etaine. "Would you like to help us distribute it? We need all the arms we can get. We give out copies in as many bars as possible before our armloads run out. It takes a few days to reach all the bars."

"I'd love to. Sounds terrific!" It did. What a windfall opening into Patpong for me! To visit every bar while associated with Empower, a friend of the girls—perfect!

She scheduled me to teach English on Tuesdays and Thursdays, 90 minutes a class. "Call me tomorrow to check if the newsletter's out."

On the way home I gloried in feeling like a Patpong insider. Then suddenly I felt guilty about not revealing my true purpose to Etaine. I hadn't been honest about my motives. I'd described myself as a student studying Thai, not a graduate student studying prostitution. After the warmth Empower aroused in me, I felt compelled to tell the truth. It would probably come out eventually anyway. Better to be straightforward from the start. I almost called Etaine as soon as I got home but decided it could wait a day.

When I called the next afternoon, she said, "No, the paper hasn't arrived yet but we're going to Patpong tonight to visit some women who have the day off. Want to come?"

Did I ever!

That night, I went to meet Etaine. First I stopped at Patpong 3 and Silom Road to look for Jek. A cheap Thai restaurant, open to the humid air, occupied one corner. The opposite corner was obscured by a jackfruit vendor, a shelf of bootlegged Marlboros, and a row of parked motorbikes in front of which sat a one-legged beggar bowing his head to the ground, causing the flow of tourists to course around him. By his side, a pom-pommed hilltribe woman sold handicrafts.

Unlike Patpong 1, which was barred to vehicular traffic at night, Patpong 3 had cars parked on both sides; but, being a dead-end street, only touts stood in its center.

"Oah," Jek said and offered his hand. I'd never liked shaking hands, and I liked it even less now that Patpong had me doing it so often. But shaking adorable Jek's hand wasn't too bad at all. "We go for coffee?" he said, pointing down

Silom Road to the countless neon-lit fast-food places.

"No, no. Not tonight. I have an appointment." I had no intention of ever going for coffee with him. Chatting on the street was fine, but becoming too cozy with a pimp, especially such an enticing one, didn't seem like a good idea. I appreciated, though, that he'd switched from inviting me to a hotel to inviting me for coffee.

I continued round the corner to Rififi, a ground-floor bar on Patpong 2. Most of the ground-floor go-go bars dressed their dancers in bikinis or one-piece suits and didn't have trick shows. The bars with naked dancing, trick shows, and sex shows were all on the second floor. The staircase gave the management time to clean the act if the doorman downstairs rang the bell signifying police were on their way up. Technically, obscenity and prostitution were illegal in Thailand. Though the police undoubtedly knew what transpired in the second-floor bars, bribes and the concealment of overt acts allowed the practice to continue.

In the case of ripoff bars, both the bribes and the rank of police who accepted them were on a higher scale. Only a handful of Patpong establishments actively cheated their customers, though. The rest, while not necessarily law abiding on carnal matters, were honest in business.

Inside Rififi, twelve bikini-clad girls danced on the center stage with another two dancing near the far wall. Etaine sat at a table surrounded by Thai women who looked at her with affection.

When I found a moment to have a word with her, I said, "I have to tell you something. I'm in Thailand to research prostitution. I thought you should know that." Her face emitted a weird smile and she turned away. She made no comment. Uh-oh. I should have said it better than that. I wished I possessed better diplomacy skills.

A half hour later, Etaine and I left with three bar girls who had the day off. As we journeyed to a restaurant, the four of them rocked the taxi with laughter. The Thais seemed to adore Etaine. But I felt a tinge of coldness from her.

The next day I called Etaine to find out about the newsletter. She didn't sound pleased to hear from me and said with a sigh in her voice, "Yes, the paper's out, but we're not going to distribute it tonight. I have to go somewhere." Then she added, "What else did I want to tell you? . . . Oh, yes, we've discussed it and we don't need more teachers for next term. Maybe the term after that. You can call us then."

I knew she wanted to get rid of me. I'd blown it when I'd mentioned the research, blurting it out like that. I shouldn't have mentioned it at all.

The next day I called again, braving another rejection. I hated to lose Empower.

"Oh, sorry," said Etaine. "We changed our minds last night and decided to give out the paper after all." Since she'd told me before it took several nights to go to all the bars, I knew I had no hope left there. Empower had closed me out.

That evening I received a phone call from Seymour. "Listen, you gotta watch out. The Mafia is looking for you," he said.

"Mafia!" Oh, no. Now what?

"Tik was in the Limelight Bar this afternoon when a Mafia dude entered and showed your picture to everyone asking if they knew you. I've heard about these guys. Real mean. They asked Tik if she knew you but she told them no. You have to stay away from Patpong. They don't like people asking questions. Wait till Tik makes connections for you."

"What kind of picture? Who was in it?"

"You and a bar girl in a bar. That's all I know."

Me with a bar girl? It couldn't have been at Rififi because I'd never been with just one Thai girl alone. It could only have been at Winner's with Pong. Though I had no doubt the pesty manager of that ripoff bar would have links to unsavory types, he had my phone number and could have called. And I'd pointed out my street to Pong when we passed it in the taxi. I was the only blond female living in the area, as far as I knew, so anyone could have found me had they so desired.

Could this be possible, then? I had assumed there'd be hazards on Patpong, but I never imagined anybody would view me as a threat. Nobody in my life had ever taken me seriously, much less considered me a menace. Consistently perceived as a dumb blond, I was convinced I could pass through events like a ghost whom no one would pay heed to, except horny males.

I didn't doubt Seymour believed the story, but it sounded like Tik would tell me any old whopper to secure herself the job of assistant and translator. Should I forget about working with Tik? Assistant and translator, she'd never be. She had definitely lied about being on Patpong that afternoon. I knew the Limelight Bar would have no more than a cleaning crew there during the day. She could not have been conducting interviews.

But not only was she lying to me, she was also lying to Seymour. Come to think of it, that was just the sort of data I was looking for. Rather than viewing Patpong prostitutes as helpless victims of circumstance, I believed them to be clever women who saw opportunity and grasped it. I wanted to demonstrate how, as actors in their own shows, they chose logical courses for their lives. In this vein, Tik was proving herself a prime subject. Besides, she was the only one I had.

"Well, thanks for the warning," I told Seymour before hanging up. I wouldn't tell him my hunch about his wife. I had to side with the women, no matter what—even if they invented stories to scare me to death, like Tik apparently had no pangs about doing.

3.

In a panel discussion on Third World tourism, Dr. Yupha (Thai Development Newsletter, 1986: 12) stated that it was the prostitutes "who attract most of the tourists, and the money earned subsequently is to their (the prostitutes') credit. They have saved our economy from bankruptcy, really."

Sereewat (1983: 7) gives these figures on the increase of tourist arrivals:

Year	1965	1976	1979	1980
Arrivals	250,000	1,100,000	1,600,000	2,200,000

The estimated number of foreign visitors for 1988 was over 4,250,000 (En Route: Tourism Business Newsletter, 1989).

How should I deal with Tik's Mafia story? Ignore it? Check it out? I didn't believe it but . . . what if it were true? My project could be in jeopardy. Maybe that was why Etaine didn't want anything to do with me. Had she heard a rumor that I was on someone's hit list and wanted to distance her organization from trouble?

Before paranoia could set in completely, I decided to plunge back into the job. The next day, I went to the supermarket on Patpong 2. Tik had to be lying. But in case someone was looking for me, it was best I went to Patpong and let him find me in public.

Nothing happened.

I walked out of Foodland with bags of canned American food, French cheese, and Thai fruit—and without a peculiar glance from anybody. My skepticism about Tik's honesty resurged.

That night I talked myself into one more trial venture to the street. I looked for Jek on his corner but didn't see him. I walked on to Patpong 1 and strolled slowly down it, parading myself in open view. I felt like a duck in a rifle range as I conversed amiably with the touts who wanted to take me to another show. When the doorman of the Firecat called me over, I seized the chance to stop and look around for lurking mobsters.

A short man in his forties, wearing a shiny black jacket, the doorman asked, "Are you an American chick?" Somehow, tourist-industry Thais could always tell an American from a German or a Swede. "I'm from L.A., man. How ya doing? My name is Charlie. Choo Choo Charlie they call me. Nice to meet ya." He spoke fast and fluently but with a heavy Thai accent.

"Los Angeles? I'm from New York. How long did you live there?"

"I left Thailand at age fifteen. Just came back a few months ago. It ain't easy here man. Can't make no money. And Thai people don't understand me. I'm too American. I miss the States. This place is a drag. You know L.A.?"

"I lived there a while." Tourists and touts bustled by but no one seemed interested in me. Western men had only Thai girls on their minds, and Charlie's presence kept the Thai men at bay. Nobody gangsterish spied on me from a doorway.

"You know the Whiskey-A-Go-Go?" Charlie asked. "Groovy place! I parked cars there. Good blow at the Whiskey. John Belushi. You know John Belushi and Cathy? Dynamite people man. Good friends of mine. Far out."

Charlie was a jabberer. He jabbered on while looking left and right, trying to hand out cards advertising the Firecat. If someone accepted the card, Charlie would invite him to the club. Most passers-by ignored him. Charlie kept up the dialogue with me without needing more than a grunt of encouragement. I had time to check out the people around me. No Mafia. Or at least nothing that looked like an Italian with a machine gun or what I imagined to be his Thai counterpart.

Choo Choo Charlie

By the time I took leave of Charlie, I felt rejuvenated. Nobody was looking for me. I had proved Tik a liar—and in the process had met a friendly Patpong person. Now I had a Patpong contact I could find every night who'd be happy to speak with me, and without my having to buy him a drink. And without my having to worry that he was too temptingly attractive, like Jek.

Walking home, I encountered Jek on his corner. "Are you from Bangkok?" I asked him.

"Yes but far from here. My family live in slump, many poor people, have nothing."

"*Slum*, I think you mean."

"What did I say?"

"Slump. Do you give your parents money?"

"Of course. Children must give money to mother."

"Do you have brothers and sisters?"

"Mother have seven children. Father is mother's second husband. I have two older brother and two older sister from mother's first husband. He was rich Danish man. His children don't want see me because my father poor, have black skin. Mother marry my father after Danish husband die. One time I work for half-brother as mechanic. He treat me like employee. Last year he stop speaking to me. If I call, he no answer phone."

"Was your family poor when you were growing up?"

"I born in slump. My whole life have to work, make money to eat. When I five year old, I sell chewing gum on the street. Sometimes I want to cry. Sometimes I feel like crying when I walk this road. I have pain here, how you say. . ."

"Appendix?"

"No."

"Stomach?"

"Hole, how you say?"

"Ulcer!"

"Yes. I get because family so poor, my stomach always empty when I growing up. How old are you?" he asked.

"Uh, twenty-seven," I lied and searched his face for signs of disbelief. There weren't any. "How old are you?"

"Twenty-five. We go for coffee?"

"Uh, no, I gotta get home."

He shook my hand again. This guy was way too cute, I thought, and now I had put myself in his age group. I should have told him the truth and scared him away.

When I returned home that night, I created a database file for Patpong men. I entered Jek, pimp, Patpong 3, dangerously good looking; and Choo Choo Charlie, Firecat doorman, plus the number of his badge, 99. For Charlie, under "Miscellaneous", I wrote: Friend of John Belushi.

Jek

Seymour called to inform me his wife had come to my apartment twice with a Patpong girl for me to interview but that I'd been out both times. The receptionist in my building had no record of the visits. Poor Seymour, I thought. If *farangs* were treated this way by their Thai girlfriends, maybe Thailand wasn't such a paradise for Western men after all. A week later, Seymour called again to say his wife had been by with another girl but that again I'd been out. I was certain Seymour believed these accounts. While Tik had supposedly gone "to work," Seymour had stayed home with the children.

The next week, Seymour called once more, this time to alert me his wife would be by that afternoon with a girl. Tik came alone. But she ended up discussing her own life, which was just as well, since she was ex-Patpong herself.

"Before See-mon, I marry five year to Thai man," she told me. "I no love him. My mother, she arrange marriage. I break face—no feel good when walk down street with him because he have black skin. I want divorce. I give him everything to end marriage. Have nothing left."

I remembered Jek saying his half brothers and sisters rejected him because his father had black skin. Thais seemed to classify each other by skin shade.

"How much money did you give him to end the marriage?" I asked her.

"Five million dollar. Now my family no trust me with money. They afraid I do same thing with See-mon. So I have to wait until I'm thirty to get money."

I hoped I'd remember the things she was telling me, though I disbelieved them. Five million dollars was a nifty piece of data. I didn't want to take notes in front of her for fear she'd stop talking if she became self-conscious.

"After divorce from Thai man, I work Patpong because I no want go home. Then I meet See-mon and stop work. First time with See-mon, he pay 500 *baht*." She laughed. "I tell all my friend to work Patpong. In Patpong, easy to find husband. What is that?"

Her eyes had been darting around the room, examining everything. The low cost of living in Thailand allowed me luxury in Bangkok. The living room equaled the space of a two-bedroom apartment in Manhattan. The bedroom was also large, and a balcony ran the length of both. With the difference between the Thai and American economies, an American welfare recipient could have lived there in grandeur.

"That's my computer," I told her. "So how did you and Seymour get along at the beginning?"

"At first, See-mon go with other girl. Then he take me. He want me to stay with him. I ask for how long—one, two month? He drink too much then. After one year, See-mon want to marry. I say no because he always drunk. See-mon leave Thailand. I go back to Patpong. I think you like elephant too much, uh," she said suddenly.

"I love elephants," I told her. Brocaded elephants hung on the walls, mirrored ones sat on tables, and a tall ceramic one stood on the floor.

"Thai people have saying—woman is hind leg of elephant."

I put disgust in my voice. "Right, and men are the front legs! That's gross. I wouldn't want to be the back end of anything." I lifted my leg. "Look, I have also an elephant tattooed on my foot. I had it done in India during my reckless years."

She looked at it with a grimace and said, "In Thailand, only criminal have tattoo. But you, *farang*. *Farang* do anything, never mind."

"So how did you and Seymour get back together after he left Thailand?"

"He come again. I say okay we marry. We go to embassy."

She stood up, went to the balcony, and looked down. "Swimming pool!" she exclaimed.

I realized she couldn't help but view me as super rich. I'd never be able to convince her I was living on a measly student loan.

"But you loved Seymour?" I prompted.

26

"Many time I want to leave him but my friend, she say no good. Must stay marry because have baby, uh. Baby mixed. People call it *farang dong*. Bad name, also mean baby have no father. School too much expensive, maybe 20,000 *baht* one year. Government school 5,000 *baht*. Monk school 6,000."

I wondered how Jek had afforded school and college.

"Sometime I very angry," Tik said. "See-mon stay quiet. I get crazy. Use bad language, uh. I tell him, your face is like my pussy."

Then she presented me with a bill totaling 889 *baht* in expenses for the girls she interviewed but whose stories she forgot because she hadn't taken notes.

"You give me money, I buy tape recorder, uh," she suggested.

"Well, I don't know about that tape recorder," I answered, convinced she would use it only to entertain herself with music. How much should I give her? At the beginning I'd said 500 *baht* a week plus expenses, but I had no intention of paying for four weeks worth of nothing plus 889 for imaginary expenses. On the other hand, she was the only live Patpong prostitute informant I had. I gave her 1,000 *baht* ($40, possibly her month's rent) and let her keep the change. She didn't object.

Before going out the door, she reminded me, "Girl no talk to you. They talk to me. I make good interview for you."

Not too bad a session, I thought after she left. Before I forgot, I scribbled down as many quotes as I could remember, such as face like pussy.

Did Seymour think he got a bargain marrying Tik? I wondered how Thai men felt about *farang*s taking their women. I'd ask Jek.

That evening, I went to Foodland on Patpong 2. I'd decided to go shopping at night so I could pass Jek.

"Oah!" he said as he saw me approach weighed down with bags.

"I want to ask you about *farang* men and Thai women," I said to him.

"Yes. I take *farang* to massage parlor. Buy plain woman, 400 *baht*; okay woman, 500 *baht*; beautiful one, 750 *baht*. Parlor have arrangement with me. Charge *farang* 1,000 for plain one, 1,200 for okay, and 1,500 for beautiful. Extra money is my commission. I ask *farang* to buy girl for me too, but we no make love. I give her 100 *baht* and keep the rest."

Massage parlors in Thailand were brothels with dozens to hundreds of women on display behind glass windows. I'd passed an opening door to a Patpong parlor once and seen them. "Oh, um . . . very clever," I murmured. He hadn't answered the question I thought I asked.

"If *farang* no want go massage parlor," he continued, "I can bring girl to hotel. For beautiful one, 2,000 *baht*; for ordinary one, 1,000."

"But what do you think about Thai women going with *farang* men?"

"Patpong woman no good. Very dirty. I never go with Patpong woman."

"Oh." We looked at each other for a silent second. I wondered what kind of women he liked. "Who do you go with then? *Farang* women?"

"No."

No? Did that mean he'd never been with a *farang* woman or that he didn't like them? "So you only go with Thai women?"

He rubbed the tips of his fingers together. "Thai women want you pay."

I knew Thai society forbade women to be sexual beings outside of marriage. Thai men, therefore, could only have sex with prostitutes. I had the feeling, though, Jek was avoiding telling me something. "Well, gotta go. See you next time."

"Wait, we go for coffee."

"Uh, no. I'm in a hurry."

Seymour called to inform me Tik would be by with a woman who'd formerly worked on Patpong but who now worked as a prostitute on cargo ships. Once again Tik arrived alone. This time she handed me a bill for 1,304 *baht*. She'd had to buy food for the women at the dock, she explained. I paid but told her I didn't have much money and was waiting for the next student loan check. She acted concerned and reluctant to accept the money, but her lip had that pinch. I decoded it as saying, "Thanks, sucker."

I really had to find myself another angle into Patpong.

I soon did. I met Dudley Dapolito.

For people wanting to learn Thai, the A.U.A. language school offered lessons in what they called the "Natural Approach," in which students watched two or three Thais act out easy-to-understand scenarios describing Thai customs. That's where I found Dudley, a twenty-six-year-old computer programmer from New Jersey. Dudley wore glasses and had red hair and a red mustache and beard. Dudley wasn't there to study Thai but to look up a friend of a friend, a missionary. A.U.A.'s Thai courses were overrun with missionaries. Dudley and I met on the balcony outside the classrooms.

Like many *farangs* who heard about my work, he immediately related his most recent escapade with a Patpong prostitute. "You should meet this hussy of mine at Queen's Castle," he said. They all had someone I just HAD to meet. "I bought her out of her bar seven nights in a row. On top of the 325 *baht* bar fee, I paid her the 500 *baht* she asked for, plus a 100 *baht* tip. I always tip them, whether they ask for it or not."

Farang men loved to tell *farang* women about their sexual exploits with Thai bar girls. Since leaving the States two months before, Dudley Dapolito had indulged himself in the sex market as much as possible. Unlike in the West, where no one would admit frequenting prostitutes, in Thailand *farangs* quickly adopted the vision of this country as a man's playground for sexual adventure. As they chalked up sexual points, they also became knights in shining armor who supported not only the prostitutes, but also the girls' families and, sometimes, entire villages in the provinces.

Exasperated by Tik's manipulations, I jumped at this chance to hear about Patpong from someone who hadn't a reason to take advantage of me. Perhaps I

28

could acquire insight into Patpong by way of its customers. Previously, I'd considered *farang* men's war stories only a nuisance.

"Why don't you come to my apartment and tell me about the hussy," I suggested.

Eagerly he accepted the invitation and followed me home. As we walked through Lumpini Park, I had trouble stemming the flow of experiences he couldn't wait to tell. He didn't even object when I asked if I could take notes. "Wait, wait, then," I said. "Don't tell me more till I get hold of a pen."

As soon as we settled on the couch and I turned on the air conditioner, he began, "Sex the first time with her was sensational. She was lively and fun. Boy oh boy, what a gal. The second time, though, was less fun, and after that it became worse and worse. We'd rent a short-time room for four hours but only stay two. She'd rush me, saying, 'Are you finished yet?' She always asked for extra money and presents. One day, she said she was sick and needed an additional 800 *baht*."

"Did you give it to her?"

"Yeah, sure. I feel sorry for them. And what's 800 *baht* to me? These people have nothing, you know. It's so sad. Then one night she talked me into buying her lady-boy *katoey* friend out of the bar too. The two of them took me to a couple of expensive nightclubs. By this time, when it came to sex, she would say, 'Hurry hurry, so we can go do something else.' One day she said she needed money for her baby."

"You gave it to her?"

"Yeah, 1,000 *baht*. Listen, these people are really bad off. Gruesome poverty here, you know what I mean? The girl supports her mother upcountry and sends two brothers to school. They have no electricity, no running water—what can I say? But hold on, listen to this—she then asks me for another present, saying, 'Tomorrow you no have to tip me.' But next day, sure enough, she asks for the tip anyway. When I reminded her of what she'd said, she pleaded that she needed food for the baby. So I gave her an extra 500 *baht*. She said she'd take me to see the kid."

I hurried to write things down, regretting I never learned shorthand.

"Meanwhile, this friend of mine tells me the girls often RENT babies in order to finagle more money. Can you believe that? I decided not to see her again. But wouldn't you know it, she came to me. Eventually I made her admit she didn't have a baby."

With only an occasional glance at my notebook, Dudley gabbed on about his trysts and their complications. Overwhelmed by the availability of gorgeous women, Dudley had tried out massage parlor sex, sex-and-shave barber shops, and had paid 65 *baht* a half hour to sit with girls in a Japanese bar. Once, he went down an alley for a 100 *baht* blow job. "But the woman turned out to be a *katoey*, you know, and after the blow job, he and his friends robbed me. I can't believe I fell for that one."

Soon I had pages of scrawlings, too many pages. It would take hours to type them into the computer. I thanked Dudley for his help and told him I'd appreciate it if he kept me up on his affairs. He strutted out the door like a rooster who'd given the neighborhood a sample of his cock-a-doodle-doo. His being robbed and hustled didn't detract from his self-image as a potent male practicing his right to sexual fun.

Before I'd typed halfway though Dudley Dapolito's notes, Seymour called to say Tik would be by with a woman who performed the Fucking Shows at Pussy Galore. Tik came alone. She spoke about her conversation with the Pussy Galore woman. "I tell her to marry *farang* then leave him." As usual, she handed me a bill for expenses.

After the successes with Dudley Dapolito, Jek, and Choo Choo Charlie, I wasn't so willing to pursue this unproductive contact. I paid her, then said, "I can't afford more right now, so don't bother to interview anybody else." I didn't want to sever the relationship completely, though. "Maybe next month we can work together again," I added. "After I get my student loan check."

"See-mon say you get money in November."

"Oh, ah, yeah. Well, whenever it gets here." She'd caught me in a lie. I hoped she wouldn't ask again how much rent I paid. She'd asked before and I couldn't remember what I'd said. I'd been telling different amounts to different people. The rent was impossibly high for a Thai, though it was a third of my rent in New York. Thais gasped at the sum even when I cut it in half, so I ended up lowering the amount every time someone asked. We were all liars, it seemed.

4.

Since the interview with Dudley Dapolito had gone so well, I decided to get more reports on Patpong women from *farang* men. I printed signs stating: "I am a graduate student studying Patpong prostitutes. If you have interesting, funny, or sad stories about them, please call me." I went to Kao San Road to post them. Would a government official spot one and come after me? Hopefully, nobody from the National Research Council would have reason to go to that area. Not many Thais did.

I knew Kao San Road was not the ideal place to reach the appropriate people, the high-budget tourists. The road catered to low-budget travellers, the only group of foreigners in Thailand composed of equal numbers of males and females and the least likely bunch to seek the company of prostitutes. But I figured it would be a good test spot. From a questionnaire I once wrote, I knew that questions I considered simple and clear could be misinterpreted in bizarre ways.

True to form, something unanticipated happened. Instead of hearing from Western men willing to discuss their experiences, the notice attracted Western women curious about my findings.

Kao San Road hosted a multitude of hostels and cheap restaurants as well as trek-and-camp travel agencies. Before I'd tacked signs in half of them, two Australian women, with straggly hair and bangles, came running up to me.

"Hi," said one. "We read your poster and would like to invite you for a yak. Would you join us for tea?"

The three of us went to the café where they'd left their belongings when they'd charged out to find me. They asked my opinion of bar girls and wanted the scoop on Patpong. Though hardly knowing anything yet, I felt like an expert as I told them, "Well, you have to watch out for the ripoff bars. They overcharge you and send the bill with a gigantic man in a dress."

They had information for me too. They advised me to look up the New Zealand owner of the Cleopatra Bar. They'd visited Patpong once and had met him. He'd taken them on a tour. The Australians poked elbows into each other laughingly. "The bloke just wanted to show off. What a wanker. You've got to meet him yourself." One woman guffawed and slapped her leg. "Wait till you see his mustache—a beaut—waxed and curling round his cheek. A bloody riot this one is. His name is David. A ripe example of a foreign bloke in Thailand."

After thanking the Australians for the tip and the tea, I continued posting.

Soon after arriving home, I received a phone call from an American woman, Linda. She too had read the notice and wanted to talk. Women were not what I'd

31

Diagram of Patpong 2

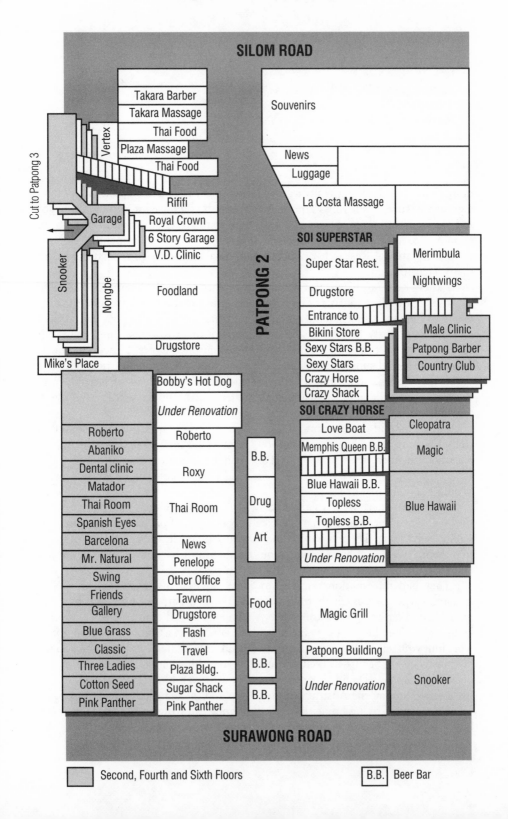

SILOM ROAD

Takara Barber
Takara Massage
Thai Food
Plaza Massage
Thai Food
Vertex

Souvenirs
News
Luggage
La Costa Massage

Cut to Patpong 3

Rififi
Royal Crown
6 Story Garage
V.D. Clinic
Garage
Foodland
Drugstore
Snooker
Nongbe

PATPONG 2

SOI SUPERSTAR

Super Star Rest.
Drugstore
Entrance to
Bikini Store
Sexy Stars B.B.
Sexy Stars
Crazy Horse
Crazy Shack

Merimbula
Nightwings
Male Clinic
Patpong Barber
Country Club

Mike's Place

Bobby's Hot Dog
Under Renovation

SOI CRAZY HORSE

Love Boat
Memphis Queen B.B.
Blue Hawaii B.B.
Topless
Topless B.B.
Under Renovation

Cleopatra
Magic
Blue Hawaii

Roberto
Abaniko
Dental clinic
Matador
Thai Room
Spanish Eyes
Barcelona
Mr. Natural
Swing
Friends
Gallery
Blue Grass
Classic
Three Ladies
Cotton Seed
Pink Panther

Roberto
Roxy
Thai Room
News
Penelope
Other Office
Tavvern
Drugstore
Flash
Travel
Plaza Bldg.
Sugar Shack
Pink Panther

B.B.
Drug
Art
Food
B.B.
B.B.

Magic Grill
Patpong Building
Under Renovation
Snooker

SURAWONG ROAD

| | Second, Fourth and Sixth Floors | | B.B. | Beer Bar |

hoped for as a response, but . . . what the heck. I agreed to meet her the following night.

In her thirties, tall, big-boned, with short blond curls framing her face, Linda came from Santa Barbara, California. She'd been in Thailand one and a half years, working as a cook on a sailboat anchored in Phuket, a tourist resort island. The bar girl scene had upset her and she needed to discuss it.

"I'm leaving the country next week," she said. "It's not healthy for me here with those women. In the end, I had to completely dissociate myself because of the effect it was having on me."

"What effect?" I asked.

"Hostility. Toward Western men. They really dig in the knife about women's place. They made me feel worthless. The Thai girls do anything for them. The laundry, anything. The men accept this as their due. Pampered and indulged. They have 'major' and 'minor' girlfriends the way Thai men have major and minor wives. As a Western woman I felt despised."

"I know what you mean. Men treat me like I'm not supposed to be here either. Were there bar girls on the boat?"

"All the time. The English captain had his major girlfriend, one he met in a Bangkok bar, living onboard. Then he'd go ashore to see his local minor one."

"What was he like?"

"A doll actually, which made everything especially hard to take. He gave out barrels of money to both girlfriends to help their families. It wasn't that he was disagreeable to me. He'd never think of me as a woman to go out with, of course. Why spend time with me, with the shore full of slave girls ready for a master to give them socks to wash?"

"They were all prostitutes?"

"The first night is pure paid sex. But their goal is to get a 'boyfriend,' and they change the relationship to 'love' very fast. Then they collect money as maintenance for themselves and their dependents."

"So you're leaving Thailand for another country?"

Linda sighed. "No. My original plan was to work my way around the world on sailboats. But Phuket totally demoralized me. I'm going home to crawl under a rock for being the wrong sex, the wrong nationality, too big, too liberated, too curly. I can't bear the sight of one more foxy Asian girl. Look at this." Linda reached into her handbag. "I can't even get away from these sex goddesses in my own hotel room."

She handed me a picture of a bare-breasted Thai girl standing in the sea. On the back was written: "With love . . . , from me . . . , to you . . . , Please remember me . . . , when you feel sad . . . , or lonely . . . , I don't love you but, I miss you, Thailand love you."

With frustration in her voice Linda said, "I found it on the wall above my bed at the guest house."

I decided to look up David, the bar owner the Australians had told me about. I figured the Cleopatra, an upstairs bar on Patpong 2, had nude dancing, trick shows, and two sex shows a night. All second-floor bars were kept locked, but tourists weren't aware of it. The man peeking through the glass would open the door as soon as he saw foreigners coming up. As I reached the top of the stairs to Cleopatra, the door swung open.

"You know David?" I asked the gatekeeper. "New Zealand man? With mustache like this?" I mimed a twisted mustache curlicuing on my cheek.

"Not here. You come later. Four o'clock."

I knew the man meant 10 o'clock, not 4 o'clock. Thais divided the twenty-four-hour day into four six-hour periods, not the two twelve-hour periods of the West. I'd learned not to make that mistake anymore.

Descending the stairs, I thought I spotted David at an open-air beer bar. How many Western men could there be that sported a Colombian hat and a waxed mustache? He watched me round the corner with that interested male look.

When I went over and asked, "Are you David?" he nodded as if expecting to be known by strangers. "Hi. I'm Cleo—like the name of your bar. I just came from there looking for you." I mentioned the two women who'd suggested I meet him. He appeared pleased to death that someone recommended him. I said I was a student but didn't say I was doing research. I wanted to behold him in his normal environment behaving naturally. After the Empower disaster, playing the naive tourist seemed prudent.

"They said you're the maven of the street," I told him. I widened my eyes to a look of awe, hoping to steer the conversation away from myself and my motives. I needn't have bothered. David had only one topic to talk about, himself. Great! That's what I needed—a profile of a Western bar owner in his everyday habitat. He ordered me a club soda.

"I'm a demigod here," he said. "All the Patpong women are in love with me. The men hate me."

Perfect, I thought, just perfect. I couldn't wait to run to the Ladies' Room to write "demigod."

"Oh, yes?" I said.

"I'm a pimp," he said next, peering at me to gauge my reaction. He recounted his recent trip upcountry to find new girls to supply Cleopatra.

"How long have you been in this business?" I asked.

"'Bout a year and a half. I own only a third of Cleo's. I have two Chinese partners. Originally I was an anesthesiologist. I left New Zealand and worked in the Israeli army and then in an African army. I gave up anesthesiology when I was thirty. Now I'm thirty-seven and a gynecologist." He laughed and gulped down his gin and tonic. "I do the weekly check-ups for Cleo's, but only for gonorrhea. Don't ask me about AIDS. I know nothing about AIDS."

"Do you do your own lab work?"

He hesitated a moment. "Yes. But you can tell by looking if there's an infection." He took another drink and I made a mental note that his exams were done by sight alone. He reported a low incidence of VD. "The girls wash themselves all the time," he explained.

"Ah."

After more background information, he paid for our drinks and escorted me to the street for a tour. First we went to the Pussy Galore Bar. As we entered, he predicted the women would go crazy with jealousy at the sight of him with me. We sat at the bar, and the naked dancing girls onstage did, in fact, gape at us.

One shouted down to him asking, "She your *fan*?" (girlfriend). Another made a circle with one hand and poked in and out of it with a finger of her other hand and asked, "Tonight, you do this?"

David signaled no but put his arm around me, and I suddenly wondered what I'd gotten myself into. After he paid the bill and we left for another bar, I realized it was imperative I pay for the next drinks. I had to break the format of a "date" or I'd be in trouble.

We went across the hall to Pussy Alive. Again we sat at the center bar.

He pointed to a dancer onstage who held a lit cigarette. "She's taking too long to take off her bikini. She should hurry and remove it and get on with the show."

Though I'd seen the cigarette show at Winner's Bar, witnessing it with David made it different. It suddenly became personal. The performer was female, and next to David I was conspicuously female too. I squirmed with embarrassment as she lowered her pants and speared herself with the filtered end.

David called my attention to two men directly opposite us at the bar. "They hate me," he said, "because of my looks. I always have problems with men challenging me because of my appearance."

I hadn't found David's appearance wonderful. His self-concept was typical of Western men living in Thailand. They saw themselves as Super Hunks and highly valued beings, an idea fostered by bar girls out for money.

"What do you think of the Thai men of Patpong?" I asked him.

"What Thai men?" he said as if he'd never noticed one.

"Patpong is full of Thai men! Outside. Over there." I pointed to the long-haired disk jockey playing records in a raised booth.

"Them? Chicos! Slime! They're not men," he said forcefully. "A bunch of lowlifes. They should be put against a wall and shot. They try to live off the girls, but the girls don't want anything to do with them."

Suddenly David's attention focused away from me to a man on the other side of him. A long time passed during which he ignored me completely. Finally, half-turning, he mumbled from the side of his mouth, "This guy wants to kill me. I can't look away from him."

A tremble crept over me as I perceived the fright in David's eyes. Oh, shit. All my fears from Tik's Mafia story came back triple strength. Had David encountered an old–time enemy out for revenge? Or was the man after me? I snuck a glance at him through a mirror and checked his hands for a weapon. Nothing in his hands, but maybe in a pocket? Was he alone or had he accomplices in the room? Could I fake an illness and leave? Should I inch myself to a further seat?

The man stood up. I imagined the bullet that would travel through David's head into mine. I debated throwing myself to the ground and crawling through the bar stools to the far wall. But then the man left—without paying his bill.

I had said I'd pay for this round, but now David grabbed the bill and, with relief lighting his face, he pointed to the man's drink and motioned to the bartender that he'd take care of that one too.

"So, did you two settle your argument?" I asked, breathing deeply to get my heart rate down.

"We had no argument. I never saw the guy before in my life. He challenged me on the spot because of my looks."

My relief became tinged with annoyance that maybe David had made me feel terror for nothing.

Next, David took me to Cleopatra. The bar didn't have trick shows after all. Only fourteen naked women dancing. "But we have two Fucking Shows a night," he told me. "The first one should start any minute."

"Oh yes?" I did want to see the show. I wanted to see everything that happened on Patpong. But I didn't really want to see it with David. When he ordered drinks, I insisted on paying for them.

"Go right ahead," he said. "I've been drinking since noon and it gets expensive. I drink every day, all day until closing time." He held his arm out and made it twitch to demonstrate how he felt when he woke in the morning.

I realized how drunk he was when he couldn't place his drink on the table without crashing it into the candle dish. The bad feelings aroused in the other bar returned. Did I really need to add a bar owner to the study? How could I get out of this?

A sign by the stage announced, "All Our Girls Are Clean And Have Weekly Check-Ups." Right, I thought—a weekly peek by this juiced character next to me. On the other hand, these details of David's life were pretty spectacular. I memorized the check-up sign and dashed to the Ladies' Room to write it down.

I returned just in time for the show. Two mattresses were placed on either end of the stage with a tub of water in between. The show began with sparklers—three naked women hanging upside down from poles, legs wide with sparklers shooting from their vaginas. The lights in the club dimmed and the disk jockey played "Happy Birthday." I wondered if the fireworks burned the women or singed their pubic hair. Then, on one mattress began a male-female Fucking Show; on the other, a female-female show. A girl bathed in the tub between them.

Should I act like a shocked newcomer? Or as if I saw this kind of thing every day? I glanced at David and was comforted by the realization that HE saw it every day. It seemed to have no more impact on him than a juggler or someone doing card tricks.

But, in truth, the male-female show was unerotic. Looking bored, the participants were clearly not enjoying themselves. The man performed cunnilingus for about ten seconds, then the woman fellated him for the same length of time. At one point the man craned his neck to fix his hair in a mirror across the room. The couple had intercourse in every position possible but the man only thrust two strokes in each. When the couple stopped moving, the bartenders applauded, signalling the end of the show. The man pulled out and left the stage holding his erection.

"The guy never comes," commented David, as if noting the impossibility of getting a repairman in to fix the phone.

"How many shows does he do a night?"

"Two here, but they work several clubs. Maybe six or eight shows a night. He rubs a Burmese balm on his penis to stay hard."

When the dancers came back onstage, David pointed out the new girls, as well as a *katoey* who'd had breast injections but had not yet undergone the genital sex-change operation. Then he grumbled because three of the dancing women wore bikinis. "It's understandable for the *katoey,* but my customers come to see naked women. They want to see the women naked and humiliated." His fist pounded the table, sending an ashtray cartwheeling across the floor.

Soon, one of the girls who'd been dancing in a suit passed our table. David called her over and made a grab for her bikini bottom. She backed away. He gestured at her and demanded she take it off when dancing.

"I'm shy," she said and walked on with a smile, as if David were not to be taken too seriously. His fury vibrated the air around me. He finished his drink and slammed the glass down, knocking off his slice of orange. With his forearm he batted the orange across the room, where it hit a pillar and left a gooey blotch. "Tomorrow she's gone," he pledged.

But now I wondered if David had anything to do with running Cleopatra at all. The Chinese partner whom he'd introduced to me seemed in charge of the place. David's rage, however, was quite real, and as he glared about, looking for a target to retaliate on, I quickly laid out the money for the latest bill. I wanted to run away but didn't want to call attention to myself by standing up.

David cursed loudly in no particular direction and said, "Goddamn broads. You have to put them in their place."

I wished I could shrink and disappear to avoid his turning the anger on me. It seemed ready to explode at anybody.

"Let's get the hell out of this joint," he said.

Outside, I tried to think of a way to end the evening gracefully. In his tipsy huff, David pressed his hat down on his forehead. He had to lift his chin and look under the brim to see. Instead of walking straight, he frequently stepped right or left as he lost his balance. I followed. The two of us proceeded down the street like a knight in a chess game: three steps forward, one to the side. Perhaps I should have studied rice farmers.

Before I knew it, he grabbed my arm and pulled me into the Memphis Queen. I didn't have a chance to talk him into going somewhere else. I knew the Welsh owner of the Memphis Queen from A.U.A., where we'd had a class together the year before (he'd dropped out midway). Many Patpong bars were owned by *farangs*. Technically, foreigners weren't allowed to own more than 49% of anything in Thailand, so they often put the papers in the names of their wives or girlfriends. I'd also met the Welsh owner's Thai wife. I would die if either of them recognized me and mentioned my research to the already crotchety David. How would David react to finding out I was studying him? Not pleasantly, I feared.

We sat on a couch in front of the stage, and I tried not to gaze at the bar, where I might catch the eye of someone I knew.

Now David's nasty mood transformed into good humor and, unfortunately, lust. Oh no, I thought, as his arm snared my shoulder and yanked me close. I'd hoped to avoid this. Even anger was preferable to amorousness. I had to learn to keep out of these situations. I tried to think of a way to tell him I wasn't going to sleep with him. A boy came by selling roses. David bought me three and received two more free. Now I was in real trouble, sitting there with five roses in my hand, courtship-style.

I tried to visualize myself as an acclaimed undercover ethnographer discovering important social phenomena and turned to watch the go-going girls in front of me. One was contorting her face grotesquely at David. She pulled her lips back, exposing her gums.

David explained, "I punched her in the face once and knocked out her teeth. Had to pay 5,000 *baht* to buy her new ones."

I didn't know how to answer that. This *farang* seemed a bigger danger to me than Thai gangsters or government officials. I debated sprinting for the door. But I couldn't make an enemy of David. I had another year to study the street and couldn't chance something going wrong at this point. An irate bar owner could ruin my plans.

When the girl with false teeth finished her set, she sat with us. I felt certain she was stoned on something. She kept pulling back her lips at David and ha-ha-ing into my face. David joked with her. He put his hand on my breast. I took it off. Get me out of here! Bravely I told him I'd like to leave.

But it wasn't even close to midnight, and I figured I had another half hour before I could respectfully plead exhaustion and head home. So I let David lead me to the Thigh Bar. By this time, he was slurring his words. We sat at the end of the bar, where a glass stood alone on the counter. David pushed it away.

He leaned over and shoved his tongue in my mouth. I tried to appear amused and playful as I edged away from him. I didn't want him to be both lustful and angry at the same time. Demurely, I kept my face averted and out of reach. "Now, now," I said in a baby tone as I waggled my index finger at him. Doris Day could not have been more syrupy. I felt retarded. A dancer stared at me, completely fascinated by my behavior. I felt ridiculously like the "good girl" among the whores. If word of this got out, it would ruin my reputation with the women.

"I can't sleep with you tonight," I said to David.

His "Oh, I don't expect you to" was not reassuring, as I heard a leer in his voice.

Ten minutes later he said, "Just spend the night at my house. No sex. I'll give you the massage of your life." He put his hand on my leg.

"Tonight, it's impossible," I said, stressing "tonight" so he wouldn't be miffed that I meant "Never in a million years, you creep." I took his hand off me and wrapped it round his gin and tonic. All the go-gos stared at me. Doris Day on Patpong—I felt a complete fool.

The Swiss owner of the bar showed up and frowned at us a moment. We were sitting in his spot. The glass had been his. Though the man signalled it was okay, David moved us over. Soon, the owner began yelling at an older Thai woman who'd been standing nearby doing calculations. The woman cowered. The man continued ranting.

"Someone's going to get a beating," David said. "You have to beat them every now and then, you know."

Suddenly David became afraid himself. His eyes bulged and darted about. In a whisper, he called my attention to the owner's bodyguard behind us. I turned to see a muscled man standing in the corner. He did look ferocious, but he wasn't looking ferociously at us. But now David became terrified. "We might be murdered here tonight," he said in a quivering voice. As the owner continued to yell at the woman, David continued to accept the rebuke as directed at himself. When the bodyguard shouted something across the room, David's hands shook. He could hardly hold his drink.

"I'm sorry," David said to the owner. "I'm really sorry." The man waved that it was no problem. "Truly, I'm sincerely sorry. Let me buy you a drink." The owner declined. David steepled his hands together and bowed at him Thai style. "I'm sorry, I'm sorry."

David whispered to me, "Let's try to leave here." He put the drink money on the bar and looked side to side. He breathed in shallow pants. We stood up and approached the door cautiously. David started to dance. "We've got to dance our way past the bouncer," he advised.

So I danced. The two of us danced in the aisle, trying to look giddy and carefree. I tossed my hair and shuffled my feet. I waved the roses in the air. David snapped his fingers, closed his eyes, and joined Madonna in singing, "I'm a material, a material girl . . ."

The bouncer moved away, but we danced on. Finally David danced us out the door and we danced on the sidewalk. Glad to be still alive, David joked with the doorman. Clowning with the glee of a reprieved inmate, he pantomimed being shot in the stomach and threw himself flat on the pavement.

Finally, he got up and followed me as I walked to Silom Road.

I turned back to him. "I'm going home now. Goodnight. Thank you for a lovely evening."

Leaving him on Patpong 1, I hurried to Patpong 3 in urgent need to see Jek and clear the awful night from my brain. What emotional calisthenics! Fear, relief, embarrassment, shame, dread, anger, fear, relief. My adrenal gland felt sprained. In the future, I'd stay away from Western men on Patpong. The Australians had been right that David enjoyed exhibiting Patpong to Western women in order to show off. I wouldn't allow another one to use me as an audience for his godlike delusions.

Spotting Jek on his corner instantly refreshed me. "Hi! Wow what a night I just had," I said to him.

"Oah! Me too. I walk many kilos back and forth."

"Are you making money?" I asked.

"Some night yes."

"How did you pay for college?"

"I do everything for myself. I always work to make my way."

"But you weren't on Patpong then, right?"

"No. I make business."

"Does Patpong pay better?"

"Patpong, can make very much money. Sometimes I feel bad when make too much. Not honest, not acceptable, not, how you say. . . ?"

"Legitimate?"

"Yes. I will only work Patpong until my next birthday, when I'm twenty-six. Twenty-five is bad age for Thai people. Bring bad luck. Next year I work office job, liga . . . ligament?"

"Legitimate."

"Yes. You good for me. I learn English. I teach you Thai. When I work in office, make no money. Maybe only 1,700 *baht* one month. Not enough to live, to give mother. But mother have happiness when I make business ligament."

"Le-git-i-mate." We mouthed the word together and laughed. "How do you say it in Thai?" I asked.

"*Sujareet*. You can say?"

"*Sujareet*?"

"Almost."

"Good enough?"

"Good enough for *farang*. Today we go for coffee?"

"Uh, no. I have to hurry home. See you next time. Bye."

As I trudged through the clogged sidewalk on Silom Road, I had to elbow my way past shoppers inspecting peddlers' wares. Maybe one day I would go for coffee with him. I think I liked the Thai men of Patpong better than the *farang* men. Jek's story could also provide information about poverty in Thailand. I'd heard before that Thais considered age twenty-five to be inauspicious. Why would Jek want to work Patpong during an unlucky year? Maybe I could find out. Besides, I enjoyed speaking with him. He restored the balance in me that Patpong seemed to upset. I wasn't sure why.

5.

Now what? How to proceed with the research from here? The truth was, by dealing with customers, doormen, touts, bar owners, and *farangs'* wives, I was still dodging the real subject of the research—the working prostitutes of Patpong. The time had come to tackle the assignment and face my true objective—get out, go to Patpong, and meet the girls. Did I have that get-up-and-go? It seemed that no matter what I did, I'd have to accept being lied to and hustled for sex or money.

So, okay, where do I start? Rififi, the bar I visited with Etaine from Empower? Maybe I could find the people I'd met and they'd treat me like an old friend. Since I no longer had to bother about allegiance to the organization, why not use that opening to enter the arena as a volunteer English teacher? Nobody would know Empower had rejected me as a fraud.

That night, I returned to Rififi. I asked the doorman his name. It was the same name as the *katoey* I'd met with Pong at Winner's Bar. Thai first names were usually long and only used formally. At an early age, short nicknames were given to children by family or friends. These nicknames were not gender specific and could be used for males or females. Actually, the *katoey* was not a specific gender herself.

I entered Rififi, sat at the bar, and looked around. I didn't recognize anybody out of the sixty or seventy females who worked there. It was hard to tell one beautiful tiny Thai with waist-length black hair from another. The girls who went to the restaurant with Etaine and me had been dressed in conservative street clothes and had worn no make-up. These were bikini-clad and painted up. Maybe one would recognize me and say hello.

Then I glimpsed someone familiar. The sex goddess! It had to be the sex goddess whose photograph Linda had given me. Few Thai women had their top layer of hair dyed blond. She wasn't in a bikini, though. She wore a strapless, clinging top and a very short miniskirt. She was even more ravishing in person than in the photo.

I went over and said, "Hi." She had gold rings on her fingers and a gold heart dangling into her cleavage from a gold chain. "I saw a picture of you. I have

The Sex Goddess

Diagram of Patpong 1

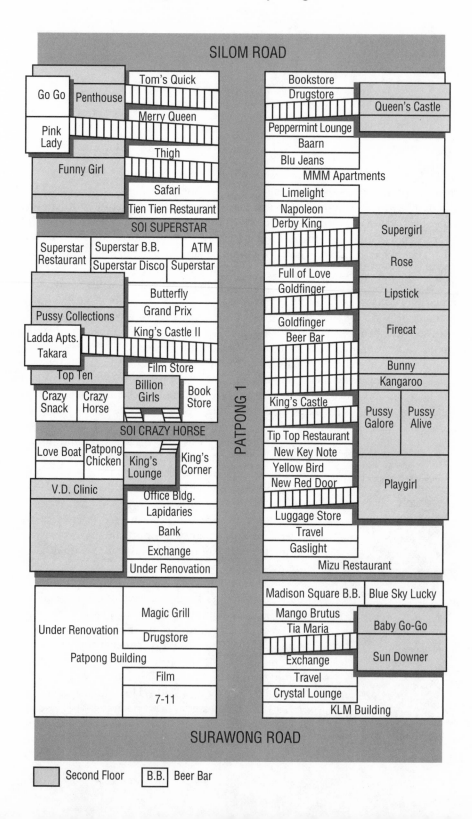

it at home. You looked terrific."

She seemed delighted. "I used to model."

I offered to buy her a drink but she said no, she wasn't working. Her boyfriend had bought her out for the night and she was waiting for him to pick her up. Her English was fairly good and we stuck to that language.

"Is your boyfriend *farang*?" I asked.

"I only go with *farang*. Never with Thai man. Don't like Thai man."

Just then, the boyfriend appeared, a good-looking *farang* in a pastel-blue "Miami Vice" suit. I was sure the sex goddess would have no trouble selecting only the choicest *farangs*. She introduced us, but he could hardly tear his eyes off her. He seemed totally smitten. He moved her front strands of hair behind her ear as if he couldn't bear to be close without making skin contact. She waved good-bye to me and her friends, and the two of them left arm in arm. It was against Thai propriety for a male and female to touch each other in any way in public; but Patpong women adapted to foreign customs.

After a trip to the Ladies' Room to write notes, I left. Meeting the sex goddess had bolstered my confidence. I felt exhilarated as I walked down Patpong 2 to my next stop, Choo Choo Charlie. This research wasn't so difficult after all, I thought. Slowly, slowly, I'd build a database of Patpong women. Now I had another one to add to my list. I even had her picture!

Music blasted me as I passed the open doors of SuperStar Bar and Crazy Horse. Between the doorways, music from upstairs bars, downstairs bars, and outside cassette vendors blended into one rhythmic noise. Turning into *Soi* Crazy Horse, I hoped I wouldn't run into David at the beer bar beneath Cleopatra. I didn't. The touts from Winner's and the ripoff place next to it tried to block my path and drag me in to see their shows.

"*Du leeow* (Have seen already)," I told them. This time I wasn't lying.

I joined Charlie in front of the Firecat. "What's cooking? How are ya? How ya doing?" he asked.

"Just divine. How are things with you?"

"Last night, man, I got twenty Japanese to come in. They left with nine chicks. Dig this." He showed me the back of one of his Firecat cards. "I have some words here in Japanese. *Domo arigato,* man. How's that? They like it when you can say something in their language. Then we had some jive here with an Italian. The chick accused him of paying her only 500 *baht* when he promised her 1,000. She throws the 500 on the floor and is gonna hit him with a bottle. I'm standing there in case there's a fight."

"Did she get her money?"

"You betcha. The bar kept his passport till he paid her."

I left Charlie with my head bursting with stories. I didn't want to hold them in till I got home, so I stopped at an outdoor bar/restaurant on Patpong 2. I wrote a bit and watched the cowboy video playing there. With the open bar in the center of the street, the thumping rock-and-roll from various go-go shows competed with the sound of cowboys' gunshots.

43

On the way home, I found Jek talking to a Thai with a pockmarked face. "This my older brother," Jek said, indicating the person I now recognized as another Patpong 3 tout. A total of twenty touts worked that corner. Jek's baby face made him the most guileless looking of the lot. "He teach me the job," Jek told me.

"How long have you been working here?" I asked the brother.

"Nineteen year." He was older than Jek and had a brutish look.

When Jek asked me to go for coffee, I agreed. I told myself it was to get away from the older brother. Was he really Jek's brother? He didn't look half Danish.

We went down Silom Road to Kentucky Fried Chicken. Thais loved American fast-food restaurants, all clean, brightly lit, air-conditioned places associated with Western culture and viewed as modern and extravagant. Jek paid the 30 *baht* for our coffees, which left his wallet empty. Thai convention dictated that males always treated females.

"Was that really your brother?" I asked him as we sat at a plastic table.

"Not real brother. Is Thai custom I call him that. He speak good English."

"Nineteen years on Patpong, he should."

"He travel all over—Hong Kong, Japan, Australia, Germany."

"Selling women?"

"He take group of girl, work for some time, come back. Who do you think more handsome, him?"

"Oh no! You, for sure. He's ugly. You're beautiful." I hurried to cover that up with, "Tell me more about your work." Since I never condemned Jek for fleecing tourists and often praised his resourcefulness, he seemed to relish recounting his financial ventures.

"I make commission in many way. Massage parlor. Boxing match. I even organize tour on Chao Praya River. Last night, I meet Iran man. He want I bring boy to his hotel room. I go to Robinson and find boy. Bring to hotel. Make big commission."

Robinson was a nearby department store on Silom Road in front of which Thai boys-for-sale gathered.

"Do you have a bank account? Do you save money?" I asked.

"When I twenty-one, I was success," Jek said. "But then have trouble. My Japanese partner, Mr. Tam, he invest my money. Something go wrong, I lose everything and owe 200,000 *baht*. I now work to pay back."

I found it hard to believe he owed that much money. "You said you had a degree in business administration from Chula, right?" I probed, doubting that too.

"Yes. I tell you how I do. Sometimes man ask for marijuana. I get him marijuana cigarette from Mr. Tam but I no charge him. Give free. This way he think he owe me. I make more commission later. Good business plan."

"Ah. Very clever," I said, thinking his strategy didn't sound like Economics 101. It sounded like street smarts. Now I was convinced his university story was a lie. "So you sell drugs too?"

"Never! Drug very bad. I don't want go to jail."

"Do you ever take drugs?"

"Never."

"Does Patpong 3 have gay ripoff bars?"

"No, I take guest to other place. To Stockholm Bar, you know it?"

Patpong people called customers "guests." "No," I answered.

"Very famous."

"Famous for cheating people?"

"Yes. Have to change name all the time. People hear story, won't go."

"Infamous. When it's known for something bad, it's called infamous."

"*Chu siang.*"

"*Chu siang?*" I tried it out.

"Almost."

Before we parted, Jek accompanied me to where I had to turn off Silom to my street, Saladaeng Road.

"You live with someone?" he asked.

"Yes," I lied so he wouldn't think he could come over.

"Oah," he said and shook my hand goodbye.

When I got home I added the sex goddess, Rififi's doorman, and Jek's older brother, the export pimp, to my growing file. A productive evening. Coffee with Jek had been informative too. And a lot of fun. I loved this research!

The next day, I set out a plan of action. I would visit Patpong every night and build a collection of people whose lives I could follow for the rest of my time in Thailand. I'd counted twenty-four downstairs bars and twenty-two upstairs bars on Patpongs 1 and 2. I would go to every one and find a contact in each. I would get a sample of different age groups, places of origin, and styles of work. What else did I need? Different genders. I'd have to add a male prostitute and a *katoey* to the group.

I decided to return to Winner's Bar, this time to see Pong's friend the *katoey*. I needed statistics on age and length of time in Patpong, and I hadn't asked her that the last time. I looked for Jek on the way but didn't see him.

"He take *farang* to bar," the older brother told me. "He won't be back till late." The other touts gathered round to shake my hand. Some held my hand too long. A Chinese-looking one scratched my palm with his middle finger. Very annoying. Those other touts were really scuzzy.

I heard one tout ask the Chinese-looking one about Jek's wife and baby. He shook his head and said that was finished. They seemed to think Jek and I were involved in a relationship.

I hurried away, pondering the existence of Jek's wife and baby. He'd never hinted anything about them. Well, so what? It wasn't anything to me that he had a family. I had no reason to be upset that he didn't tell me.

At Winner's Bar, I followed protocol by first asking for the manager. He wasn't in, they said. Then I asked for the *katoey*. But I didn't have her number and they didn't know whom I meant. Next, I asked for Pong, but I didn't have her number either, and again they looked confused. Maybe I used the wrong *p* or the wrong tone. I tried a few variations of *Pong* but with no success. A hostess took my hand and escorted me across the room to look at the girls. I found neither of them. On the verge of giving up, I was led outside and around the corner to Pussys Collections, an upstairs bar on Patpong 1.

I entered to find Pong performing Pussy Blow Whistle, which she concluded by taking the whistle out of her vagina and blowing it loudly with her mouth. When Pong came off stage, she gave me a hug and joined me. I bought her a drink. Under the same management as Winner's, Pussys Collections was also a ripoff bar, but I was now considered a friend and would no longer be overcharged.

Ong, Pong's husband, had also switched bars; he worked downstairs at the door. He came up to say hello. I asked about the *katoey;* she'd been transferred to yet another ripoff bar.

Then they gave me the news. "Manager die. Very bad," said Pong.

"Dead from motorbike. Near there," added Ong.

"Who's dead?" Again I felt the inadequacy of my Thai as I tried to figure out what they were telling me. It turned out the manager of Winner's Bar had been murdered, shot dead a few blocks away by two men on a motorbike as his car stopped for a red light. His wife—whom he'd never mentioned to me—now ran the bars.

"Why was he killed?"

Ong looked around, then whispered that they thought the mother-in-law had arranged it because he'd beaten her daughter. Apparently, the mother-in-law had connections on the street.

What a story! Maybe Tik's Mafia tale and David's paranoia were not so absurd. And how typically Thai male of that man to woo me while married to someone else, and someone apparently related to the bar we'd been sitting in at the time. Thai men often acted single despite the major and minor wives they already had. Thai culture accepted this as normal and even had a weekly TV soap opera called *Mia Noi* (Minor Wife). Good thing I hadn't reciprocated his attentions. In the future, I'd have to be wary of Thai men. Including Jek. He'd never mentioned his wife and baby either.

At the end of August, Dudley Dapolito returned from seventeen days in Pattaya, a seaside resort two hours from Bangkok. With him was Sow, a Pattaya bar girl. The word *Sow*, pronounced like the English female pig, meant "young woman" in Thai. Dudley left Sow in his hotel room and came to visit me.

"I met her my second day in Pattaya," he told me, blurting out the news before I'd had time to open my notebook. "I paid 100 *baht* to buy her out of the bar and then paid her 500 *baht* even though she only asked for 400. Sow suggested I take her for the next day too. I declined, saying I wanted to be a butterfly for the rest of my time in Pattaya. A butterfly is what the girls call someone who has lots of lovers, did you know? Anyway, she cried when I said that."

One hundred *baht* was four dollars. "She cried?"

"A little. You know. Then I took other girls from Sow's bar, including her little sister. But before I left Pattaya, Sow persuaded me to bring her to Bangkok, which is not what I wanted to do. I don't know how I let her talk me into this. Anyway, Sow told me she had to pay the mamasan 150 *baht* a day for room and board on top of what I paid the bar. If I took her for a week, though, she could have it reduced to 100 *baht* a day."

"So you have her for a week?"

"Yup. Altogether I gave 700 *baht* to the bar and another 700 to the mamasan. I pay Sow 500 a day. Actually, I'd like to get rid of her but I don't want to hurt her feelings. I get bored with just the two of us. I don't speak Thai and Sow speaks little English. But she has a good heart. She buys me things like fruit, or 10 *baht* worth of something or other."

"So you won't be going to Patpong?" With a smile I added, "No more visits to your lover at Queen's Castle?" I remembered he'd been scammed by that one.

"Don't remind me of that woman with the make-believe baby."

That night, I decided to see Queen's Castle for myself. The hostess who led me to a seat was male. It appeared to be a popular practice to have a transvestite (or transsexual) at the door. Despite their range in appearance, from huge and intimidating to petite and dainty, these hostesses were recognizably male. In contrast, the male go-gos couldn't be recognized as male until in bed with a tourist-customer. Resident-customers recognized them by their narrow hips, biceps not covered by female fat, and occasionally an Adam's apple. Resident *farangs* chuckled over the unsuspecting tourist who landed in bed with a *katoey*.

The 8 p.m. opening act of Queen's Castle was just ending—all one hundred go-go girls dancing nude at one time. Quite a sight to see on the small stage. Packed shoulder to shoulder, they hardly had room to wiggle anything.

Soon, all but two dancers climbed down and put on their bikinis. One came to sit with me, moving close so her arm touched mine. She had long black hair and a brown beauty mark on her nose. She introduced herself as Nok.

Above the loud disco beat, I yelled the name of Dudley Dapolito's ex-lover, asking if Nok knew her.

Nok lowered her head like a bull facing a matador's cape, as if threatened she'd lose the drink she was about to get me to buy her. On top of their salaries, the girls received commissions from drinks bought them. "Her number is what?" she asked.

"I don't have her number. Is there someone here with that name?"

She shook her head, but the defensive tilt made her denial unbelievable. I gave up and offered Nok a drink.

She smiled, thanked me, and, that job over, seemed to relax.

"Do you have a boyfriend?" I asked her.

"Have Japanese boyfriend. He give me this." She touched one of her gold earrings, a dangling star.

"Nice. Are they real gold?"

"Real. He rich man."

Suddenly she caught hold of another girl and sat her down on my other side. "I go make show," she explained. "You buy drink for little sister. I come back."

Before I had time to object, the new girl *wai*ed me (steepled her hands prayer-like before her face) and ordered herself a drink.

Oh no, I thought, events were rushing away from me again. And Queen's Castle wasn't even a ripoff bar! I had to learn how not to be milked for my last *baht* every time I entered a bar.

Nok mounted the stage, spun toward a shrine across the room, and *wai*ed it so fast, the audience received only the impression of a sexy move. Every bar had a shrine, usually situated high on a wall near the ceiling. The *wai* connoted respect and was made to people in greeting as well as to religious objects. It also served as a "thank you" when you duped someone into buying you a drink.

After the initial dancing song, Nok and three others took off their bikinis and inserted chopsticks into their vaginas. A carton of muffins was placed in the center of the stage, and they took turns skewering two muffins. Nok went first, dipping ungracefully for the stab and then waddling to the edge of the stage, where she slid the muffins off. The next girl offered her muffins to the bartender.

When Nok left the stage, she stopped by a Japanese man. She sat on his lap for a minute then came back to me. Pointing to the man, she said, "Nok's boyfriend." From her laugh, though, I suspected she just met him.

"Is he the one who gave you the earrings?" I asked.

She giggled. "No. Another one."

"Why did you *wai* the shrine?" I asked next.

She answered, "For good luck. Get good *farang.*" Used in an economic sense, the word *farang* could mean a customer from any nationality. She motioned to the melted ice cubes in her glass and said, "You buy me better drink."

"Can I see that?" I asked, pointing to the VD book she had with her.

When she handed it to me I let her order her drink.

All Patpong girls had VD books. The three- by four-inch grey booklet displayed Nok's picture on the back inside cover. Date stamps and signatures filled most of the dozen pages. The dates showed she went for a test about every other day but the results were not revealed. I'd heard that no girl would turn down a customer just because she tested positive for venereal disease. I wanted to ask Nok but doubted she'd tell me the truth till she knew me better.

"Do you use birth control?" I asked her instead.

"No need. Cannot have baby." She looked sad.

"Oh? Why?"

She shrugged. "Fortune teller tell me. He no say why."

When she slurped the last of her new cola, I hurried to pay and leave before she could talk me into ordering yet another one.

I left Queen's Castle feeling abused. Ridiculous, I told myself. What did it matter if I bought a few drinks?

CLEO ODZER

I accepted Jek's offer to go for coffee. At least with him, I didn't have to pay.

As we sat in Dunkin' Donuts, I noticed him hold his side. "Your ulcer hurts?" I asked. Jek nodded. "Can't you go to a doctor?"

"Too expensive for medicine. When I growing up my mother take me to *maw du,* how you say?"

"Psychic. Fortune teller. Did that help?"

He shook his head with brows furrowed. "I had a burn. Never get better. Finally I go to hospital. Now have bad scar. Too poor always. Can never do anything right because always too poor."

"What work did you do before Patpong?" I asked. He'd never made that clear.

He raised his head from where it had been aiming gloomily at his cup. He paused a second, then gave me a playful look. "You want to know?" His line of bushy eyebrow drew together as it always did when he had an amusing anecdote to tell me. By now he knew how to make me laugh. "No, you don't want to know," he said, which by now I recognized as his routine for building drama and suspense. His baby face lost its crease of worry as he teased me by withholding the story. "Maybe I don't tell you."

I rapped his wrist. "Tell me!"

"Is very funny." He twirled his plastic stirrer and said no more.

I grabbed his arm and shook it till the stirrer rattled the cup. "TELL ME!"

He beamed. "All right. I tell you. I sell air conditioner for a ripoff company called Dynamic. Dynamic air condition no good. Only work first month."

I laughed.

"People always call to complain about their Dynamic air condition. Every day I get phone call. One time big shopping center do business with me."

I covered my face with my hands. "Oh no! Don't tell me."

"I sell air condition for whole shopping center. Many many! On many floor. All air condition stop!"

We laughed together over the image of a slew of air conditioners breaking down one after another.

"Smoke come out. Make noise like tractor. BRRRmmm, BRRRmmm. Very loud. Sometimes piece fall off."

I had to rest my head on the table from laughing.

Then I said, "Tell me about your wife."

"How you know?"

"I heard your coworkers mention her."

"I marry for six year but now marriage finished," he said. "No more live together."

"And the baby?"

"My son named Thanakan. *Thanakan* means bank in Thai language. Bank is his nickname. I want my son have money and not be poor. You want see picture?" He took out his wallet and showed me.

"Cute. How old is he?"

49

"One year. My wife thirty year old."

"You see her when you visit your son?"

"No, I never see her. My son Bank live with my mother."

"Where do you live?"

"On Silom Road between Patpong 2 and Patpong 3. My partner Mr. Tam has place. He sleep in bed at night and I sleep in it during day."

"Does your ex-wife go to your mother's to visit Bank? Bank, I like that name."

"No. She don't go."

"No? Why?"

He didn't answer.

"Why did your marriage end?"

"She always fight with me. Want to kill me. I tell you *samnuan*. How you say *samnuan* in English?"

"Proverb." I knew that word because Thais loved to recite them, along with clichés, mottos, and any old outdated slogan that came to mind.

"I tell you Thai proverb. A woman must have two eye open when she fall in love. After she marry, she must close one eye because men are butterfly."

Later as I walked home, I considered Jek's thirty-year-old ex-wife. Since she was five years older than Jek, he wouldn't view me—at twenty-seven—as an older woman.

Immediately I scolded myself for thinking of Jek as an available man. He was not a man! He was an informant, to be observed only—a tout, a pimp, a Thai male raised to amass major and minor wives. He expected women to keep one of their eyes closed. He probably had gonorrhea, syphilis, herpes, crabs, and AIDS. Banish him from my mind!

6.

Dudley Dapolito called to say he'd be leaving Thailand soon to visit Hong Kong and China. Sow had returned to Pattaya after spending a week with him.

"Guess what I have," he said. "Herpes. I just broke out with herpes. What a bummer." He gave me a list of his symptoms, a description of his sores, and a report on the medical procedures at the VD clinic. Then he said, "But I don't believe I caught it from Sow. She said she's never had it. It must have come from someone else. I've narrowed it down to three other girls from her bar. I feel guilty because I may have passed the herpes to Sow. She had a cold sore beginning on her mouth the day she left."

"What about AIDS? Aren't your afraid of catching AIDS?"

"Yeah. Have you run across AIDS cases on Patpong?"

"Nobody mentions it. I don't think they've heard of it."

"The girls I met never heard of a condom."

"What about you? Coming from the States, you should be saturated with information on safe sex."

"I am. I know about it. I just haven't practiced it." He laughed. "I don't know why. Well anyway, before I leave Thailand, I'm going back to Pattaya. I want to make sure Sow gets herpes treatment. I feel responsible for giving it to her."

One day at A.U.A., as my classmates and I waited for our lesson to begin, two guys snickered over Patpong's sex-on-the-spot bars. On one side of the room sat a middle-aged economics professor from Montreal. He kept a permanent apartment in Bangkok where he stayed once or twice a year. On the other side stood a thirtyish English real estate broker. Between them sat three women, a Japanese, an Australian, and me. The men looked slyly at each other over our heads.

"Ever try the Rose Bar?" shouted the Canadian in a stage whisper while checking to see if we females were listening. He covered the Japanese woman's ears with his hands and said, "Don't listen to this." Both men laughed raucously. "It's a blow job bar," one said, and they laughed some more. "Forget you heard that, ladies."

That night I decided to check out the Rose, situated midway down Patpong 1. Next time, maybe I'd have a thing or two to tell the guys.

The doorman outside the locked door wouldn't let me in until I made it clear I knew where I was going. As I mounted the dark narrow staircase, I wondered if I shouldn't have saved this place for when I became more accustomed to my work. The tiny second-floor room had hardly more illumination than the stairs, save for

51

Diagram of Queen's Castle Bar

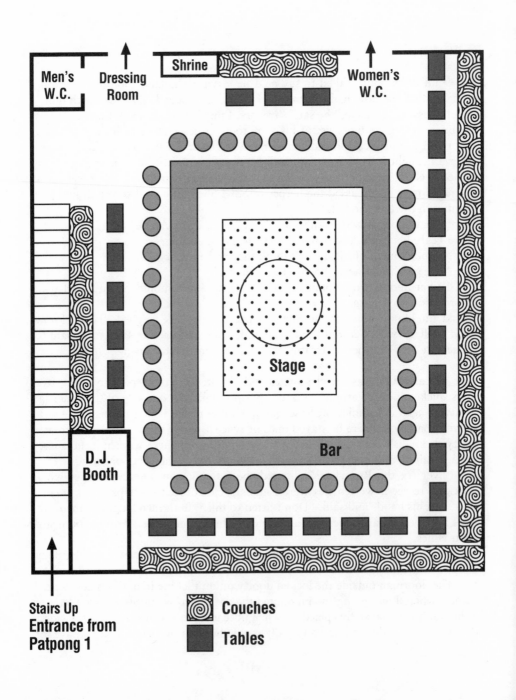

Men's W.C.

Dressing Room

Shrine

Women's W.C.

Stage

Bar

D.J. Booth

Stairs Up
Entrance from Patpong 1

Couches

Tables

the small bar and the spotlighted stage, where one girl danced with her bathing suit top pulled down to expose her breasts. Only one man sat there. A hostess in a green gown led me to a bar stool. About fifteen girls in bathing suits occupied almost all the couch space.

Two girls joined me. I picked one and offered her a drink, determined not to buy anyone else anything.

When she received her cola, the girl kissed my cheek (not a Thai custom), then shook my hand. She had shaggy bangs over a round face and long black hair. "What you do in Thailand?" she asked. "You make holiday?"

"No, I live here. Have you heard of Empower? I went there to volunteer as a teacher." I thought I'd try out the Empower angle and see how it went over.

She lit up like a sun rise. "EMPOWER!" She kissed me again. "I go before, study English. Etaine. You know Etaine?" She hugged me. "Long time now, I no go. One time Etaine come here. She say, 'Dang, why you no go to school? We miss you.' But I have no time. Start work one o'clock in afternoon."

I felt comforted to know that Etaine had come to the Rose Bar. Though I'd heard *farang* women occasionally came to check out Patpong and that some even bought out a bar girl for lesbian sex, I'd never seen any in the bars so far.

Very shortly, I suspected Dang was on amphetamines. She chattered non-stop. So did the other girl. They either interrupted each other or they both talked at the same time. Did the bar give speed to its staff?

I didn't have to ask questions to find out Dang was twenty-three and had been working there two years. All the girls in the Rose came from Udon, in the Northeast, and had heard about the job from each other. The female owner was herself from Udon and also owned the Kangaroo next door (another sex-on-the-spot bar, according to my classmates). Dang pointed out her "older sister," who'd taught her the trade.

When three *farang* men came up the stairs, Dang moved me to the couch against the wall. The other girl wrapped her arms around one of the men.

Two blow jobs commenced. One man sat at the far corner of the bar. A hostess, with the top of her dress pulled down, unzipped his pants and bent over to take his penis in her mouth. Her head pumped up and down and the hand that held his penis moved vigorously. The man frequently looked down to watch her. Then he'd gaze casually at the bar. The hostess worked without breaking stride, slowing down, or changing position for seventeen minutes. I wondered if my presence made it take longer than usual. When the man ejaculated, she unrolled a few sheets of toilet paper from the many rolls that lined the bar and cleaned him up. Then she refastened her dress.

At the same time, another *farang* was being serviced on the couch. One girl kneeled on the floor between his legs fellating him, while another kneeled on the couch to his left offering her breast to his mouth. When he ejaculated, the girl on the floor cleaned him up with toilet paper. I noted: lots of toilet paper; no condoms. Meanwhile, Dang's friend had escorted her *farang* to sit on the other side of Dang, and she crouched on the floor between his legs.

Since Dang was seated between me and the action, I had a front-row view of events. Dang chattered; I watched. I barely heard a word she said. I wanted to go to the Ladies' Room to write but a kneeling girl blocked the way.

On leaving the Rose, I stopped by Choo Choo Charlie to readjust my frame of mind.

"Dig this, man," he began. But I had trouble listening. A cloud of furor sat on my chest. What did I feel? Angry with the men? Maybe a bit. Sorry for the girls? Maybe that too. Jealous that men had this sort of thing available to them? Yes, very. And what else? Elated that I'd entered this strange world. Excited that I was trespassing into male territory. Resentful that being serviced by a woman was considered male sexuality. And even more resentful that women didn't have this same right to sexual gratification.

I didn't stay long with Charlie. After a quick stop at the outdoor video restaurant to jot notes, I headed home. I contemplated the Rose Bar and the freedom *farang* men had to indulge their sexual desires. Actually, as a single *farang* female, I did have the same freedom to follow sexual whims. I could go right now and take Jek to a short-time hotel. I could collect as many species of VD as I wanted.

As I approached Jek's corner, I saw him showing a card to a Western man with a protruding stomach and a Yankee baseball cap. Jek had the thin, sexy body of a Thai. He probably had droves of women after him, especially since beautiful females were his trade. Jek plucked the man out of the Silom crowd and maneuvered him a few feet down Patpong 3. He didn't see me as I passed.

Early the next night, I went to Rififi to visit the sex goddess, the woman whose picture Linda had given me. I found her dressed again and not working. She let me buy her a drink, though, while she waited for her boyfriend. She seemed happy I'd returned to see her. She told me she was twenty-one and from the Northeast. She'd been working in Bangkok two years, four months at Rififi and six months at the Memphis Queen.

Dang from the Rose Bar

"I have your picture with me," I said, fishing for it in my bag.

She took it eagerly and held it under the yellow light from a Singha Beer advertisement. Then she blinked. Her mouth crimped.

My bones froze as her devastated expression told me I'd made a terrible mistake. Of course she knew who the picture had come from, and of course she was crushed that it had been discarded and left behind in a guest house. Why hadn't I considered that?

"From Europe man," she said in a voice sounding like an ox had trampled her soul. "Take picture on Ko Samui last month. He have girlfriend in Europe." She handed back the picture as if it were a platter of joy now ravaged.

I left Rififi feeling inadequate, insensitive, and such a failure as a social scientist that I went straight home. How could I not have known she would be hurt by someone tacking her picture to the wall of a guest house? And someone she'd apparently cared for too. What a miserable, unthinking person I was.

Jek wasn't on his corner, and I was glad. I felt too hopeless as a human being to see anyone.

On the other side of the world, British television aired a documentary about prostitution in Thailand, called *Foreign Bodies,* that portrayed the country as the brothel of the world. News of the film scandalized Thailand, whose policy had been to hide and underplay the industry on which much of its foreign income rested. On top of that, Cooper and Porteous, the filmmakers, had lied to the Thai government about their topic, saying they were interested in refugees from Indochina, not prostitutes in the port of Pattaya.

One night, the Foreign Correspondents' Club planned a screening of the film to be followed by a panel of Thai officials discussing the repercussions of such underhanded reportage on the reputation of Thai people.

One of my journalist neighbors invited me. "This is for you too" he said, jokingly referring to my unsanctioned status. He knew the Thai government had denied me permission to study prostitution.

The Foreign Correspondents' Club occupied the top floor of the luxurious Dusit Thani Hotel. Three walls of windows, high above the city, provided a spectacular view of Bangkok: Lumpini Park below us, and miles of avenue stretching left and right dotted with stationary red lights—a routine traffic jam.

The male journalists who attended the screening viewed the evening as a joke, since they patronized the sex spots as much as anyone; matter of fact, with Patpong only a few blocks away, they'd probably head there at evening's end. As they munched the superb meal, the foreign journalists—who lived in this Third World country on First World salaries—watched the film's opening shot of a Thai girl whose impoverished family had sold her to a brothel at age thirteen. The sale of daughters was a familiar story to them. Though the prostitutes who worked with tourists were mostly in the business of their own will, newspapers frequently reported on the underaged girls who were locked in brothels geared to the local clientele, Thai and Chinese men. The Chinese particularly adhered to the belief that sex with a virgin prolonged one's life. As the film's narrator explained the Buddhist low opinion of women, the *farang* males laughed. The narrator noted that if women lead "a blameless life and are very lucky, they might just make it back as a man in the next life." The foreign correspondents laughed throughout the film.

For the most part, I found the documentary accurate in depicting Thailand's sex tourism and in rooting out Thailand's depreciation of women as a crucial factor. Racy music and gyrating, half-nude bodies jazzed up the drier details of VD statistics and police corruption. Thai professionals were filmed stating outright that the government repressed the true picture of AIDS infection for fear of hurting the tourist industry. The journalists in the audience already knew that to ask too many questions about AIDS might mean the loss of their work visas. In Thailand, AIDS was a taboo subject for the press. As far as the populace knew, the disease was not a problem in their country.

Though I hadn't heard of AIDS cases on Patpong, I wondered if it was making its way into the bars via *farang* men. Then it would spread to the Thai men on the street. Jek said he never went with Patpong women, but I found it hard to believe he'd turn down those exquisite beauties. Was my adorable Thai friend doomed to die one day of AIDS?

Much of the film's footage came from Pattaya, whose entire resort and port centered on prostitution. The part that caught my attention starred a bar owner named Tom. In his interview, he said that older Western men—"dumpy and not loved by anyone," men who would be "spit on" back home—came to Thailand and had their "good hearts" appreciated by the women. I decided to meet Tom and interview him myself.

Two hours south of Bangkok, the public bus pulled into the coastal town of Pattaya. It drove along the waterfront past a continuous line of bars, chock-full of scantily clad Thai women even in the afternoon. For three streets from the water's edge, all establishments served tourists: guest houses, pizza parlors, souvenir shops, and countless places called taverns, pubs, cocktail lounges, and saloons.

I checked into a guest house and set out to track down Tom. The name of his bar hadn't been mentioned in the film, but he was known by the *farang* bar owner community, all of whom had seen a bootleg copy of *Foreign Bodies*. I received directions to his Wild Elephant at the first bar I stepped into. Despite the crush of tourists in the streets, Pattaya was a small community, and foreign bar owners of the same nationality generally knew each other. The Germans met for schnitzel; the Aussies to watch Australian-football videos; the Brits for rugby. Many English speakers went to Tom's Wild Elephant Bar for CNN news out of Hong Kong, only one day old.

Passing under the elephant sign hanging above the sidewalk, I recognized Tom's balding head and hairy arms from the film. I approached him and told him about my project and that I'd seen him in *Foreign Bodies*.

His eyes narrowed in a fierce glint. Then he pounced on me with a loud voice. "THEY USED ME! THEY SAID THEY WERE FILMING THAILAND AND THEY WERE ONLY INTERESTED IN SMUT!" Heads flicked toward me as Tom's patrons turned to see whom he was shouting at. A man about to shoot at a billiard ball halted and straightened to get a better look. "THAT FILM IS PURE SENSATIONALISM. I TOOK THE CREW OUT JOGGING WITH MY FRIENDS, SHOWED THEM AROUND TOWN, AND THEY CUT IT ALL OUT OF THE MOVIE! ALL THEY WANTED WAS FLESH!"

After a long tirade, Tom stormed off, leaving me in the company of his

CLEO ODZER

Vietnam vet friend, who'd joined the table to observe the hoopla. I paid my bill and left as soon as the occupants of the Wild Elephant stopped glancing at me.

Before returning to Bangkok the next morning, I spoke to a few other Pattaya resident *farangs* about *Foreign Bodies*. They were indignant about its portrayal of their adopted home. The heterosexuals among them expressed disgust over the accusation of rampant homosexuality. And they all assumed a protective stance toward the Pattaya women. One of these staunch defenders sold T-shirts with his bar's name. The shirt depicted a fully dressed *farang* male—complete with hat and shoes—draping his arm around a topless dark Thai female in a bikini bottom. "Pattaya, Thailand" was printed beneath.

None of the resident *farangs* appeared pleased to meet me. Even more than the ones in Bangkok, they made me feel like an intruder.

"How do you like living in Thailand?" one asked with a sneer. "It's not the place for a Caucasian girl, you know."

"I like it a lot."

"Do you now?" he said sarcastically. "I've seen newlyweds come here and the wife ends up flying home alone." Ha ha ha.

On my return to Bangkok, Jek welcomed me back warmly. "I missed you," he said.

"You did? I've only been gone two days."

I continued the nightly routine on Patpong. I went there early, before the crowds of men turned up. I figured if I arrived as the bars opened, the girls would be happy to have someone buy them a drink, and then they'd be free of me by the time the real customers came. I stayed only ten or fifteen minutes with each person. Longer than that and they grew bored.

Whenever I passed Patpong 3, I looked for Jek. Sometimes I'd see him scanning the congested pathway through Silom's street vendors. Other times, I'd see him latch onto a passing *farang* and embark on his hustle. Most *farangs* looked at him with repugnance and ignored him or told him to go away. Often when this happened, Jek's face flashed anguish before a blankness covered it. Then he'd spot me and the hard edges would soften as he broke into a smiling "Oah!"

Sometimes we went for coffee, but other times he couldn't afford it, either in time or money. "I can't take break now," he'd say. "Already is late and I have no money yet to bring my mother."

"Do you give money to your ex-wife too?" I asked once.

He hesitated a second, then said, "No." I felt a lie existed there, but I didn't want to press him about his ex-wife. I told myself it had no relevance to me.

Sometimes, though, I worried that I cared too much about him. I thought of him often. Did he sample the women he marketed? They must have found him as attractive as I did. I wondered why he was no longer with his ex-wife when their baby was only a year old. I'd heard stories and seen TV shows that portrayed the birth of a baby as the time when Thai husbands left to find a new wife. Why didn't I see Jek as the exact type of male who made women's lives hell? Why did

I find his vocation justifiable? For sure, I liked him too much. I'd been planning my schedules around the times I'd see him, and if we didn't meet, I felt let down.

I had to admit my feelings about him were not as objective as I'd have liked. He was the bright spot of Patpong for me, a friendly island in a sea of crocodiles.

Alex

One night I received a call from someone named Alex. He'd read my notice asking for stories about Patpong women. He was living with a girl he'd met in a Patpong bar four months before, and he seemed desperate to talk about her. We arranged to meet in the Dusit Thani coffee shop the next day.

Alex was twenty-two, from Belgium, with light blond hair. Soft-spoken, he had a funny sense of humor and perfect manners. His flawless English had a charming French lilt. With his intelligent and perky brown eyes, he could have been described as gorgeous. Alex refused the breakfast I offered to order him, and over one cup of coffee, he related his past four months with Hoi.

"I met her at the Zoo Bar on Patpong 1 my second day in Bangkok. I asked her to accompany me to the mountains of Chiang Mai in the North the next day, and she agreed. At first we didn't have sex. I invited her to travel with me only as guide and interpreter. When she asked for money, I'm certain she was embarrassed because we weren't sleeping together."

"She did ask for money though?"

"But of course," Alex said in humorous sing-song. "Eventually we did make love, but only when she wanted to. We stayed in Chiang Mai one week and then, since Hoi said she didn't want to go back to work, we went to visit her family in Ubon. We stayed upcountry one month with her father and his girlfriend." Alex raised his eyebrows. "Have you been to Isan?" he asked me.

Isan was the local name for the Northeastern section of the country, the poorest in Thailand. Many Patpong women came from Isan. "Not yet."

"What a horror. Nothing grows there. The rain doesn't fall. It's really awful. They have no work. Her father drank and gambled continuously. They all smoke marijuana. Hoi and her father smoked with the police."

"How did her father act toward you?"

"The whole family expected me to give them money. Hoi's father asked her to get money from me. Her brother arrived in town and asked me for it himself. Then Hoi's sister wanted some. This time I said no. Instead, I offered to lend the sister an amount so she could buy things to sell at the Laotian border."

"Did she take you up on it?"

"Yes. There's a market there every other Thursday. She made a tidy profit.

58

You see, it's not hopeless for these people if you show them how to do something. They can succeed with a bit of direction."

Alex seemed proud of his feat in demonstrating capitalist know-how. "So, what happened when you and Hoi returned to Bangkok?" I asked.

"I was supposed to pay the Zoo Bar for the time Hoi had been away but I didn't because they cheated her. When she collected her 3,000 *baht* salary, they gave it to her in 10 *baht* notes, knowing she didn't know how to count. Instead of paying the bar, I told them I had to go to the bank and would be right back. I never returned."

"You've been living together ever since?"

"Yes, but we're not really boyfriend and girlfriend. I wouldn't be with her if we were in Belgium. Sometimes it's a nightmare. She is so impolite. She spends all my money. Sometimes she's funny and good, but sometimes she's wicked. She's lazy. She speaks the worst Thai. My Thai friends frown whenever she opens her mouth."

"Maybe you'll be a good influence on her."

"I try to teach her manners. I brought in a private teacher once, but Hoi was rude and lazy and it didn't work. She didn't want to learn. I bought English books to teach her English and another time tried to teach her math. Lazy." Alex smiled and said, "When I taught her the Earth was round and revolving, she said I talked too much. Sometimes she reads Thai children's books. She thinks like a baby. Her actions and reactions are those of a spoiled brat."

"But you get along?"

"We argue all the time. About everything. If she were my girlfriend in Belgium I would have gotten rid of her within a week. But after I heard her life story I decided I couldn't abandon her. Now it would be too painful if Hoi had to revert to Patpong. And she doesn't want to." Alex looked away a moment, then added, "To tell the truth, she wasn't unhappy working Patpong. She often threatens to go back. She doesn't really want to go. She just says that to get something. She smokes marijuana—as much as she can get. She eats continually, which I think is a fear of not having food in the future. She's blown up like a balloon. When I met her she was very slim."

"Does she cook for you?" I asked. Part of the allure of Thai women for Western men was the vision of passive little women who cooked and cleaned and catered to men's needs. I was beginning to suspect, though, the brazen bar girls only fulfilled that role to the extent it served their purposes.

"When we first moved in together, we agreed to share the housework fifty-fifty, but I do most of it. She's dirty and lazy. If she does something one day, she does nothing else for four days. Sometimes she cooks or I cook, but mostly she buys ready-made food. She buys Isan food and doesn't care if I like it or not."

"Does she support her father?"

"Yes, she sends him as much as she can, maybe 1,000 *baht* a month when she has it. I've been sharing my money with her. In the four months we've been together, I've spent $6,800 and have only $400 left. I don't know what I'll do when that runs out."

"But you like her? Do you love her?"

"I feel bad for her. Middle-class Bangkok people look down on prostitutes as the lowest form of life. Thais take one look at Hoi and label her a prostitute even though she doesn't dress like a whore anymore. Hoi doesn't like to be seen in public with me because she feels people view Thai women with European men as prostitutes. When they see her dark skin, they know she's from Isan and scorn her more."

As Alex and I left the coffee shop, he stated again his determination to always be available for Hoi. "I want to give her a future. I promised her I'd never leave her and that she'll never have to go back to Patpong."

"How long are you planning to stay in Thailand?"

Alex squinted in a comic gesture and said, "Actually, I only came to Thailand for two weeks. Then I met Hoi and cashed in the return ticket. A month later I sent for the money my parents gave me as a present for graduating university. It was supposed to buy me a little car to get around in. Instead of a Honda, I have Hoi."

I laughed at the familiar story—vacationers in Thailand staying indefinitely.

He asked if I'd like to visit him one day and meet her.

"I'd love to!"

Hoi and Alex lived in a ground-floor apartment by a canal in a Bangkok suburb. Since it was an expensive taxi ride away, I went there by *tuk-tuk,* an open-air, three-wheeled, motorized rickshaw. A ride in a daredevil *tuk-tuk* caused terror in tourists, but I'd conditioned myself out of that reaction. The little vehicle was cheap and the fastest way to zip and zag through Bangkok's impossible traffic.

When I arrived, Alex sat on the patio reading. We entered to find Hoi asleep on the floor in the front room. After what he'd told me about her gaining weight, I expected a hippopotamus. An inch or two shorter than I, she couldn't have weighed more than 115 pounds. She was beautiful and healthy looking, *farang*-sized rather than tiny Thai, with big eyes and long wavy hair. Alex made us coffee, then left to buy pastries so Hoi and I could be alone. She spoke about her hometown in Ubon Ratchathani and offered to take me there.

"Great! When?"

"Tomorrow," she suggested.

"Whoa! How about in a few days?"

I liked her immediately, much more than Tik, Pong from the ripoff bar, Nok from Queen's Castle, or Dang from the Rose. Hoi made me laugh. Before the Zoo, she'd worked at Rififi. She mentioned the bar with a lilt in her voice, as if she had fond memories of it. She told me about a friend of hers who'd spent three months in Sweden with a Swedish boyfriend. "My friend just now come Bangkok again. She want go back to Rififi. She like Patpong better than Sweden."

When Alex returned, Hoi jumped to gobble the pastries. I told him she'd invited me to her village.

CLEO ODZER

"I'd like to find Hoi a job," he said. "What do you think of her working as a tourist guide taking people to Ubon?"

I told him I'd see how it went and let him know.

A trip to Ubon sounded like a perfect way to get out of Patpong for a few days. I needed a break. Patpong filled too much of my life, and Jek had become too special a part of it. A change of scenery would put things into perspective. If I broadened my scope on the world, perhaps Jek would shrink in importance to me.

Hoi

7.

One evening a few days later, Hoi and I boarded the train for the nine-and-a-half-hour ride to Ubon in the Northeast.

I felt exhilarated to be venturing into Isan, the home of many Patpong people. Patpong, Pattaya, and other tourist areas liked to hire Isan women because of their dark skin, which Thais believed *farang* men preferred. Thai and Chinese brothels mostly hired girls from the North, where skin color was lightest. To Thai and Chinese, the lighter the better. This was also true for the brothels and massage parlors of Southern Thailand, where big business came from across the Malaysian border. Outside *farang* areas, Isan women did not make as good a living from prostitution.

Hoi and I had a couple of hours to wait before the porter would make our beds, giving us a chunk of time to get acquainted. After leaving Bangkok, the blackness of country night sealed us intimately into the soothing rumble and clack of the wheels. I wasn't sure how much Alex had told Hoi about my research. She knew I was interested in Patpong, but I didn't know if she knew I was interested in her. In any case, I didn't feel comfortable taking notes. I wanted to be with her as a friend. If I grabbed a pen every time she confided something, she might be put off.

"So your family lives in Ubon?" I asked her as I rested my feet on her seat, facing me. She already had her feet on my seat.

"Father mother come from Khon Kaen but move to Ubon to find work when mother pregnant with me. When I baby, mother die. She step on land mine. Before this my family rich, but then father drink. We sell everything."

"A land mine! That must have been during the Vietnam War, right? You're nineteen, so that was 1969?" I said before realizing that mentioning the war might put me, an American, in an unfavorable light to Thai people, especially to one whose mother had died in a related incident. I changed the subject. "How many brothers and sisters do you have?"

"Sister sixteen year older than me. When I twelve, father bring us to Bangkok. Father work build house. I work shoe factory. From sixteen to seventeen year old, I have boyfriend. Thai boy. Then I find out he see other girl. Thai man no good. Too butterfly. I very angry. I go work Patpong. Now father no work. He wait I give money to him. I work Patpong two and a half year."

"Is Rififi a good bar?" I asked. She nodded. "Then why did you switch to the Zoo?"

"One time I stay with boyfriend. No work. If I go back Rififi, I must pay bar

Diagram of the Rose Bar

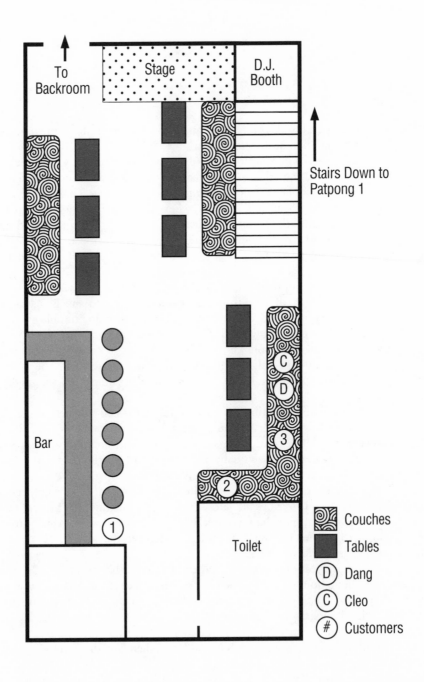

To Backroom

Stage

D.J. Booth

Stairs Down to Patpong 1

Bar

Toilet

Couches

Tables

(D) Dang

(C) Cleo

(#) Customers

for time away. So cannot go back. But I telephone every week, speak to my friend."

"I don't know the Zoo. Is that on the ground floor with girls dancing in bikinis?"

"Yes, but I no wear bikini. No dance. I wear dress. Very sexy."

"Did you make good money on Patpong?"

"Salary 3,000 *baht*. I make all together 15,000 *baht* one month."

Six hundred dollars. I'd read that the earnings from Patpong could equal the salary of a high Thai government official. "How much did you make the first time you went with a man?"

"First time, I get 1,500 *baht*. I go with man from all country. I meet whole world. One man pay apartment for me, 7,000 *baht* one month."

"What do you think of Patpong men?"

"They like money too much," she answered. "I had boyfriend, disk jockey from Rififi. Very handsome. Long hair. He always want money from me. I have to finish with him."

"I thought in Thailand the man always paid for the woman."

"He want I give him money, then when we go out, he pay."

"What do you wish for your future?"

"My dream is to buy house in Ubon." She leaned over and took hold of my hair, then felt her hair. "Not same," she said. "Your white skin beautiful. Before, I cry because have black skin. Ugly." Hoi was, in fact, a light sun-tanned shade, but to color-conscious Thais—many of whose city people were part Chinese—she was considered black.

Around 10 p.m., the conductor fixed our beds and I retreated behind the curtain to write. Since Hoi wasn't a go-go girl, she was in a class different from Pong, Nok, or Dang. A hierarchy of jobs existed on Patpong. Working in a blow job bar, like Dang, or performing in Fucking Shows was at the bottom. Next came dancing nude and performing trick shows in ripoff bars, like Pong; then dancing nude and trick shows in nonripoff bars, like Nok. Bikini dancing in ground-floor establishments was high status, but working in evening clothes without having to dance, like Hoi, was higher. A distinction existed, however, between pretty women in dresses, who were bought out often, and less ravishing, perhaps fat, older women who served as hostesses only. Hostess-only types were pitied. Attractiveness and sex appeal were major elements of Patpong prestige. Being bought by young handsome men counted more than pudgy older ones. At the top of the status hierarchy were the beauties who didn't work for a bar at all but came and went on their own time. Some of the larger establishments allowed these women to mix with their clientele. If a girl found a customer there, the man paid the bar to buy her out. If she didn't find a customer, she paid the bar herself for the privilege of sitting in it. The high cost for these girls, 2,000 *baht* a night minimum (a month's salary for an office worker), insured against the occasional loss.

Loud voices disturbed my concentration. Peeping from the curtain, I spied Hoi laughing with the porters. Now that the passengers had settled in their bunks, the train crew was eating dinner. Hoi too had ordered a meal. The men seemed enthralled by Hoi's outgoingness. From the lessons at A.U.A., I knew that mingling with strange men was considered improper behavior for young Thai women. Nonprostitute Thai women had little personal freedom.

One of my Thai teachers—a twenty-two-year-old woman from a middle-class Bangkok family—had told me she couldn't ride the train to visit friends or relatives unless someone accompanied her. I remembered the passion in her voice as she recounted how she hated the bar girls who lived in her apartment building because she was jealous of seeing them do nothing all day. To the teacher who left daily to work, the prostitutes lived a life of leisure. She also related, in sad confusion, how men preferred those types of women to her. If she and a prostitute walked down the street together, no man would look at her. She noted that many of her handsome *farang* students were in love with bar girls and none had ever shown an interest in her. While her brother went out nights with his friends, she rarely went anywhere. Off work, she spent her time caring for her younger siblings. She feared her family would arrange a marriage for her with the neighbor's son, an unpleasant man destined to take over his father's dry cleaning store. When the teacher spoke of the despised bar girls, she seemed full of resentment for the things she couldn't have, such as freedom of movement, boyfriends, and spontaneity.

I fell asleep to the lively murmur around Hoi and her occasional bursts of laughter.

Morning came in bright yellows through the window. The colorless dried dirt of the horizon took on the hue of sunrise, starkly proclaiming that no green grew here. People in Bangkok frequently laughed over the government's *Isan Keeow* project, the greening of Isan—a plan that never worked, no matter what new technology they introduced. They laughed over anything about Isan, the place or its people.

Isan, the Northeastern section of Thailand, was geographically related to Laos, and the people of Isan called themselves Lao. Their language was Lao, but they learned Central Thai in school. Because Isan was the poorest section of the country, its people were typically uneducated, considered "unrefined," and could be found in the most menial jobs in Bangkok. To city dwellers, the Lao were bumpkins. Thai movies and TV always portrayed the household servant as a bumbling ignoramus from Isan. From the way Alex had described his visit to Hoi's home, I knew I was in for an adventure. Seeing the grim expression on his face when he spoke of it, I'd decided to limit our stay to three days. Besides, it was all I could afford. Though Alex had given Hoi spending money, I paid for the round-trip tickets and expected more expenses when we arrived. Thais never engaged in "American share," where each person paid his or her bill. Instead, custom dictated that the richest, eldest, or highest in rank pay for everybody. I'd have to be careful not to be hoodwinked into treating the whole province to a steak dinner.

Hoi's village was actually two hours east of Ubon, only a few miles from the Laotian border. We arrived in Ubon early in the morning and boarded a *song-tow*, a truck with two rows of seats, to a smaller town fifty minutes away. From there, we climbed into another crowded *song-tow* for the next fifty-minute ride. Then we walked along a paved, carless road. The splendid road, with its perfectly spaced lines, reflected the government's attempt to incorporate Isan into the growing economy. The absence of four-wheeled vehicles attested to the government's failure.

Swiveling around, looking for faces to greet, Hoi seemed to glow from being in her homeland. People on the side of the road waved. A school friend bicycled by and stopped short when he saw her. They exchanged hellos excitedly. A boy on a motorbike took our bags, and the school friend insisted on lending us his bicycle.

"We ride," Hoi said to me as she leapt aboard and motioned for me to sit on the back wheel frame. She pedalled and I clung, not sure how to hold my legs so that my skirt didn't catch in the wheels.

Thai-style houses were up on stilts and made of wood. Turning off the road, she bumped us down a pebbly path to our destination, a run-down old house whose thatched roof had bald spots. The motorcycle putt-putted there, waiting for us to collect our gear. A rickety ladder with wide-spaced, irregular rungs led to a porch that surrounded three sides of the house. Following Thai custom, we took off our shoes. An insect with narrow wings tried to land on my shoulder. I climbed the splintery ladder in bare feet with my handbag, overnight bag, and snack bag on my back and wondered what kind of ordeal I'd let myself in for. I seemed far from civilization, with not a telephone pole in sight. Wasn't Cambodia near here? Weren't they still fighting there? My skirt hooked on a nail.

"Is this your house?" I asked Hoi, freeing the skirt with a toe.

"No have house. Belong to woman who sell balloon in city."

Before I could orient myself about whose house we were in and why, a mob descended on us. News of our arrival had circulated. Four older women and two men arrived first, followed by a horde of children. One dashed up the ladder to relieve me of my luggage, and I clambered to the porch on hands and knees. The wooden slats of the floor sagged and wobbled. A woman covered a corner area with tattered straw mats.

"We sleep here," said Hoi, motioning to the mats.

"Is this where you stayed with Alex? Does the woman know we're staying in her house? I thought we were going to your family home."

"No have home. I stay here before. Give woman 10 *baht* a day."

"Where's your father?"

"He live with girlfriend."

Bulges zigzagged across the walls, and I shivered thinking of the termites burrowing inside. As I arranged my belongings, trying not to brush a wall, my nail polish bottle rolled along the uneven floor and fell through the mismatched planks.

Hoi sent someone to retrieve it. She laughed when she saw what it was. "Why you bring this?"

I looked at my painted red nails. "Well . . . for when the color chips."

We settled in. Friends and neighbors appeared and sat cross-legged around us. Though they were curious about me, Hoi was the center of everyone's attention.

"Train cost how much?" a visitor asked her. Contrary to Western manners, Thai conversation often dealt with the price of things, one's income, weekly expenditures, rent, even savings. This was one of the hardest things Westerners living in Thailand had to get used to.

"Seven hundred and seventy-five *baht*," answered Hoi, disclosing an amount staggering to people who may have spent that much a year on food. "We come by Express Sleeper. Sleep in bed." For sure, none of them had ridden other than Third-Class Local.

"Train has bed?" someone asked incredulously. Even the concept of "bed" was foreign to people who slept on floor mats and had never seen a sheet.

They fingered the material of Hoi's garments and examined her jewelry. All wore dusty, frayed, and stained clothes with frazzled hems. Next to them, Hoi looked like a princess in clean modern slacks and a white sweatshirt that said "Los Angeles" in pink and black letters. More people climbed the ladder and joined us. Hoi didn't introduce me to anyone. It didn't seem an Isan custom. If newcomers arrived, someone would tell them I was an American student. When they heard I was twenty-seven, unmarried, with no children and traveling alone, they gave up trying to figure me out. I was unfathomable to them. Hoi, the local girl turned city slicker, was much more interesting.

Hoi pointed out her sister's three children: Ah, the oldest daughter at eleven; an eight-year-old boy; and another girl who was four. Ah stared at her aunt as if she were a goddess. The little girl took a fancy to me too, sitting close, often with her hand on my lap.

At the House in Ubon

"You want wash?" Hoi asked me.

"Great idea," I answered, suddenly overwhelmed by the strange smells around me, earthy dust and spices. I'd spotted the outhouse down the hill, a tilting hut of palm fronds, but had no idea where people bathed. After climbing down the ladder, it took me a while to excavate my shoes from the mountain of them piled there. By the side of the house was a rusted barrel of water half-covered by tarpaulin. As someone replenished a drinking glass from it, I noticed larvae swimming on the surface.

"You have *pa tung*?" Hoi asked me.

"No." A *pa tung* was a traditional piece

of cloth women wore to wash in.

Hoi borrowed one for me from a neighbor, then led me down the hill to a two-foot-square muddy pond topped with slime. She drew up muck with a bucket, undressed, and wrapped herself in the cloth. I followed suit, looking around to see who was watching. No one in sight. Thais were proper about not watching each other bathe.

"I'm not sure how to do this," I said.

Hoi poured water over herself, soaking the cloth. "What you don't know?" She soaped herself, washing under and around the *pa tung*. I followed her example, finding it difficult to splash the water up and underneath. I hoped my hair wouldn't come out sticky and green. Hoi laughed and we took turns emptying the bucket over each other's head. I kept my mouth closed in order not to swallow sludge.

Thais were exceedingly modest. They never undressed completely, even when alone. Becoming accustomed to nudity was one of the extreme changes the working women of Patpong had to undergo. Hoi dried herself and exchanged the wet cloth for a short shirt that exposed her sparse pubic hair. She glanced down at herself, appeared pleased by what she saw, and returned to the house where she changed into fresh clothes.

Bathing in *Pa Tungs*

We sat around all day, Hoi receiving visitors like a queen. She ate an enormous amount of food. Meals appeared frequently at her command.

"Chicken, you want chicken?" she would ask me, or "Egg, you want egg?" I knew chicken and eggs and the other dishes Hoi ordered were rare feasts for the people of Isan. Bangkokians smirked over what Isan considered edible: beetles, lizards, and assorted worms.

Hoi handed out money and sent people running repeatedly to the store for food. She'd dispatch someone to cook a huge amount of it. When it came, she'd put some on a plate for me. Country Thais usually ate from a communal dish, but Hoi knew about *farang* customs. Only Hoi and I, plus one or two of the nearest children, would eat first.

"*Arroy* (delicious)," Hoi would declare to the others who watched every biteful as it entered her mouth. Finished, she'd regally hand out the remainder to the entourage.

Throughout the afternoon, Hoi acted like a superstar with the neighbors at her service. Everyone ran to fetch things for her, especially her niece Ah. The villagers spoke to each other in Lao, occasionally addressing me in Thai. Mostly they ignored me in their fascination with Hoi. One woman pulled a piece of straw from the roof and used it to clean her ears. I wondered how long a roof lasted if people pulled at it whenever they needed a utensil.

Hoi pointed to the group of scruffy people and said in English, "Before, I look like that too." She wrinkled her nose. She did look different, sophisticated, "mannered," more self-confident, cleaner and neater.

"What do they think of Patpong?" I asked.

"They don't like. They don't like me because I work there."

I hadn't seen evidence of the villagers' disapproval. On the contrary, they seemed to idolize her. "What kind of work do they do?" I asked. "Do they grow rice?"

"No rice. No work. No have jobs here. Young people all go to Bangkok. Sometimes they make like that." She indicated slats of palm fronds. "For roof."

Late afternoon, Hoi suggested, "You want walk?"

"Definitely." Once again I felt like I was suffocating; everyone was too close. My back ached from sitting without leaning against the termite-ridden wall. This time, when I dug under the house for my shoes, I could only find one.

"No matter," said Hoi. "Take any."

So I set out in one blue thong and one white, followed by a parade of children. We visited the house next door, then strolled to the river, where Hoi took us out in a canoe: me, Hoi, and six kids, one in front of the other with water seeping into the bottom fast. Hoi propelled the craft with its one ore, while the rest of us bailed water using our shoes. Her niece Ah sat in front of me and seemed honored when I offered her the use of one of my big thongs.

Back at the house we received more visitors and more food.

That night, Hoi's father arrived with a group of men, including the village headman, a sturdy man with big lips and wide ears.

"Hello, you," the headman said as he took me aside for a chat. Whether his interest in me stemmed from his position as chief diplomat or virile man, I didn't know. When his tubby wife showed up, she clearly wasn't pleased with the situation. Among that skinny group, the heavy woman wore her fat like an ornament of prosperity.

From the thatched roof, a neighbor hung one lightbulb that was connected to an extension cord brought over from the house next door. Hoi bought liquor for everyone. Her father sat next to her and looked at his beautiful daughter with pride in his eyes. Hoi told me, "You see father's gold watch? Is present from Alex." Hoi doted on her father and made sure he had a fresh bottle of beer whenever he finished one off. He, in turn, acted as host, making sure everyone else had a drink and a cigarette and whatever other goodies his daughter bought. I couldn't understand what the headman's wife said, but the haughty looks she threw me weren't friendly. She was courteous to Hoi, though.

Hoi called my attention to five young men and said, "They no can have girlfriend because all village girl are in Patpong."

Before we'd left Bangkok, Alex had borrowed a camera for Hoi and had instructed her on composition and tableau. I'd thought it strange at the time that he was teaching artistry to someone who'd never before taken a picture. That afternoon, Hoi had shot a few, and I had to explain why she needn't use the flash in sunlight. Now, playing with the camera, one of Hoi's neighbors accidentally rewound the film, making the rest of the roll useless.

I drenched myself in the mosquito repellent I'd brought with me. "Anybody want some?" I offered. Nobody did.

Everyone drank until inebriated. Food came again, this time as a formal meal of chicken and soup. Since twenty-three people shared four bowls, each person had to haul their large tin spoon the long distance from the bowl to his or her mouth. Trails of liquid soon covered the mats. No one washed their hands before eating. Mine were filthy, but I didn't want to be the only one to go wash them. The company dug their hands into the basket of rice and then, after squashing and rolling the rice into a ball, they'd dip it into a bowl of soup. A man extracted a chunk of rice, mashed it in his dingy palm, and handed the grimy ball to me.

"Oh, thank you," I said, trying not to display disgust. I avoided looking at the ball as I forced myself to eat it. Then I grasped one of the four bowls and monopolized it, not caring if I was being impolite. Hoi had ordered me a Coke, but everyone else drank from one glass that became gunky and covered with chicken grease and stray kernels of rice. The men guzzled bottles of *Lao Kaow*, the local liquor. A guy urinated over the edge of the porch, loudly.

They went through eighteen bottles of beer and five bottles of *Lao Kaow*. Hoi bought marijuana, and they all had a smoke. Fumes of alcohol breath, mosquito repellent, and stinky mats with ground-in food set my nerves on edge. Where was that fresh country air I was supposed to breathe here? I couldn't inhale deeply because I wanted to avoid the marijuana cloud hovering over my head. I hadn't done that since my old hippy days. The uncontrolled hilarity of the drunken mob spooked me. They jerked each other around roughly. A man put his nose in my ear as he orated some story to me in Lao, which only occasionally did he remember I didn't understand. The headman mouthed words to me I couldn't make out from across the porch. Next to him, his wife cursed me with her eyes. Then she spotted my red nails and smiled sweetly as she mimed that she would like to paint her nails too. I handed my polish bottle to the person next to me, and it was passed to the headman's wife. I received no more nasty looks from her.

Fortunately, when I told Hoi I felt tired, she shooed away the crowd. Slowly they tramped off, bashing into bushes and singing.

Hoi's father, two old women, and six children prepared themselves to sleep on the porch with us. Instead of going to the toilet hut forty feet away, Hoi said, "Come, we go there," and led me and her niece Ah to the kitchen area on the other side of the porch. "You piss here," she told us. The English vocabulary of Patpong women often mimicked the speech habits of their drunken customers. Likewise, the Thai phrases *farang* men picked up from their Patpong girlfriends reflected gutter slang and brought sharp, indignant looks when the men uttered them in polite Thai society.

I noticed the floor boards there were a different color, as if used often as a toilet.

Before settling on our mats, Hoi made weak swipes to brush the spattered food off the porch, then she yelled to the neighbor to unplug the light.

In the moonlight I could see a long-legged spider inspect the food scents beneath me. I closed my eyes and let the night creatures buzz and eep-eep me to sleep.

Hoi's Father and the Village Headman

Hoi and Her Father

The thump and stomp of people moving about woke me at dawn. Hoi had dressed in a sexy negligee the night before, and she kept it on all morning while receiving guests. All of yesterday's people returned, and new ones came. At one point Hoi learned to drive using someone's motorbike; the nightie flapped in the breeze behind her. A knot of neighbors gathered to watch her progress. They seemed fascinated, though they must have seen bike drivers every day.

"O! O!" Hoi shouted to me as she zipped by. Thai nicknames were usually composed of one syllable, and Hoi had decided to shorten Cleo to O.

When we returned to the house, breakfast awaited us. "O, I get bread for you," said Hoi, who knew about *farang* food preferences. But whomever she'd sent to the store didn't know much about bread. An old woman handed me a plate of little rolls with green jelly in the center.

"Anybody want some of this, uh, bread?" I offered. Nobody did. Thais ate rice for breakfast, the same as every meal. Isan had its own style of rice, called sticky rice because it clumped together. It was the best rice I'd ever tasted, and I'd have preferred eating that instead of the awful jelly cakes, but I didn't want to seem ungrateful.

Hoi noticed a wet spot on the floor under the food. "Smell bad," she commented and moved the plates three inches away. I guessed the spot was urine from the little boy who'd slept there.

We heard a loud, harsh voice coming from up the hill, across the road. Hoi listened a moment and said, "My sister Na here." Even when Na came close, her volume didn't lower, nor did her tone soften. She consistently sounded as if she were reprimanding someone a mile away.

CLEO ODZER

I hated her on sight. Hoi's sister Na had the aura of a bulldozer. Short and fat with short curly hair, she had none of Hoi's beauty. The people on the porch seemed to tilt away from her like trees in a wind as she mounted the ladder and grabbed my T-shirt from the railing to wipe the liquid on the floor.

"How much was train?" Na asked Hoi without looking at her. She seized Hoi's bag and proceeded to make up her face with Hoi's cosmetics. As Hoi supplied details of our rail journey, Na immersed herself in the mirror, spreading gobs of rouge around her cheeks. Now she used my T-shirt as a powder puff. Next she asked, "How much money Alex give you to come here?" as she took hold of my suitcase and opened it. I could only stare in horror as she proceeded to examine everything inside.

Even if I'd had the courage to object, I had instructed myself to observe events, not interrupt—to allow myself to be integrated in the daily routine. In that manner I hoped to gain insights into the villagers' lives.

The images that struck me most, though, didn't concern foreign practices, but my own. In the presence of people who did not say "Please" and "May I?" I realized how conditioned I was to using them. I became aware of my own concepts of good manners, personal space, and private property. Na's liberties with my belongings made me realize the barriers I recognized between me and other people's things. The more I came upon these clashes of culture, the more I appreciated the colossal adaptations made by the women of Patpong.

In astonishment, I watched Na paw through my sundries and underwear. She found my hat and put it on. She came across my sunglasses and put them on too. Finished with my suitcase, she looked at me for the first time and smiled, then left.

The place became peacefully quiet without her presence. She reached only halfway up the hill, though, before she turned back and yelled something.

Hoi turned to me. "O, you go with Na. She ask you to come."

I panicked. "Where? Why? No, I'd rather stay here." In this unfamiliar environment, I felt reasonably secure with Hoi, but alone with that brute?

Hoi must have seen apprehension on my face, for she told her sister I didn't want to go. Na left by herself.

"Thanks," I said. "That woman is scary. She's Ah's mother? What about her husband?"

"Husband, no have."

"Was she ever married? She has three children."

"Different father."

"Did she have three husbands?"

"No have husband."

Maybe I wasn't asking the right questions. Sometimes I couldn't get the information I wanted. "Did Na ever live with a man?" I asked.

"Man go."

I gave up on Na's matrimonial status as children and women began arriving in fancy, but shabby, clothes. Hoi and I had planned to visit a cave with prehistoric drawings, but it turned out Hoi's father had found me a truck instead of a

73

car, and he'd invited the whole village to come along. None of the children would go to school that day, though it was a school day.

Na returned with a pink dress for her youngest child. She dressed herself in Hoi's Los Angeles sweatshirt while Hoi put on a blue blouse of mine.

When Hoi's father arrived with the truck, Na herded us out like a drill sergeant.

"O, you sit in front with driver," Hoi said. My relief at not having to sit near Na was dashed as I saw that Hoi, her father, me, the driver and the driver's daughter were all to squeeze in side-by-side.

As we drove off, Na called out deafeningly to men walking by, and we added four policemen to our party. Again, nobody was introduced to me. I thought of the automatic way I performed introductions. The robot in my mouth would have said, I'd like you to meet . . .

As we cruised around the village, going nowhere and sitting for long periods in the truck while Na accosted people on the road, I grew irritated. Na made us park, it seemed, at every house and store in the vicinity. She stockpiled bags of fruit and cakes, which she let Hoi pay for. When we stopped at a barracks so the policemen could run in and change clothes, I gave Hoi an exasperated look.

"Your sister is getting on my nerves," I couldn't stop myself from saying. A while later I added, "That woman is terrible. I dislike her intensely."

Hoi nodded in agreement and, looking away, said softly, "She always like that. What can I do?"

Calm down, Cleo, I admonished myself. All experiences were valid data, even sitting squashed for hours in the front seat of a truck. I reminded myself that I was the guest in these peoples' lives. I should not insult anybody's relative. Luckily, nobody understood my English dialogue with Hoi.

"What work does Na do?" I asked. At least I could use the time to extract information.

"No work," Hoi answered.

"How does Na get money?"

"She sell sometime."

"Sell what? Where?"

Hoi shrugged. "Maybe food."

"Oh, yes, Alex said he gave her money to buy things to sell at the border market, is that it?"

"She do once."

The conversation told me zero, and I resigned myself to watching Na through the rearview mirror as she organized seating arrangements.

Finally we set out. Arriving at the archaeological site, Na jumped from the truck with mats in her arms and shouted for us to come eat. I ignored the dreadful woman and walked off toward the caves. Hoi's niece Ah followed me, then Hoi joined us, and then everyone else except Na and three men she was able to shanghai.

Ah insisted on carrying my bag, which I let her do. She held it as if it contained the crown jewels. A fence cordoned off the caves, but no one seemed interested in the prehistoric art but me anyway. From afar, I could make out fishlike forms, figures with flat heads, and squiggly lines painted on limestone.

"O, O," I heard someone shout in the distance. I paid no attention to it. Ah tapped my arm and gestured toward Hoi, who was calling me.

"Sorry," I said to her when I caught up. "But I don't think I'll ever respond to O. It sounds like someone is surprised about something. Why don't you call me Cle. I like Cle."

"No. O is good name."

We returned to find the meal set out on the same mats we'd slept on. Plates were piled with chicken, rice, and blood, a local delicacy. Blood of what, I never found out. Before I could sit, Na led me to the food stall, where the vendor waited for me to pay the bill. Since they viewed me as the richest among them, I accepted the responsibility and paid as custom dictated.

"I need a Coca-Cola," I said. Na obliged me by ordering one, along with five king-sized bottles for everyone else.

Banquet over, we drove to a waterfall, where Na ordered another meal, which again I paid for. This time I felt less honored by the status of benefactor. Though I was the only one who changed into a bathing suit, everyone went for a swim. At A.U.A. we'd been taught that, for modesty reasons, Thais generally swam with all their clothes on. Next, we went to a river bank, where we had yet another full feast of rice and meat complete with sauces, dips, and various vegetables in plastic bags. By this time, Na no longer asked me to pay; she just walked off, leaving me with the vendor. I didn't like this system one bit and thought it

At the Waterfall with Hoi

wouldn't hurt them to learn about "American share."

Though Na was fat, the others were skinny, and I wondered where they put all that food. The company consumed each massive meal as if it were the first of the week. Before we piled into the truck for the return trip, Na picked up chili snacks and pink pudding-like sweets to eat on the way.

Driving back, I felt remorse over criticizing Hoi's sister. I knew I'd done a mean thing by telling her I didn't like the sister who'd raised her. Though I disliked Na as much as ever, I said to Hoi, "I changed my mind about Na. She's great once you know her."

Hoi's "Thank you" made me feel even more tactless and rude. I promised myself to be nice to the horrible witch in the future.

Near the house, we stopped at an open-air market to buy food for dinner. Strange things lay arrayed for sale, most of them still alive. I managed to steer Hoi and one of the policemen away from Na and the others. I didn't want Na to get me to buy out every stall in the marketplace.

"You like frog?" Hoi asked.

"Frog! Oh, yum. I love frog." I thought of the delicious frog's legs I'd eaten in an expensive French restaurant. Hoi bought a paper sack of frogs, all thankfully dead. She paid for them herself.

That night, three of the policemen invited Na, Hoi, and me to an outdoor nightclub an hour's motorbike ride away. I didn't really want to go, but I didn't want to sit through another drinking hullabaloo like the night before either. Afraid of motorbikes, I had to tell my policeman repeatedly to slow down. The road wasn't lighted, nor was there other traffic.

At the nightclub, hostesses in heavy make-up and short skirts showed us to a table, and four of them sat with us, a reminder that prostitution was part of Thai culture even out there in the bush. I watched how Hoi, dressed in a floppy sweatshirt, pants, and a baseball cap,

Hoi and Frog with Policeman, and Her Sister Na

responded to the women. She spoke to them hesitantly and behaved in a subdued manner.

I'd wondered what happened to the food we bought at the market, and I soon found out. Upon arriving, Na had handed a package to a hostess, and now a waitress placed a big bowl in the center of the table.

"Eat," said Hoi with anticipation on her face. "Your frog."

Yes, it was frog. But not the gourmet frog's legs I'd envisioned. This was the entire frog, with head, feet, and every bone intact and in place.

I picked out a portion and tasted it. Definitely not frog's legs, but not bad. However, it presented a problem. Where to put the bones? I didn't want to deposit them back in the bowl, nor did I want to place them on the table cloth. I watched the others, but without seeing a solution. What did they do with theirs? Eat them? Throw them on the ground? I never found out, and after that first frog I didn't take a second. With bones stacked on the table in front of me, I felt like a slob.

"*Arroy mai?*(Is it delicious?)," asked Hoi.

"*Arroy* (delicious)," I answered.

"Why you no make friendly?" Na said, aiming her finger at my face and reaching across the table to bop my policeman on the shoulder.

Actually, my escort and I could not understand each other at all. He couldn't decipher my Thai and I didn't know his Lao.

Na, Hoi, and their two men made boisterous fun of us. They snickered, poked at us, and winked suggestively. Na shoved me so that I fell against my "date." I restrained myself from throwing frog bones in her face.

Hoi and the policemen boozed up on *Lao Kaow,* and I worried about the ride back.

"I'm afraid of drunken drivers," I told Hoi. "I don't want to ride behind someone who's been drinking." Hoi, hardly more sober than the men, looked at me as if she'd never heard such a complaint before. "Really," I continued, "drunk driving is dangerous."

Suddenly her face lit up. "You want we sleep in hotel?" Instantly, she fell in love with the idea, and before I could answer, she informed the others we were going to spend the night in a hotel.

"No, I don't want to stay in a hotel," I exclaimed, equally aghast at the thought of dividing into three couples and of getting stuck with the bill for three rooms. "No. No, I don't like that idea." Meanwhile the others were thrilled with it. "No," I pressed. "I don't want to sleep here. I'll take a taxi back to the house then."

Hoi chortled. "Taxi? From where you get taxi?" They all laughed.

Na slapped me on the back. "Taxi. No have."

"I want to go back to the house," I said firmly. "I don't have my toothbrush, the wetting solution for my contact lenses. Insect repellent!" They fell on top of each other laughing. "I'm not staying here!"

As their laughter subsided, disappointment set in. They debated with each other what to do—how to convince me to stay, or where else should we go? I found out that Na could drive a motorbike and that she hadn't had any alcohol.

"Please take me back," I begged her. "I want to ride with you. Can you take me back now, I'm so tired." They looked at each other defeatedly, as if grand plans had been ruined. "I'll go pay the bill," I said, trying to assume authority. I had no doubt the bill was destined for me anyway.

We left. Hoi, who could hardly walk, insisted on driving a motorbike with the policeman riding behind her. For the entire journey back, she zoomed into the darkness of the unlit road and then zoomed back to taunt us for the modest speed I insisted that Na maintain.

"O go too slow!" Hoi bellowed as she sped past roaring with laughter.

With my arms around Na's waist I told her, "Thank you for driving me. You're a wonderful person. I'll send you copies of the pictures I've taken." Truthfully I felt grateful.

The dilapidated old house looked like a castle to me—I was that pleased to see it.

The next morning, Hoi was the last to awaken. She, her father, and I were supposed to visit his family in Khon Kaen, two hours by train from Ubon. He wanted us to stay overnight, but we were due to return that evening to Bangkok.

When her father was ready to go, I had to hunt for Hoi. I found her at the house next door, talking to a man. They sat close on a log, and Hoi didn't seem happy to see me approach.

In mock surprise, she said, "You don't really want to go to Khon Kaen, do you?" Obviously she no longer wanted to.

"Yes, I do. So does your father."

With frown lines in Hoi's forehead, we left. Nobody said goodbye or thanked us for anything. Goodbyes and thank-yous weren't Isan customs.

During the ride to Ubon, Hoi told me about the man next door. "He very rich. He like me too much. Can you see? He have big car. He make good money. Do you think he handsome?"

Opposite us in the *song-tow*, a well-dressed Thai woman conversed with Hoi's father.

"She teacher," Hoi's father informed us. Teachers were highly honored in Thailand. The job, though, was mostly restricted to the elite who had the money and influence necessary for education. In Thailand, jobs were not acquired so much by capability as by connections. For this reason, it was almost impossible for poor people to move across class lines.

Hoi put her hands together and *wai*ed the woman respectfully.

The woman asked Hoi, "Do you live in Pattaya?" which meant she assumed Hoi worked as a prostitute. Hoi didn't answer, only shook her head with a defensive hunch to her shoulders.

Even without their fashionable clothes and healthy bodies, Thai prostitutes could be immediately recognized. Long after a woman stopped working in a bar, she was labelled a bar girl, almost on sight. Having often jumped to this conclusion myself, I tried to isolate the characteristics that were so identifiable. It seemed to involve the way they interacted with others—more forthright and confident, more demanding and outgoing. Thai culture viewed these as marks of dishonor for a woman, symptoms of prostitution. A proper woman was supposed to be shy and reserved, nonassertive and pliant.

Halfway to Ubon, as we changed *song-tows,* Hoi bought herself balls of meat on a stick and discussed the folly of voyaging to Khon Kaen for only a few hours' stay. Since I knew Hoi's mind was overrun with fantasies of the man next door, her arguments didn't convince me. They convinced her, though, and by the time we arrived in Ubon, she decided not to go to Khon Kaen or even to Bangkok. She announced she was returning to the house. She offered the excuses that she would "help sister sell" and "check out hotel to be tourist guide for Alex," both of which I was positive she had no intention of doing.

Hoi boarded the first *song-tow* back. Without her as a buffer, I didn't want to face the family in Khon Kaen. Her father waited the nine hours with me in Ubon for my train to Bangkok. I bought him a bottle of *Lao Kaow* and took him to a theater, where he slept through four hours of movies, one Thai and one Chinese.

At last on the train, in a bunk with curtain drawn, I savored the feeling of not having a crowd underfoot. Upset at Hoi's abandoning me, I nonetheless relished the freedom to turn off my brain. How wonderful to be alone. Thais didn't understand the luxury of this, probably because they never had the chance to experience it. Growing up in large families, they ate and slept in packs. Their religion, too, fashioned them into teamlike family units. Even after a parent's death, children had to "made merit" in the parent's name. The amount of accumulated merit decided what one's fate would be in the next incarnation. The more children to make merit, the better one's next life. Thais needed large families for economic reasons also. Without Social Security or welfare, old folks depended on relatives to care for them. Children were mandatory for one's old age. They were, in fact, expected to support their parents as soon as they were able. Thai culture decreed that Hoi support her father. That she did it by prostitution was less important than that she did it. It was the same for Jek, who supported his mother by pimping.

So, had I succeeded in getting Jek out of my system? Maybe. The world did seem a different place than before I'd left Bangkok.

8.

Much of Thailand's hinterland is living in poverty and under-privileged conditions. Isan, the Northeastern sector, which occupies about one-third of the country's total land mass, is especially cited as barely able to maintain a subsistence-level standard of living (Keyes, 1967; Boontawee, 1988). A flat limestone plateau with poor soil and insufficient irrigation, Isan's natural vegetation is limited to shrub, grasses, and weeds. Isan has the lowest annual per capita income in Thailand—8,321 baht in 1986 (US $333) (Inbaraj, 1988: 31). The average peasant family barely survives by primitive methods that include hunting and gathering in the forests and doing odd jobs for irregular wages.

The morning I arrived back in town, I called Alex. "I'm back, but Hoi stayed."

"She didn't return with you?" he exclaimed in a high pitch. I thought I detected hurt in his voice. He wasn't so unattached to Hoi as he led me to believe. "Why? Did she say why?"

"Don't worry. She's coming back," I told him. "She promised to be here in two days." More likely, I thought, she'd return when she ran out of the money Alex had given her. I didn't tell him I thought she stayed to flirt with the man next door.

"What do you think about her being a tourist guide?" he asked.

"Well . . . I don't think that place would please tourists. All those people hanging around. No running water . . ." When I heard Alex sigh, I hurried to add, "But I had a wonderful time and I loved Hoi. She's great."

His pleasure at my approval radiated through the telephone. "You think so?"

After the call, I went through the mail and found a letter from Dudley Dapolito in Hong Kong. "Howdy Cleo," it began. He wrote: "I've had some awful experiences with the massage parlors of Hong Kong. I'm never going back to one. I felt like a piece of meat on an assembly line. They gave me no opportunity to treat them as human beings. It's a hardened business here. I'm not sure who felt more degraded, them or me.

"For some reason I don't feel the same way in Thailand. Do you think I'm drawing some kind of line where none exists?"

Dudley's question made me think. He said he didn't know who felt more degraded, him or the prostitutes. So if Thailand made him feel better, did that mean it wasn't Dudley who felt degraded in Thailand? Or did he mean everyone in Hong Kong had felt degraded but no one in Thailand did—not the girl who borrowed a baby to get money from him, not Sow who said she didn't give him herpes, and not the *katoey* who took him down an alley to give him a blow job and rob him? Where exactly was that line he drew?

Did I draw lines too? Didn't I think prostitution was, in fact, degrading but less degrading than being someone's poor and powerless *mia noi* (minor wife)? Were my lines more meaningful than his?

The letter ended, "I hope you're not upset: I took the liberty of using you as my forwarding address. Thanks for the help. I'll be back at the end of October. Cheers, Dudley Dapolito!"

Clanging buckets outside the door signalled it was time to take my morning break from typing. The two Thai maids who cleaned the apartments were too friendly for me to tolerate staying inside while they made the bed, washed the dishes, and threw water around the bathroom. Since Thais couldn't believe anyone would deliberately choose to live by themselves, much of the maids' conversation centered on how lonely they imagined me to be. They'd ask why I didn't write my mother to fly over and stay, to shelter and protect me. Whenever a friend visited, they'd twitter with joy and plead with the person to move in and keep me company. To escape their frisky devotion, I used this time to go downstairs and read the newspaper.

As with most modern buildings in Bangkok, quite a few foreigners lived there. We had a Burmese businessman, a diplomatic couple from Bangladesh, and the usual array of *farang* men. In Thailand, much of the local population lived in poverty, cramming large extended families into one house. In contrast, a small number possessed outrageous fortunes. These Thais traveled abroad extensively and, besides their country estates, owned apartments in Bangkok. Their style of living set the standard for the privileged life resident *farangs* followed. Given the low cost of living there, few *farangs* did housework, and all apartment buildings had a swimming pool. The student loan that wouldn't support me through four months in New York City provided me a sumptuous life in Thailand, including the periodic visa trips I had to make. Though I didn't have extra cash, I lived well.

Downstairs, one or two foreign residents could always be found in the lounge area by the pool reading the newspapers that were kept there. Saturday mornings brought more residents than usual as they discussed with amusement the latest editorial by Trink.

Bernard Trink, an American, had been writing a column on Bangkok's nightlife since 1966. His Saturday column took up an entire page, about a quarter of which was dedicated to Patpong. Trink's column reflected the arrogant, elitist, sexist, and often racist attitude of resident *farang* males. It supported the view of Thailand as a foreign male's sexual utopia. Trink geared his critiques to English-speaking foreign men. He advised where to go for the best service, best girls, best food and drink. He wrote contemptuously of the Thai men of Patpong, whom he loathed, as did most *farang* men. He belittled them, which added to the image of *farang* men as superior and most desirable. Though Trink described the bar girls as pathetic victims of circumstance, he also warned that they were out to get what they could, which contributed to an "in-the-know" feeling among residents as opposed to tourists. He praised the women who best pleased men and noted where to find them.

Though most *farang* males had nothing but snide comments to make about Trink the man, they nonetheless seemed to delight in reading his column. It provided an opportunity to offer each other advice on where to go and what to watch out for. They may have disliked Trink's pompous tone, but his portrait of Thailand's entertainment industry tickled their egos.

That morning, as I crossed the pool area, I overheard my Australian neighbor say, "Give a listen to this," to an alcoholic American whose facial scabs attested to his latest encounter with a floor. "Trink writes about old men and young Thai women in Pattaya. I quote: 'The exchange—his money, her youth—is not without its drawback'." Both men laughed, though the American was gay and had two Thai boys living with him. In Thailand, *farang* men respected each other's freedom to live out their sexual fancies. "Bloody hell, there's a drawback," the Australian exclaimed, "but it's worth it for a sweet young thing who doesn't talk back.'"

A freelance journalist who'd been living in Thailand eighteen years, the Australian knew well about older men and young Thai women. His second Thai wife had just divorced him the year before. I couldn't blame her. I ran into him daily and had several brusque encounters with him. He too liked to drink, but unlike the American, who became puppyish and talkative, the Australian turned mean and combative. Spotting me, he said, "Here, kiddo, there's news for you too. It's about Patpong. Trink says the Limelight Bar has started using pasties. Did you know that? The girls who wear them get a bonus. How 'bout this one—the SuperStar Bar has a new 26-inch video." He chuckled. "You should study Trink's column, kiddo. He's just what you need, the bloody twit. Why don't you go meet the arsehole? He's just around the corner."

Sitting down with a newspaper section, I waved at the whiskey air in front of the American's face as he held a satirical cartoon for me to read. Sometimes the American surprised me with witty remarks. Foreign residents who seemed like misfits and derelicts often revealed themselves as on-the-ball. Nobody was sure how the American supported himself, but he did little but drink and bring Thai boys to his apartment. He'd been living that way close to twenty years now. As for the Australian, on the rare occasion when he had an article published, he proved himself talented. Mostly, though, he succeeded only in getting himself fired from one editor's job after another. Thailand hosted a myriad of publishing houses that printed tourist and business-traveler magazines supplying hotels and airlines for all Asia. By now my neighbor must have made enemies of them all.

I considered his suggestion about Trink. I wasn't ready to expose myself as a researcher yet. For one thing, I didn't want to chance the government's hearing about me. Meeting Trink would be disastrous if word got out I was meddling in Patpong. Investigating Trink's columns from the past, though, sounded like a good idea. Perhaps I could get background information on the Patpong streets. With the *Bangkok Post* just around the corner, I could spend an hour there a day.

"Does the *Post* have a library?" I asked the Australian.

"Natch. If you want to go, I'll give you the name of someone to ask for. But don't mention me, kiddles, they'll throw you out for sure."

I had no doubt they would. I'd seen him turn ornery a number of times. Our switchboard operator pursed her mouth nervously whenever she saw him. She was no more pleased by the American, who frequently lurched into her booth when he needed someone to listen to him. The Thais who worked in the building thought we *farangs* were all a strange lot.

That afternoon, I went to the *Bangkok Post*. Following the Australian's advice, I said I was doing research on entertainment when I filled out the admission form. Pinned with a plastic card that said "Visitor," I spent two hours reading Trink's columns from 1972. I picked that year to see if I could dig up bits on the Vietnam War.

Instead, I learned about the growth of the sex industry and how the Thai government had tried to stop it. In 1972, as it became apparent that a sex market for foreigners was blossoming, Thailand created laws to control it. Much of the fuss concerned Patpong establishments, of which only a handful existed.

In January 1972, Trink noted that Patpong bars were busted for staying open late, having indecent shows, and being premises of prostitution. Though business was booming, proprietors were growing nervous about the new decrees the government planned to initiate. A week later Trink warned his readers there'd be a 5,000 *baht* fine for breaking the curfew that would soon begin. The following week, he noted bars that were trying to figure out what to have during curfew—darts, films, scrabble, go-go?

In February 1972, "Fun City Passes Away: A Gloomy Outlook as Decrees Take Effect" headed Trink's column. Entertainment people were fired by the hundreds, staffs cut by 50 percent. People were thinking of moving to another country. Patpong was hit hardest. Club and bar owners were looking for buyers. Buyers did exist, Trink claimed. They were mostly Americans from Vietnam who'd had bars in Saigon.

In March 1972, under the heading "Police Miss Their Payoffs," Trink wrote that the police could no longer collect the 2,000 *baht* minimum a month they'd extracted from bar owners. In April, another three bars were busted and closed for ten days. But by June, Trink reported that the trend to pack the bar and move elsewhere had halted. By July, for every bar closing, two were opening.

At the end of 1972, Trink reported business was back to normal, with bars operating after-hours and having naughty shows. Once again, bribes changed hands. Now everybody was happy: the bars had peace, the police had payoffs, and some government officials were richer than they'd been the year before.

Trink often criticized the Thai system of government by pointing out the corruption of its officials. Though not inaccurate, it contributed to the notion of superior *farangs* in a primitive land of ineptitude. Trink's column helped shape the mentality of foreign males in Thailand. In that Third World country, they lived as exalted beings, on the level of Thai aristocrats, but without having to respond to Thai morals—nor to those of their homelands.

I signed myself out of the library, satisfied with the day's work. I made plans to return there for more insights into Patpong's past.

That night, when I stopped by Jek's corner, I asked him, "Have you ever seen Trink come by here?"

"Trink? Who that?"

"You never heard of Trink? He writes a column on Patpong for the *Bangkok Post.*"

"I don't know about him. We go for coffee?"

We went to Dunkin' Donuts and sat at our usual table.

"I have some pictures to show you from my trip to Ubon. Here. This is Hoi."

"Oah! Isan people dress no good," he said noticing Hoi's friends and neighbors.

"This is Hoi's sister Na, a witch."

"*Pee?*"

"No, no, not a ghost. Just a horrible woman." Thais believed in ghosts, and I'd learned to be careful about referring to them. Once, I'd jokingly speculated that a slammed door had been caused by a ghost. Seeing the fear that caused, I now avoided the word.

"Oah! Sexy," he exclaimed looking at me and Hoi bathing in *pa tungs*. I didn't think the dull cloth was sexy at all, but apparently it had significance to Thais. I liked his approving nod.

"Here's Hoi buying frogs at the market," I said.

"Frog!" Jek made a lemon-tasting face that looked adorable on him. "Isan people eat anything."

I laughed at his expression. "Frog can be delicious. It's a delicacy in France."

"French people eat frog too? No, you make fun of me. Oh, I forget to tell you," he said suddenly. "I meet your friend."

"Who?"

"His name Charlie. He speak good English. I see him on street. I think he tourist from Singapore. We talk and he say he know you."

"Choo Choo Charlie! He's the doorman at Firecat." I didn't like that at all. I didn't want Patpong people to know I talked to many of them and asked questions. I was afraid to find out what Charlie told Jek about me. "Have you been to Isan?" I asked instead.

His adorable lemon-tasting look came back. "Don't want to go there."

This time when we parted, he said, "Why you never kiss me goodbye?" He leaned over and tapped his cheek. I kissed it. "Oah!"

At home that night, I thought, no, the trip to Ubon hadn't gotten Jek out of my system. Well, okay, as long as I didn't act on the feelings he stirred, I might as well enjoy the way they invigorated my life. I just had to be careful not to let it go further.

By the end of September, Alex called me daily in despair because Hoi had not yet returned. "Don't worry," I told him. "I'm positive she'll be back any minute." I was. For sure, she'd leave Ubon as soon as she ran out of money.

My research expanded to full-time. At night, I continued visiting new bars, meeting new people, and returning to see old ones. In the morning, I typed notes and had a Thai lesson. In the afternoon, I poured through Trink's back issues, then sometimes I'd go to Patpong to draw maps.

On Patpongs 1 and 2, I counted forty-six go-go bars, twenty-three cocktail lounges, nine beer bars (open-air bars), two country & western bars, two discotheques, three massage parlors, three (shave and sex) barber shops, three short-time hotels, three VD clinics, eleven restaurants, nine fast-food places, six drug stores, and two of what Trink called "meat markets," after-hour places for bar girls who hadn't yet found a customer for the night. I included the drug stores in the list of Patpong establishments because of their lax manner in dispensing amphetamines, barbiturates, sex enhancers, etc. Thailand, in general, was liberal in supplying drugs without prescriptions, but Patpong even more so.

Patpong 3 had twelve cocktail lounge/bars, one go-go bar, eight restaurants, and a two-story discotheque.

I drew the maps in the daytime, when no touts, peddlers, or mobs of shifty people were around to disturb me. During the day, it took two minutes and forty-three seconds to walk from one end of Patpong 1 to the other. At night, no less than fifteen minutes were needed to sidestep through the obstacle course of what collected there.

Plotting doorways and marking building lines weren't easy tasks for someone who'd never studied cartography. I had to return repeatedly to measure distances.

One afternoon on Patpong 3, I met Chai. He half-sat, half-leaned on a gold railing in front of a big structure called the Rome Club. With fuzzy short hair brushed back above a wide face, he looked easy-going and kind.

"Do you know where this bar ends?" I asked him as I tried to peer through the black window of a door.

"Upstair," he answered.

"No. This one." I tapped the name on the glass. "I'm trying to figure out where the bar ends and the restaurant begins. It's locked, so I can't go in and check."

"Bar upstair. Here only door."

"Oh." I looked left and right to see how that worked, then went to his rail to use it as support as I erased lines and scribbled new ones. "Do you work around here?" I asked.

He pointed over his shoulder and said, "At the Apollo Inn."

Since I hadn't yet visited a Patpong 3 bar, this news roused my interest.

"Are you gay?" I asked. Thais used the English terms "gay" for homosexual and "tom" for lesbians. The Thai word *katoey* denoted a homosexual male in its broad usage, but specifically an effeminate homosexual male or transsexual.

"Yes."

"What work do you do there?"

"I dance go-go."

I looked up at the four story building. Apollo was the god of manly beauty— a good name for a male go-go bar. "All this is the Apollo Inn?" I asked.

"Yes. First floor is restaurant. I work there serve food for lunch. Second floor is bar. I work dancing nighttime. Third floor have private room for massage, for make love. Fourth floor have locker for clothes."

"You live there?"

"Yes. Sleep in bar. Will you help me write letter please?"

"Sure. What can I do?"

"Just read. See if okay." He pulled a letter from his pocket and handed it to me.

Addressed to a man in New York, the four pages were written in English script. "Is he your boyfriend?" I asked.

"Guest. I give him massage. He holiday in Thailand six month ago and say he come back to see me. I just get letter say he no can come."

I perched myself on the rail next to Chai and read.

The letter stated that Chai was sitting under a tree in Lumpini Park very sad the man wasn't coming. I love you, miss you, I remember the time you lay next to me at the Apollo Inn. I want to kiss you, hold you . . . Your picture is on the wall by my bed. All my friends say you handsome. I sing the song "Welcome to Thailand" because it makes me think of you. In just one line, the letter also asked for money.

I made a few grammar and spelling corrections, then put a suspicious look on my face and asked, "Do you really miss him?"

He laughed. "No, he not really handsome. He forty-two."

"Has he sent you money before?"

"No. This first time I ask."

A few nights later, I headed for the Apollo Inn with a present of stationery for Chai. Now that I'd made a contact on Patpong 3, I wanted to follow up on it. First I stopped by Jek's corner at the entrance to the street.

"Where you go now?" he asked as always.

"Today I'm going down here."

"I see you when you come back?"

I nodded. Actually, I didn't have to pass that way when I left the Apollo Inn. The afternoon I'd met Chai, he'd shown me a shortcut to Patpong 2 through a bar and a parking lot. Maybe I'd go the long way, though, for the extra chance to see Jek.

Inside the Apollo Inn, a sign in Thai said, "No Women Allowed." Though nobody knew I could read it, it increased my feeling of being a trespasser, a female in a man's gay bar. I already had an acquaintance there, though, so I forged ahead and climbed the stairs.

It was too early for customers; the seats were filled with employees. The place was packed with Thai boys in their late teens and early twenties wearing kimonos over bikinis, watching a Kung Fu video. There must have been seventy of them.

I asked the nearest one for Chai.

"CHAI!" he shouted, distracting everyone's attention from the movie. Once they saw me, none of the seventy turned back to the screen. They seemed to be smirking at the sight of the dumb tourist who must have made a wrong turn somewhere. I was relieved to see Chai make his way through the crowd to join me.

He led me to a booth where one boy had to sit on another's lap to make room for us.

"How old are you?" I asked Chai after I offered him a drink. A drink for the boys, I noticed, meant a beer, not a cola or an orange juice.

"Twenty-one," he answered.

"Where are you from?"

"Udon. In the Northeast." Udon was short for Udon Thani and wasn't the same place as Hoi's town of Ubon, or Ubon Ratchathani. Thais shortened long names.

Since Chai had caught me mapping Patpong, I'd no choice but to tell him about the research. So far, except for Empower, he was the only one on Patpong who knew. This allowed me greater freedom to ask personal questions.

"How much money do you make here?"

"I get 600 *baht* a month salary, plus 20 *baht* if I go with guest and 10 *baht* for every drink someone buy me."

"And for sex?"

He smiled. "Everything I get, I keep."

"How much?"

"Short-time, I get 200, 300, or 500 *baht* from *farang*, 200 *baht* from Thai. Last month I have good luck. I get 1,500, then 2,000 and again 2,000 from same guest. When man go home to England, he give me 4,000 *baht*. He like me, give tip. Another guest give me 800 *baht* each time and take me ten time. Another take me eight time, three time at 400 *baht* short-time and all night five time."

With the exchange rate of 25 *baht* to the dollar, 200 *baht* meant $8 was the minimum for short-time. "How many guests do you have a month?"

Chai made counting wiggles with his fingers and answered, "About fifteen."

"Do you send money home to Udon?"

"When I have. Maybe 5,000 *baht* every three month. Family don't know I'm gay or go-go. I tell them I'm waiter in restaurant."

"Do women come here? I saw that sign downstairs."

"Not so many. Manager don't want. Bar charge *farang* women 30 *baht* extra for drink. Thai woman pay 70 *baht* extra."

"Do you go to Udon for visits?"

"Expensive," he answered. "And I have to work."

We seemed to be getting along well. I didn't think he minded my questions. So I asked, "Would you take me to your home? Just for a few days. I'd pay the bar." The trip with Hoi had shown me the importance of establishing background context for the people I met. The more insights into upcountry life I could get, the better.

Chai smiled and nodded but didn't seem to take me seriously. In his job, he probably had loads of people saying things they didn't mean. I told him, "I'll come back and tell you when I can leave Bangkok. We'll arrange it, okay?"

He nodded a yes-yes that I could tell meant "I'm not holding my breath."

"Really," I said. "For sure. I promise. Okay?"

A glint flickered in his eye, but I didn't feel he was convinced.

When I left the bar, I didn't take the shortcut to Patpong 2. At the corner, I looked for Jek.

"He go massage parlor with *farang*," another tout told me.

Just as well, I thought. How ridiculous that I now found ways to meet Jek more often. I really had to do something to cool down.

Since I'd already entered a new bar that night, I decided to revisit Dang at the Rose. How many blow jobs would I see tonight?

The doorman remembered me. Since the first time I'd been there, I'd passed the Rose many times, and I always greeted Patpong people I'd met before. He opened the door and rang the bell that alerted upstairs someone was coming. In the smaller bars—especially the sex-on-the-spot ones where clientele didn't stick around longer than necessary—the stage entertainment ceased until the bell signalled a "live one" was on the way up.

I climbed the stairs to find the bar empty of anyone but employees. When Dang saw me, she flew over and wrapped me in a hug. The intensity of her embrace overwhelmed me. Was it amphetamine affection or was she that glad to see me?

I ordered two drinks and followed her to a table.

"I very happy you come again see Dang," she said. "How is Etaine? Everything good at Empower?"

"Well, actually, I haven't been there lately," I answered. I'd forgotten I told her I worked there. I changed the subject. "Do you have a boyfriend?"

"Have French boyfriend. He forty-five. Send me money every month."

"He doesn't live in Thailand?"

"No. Only come for holiday last year."

"So he's been sending you money every month since last year?" She nodded. "What about a Thai boyfriend?" I asked.

"Thai man no good," she said forcefully.

"Oh?"

"No good!" she said again. "Only few good."

"I know a nice one. He works on Patpong 3." I thought saying that would make me more a part of the Patpong scene. I also had an irresistible urge to discuss Jek. "His name's Jek. Do you know him?"

"No. Patpong man very bad. You watch out."

"What's wrong with Patpong men?"

"Thai man have many girlfriend at same time. *Farang* only want one."

Just then, two *farang* men exited a door near the stage. They continued down and out without stopping in the bar. "What's back there?"

"Private room."

"Do you have a bank account with savings?" I asked her next.

She shook her head. "Send money for mama."

"How much?"

"Depend how much I make, 3,000 *baht* or 10,000 *baht* a month."

A *farang* entered and went straight through to the private rooms.

"Did you go to school?"

"I finish grade four then run away when eleven year old. My father beat me too much. I think he no love me because he beat me. I wash dish in Udon for 300 *baht* a month. I never go home. When father sick, I still no go because I think he no love me. After father die, I go home. Mama tell me he always love me the best."

Time to leave the Rose; Dang escorted me to the top of the stairs and gave me the warmest hug I'd ever experienced, as if I were the only person who'd ever visited her just to say hello.

"Thank you for come see Dang," she said.

I promised I'd be back.

Next, I stopped at the Firecat to see Choo Choo Charlie and find out what he'd told Jek. How could I explain my sorties into the Rose Bar to Jek? He might think I was gay or perverted. I didn't care what Charlie thought. Oh no, was I now going to tailor my research activities to fit Jek's approval? Ridiculous. Here I was campaigning to make prostitution a valid occupation, and suddenly I'm concerned about my reputation in the eyes of a pimp. What foolishness.

"Charlie no work here anymore," the new doorman told me. "He quit."

I didn't like losing an informant, but I liked it even less that Charlie was on the loose and telling people about the blond American he knew.

On the way home I looked for Jek, but he hadn't yet returned. I hated myself for feeling disappointed.

Walking on, I contemplated how happy Dang had been over my visit. I'd thought that anthropologists observed their subjects, then left without changing anything or affecting anybody. That didn't seem the case with me. My presence did seem to affect some of the Thai people of Patpong. Worse than that, one was definitely affecting me.

9.

After several frantic calls from Alex asking me again when Hoi would be back, one day he called to invite me to the Weekend Market.

"Remember I told you about Sumalee and her Israeli boyfriend, Shlomo? Well, they're back from the Philippines and staying with me. We can all go to the Market together."

"Sounds nifty," I told him. I felt sure he'd invited me just to have someone to talk to about Hoi. Clearly he was cuckoo over her. That was fine with me.

Sumalee, I remembered, was the one Alex had hoped would teach Hoi to "be a lady." He had met Sumalee while she was traveling in the North with a thirty-nine-year-old Danish man whom she'd picked up in the bar where she worked. She quit the bar when the man requested she spend the rest of his vacation with him. When Alex heard the Dane was leaving the country, he offered to let Sumalee—who was from Bangkok and had two years of college—stay in the apartment as a role model for Hoi. A few weeks after she moved in, Alex went to India for a month. He left 6,000 *baht* with Hoi and Sumalee, and they spent it all in two weeks. With the money gone, Sumalee went to work on Patpong. Within days, she met Shlomo and quit that bar too. Sumalee and Shlomo had now known each other two months. During their recent trip to the Philippines, Shlomo asked her to marry him.

It was a common occurrence to hear about foreign men enamored of Thai women they'd bought from a bar. Some married them; others returned to their home countries but sent money for years to support them. Sumalee belonged to the small percent of Thai people who adhered to the Islamic faith. She was Muslim, Shlomo Jewish. These two sounded like a couple I just had to meet.

I *tuk-tuk*ed to Alex's apartment and found him in the small front room. He'd given the bedroom to Sumalee and Shlomo.

"Any news from Hoi?" I asked.

He shook his head like a wounded sparrow. Then he called Sumalee and Shlomo to come meet me. Sumalee, with bobbed shoulder-length hair and a jeans outfit, looked more Bangkok middle-class than Patpong prostitute. From the poised way she handled his introduction, I understood why Alex thought she could teach Hoi manners. Wide-shouldered and muscular, Shlomo looked like your typical Israeli on the road after completing army duty. Kao San Road, the Bangkok district catering to low-budget travellers, had hordes of those Israelis, out for a global romp now that they'd proven themselves as patriots. Shlomo was twenty-three, Sumalee twenty-two.

Diagram of Patpong 3

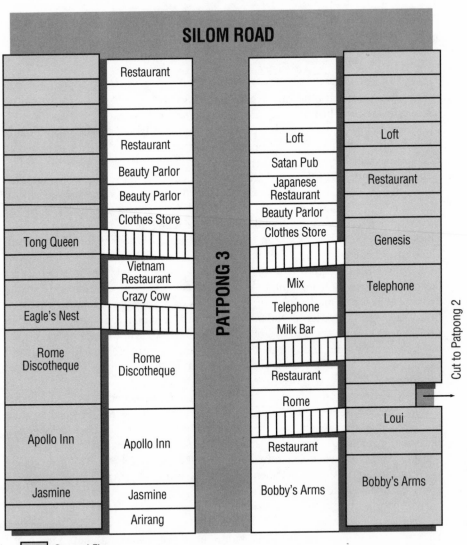

SILOM ROAD

PATPONG 3

Cut to Patpong 2

Restaurant

Restaurant

Beauty Parlor

Beauty Parlor

Clothes Store

Tong Queen

Vietnam Restaurant

Crazy Cow

Eagle's Nest

Rome Discotheque

Rome Discotheque

Apollo Inn

Apollo Inn

Jasmine

Jasmine

Arirang

Loft

Satan Pub

Japanese Restaurant

Beauty Parlor

Clothes Store

Mix

Telephone

Milk Bar

Restaurant

Rome

Restaurant

Bobby's Arms

Loft

Restaurant

Genesis

Telephone

Loui

Bobby's Arms

Second Floor

Shlomo's eyes followed Sumalee as she put on her shoes and prepared to leave the apartment. Though Sumalee looked at him sweetly, she didn't have the same love-lust.

The four of us went to the Weekend Market, a giant affair that took place every Saturday and Sunday under tents in Jatujak Park near the outskirts of Bangkok. Crowds of people prevented us from progressing more than a few shuffled inches at a time. My blond hair and Alex's prevented us from losing sight of each other, and we kept track of Shlomo by his height. Though it was bad Thai form, Shlomo held Sumalee's hand.

We jostled our way through hilltribe handicrafts and mounds of smelly purple fish-paste and found ourselves in the animal section. A baby orangutan looked at us with sad eyes and extended an arm through his cage.

"They kill the mother to get the baby," Alex commented. "It's so mean. Those hunters should be put in jail."

"Poachers are jailed and fined," Sumalee said in excellent English. "But they're poor. They have no choice. It's also illegal to transport the animals over borders. This little fellow comes from Borneo. Sometimes, to survive, people have to do things they don't want."

"Look at this one," said Shlomo with a baby gibbon nuzzling his knuckle.

"Aw," murmured Alex.

When we paused at a box of fighting beetles, I positioned myself near Sumalee to get acquainted with her. A group of Thai men egged the beetles on.

"You're from Bangkok?" I asked her.

"Yes, my family owns two houses here."

"Where did you meet Shlomo?"

"At the Memphis Queen."

"Did you like working there?"

"It wasn't fair. When I went with a man I made 500 *baht*, the bar made 300."

The beetles snapped fearsome pincers at each other. From further off, Alex called our attention to a tank of fighting fish. Shlomo frowned and suggested we sit somewhere for a drink. Foreigners who weren't used to Bangkok's heat needed to stop frequently for liquids. We pushed on, single file, through the shoppers till we came to a juice stand.

As we sat at an empty table, I asked Sumalee, "How did you like the Philippines?"

"Show her the pictures we took," Shlomo told her. I noticed he was still holding her arm, even though she was using it to lift her glass.

"I left them in the apartment."

"I wanted to take Sumalee to Japan," Shlomo told me, "but they wouldn't give her a visa."

No one but me could hear Alex over the din as he whispered, "It's almost impossible for Thai women to get visas for most countries because it's assumed they're traveling for prostitution. The world thinks all Thai women are whores."

"The Japanese embassy put us through an ordeal," Shlomo continued. "And for nothing. First they said Sumalee had to have $500 in traveler's checks. So I bought her the checks, but then they said she couldn't get a visa until six months after her Thai passport had been issued. The passport had only been issued that month. I also wanted to take her to Israel, but the Israeli embassy wouldn't give her a visa either. They said we had to be married."

"So we plan to marry next month," said Sumalee. "You're invited to the wedding."

"It will be a Muslim ceremony," Alex explained, "because of Sumalee's family."

"Then we'll go to Israel," said Shlomo. "Maybe Sumalee will find a waitressing job in Tel Aviv. She can learn Hebrew in six months. She already knows a few words. Show them how you can speak Hebrew," he urged her like a boastful father.

"*Shalom. Can. Lo. La chaim*!" she uttered. (Hello. Yes. No. To life!) Shlomo looked pleased as punch.

"So you think Thai-*farang* relationships can work?" I asked.

"Sure. Why not?"

"What about a Thai man and a *farang* woman?"

At this, both Alex and Shlomo made drawn-out throat noises.

"That's different."

"That's another matter entirely."

"No. I don't think so."

"Forget it."

Sumalee didn't say anything.

"In Thailand, a male is much higher than a female," explained Shlomo. "A *farang* woman would never stand for it."

"The man would never change," added Alex.

"Not possible."

"Come now, I want you to meet my friend who works here at the Weekend Market," Alex said while standing up and paying for our lemonades. "I hope I can find him." We traipsed back through the tiny aisles that should not have fit more than two people across but had four or five plus a variety of food vendors who planted themselves in the spots most likely to block traffic.

Apparently Alex often visited this friend of his at the Market, and he led us straight to his stall. Half-Thai, half-Chinese, Alex's friend sold antique watches and bric-a-brac; he was assisted by his Thai girlfriend. She too wore a jeans outfit. Imported and expensive, they were a Thai marker of status. She looked even more classy than Sumalee.

"She's leaving next month for a university in Japan," Alex told me.

I knew that meant she belonged to the moneyed minority of Thai society. Those women had more freedom to be their own people, traveling abroad and assimilating foreign lifestyles.

Alex's Thai-Chinese friend was chipper and friendly. He showed us an intricate cigarette lighter and offered to take us on a tour of Chinatown one day.

A few days later, I answered my phone to hear a babble of rapid Thai. It seemed to be carrying on about how bad the Bangkok air was.

"You have the wrong number," I said in English, annoyed that the switchboard operator had misplugged connections. The voice babbled faster. "Wrong number!" I repeated and hung up.

Seconds later, it rang again. This time it was Alex. He had ecstasy in his voice. "Hoi's here! She arrived this morning."

"See. I told you she'd be back."

His ecstasy lessened as he added, "But she's not alone. She brought her sister Na and one of the policemen you told me about."

"Oh no! You have Na and the policeman as houseguests?" Poor Alex, I thought. We had discussed how irritating Na could be. He'd hated her on sight, the same as I had. "What about Sumalee and Shlomo?"

"Everybody's right here. Na just called you. What happened?"

"That was Na?" I laughed. "You have to tell her that when she uses the telephone, she must identify herself. Tell her to say, *Na poot, ka*, this is Na speaking." Alex and I giggled. *Ka* was a polite particle of speech used by women at the ends of sentences. Few Patpong or Isan women used it. The image of Na saying *ka* flared amusement in us. Even foreign men who didn't speak Thai knew about *ka*. All foreigners tried to learn at least how to say hello in Thai. From women, men picked up *Sawatdee ka*. But males were supposed to say *krab*, not *ka*. The peals of laughter caused by their saying *ka* imprinted that word forever on their brains.

"Why did Na call me?" I asked.

"I think she believes you two are good friends," he said with a humorous undertone. Alex had a knack for making statements burst with comic meaning.

"Oh no! Since my urge was to strangle her, I went out of my way to be nice."

"You may have overdone it. Me too. I think she feels the same about me."

The next afternoon, I *tuk-tuk*ed to his apartment. Now Sumalee and Shlomo had the front room, with Hoi, Alex, Na, and the policeman in the bedroom. Na greeted me like a long-lost friend. She took hold of my wrist and held on.

Hoi said to me, "My sister Na very happy with picture you sent her."

"I wanted to thank her for driving me that night." I made a little bow movement at Na.

"*O nisai dee*," Na said with a grin. (Cleo has good character.) She bopped my shoulder.

"Father happy you send him picture too. He said you write Thai very pretty."

I remembered that when Hoi's father gave me his address at the train station in Ubon, he had the station master write it for him. He was probably illiterate.

"O have mascara?" Hoi asked, squinting at my lashes. "I can use?"

"Sure." I searched my bag and gave it to her. "Don't you have any?"

"I throw away. Alex no want I look sexy anymore."

"You're beautiful without that make-up you used to wear," Alex said. He had the same enraptured face when he gazed at her that Shlomo had for Sumalee.

Hoi looked at him playfully and coquettishly but without much passion.

As Hoi went to the bathroom with the mascara, Alex brought me the pictures she'd taken in Ubon. "There's only a few because that guy rewound the camera." He shook his head as if in frustration.

"How'd they come out?"

He clicked his tongue. "She didn't listen to anything I told her about subject placement and perspective."

"She never used a camera before! Don't expect artistic genius at first try."

When everyone was ready, all seven of us piled into a taxi, a standard practice in Thailand. Newcomers were astounded by how many people, babies, farm animals, and produce could be shoved into taxis and *tuk-tuks*.

We met up with Alex's Thai-Chinese friend for a tour of Chinatown. Chinatown in Bangkok, called Yaowarat, was near the train terminal. Alex's friend led us down an avenue lined with gold stores with signs written in Chinese characters. I couldn't seem to shake Hoi's sister Na and the policeman from my elbow. Bangkok was more foreign to them than it was to us *farangs*. When a bus passed, trailing a comet-tail of black smoke, the policeman's eyes bulged and he grabbed his throat. Na held her nose. We Bangkok dwellers ignored it. All public buses did that. After being caught various times at a five-minute red light in an open air *tuk-tuk* behind a bus spewing black smoke, we'd learned the only way to deal with it—pretend it didn't exist. At some intersections in the city, the air pollution was rated at twenty times greater than the danger limit. You either ignored it or you moved away.

Hoi walked at my other elbow, occasionally smiling across me at Na.

When Shlomo and Sumalee stopped to look at gold necklaces, Na and the policeman checked out a cart of round Chinese pastries.

Alex came over to me. "My friend wants to show me one of those brothels with young girls, ten and eleven years old," he said. "They're here in Chinatown."

"Are you going?"

"No, I don't want to see that. It's sick. It would make me feel bad."

"I'll go."

"I don't think they'll let you in. It's not like Patpong. The doors are locked. The prostitutes are prisoners."

"THEN THEY'RE NOT PROSTITUTES," I exclaimed. It infuriated me how Thais labelled nonvirgins whores, ruined, and bad, no matter how they got that way or how old they were. In their haste to make sex a male privilege, they faulted females for not being "pure" and rationalized their fallen status as reason to abuse them. "Ten-year-old girls sold to a brothel and prevented from leaving— that's SLAVERY and RAPE. Prostitution is exchanging sex for profit."

"I agree. That's why I can't go. It would give me nightmares."

"It would give me nightmares too, but I could use the information to show what happens when a culture has low regard for females and adheres to a double standard."

Next we stopped at a coconut stand so Shlomo could get something to drink.

Hoi took me aside. "Alex's friend and his girlfriend no like me," she said.

"Why?"

She gazed down and looked about to cry.

When I later mentioned this to Alex, he said, "It's true. They find Hoi low class. They tell me I should leave her and take her back to Patpong. Bangkok people look down their noses at Isan people. They say she's too impolite."

"I think Hoi's great. Then what do they think of her sister Na?"

Alex rolled his eyes.

Saturday afternoon, the phone rang. "Are you in?" said a male voice in Thai.

"Who is this?" I asked, worried it might be the policeman and Na wanting to invite me for something I would pay for.

"Chai and a friend."

It was the go-go boy from the Apollo Inn. "Oh. Where are you?"

"Downstair."

"Well, okay, come up."

Visitors entering my building had to pass the switchboard operator, who didn't let anyone up without being announced. Since Chai came from the Northeast, I knew he had to be as unaccustomed to using the phone as Na. He never would have thought to call ahead before coming. Unforewarned visiting was, in fact, a habit of Thais and something I found really irritating. I made an effort to repress my ill temper at being imposed on when I opened the door.

"Welcome," I said, hoping I didn't sound crabby.

Chai's friend looked young and fresh, like a preteen at a gym dance.

"He seventeen," Chai said.

"Do you work at the Apollo Inn too?"

"I work there eight day now. Before that I sleep in Lumpini Park because no have money."

"He's not gay," said Chai. The seventeen-year-old echoed firmly, "Not gay."

"But you still go with men?"

He shrugged. Chai explained, "It's job. Many boy at Apollo are not gay. They need money."

I fetched them Cokes and we sat on the couch in front of the TV. The Olympic games were starting in Korea, and I wanted to watch the opening ceremonies.

When a bra commercial came on, the seventeen-year-old's eyes popped. Chai laughed. "He like female too much."

The boy agreed and showed me a nudie photo of a Thai woman he had in his pocket. "Maybe tonight I go to discotheque, meet girl," he said with bravado.

"He's dreaming," said Chai. "If he no work, he no eat."

Fanfare began at Seoul Stadium—waving banners and women in traditional dress. I was terribly impressed but the boys couldn't have cared less. They weren't interested in how a country devastated by war a few decades back could create a spectacle so massive and organized. They'd rather have watched a program on how the Thai government planned to develop Isan.

To entertain my guests, I took out a Thai Monopoly game. The board didn't have Patpong, but it had Silom Road, and all three of us wanted to land on it. They'd never played Monopoly before. Chai's friend couldn't read the Chance cards, and neither of them was good at counting money or making change.

"Udon!" Chai declared. "I land on Udon. My home! I buy."

"No, you can't buy it. I already own it," I told him. "Matter of fact, you owe me rent."

"You exchange with me? I give you Chiang Mai."

"Uh-un. Give me my 1,000 *baht* rent."

Chai's friend landed on a Chance card. Chai and I read it and told him he had to pay 1,500 *baht* for *wat* (temple) tax.

"Nobody pay 1,500 *baht* to go to *wat*! You two cheat me," he accused us.

"It's a tax. They use the money to make repairs, put new gold leaf on the Buddhas, build rooms for the monks," I explained.

Chai asked me, "When you take me visit my family in Udon?"

"Uh . . . how about in three weeks?"

He beamed. The two of them had been unable to stop glancing around my apartment. To them, it must have seemed the home of a millionaire.

At night on Patpong, I decided to revisit Pong and her husband Ong at Pussys Collection but it turned out both had the day off. That was fine with me; I wanted to hurry home so I could stop by Jek.

I found him on Silom Road speaking to a foreigner. I didn't want to interrupt the sales pitch I recognized from his gestures, so I waved and moved off. Jek called me back.

"Where you go now?" he asked, extending his hand.

Instead of shaking it, I grasped it and moved in close. "Home," I answered. Now we were just standing there holding hands.

The foreigner didn't seem pleased that he'd lost Jek's attention. I didn't want Jek to lose him because of me. In his line of work, I knew Jek put up with abusive looks and people telling him to drop dead before he found someone who'd listen to him. "See you tomorrow."

We stood looking at each other a moment, then I kissed his cheek and broke away.

"Oah!"

Uh-oh, I really had to do something to end this or I'd be in trouble. I seemed incapable of not responding to my attraction to him.

The next day at Pussys Collection, Pong and Ong were in. Ong followed me up the stairs from his job at the door and stood in the aisle a few minutes while I sat with Pong. On this occasion, I noted the interaction between them—close, in love, intimate. She asked him to get her handbag from the back room and he ran the errand as if happy to do anything for her.

"I have a map of Thailand with me," I told her, unfolding the oversized thing that spread the width of two tables. I had to be careful that the candle didn't set it on fire. "Where did you say your home was?"

"Phichit," she said, hunting the map with her finger.

The map was written in both Thai and English, but when Pong started looking in Southern Thailand when she'd told me she came from the North, I thought she might need assistance. "This is Chiang Mai up here," I said, pointing to the Northern capital. "Is Phichit near Chiang Mai?"

"Not so far. More close Bangkok." Now she was looking in Burma.

I hadn't realized a map could be so confusing. Maybe she hadn't seen one before—except perhaps the weather map on TV, which, with its little umbrellas and smiling suns, may not have translated well to paper.

"This is the railway line," I told her. "Is Phichit near the train?"

She nodded and followed the speckled line. "Here," she said finally.

"If you want, I can take you there for a few days," I offered. "Not now, in two or three months. Would you like that?"

"Yes. Ong come too."

Ong too? I thought of the extra expense that would be. Another set of train tickets. More food. And maybe the love birds would ignore me and talk only to each other. I noticed a letter in her bag. "What's that?" I asked.

"Letter from German man."

"Can I read it?" I needed time to think about taking both Ong and Pong to the North. I wasn't ready to commit myself to treating them to a honeymoon.

She handed me a postcard and a letter and said, "Few month ago, man spend four night in Thailand. Come bar."

The postcard stated he was fifty years old, 1.85 meters tall, and lonely. The letter continued about loneliness and that he was looking for a faithful woman. He wrote that he didn't like German women's attitude. He wanted Pong to be with him in Germany.

Since the letters were so complimentary, I didn't understand why she made grumbling noises until she said, "He come back Bangkok already. He take other woman. Man no good."

Ready to leave the bar, I had to wait because a group of *farangs* blocked the exit. It took ten minutes for the club to convince them they wouldn't get out the door without paying their inflated bill.

Finished for the night, I stopped at Foodland on Patpong 2 before heading home. Reaching the check-out counter, I spied Jek on the phone by the door. He saw me at the same time and signalled for me to wait. His face looked upset.

After banging down the receiver with what seemed like woe, he motioned, without looking at me, that we were going for coffee. This was different from his usual graciousness. He didn't even shake my hand. I knew something was wrong.

As we walked down Patpong 2 toward Kentucky Fried Chicken, he repeatedly ran his hand backward over his head as if trying to alleviate a burden resting there. I wondered if he were angry with me. Had Choo Choo Charlie said something? Had Jek found out about my research? Would he feel betrayed, thinking I spoke to him only to collect information?

I had to walk behind Jek, since the narrow congested street didn't allow for two abreast. I didn't like that he just walked as if alone, but when he turned back to me, his face was so dismayed I felt worse.

As soon as we sat, I asked, "What's the matter?"

He looked out the window and shifted around.

"Tell me."

He started to speak, then stopped.

"Did I do something?"

"No. Is not you. I have trouble with massage parlor. Guest decide he no want girl but I leave with money already. Now I have to give money back. I don't want bad reputation with parlor. But I no have. I need 500 *baht*. Can you lend me?"

"Oh." I didn't like feeling that maybe I was being scammed. On the other hand, he looked seriously upset, and as a friend, how could I not help? He may have already spent 500 *baht* ($20) on coffees for me.

I hesitated, though, because I knew lending money, in itself, damaged relationships.

Perfect, I thought. Hadn't I been worried over how to rid myself of the dangerous urges I was having for him? Here was the way out. Probably I'd never get the $20 back. Since I could never tolerate being hustled by Jek, that would end the liaison once and for all.

"Okay," I told him, opening my purse and giving him the money.

"I give you back tomorrow for sure," he said.

We left immediately. I made a pledge to myself: if he didn't make good the loan, I'd never speak to him again. That would settle that. I felt half relieved that I'd found a way of preventing a romance with a tout and half afraid of how much I'd miss him if he didn't pay me back.

The next day I bought the train tickets for the trip to Udon with Chai. That night, Jek gave me a warm hello and a handshake. He seemed back to normal.

"You wonder about your money," he said. "I don't have right now, but I just start work. When you pass later I give you."

Sounded dubious. I entered the Apollo Inn half triumphant the plan was working—I wouldn't get the money back and the risky affair would be over. The other half felt mournful that it really might be over.

Chai was delighted when I put the tickets in his hands. "Should I pay the bar now to take you away for three days?" I asked him. I'd decided to make this journey three nights only, two on the train and one with his family. The four nights with Hoi had been too much.

"I already made manager lower price for you," he said. "No 200 *baht* one day. For you 120. I take another day as my day off, so for three day you pay 240 *baht*."

Buying out a male, apparently, was cheaper than a female.

Chai's badge, pinned to the edge of his bikini, said #9. The entertainment had already begun, and as Chai went to pay the manager, I watched five go-go boys onstage. They made circular motions with their hips, aiming their crotches at the *farang* men in the audience. They put more energy in their dancing than did their female counterparts. Trink's column often complained about the lack of enthusiasm go-go girls had for go-going.

"*Sawatdee, krab* (hello)" said a boy sitting in my booth. The place was so full of working boys, it would have been impossible to have a table to myself.

Chai returned and told me about him, "He is my neighbor from Udon. He come to Apollo few month after me. He don't know I work here. We very surprised. Many of my neighbor from Udon come work in Bangkok gay bar. But only me gay."

The neighbor confirmed, "I'm not gay."

"He is number one off," Chai told me, using the Patpong term "off," which meant a customer paid the bar to take him "off" of bar work. "He go with guest about twenty time one month. Have more guest than other boy. He very popular. Very handsome."

"Since you're not gay, how do you meet girls?" I asked Number One Off.

"I go massage parlor, pay 300 *baht* one hour."

Leaving the Apollo Inn, I went the long way around to Patpong 2.

"Not yet," Jek said. "I don't have your money yet."

I didn't stay and chat. On the way home, again he didn't have it. The next day, he didn't mention the money at all. He carried on as if the loan had never taken place.

The day after that I asked him straight out when I first saw him, "Do you have my money?"

"You still think about that? Okay, later I give you." He opened his wallet for me to see inside. It contained only 30 *baht*. "We go for coffee?" he asked. "I have enough for coffee."

"No," I said and walked away. I no longer felt mournful. Now I was just angry. Very angry.

As an anthropologist investigating Patpong, I expected to pay to keep in people's good graces. Obviously I wasn't behaving like the detached scientist I was supposed to be. I felt hurt that Jek thought of me as another *farang* to be manipulated. Ridiculous. I was acting like a female scorned in love. This relationship with Jek had gotten out of hand. I had to get out of it. I could use anger for that. I hoped he never paid me back. If he viewed me as just another *farang*, I could return to thinking of him as just another tout.

The next day, I didn't stop or look for him when I reached his corner. On the way back, he fell into step beside me as I passed at a brisk pace.

"You angry me?" he said.

I didn't answer.

"Because of your money?"

"Yes." I hoped he wouldn't say anything nice.

"I don't have money now." He looked so troubled I felt close to softening. "Did you tear up my picture?" he asked next. I had taken a picture of the two of us on his corner once and had given him a copy.

"No," I answered, surprised at the intensity of the question. "You would be upset if I did?" I asked and hated myself for asking. I shouldn't be probing for his feelings. I should just let the thing end.

"No," he said, which made me feel worse.

He walked with me all the way to the department store where I had to turn off Silom onto Saladaeng Road. "Goodbye," I said so he wouldn't follow me farther. He put out his hand for a handshake. I ignored it and walked away.

Continuing home, I felt miserable. Mostly I was miserable because he said he wouldn't have been upset if I tore up his picture. Then I remembered the misunderstandings between Thais and *farangs* over questions that called for agreement. To answer, "You don't like that, do you?" a *farang* would answer "No," meaning no, I don't like that. But a Thai would answer "Yes," meaning yes, you're right, I don't like that. It became even more confusing for *farangs* and Thais who were aware of these clashing responses because they overcompensated and ended up agreeing in the wrong way but with the right idea. I tried to remember how I'd asked him the question about tearing up his picture, but that wouldn't have mattered if he were trying to compensate for how he knew a *farang* would answer. Then I became furious at myself for caring what he thought. It was perfect that we were no longer on friendly terms. Best to keep it that way.

The next few nights, I deliberately passed without looking for him. Alas, before I had a chance to snub him, the other touts jumped to tell me he wasn't there when they saw me approach. It became more annoying as I realized they were lying. I knew he worked every day without a day off. He was there but avoiding me!

One night I stayed on Patpong later than usual. By the time I passed Jek's corner, it was late enough to have the attention of the touts occupied by the multitude of strolling tourists. No one saw me until I was in the center of Patpong 3, looking at the spot where Jek usually stood. He was sitting on a parked motorbike but didn't see me. I thought he looked adorable, very young and vulnerable.

Jek's older brother spotted me. "Jek didn't come to work today," he said. "He's not here."

The street was jammed with parked vehicles, T-shirt vendors, and ambling foreigners. Though Jek was no more than twenty feet from me, a battery of bicycles, peddler baskets, and people separated us.

"Yes, he is," I stated with a chuckle. "He's right there."

Meanwhile, someone had alerted Jek. As I watched, his body jolted from a relaxed posture to frozen stiffness. Then, without daring to see where I was, he threw himself to the ground and scurried behind a parked van.

"No, he's not here," the older brother said.

I was so horrified by the sight of Jek crawling to hide from me that I couldn't argue. As the silhouette of Jek's head appeared through the side windows of the van, I walked away.

How could he have so dreaded to see me? I didn't want him to feel like a piranha over $20, an amount he may have already spent on me. The problem was my feelings for him. I expected Patpong people to wangle as much from me as they could. Not only didn't I mind, it made me feel better that they were getting something out of the deal. I'd be getting a Ph.D. out of it. With Jek, I'd crossed the line between anthropologist and subject. I'd wanted him to treat me differently. I made a stink about the $20 to protect myself from my attraction to him. How awful that I'd made him feel so uncomfortable that he had to slink away like a reptile. To make matters worse—I missed him.

The next afternoon, I bought a small tin elephant. That night, I said to the older brother, "Here, give this to Jek. Tell him he doesn't have to hide from me anymore."

Later that night, Jek found me on Patpong 2. He had his usual merry grin, but his eyes looked sheepdogish and beaten. "You give souvenir to me?" he said.

"Yes, it's for you."

"Why?" He held one hand pressed to his heart.

"I don't want us to be enemies."

He looked down, then away, then said, "We go to Dunkin' Donut."

This time, he walked slower and we did stay abreast in the narrow street. As we sat at a table, I noticed he looked disheveled, with pimples on his face and his hair standing up, as if he'd been running his fingers through it anxiously. Even his shirt was wrinkled, which was different from his usual, perfectly ironed self.

"I'm bad boy," he said. "Do bad, have bad in your heart, have bad luck."

"Has something happened to you? You look upset."

"I'm tired. No sleep."

"How's your ulcer?" He shook his head. "Does it hurt?"

"Hurt all the time. I have to eat often to make better. No eat when growing up. When mama birth me, she have only 5 *baht* she make from selling food on street."

"What work did your father do?"

"Sometime he buy ticket for boxing match and sell for more money."

"A scalper."

"Now father is fortune teller. He don't like me. My family never want me."

Jek looked so down and depressed, I had an urge to touch his hand. I didn't, though. "Maybe one day you can come to my apartment," I said and immediately felt shock that I'd let that out of my mouth.

His face took on that beaten dog look again. His black eyes squinted as if I'd hurt him. Slumped in his seat, he asked, "Why? No, I can't do that. Maybe I'm pickpocket."

We didn't stay long at Dunkin' Donuts. He had to get back to work and seemed too mopey to have a conversation for long. For myself, I wanted to hurry off in order to take back that invitation.

He shook my hand. "I see you tomorrow?"

"No. Tomorrow I'm going to Udon."

"Oah! Udon, why you go there?"

"Just to visit. Only a few days."

"I see you when you come back Bangkok."

"Bye."

Now what had I done? I was in the same place as before but worse—he never returned the money and now we'd experienced an emotional incident together. Yet, part of me was happy too. Uh-oh, I was being drawn ever closer to a confessed pickpocket. Actually, I didn't believe he was a pickpocket. More likely he'd been thinking of the word "thief." I didn't really think he was a thief either. Though his job involved conning tourists, I remembered how he'd told me it sometimes made him feel rotten. He was poor, and Thailand as a newly industrializing country didn't have the jobs available to support its population. Jek had to make money to give his mother. As Sumalee had said, to survive people sometimes had to do things they didn't want. On the other hand, maybe that philosophy also meant that, if he had to "pickpocket" me to survive, he would.

10.

At 8 p.m., I went to the station to meet Chai, who was dressed in fancy mini-boots, black trousers, and a black jacket over a white sweatshirt. As we boarded the train for the ten-hour trip to Udon, Chai said, "Seven month I no go home. I no see new house. No meet brother's new wife." He bubbled with anticipation and seemed impressed with our air-conditioned sleeper car. Clearly, he wasn't accustomed to the space our reserved, single-person seats afforded. Third Class Local was characterized as permitting as many people as possible to squeeze in.

"Did your family build the house with money you sent them?" I asked.

"Yes. Before, my family poor," he said. "Now okay because I send money. Sister send money too."

"She works in Bangkok?"

"Yes, she is mamasan in massage parlor. We send money, family build house." He seemed proud.

"Who lives there?"

"Mother, father, my older brother and his new wife. Marry three month now. Also my brother's son from other marriage."

"He was married before?"

"Four time. He marry wife two and wife three in same month."

"How old is he?"

"Twenty-seven."

"The new wife takes care of the son?"

"No, my mother care for him. He sleep with her and my father."

"What does your brother do?"

"He write brochure for horse race in Udon and in Bangkok."

In the morning, Chai refused breakfast but was spellbound by the bow-tied waiter who brought it to each seat. "I can't eat," he said. "My stomach . . ." he made flurry movements with his hands.

"You're excited?"

He smiled and nodded.

We arrived in Udon at 6 a.m. While Hoi's village had been two hours outside Ubon, Chai lived on the outer fringe of Udon. Both Udon and Ubon were central towns in Isan. Chai's house was off a dirt road that had a canal running down its center. Green fields ranged into the distance from both sides of the road. A crooked corrugated iron fence divided his family's plot from the neighbor's and joined a wire fence marking the plot against a rice field, a canal, and the road.

"Rice!" I exclaimed. "You can grow rice here. There wasn't any near Ubon."

Diagram of Chai's House

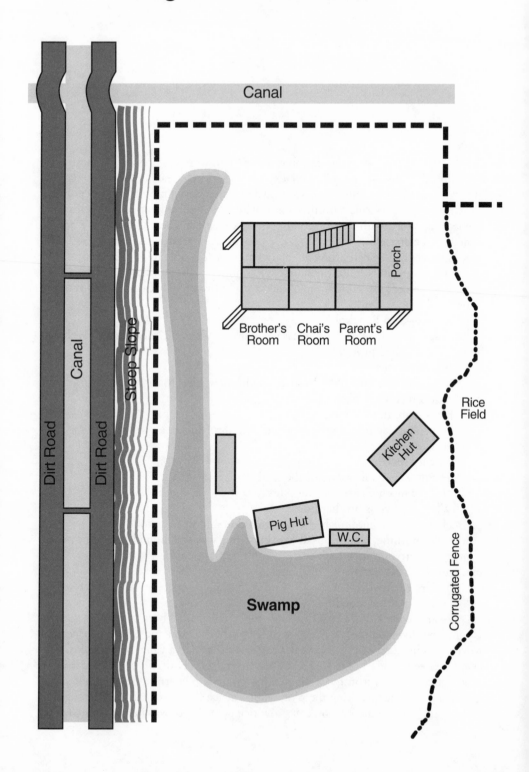

"Have canal but my family no grow rice. No land. Field belong to rich man. Rich man buy land, buy chemical, have tractor. Impossible for poor man."

A Thai-style wooden house, looking brand new, sat on stilts before us. Chai looked at it in awe. "My house," he declared. "I buy this house for my mother. Beautiful, right?"

"Beautiful," I agreed.

At odd angles nearby were two thatched-roof huts. One acted as the kitchen but had formerly been the main house, Chai told me. An electrical wire was attached to the house in a manner no more professional than a child's Erector Set. From a clump of cables haphazardly nailed under the roof, one wire ran into the house through a window. All the windows bore wooden shutters but no glass or mosquito screens.

Chai's House

We climbed a steep ladder-like staircase and joined Chai's mother, father, and nephew on the porch, which served as both living room and dining room. Woven mats covered one end of the porch, which was otherwise empty except for a plastic-covered can for his mother to spit her betel nut, which she chewed nonstop. The smile she gave Chai exposed glaring red teeth and gums. The five-year old nephew sat at her side with his chest on her lap. The father sat cross-legged while the mother sat with legs to the side, as was proper for Thai females. Chai had written them of our arrival; none of his family or friends possessed a telephone.

"Sit," the father said to me, patting the mat.

"Bring cushion for *farang*," the mother shouted to someone inside.

Chai and his parents seemed elated to see each other.

Chai with His Mother and Father

"What do you think of the house?" the father asked him, with his own love for it evident.

Chai eyed the walls with the look of a mother to a child just delivered from her body. He nodded and said, "Looks strong."

The family exchanged news and reminisced, bringing out a photo album.

"Older brother's wedding," Chai's mother said.

The pictures didn't all face in the same direction, so Chai and I had to keep turning the album upside down to view them.

Chai's brother was in Bangkok working, but we met his twenty-two-year-old

107

wife, who brought me a cushion. I didn't know if I should sit on it or lean on it. The brother's wife didn't sit with us because her duty as *saphay* (female in-law) was to be the family servant.

"Bring water for *farang*," the mother said to the *saphay*. In a moment, she presented me with a glass of water.

"*Poot Thai keng* (you speak Thai well)," the mother lied to me. Both she and the father had trouble understanding what I said. Chai told them I was a student studying Thai. They soon gave up trying to communicate with me. The father offered me a cigarette by asking Chai if I wanted one. I waved my hands, signalling that I didn't.

After a rice meal served by the *saphay*, we scraped our plates over the side of the porch and made noises to call the chickens.

"How many chickens are there?" (*Mee kai kee tua?*) I asked Chai, which made him break out in laughter. "What happened? What did I say?" I asked.

"Chicken, you know what that means?"

I looked at the animals pecking the rice, but obviously that wasn't the meaning he had in mind. Had I used the wrong *k* or the wrong tone?

"Chicken means whore," he told me.

"Oh. Yeah?" I made a note not to discuss chickens on Patpong. "Is that the toilet?" I asked, motioning to a hut just down from the porch. When he nodded, still laughing, I fetched my roll of toilet paper and headed for it.

The porcelain squat bowl sat on a mound of dirt and looked brand new. As I closed the thatch half-door, I wondered who'd designed the room's wacky set-up. The hut was long but the toilet was situated right in front of the door, which not only left most of the spacious interior empty, but, since the toilet was raised on a mound, everyone sitting on the porch had a view of the top half of anyone squatting on the toilet. Over the half-door I could see them all, which meant they could all see me. I moved farther into the hut and looked around for something to cover the top of the door. I found a torn burlap bag and strung it from the roof. I heard laughter coming from the porch and guessed it meant they'd witnessed my redecoration. I imagined Chai still laughing at the chicken question. Well, at least I was treating everyone to a jolly time. The bowl flushed manually by scooping water from a jug.

I thought of Jek. How terrible: he was like a disease I'd caught that itched in quiet moments.

When I returned to the porch, Chai commented, "You make pretty?" His family looked at me with mirth on their faces. His mother waved at the hut, where the burlap bag still hung, and flashed me a grin of betel nut.

In the afternoon, we visited a museum two hours away that none of them had been to before. Chai's father rented me an entire *song-tow* instead of a car. After Ubon with Hoi, I should have expected that. Everyone but the *saphay* came, including Chai's aunt and uncle, their two daughters, a nine-year-old daughter of another aunt, and an assortment of neighbors. Chai looked cosmopolitan in his Bangkok clothes. Like Hoi, he stood out in dress and demeanor. He didn't look like a gay go-go boy but a suave urbanite. Of course, nobody was introduced to me and nobody thanked me for the afternoon or for the restaurant lunch I paid for. On the way back, as we dropped people off in different locations, nobody turned to me for a goodbye or a nice-to-have-met-you. No goodbyes were offered to Chai or his parents either.

Back at the house, laundry covered the front and rear porches. Along with

Song-Tow

washing the dishes, the *saphay* had completed a host of chores, including filling the Goliath water jug in the toilet.

"Your *saphay* works hard," I commented to Chai. "She seems to be doing everything for everybody."

Chai blinked as if I'd said something like "Water is wet," which didn't call for explanation.

I wondered why anyone would want to marry into a family to become the household slave at everyone's call. Then again, what other options did women have besides Patpong or to be a *chee,* a female religious disciple who was in nowhere near the same league as male monks? While both the monk and the *chee* survived by begging, the populace only "made merit" by giving food to monks. No one scored Buddhist points by feeding *chees.*

The family settled back on the porch. Chai and

I retreated to his room, situated between two other bedrooms. Framed boyhood pictures hung on the wall, and Chai seemed pleased at the way his parents had arranged things. He unrolled a thin mattress that took up most of the floor space, which was empty save for a small table.

"How do your mother and father have sex with the nephew sleeping in the same room?" I asked. Sometimes I amazed myself at the questions I came up with. Chai didn't seem fazed by this one though. Perhaps he thought it was a *farang* custom to ask things like that.

The *Saphay*

"No make love," he said. "Long time already. Father have *mia noi* ten year now."

"What does your mother think of his *mia noi?*"

"She don't mind anymore but when I little, I cry often because they fight about it."

"How does the *mia noi* feel about your mother?"

"She has husband."

I was confused. "The *mia noi* has her own husband? Doesn't that make your father a *pua noi* (minor husband)?"

Chai thought that was hysterical. He fell over on his back, laughed and laughed. He sat up, threw his head forward and laughed some more. The chicken, the toilet, and now this—well, at least I was entertaining him.

"*Pua noi mai mee,*" he declared. (There's no such thing as a minor husband.) Obviously, while Thai men collected wives, the concept of a woman having more than one husband just didn't exist.

Though monogamy was declared the only legal marriage in 1935, Thai men still registered marriages to different women one after another. No penalty existed for polygamy. Since the Prince of Thailand himself was shown on TV news with his *mia noi* and his children by the *mia noi*, no Thai man thought twice about it.

In the evening, we sat on the floor in the center hallway, which housed the TV and a neon light, the only light in the house. Held down by a table at one end, unglued linoleum covered most, but not all, of the floor space. A food cabinet—sitting in four bowls of water as ant prevention—held down the other end. The three bedrooms had no light whatsoever. The *saphay* lay on her stomach in the doorway of her room, working on her husband's racing brochure and singing.

"Anybody want some mosquito repellent?" I offered, applying the odorous stuff to my skin. The room's air was thick with flying and hopping creatures.

Nobody did.

When the family spoke quickly to each other, I couldn't understand, so I left them alone and went to bed early. The only way to close the door in Chai's room, where I was to sleep, was to slide the bolt. It wasn't until I did this that I realized it left me in pitch blackness. As I groped for a nightgown, thoughts of Jek flooded my brain.

This disease would not go away, it seemed. In Bangkok, there'd be no way to avoid seeing him every day. So what should I do? What did I want to do? I wanted to be with him. I hadn't seen him in two days and I desperately missed his face. Well, why not? Why not have a fling? What better way to be part of the Patpong scene?

As I lay on the thin mat, I could hear each word spoken by the father and nephew in the parents' room to the right of me. From my left came the *saphay*'s singing. I wondered if she received credit for the work she did on her husband's brochure. Probably not. From in front came TV sounds and the voices of Chai and his mother speaking intimately.

I decided. I'd have an affair with Jek. But where? Did I trust him in the apartment with my computer and other electronic gadgets? Not really. Did I want to go to a short-time hotel? No—though it would be good data—I didn't.

I slept dreaming of Jek. I slept unaware that above the window was the socket into which plugged the neon light for the other room. The electric wire ran into the house through my window. When Chai came in the morning to unplug it, I realized the light had been on all night because no one could enter my locked room.

The next day, Chai's brother arrived from Bangkok. He didn't greet, or even acknowledge, his new wife in any way I could see. While the family sat on the porch, the *saphay* hovered in the doorway the same way she had when her husband wasn't there.

"Bring water," the mother said to her, and she ran to the six-foot clay vat outside. The house had four vats that caught runoff rain from the roof, the only source of water.

As Chai and I prepared for the trip back, we found out his mother, father, nephew, and cousin would also be going to Bangkok. They would stay with Chai's sister. I had a moment of alarm, thinking I'd be expected to pay their fares on the Express Sleeper. With relief, I saw Chai buy tickets for them on the Third-Class Local. We wouldn't even be riding the same train. Though theirs left forty minutes sooner, they arrived in Bangkok seven hours later. While they sat crammed into seats for seventeen hours, Chai and I snoozed our way to the city.

11.

In their pamphlet on the status of Thai women, Dharmasakti and Jamnarnwey (1962), of the Women Lawyers Association of Thailand, describe how women lose rights upon marriage:

> *The husband becomes the head of the family. He has the right to choose the place of residence and it is the duty of his wife to reside there with him (Ibid.: 10).*
>
> *A married woman cannot set up a trade or business or a profession without her husband's consent (Ibid.: 11).*
>
> *Adultery is a ground for divorce on the application of the husband only. . . . Thus, under the law as it now stands, the husband is still allowed scope to acquire concubines who are called "mistresses" and there will neither be bigamy charges nor action for divorce based on adultery against him (Ibid.: 17).*
>
> *A married woman cannot apply for a passport to go abroad without the consent of her husband (Ibid.: 38).*
>
> *Thai married woman's life, despite the "respectability" it offers, has much to uphold the idea that females are born the cursed sex. Wongpanich (1980) reports that the average Thai woman is pregnant every twenty-two months, while twenty-eight months is suggested as the minimal rest period needed between pregnancies.*

The first night back in Bangkok, I felt too drained to go to Patpong. I wanted to look my best when I saw Jek. Had it registered with him that I'd invited him to my apartment? Would he pick up on it? Was he feeling better than last time?

The next day, October 20th, Chai turned twenty-two. I put on a sexy dress and headed for Patpong 3, stopping at a pastry shop to pick up the birthday cake I'd ordered. Jek wasn't on his corner. A fellow tout rotated his hands, indicating that he didn't know where Jek was. I went on to the Apollo Inn.

Chai was pleased with the cake and the pictures from Udon I gave him tied in a bow. Giving birthday presents wasn't a Thai custom. I could imagine why—since Thais maximized their number of offspring, they'd end up throwing parties and buying gifts once a month. Receiving birthday presents, though, was the favorite *farang* custom adopted by Patpong people.

Chai had spent the day at a *wat*, a Buddhist temple.

"I get answer from man in New York," he told me. "Remember you help me write him? Can you help again?"

"Sure." He had the New Yorker's letter in his pocket and I read: "I'm worried about your health because you're an off-boy. You must be careful about AIDS. You must use a condom even if the customer doesn't ask for it. You can put it on him while you're massaging him."

"Do you use condoms?" I asked Chai.

He lifted a shoulder. "Guest no like."

I couldn't say anything to that. Though his job was life-threatening, he didn't have much choice; and because newspapers suppressed the topic of AIDS, Thai people didn't think it a Thai problem. Instilling fear in him would do no good at this point. If he quit the bar, another boy would take his place.

"How should I answer the letter?" I asked, accepting the pen and paper he held out.

"Tell him I know about AIDS," he said.

I'd found the man's tone patronizing, so I wrote: "I know about AIDS. I'm worried about YOU because I heard New York is the AIDS capital of the world."

Then, thinking that might be too sarcastic, I checked it with Chai. "It's okay," he said.

"What else should I write?" Chai shrugged. "How about this?" I suggested, "Since he lives on 14th Street in Manhattan, I'll ask him if he's seen Bernhard Goetz, who also lives there. Have you heard of Goetz, the Subway Gunman?"

"No."

Of course he hadn't. I explained, and we giggled about putting it in the letter. The IRT was a long way from Bangkok.

Out on the street, I thought I recognized Jek's walk from behind, but this guy was wearing sunglasses and swaggering. He passed a Thai coming from the opposite direction, and they greeted each other by slapping palms. Eek! Was this swaggering, sunglassed, hand slapper the one I'd been lusting after?

It was. At the corner he turned and saw me. "Oah!"

"What's with the shades?" I asked.

"This? I have irritate." He removed them and showed me one red eye. "Where you go now?"

"Nowhere. I was looking for you."

"Oah!" Big smile. "We go hotel?"

"Hotel? Well . . ." I made a face. "I'd rather bring you to my apartment, but I don't know . . . Last week you said maybe you were a pickpocket."

"No. I'm not pickpocket. We go?"

"Okay."

Walking home, I wondered if I was making the mistake of my life. What if he stole my computer? My project would be ruined if I lost it. Computers cost a fortune in Thailand. The old Commodore 64 I'd brought with me was a valuable item, even with its sticking keys. I could never buy a new one. I also had an Epson laptop that had been a farewell present from a friend. Though I'd stashed it in a closet, it would be easy to steal. Since I never used the laptop—it was incompatible with my printer—maybe I should put it in storage with the building's manager. Given the subject of my research, a few precautions might not be a bad idea.

"Oah!" Jek exclaimed as we entered the apartment. "How much rent you pay?" He had shock on his face. Maybe he'd never been to a Bangkok apartment before. Maybe the slum was all he knew.

"Six thousand for everything." ($260) Actually it was closer to eight thousand. I should have told him even less. That figure still represented three months' salary for a Thai office worker.

I sat on the couch, but he didn't sit next to me. He took the chair opposite. Had my apartment intimidated him?

"Oah, you have many elephant."

"Elephants are my trademark."

He perked up. "Like you give silver elephant to me." He looked around the room. "You have all over."

"That big one comes from Vietnam. I lugged it in my arms through two airports—30 pounds of ceramics. The smaller elephants are from there too."

"When you go Vietnam?"

"I must leave Thailand every three months for my visa. Every six months, I need a new Double-Entry visa. For that, I have to go to a capital city somewhere. In between, I only cross the border and re-enter on my second entry. My visa is up again next week. Last time, I took the train to the Malaysian border. This time, I'll have to be away a few days."

"Next week you leave Thailand?" he asked. Happily I noted concern in his pitch.

"I could get a one-month extension. It costs 500 *baht* and takes a few hours. I might do that."

"You go back to Vietnam?"

"No, that trip was special. When I heard Vietnam was open for tourists, I felt compelled to go. As a teenager, I marched on Washington to protest the war. I needed to see the country that had been such an issue for me." Oh shit, had I just revealed my age? I hurried to cover it up with, "For my visa, I usually take the overnight train to Penang. It's cheap. What are you doing?"

He'd found a piece of paper and was illustrating what we said. "I like to draw," he explained, showing me the train he'd sketched. Then, telling me about the massage parlor he worked for, he drew girls sitting behind a glass waiting to be picked by a customer. Next, he wrote his name, address, and phone number. The address was in a Bangkok suburb.

"This my house." He drew a house attached on both sides to other houses.

"You live there? At this address?"

"Yes." He drew the inside of the single room. Bed in the middle. A fan. TV. "*Kow dam*," he said (white black, meaning a black-and-white TV). A bookshelf. "I like to read," he noted.

I didn't mention that he'd previously told me he lived with Mr. Tam on Silom Road. As with the girls when they told me conflicting stories, I couldn't admit that I wrote down everything I heard. "You live alone?" I asked.

"Yes."

"Who does the cleaning and cooking?" I knew a Thai man wouldn't.

"Old woman come every day."

Though I knew that in Thailand almost everybody who wasn't a servant had a servant, I felt he lied. His presence had me so intoxicated, though, that I let that one go too. Why was he sitting so far away?

"Come sit here," I said. He came over and kneeled before me.

"I want to kiss you," he said.

I slid my arms around his neck and we kissed. The months of longing seemed to explode in the places where my skin touched his. I loved the feel of him; his shoulders seemed the width of mine. He tightened me against him as if he'd been waiting a long time too.

I led him to the bedroom.

He barely had time to acknowledge the size of the room before I recaptured his attention by taking off my dress. I pulled down the bed covers, suspecting the giant air conditioner made the room too cold for someone raised in a hot climate.

Naked in bed, we entwined our legs and stroked each other.

"Have you been with a *farang* before?" I asked him.

"Never," he said in such a way that I believed him. "Have you been with Thai man?"

"No."

I explored the shape of his body, which felt different from *farang* men in ways I couldn't identify. He smelled different too.

He pulled tenderly at a strand of my hair. "Narrow," he said. "Not same Thai hair."

"Thin." I giggled. "Not narrow. Yours is thick." Up close I noticed how his eyelids shaped his eyes Asian-style. "Thai eyes," I said.

He stroked my face softly and said, "Your eyes very blue." He pressed his lips to my temple. "Same like fish."

"Fish!" I laughed. "Thank you very much."

"Have many color inside. Thai people have only dark color."

I noticed his fingers looked specifically Thai too, as he entwined them with mine.

His kiss felt like a kiss, though, and as he moved on top of me I thought some things were just the same, except that he felt very light. His gentleness made me think I held a cloud, and I lost myself in a blend of East and West.

116

An hour later, I heard him go to the refrigerator. I followed.

"I need to eat for my stomach."

"Your ulcer hurts?"

"All the time."

I rested my chin on his shoulder, and he tilted his head against mine as we peered into the empty refrigerator. "I don't keep food here," I said. "I don't cook. This is all I have." I opened a bag from the Dusit Thani pastry shop. "One roll. Do you like bread?" Thais weren't crazy about bread, which wasn't a Thai food.

"Anything is okay."

With my arm around his waist, I laughed as he bit into the hard roll, which he probably didn't like at all. Thais—accustomed to spicy food—called *farang* food tasteless.

"What's that scar?" I asked, pointing to an ugly thing on his shoulder.

"Boiling water fall on me when I young. Here have another." He showed me his inner arm. "Mirror break. I have too much bad luck in my life. Always have pain."

I touched his scarred skin, and we ended up making love again. This time I remembered AIDS, but I didn't fetch the condoms I kept in a drawer for such occasions.

After it was too late to do anything about it, I said, "I worry about AIDS."

"If I sleep with prostitute, I wear condom."

"You sleep with prostitutes?" My skin recoiled where moments ago it seemed welded to his.

"Sometime have to. *Farang* buy for me. Sometime can't say no."

I thought he'd told me he never slept with prostitutes. I also found it hard to believe he always used condoms. Or ever did. Now it wasn't only my Commodore 64 at risk, but me too.

I remembered something from my A.U.A. lectures on Thai custom. In Thailand, a woman was supposed to sit or sleep on the left side of a man, as suited her subordinate position. I was on Jek's left side. I didn't want to go along with Thailand's depreciation of women, but his right side was next to the wall, and I didn't want to be there either. No, I wouldn't move to his other side just to make a point. I'd have to let him know in other ways he couldn't treat me like a Thai woman. Or maybe it didn't matter anymore; I hated the thought of his having sex in massage parlors, who knew how often. I fell asleep not touching him and not wanting to.

I awoke early as usual. I let Jek sleep and closed the bedroom door so he wouldn't hear the computer beep.

I typed notes about the New Yorker's letter to Chai. The phone rang.

"Hello O," said Hoi. "You want go Sunday to Sumalee and Shlomo's wedding?"

"I'd love to. Thanks."

"You come here first. We go together. It's outside Bangkok."

The wedding between Shlomo the Israeli and Sumalee the Moslem Patpong prostitute sounded perfect for my research. After hanging up the phone, I looked through the file on them. Should I keep my Patpong files locked from Jek? Or should I tell him about the research? Should I write what Jek told me the night before? I'd feel sneaky recording what someone said in bed. On the other hand, I wasn't sure I'd be with him again. Maybe once was enough. I didn't want someone who couldn't refuse sex if a customer bought it for him. Was I afraid of VD or was I jealous?

Jealous. I hated the idea of some other female touching him.

I wanted to go down and read the newspaper but didn't feel comfortable leaving a "pickpocket" alone in my room. Even if Jek were trustworthy, what about those sleazy characters on his corner? Would they rob the apartment now that they could find out where I lived?

How long would Jek sleep? I wanted to go do things. I wanted to go to the *Bangkok Post* library before my Thai class later that afternoon. Maybe I could check out the Thailand Information Center that the Australian neighbor told me was in the library of Chulalongkorn University. Should I ask Jek about the Center? Jek said he'd graduated from Chula, but I didn't believe it. Chula was the most prestigious university in Thailand. I didn't believe much of what Jek told me. Where did he live? With Mr. Tam or in that house he drew? Had he lied about using condoms with prostitutes? How long was he going to sleep?

I looked in on him. Dead to the world.

The hell with him. I opened his computer file and typed in the address and the other things he'd written the night before.

Around 10:30, I heard the maids in the hall. They used their key to open the door but didn't get in because I had the bolt secured. They couldn't make the bed with Jek in it, so I didn't open. I hoped they'd return later. What a pain having a sleeper in my bed. No, I didn't need to do this again. Once was enough.

At 1 p.m., I tired of waiting for him to wake. I banged things around, but he didn't stir. Finally I sat on him. I dressed first so he'd know I wasn't in the mood for sex and to show him I had to leave. I wore a Tweety and Sylvester T-shirt with Tweety's yellow face covering the entire front. Jek wasn't easy to wake—I had to jump up and down on him.

"Oah!" he exclaimed at last, looking up at me and Tweety. "Big bird."

"No, this is Tweety. Big Bird is bigger."

"Who?"

I laughed, remembering Thailand didn't have "Sesame Street." "Never mind. I have to leave. I'm going to check out Chula's library." I waited for him to tell me where the library was situated at Chula.

Suddenly I remembered something else from my A.U.A. class. A woman wasn't supposed to go over a man. To get to the other side of her husband in bed, a wife had to go around him, not over. I wondered if I was breaking a taboo by sitting on Jek. Good—that would make up for sleeping on his left side. Following a tradition that demeaned women was taboo for me.

He didn't seem to mind; he pulled me down for a hug. Mmm, very nice. It wasn't too bad having him in my bed after all. "Up, up," I said, though, pulling him out of bed jokingly. "I have to go."

We left the house together. "You hungry?" he asked. "I must put food in my stomach."

"No, I'll eat later."

At the corner, he turned left toward Patpong and I went right. I felt relieved to be away from him and angry about his prostitutes, but also energized.

I knew where Chula University was, and the library was easy to find. I didn't stay long, though. I still felt his touch on me and couldn't sit still and read.

That night, on my way home from Patpong, Jek had a special smile when, from half a block away, he saw me approach. Had he been watching for me? He brought me to a Thai magazine stand and said, "This is dirty-joke book I tell you about last night." He had suggested I read the joke book to improve my understanding of colloquial Thai.

He expected me to buy it, so I did—2 *baht* (8 cents). Money would be a problem between us, I realized. His concept of a *baht* and mine could never correspond. A *farang* man would never quibble over 8 cents and would have bought the magazine for me.

Jek walked with me as I went home. Was he planning to come up? I didn't really want him to. At the entrance to my building, I stopped and said I had to get up early.

"Is okay, I can't stay. Must work." He kissed me goodbye. "I think about you all day," he said. "You sit on me this morning, very cutesy. I like very much."

"Yeah?" He was cute himself, I thought. He kissed me again and headed back to Silom.

The next night, after a round on Patpong, again I noticed he spotted me from half a block away.

"I don't look for guest anymore," he said. "I only look for you." He took my hand to steer me across the street. It was much easier to walk on the other side of Silom, which wasn't jammed with crowds and street vendors. His older brother saw us hop through traffic and hailed him.

"I back in three minute," Jek yelled over his shoulder.

Again I didn't want Jek to come to the apartment and felt relieved to hear this. The next morning was Sumalee and Shlomo's wedding. I didn't want to leave him alone while I was away. What if I returned to find things gone? It was nice to have him walk me home though. Rather than a visitor to Patpong, I felt more a part of it, as if Patpong itself walked me home.

As we approached Saladaeng Road, I told him his three minutes were up. "You can leave me here."

"No, I walk with you to your door."

We kissed goodbye at the building's gate. My arms didn't want to let him go. As he turned back to Silom, I thought maybe next time I would invite him up.

Before going to bed, I took the Epson laptop out of the closet to remind myself to put it in storage.

12.

From olden times, men in Thailand had opportunities women had not. While boys studied in the temples, it was not deemed necessary for females to be educated (lower-class males were also mostly illiterate) (Chulachart: 1980). During the Ayuthaya (from the fourteenth century) and early Rattanakosin periods, women had no rights to be independent or self-possessed. They "could be beaten and scolded or even sold to other people without their consent" (Thai Development Newsletter, 1984: 11). Thailand has not changed much in this regard. A contemporary study in a Bangkok slum "found that 50 percent of these women are battered by their husbands regularly" (Thai Development Newsletter, 1986: 26).

Today, the more valued employment in Thailand is dependent on a degree of education that is restricted to the elite classes (Ward, 1963). What is left for unskilled Thai women are the limited jobs in factories that, despite the grueling and time-consuming labor involved (Nash and Fernandez-Kelly, 1983), some women nevertheless find a decided improvement over their home lives. In her research into the motivation for female migration to urban factories, Ariffin found that the desire for freedom and independence was second only to economic factors (Fawcett, Khoo, and Smith, 1984).

At 9 a.m., I went to meet Alex for the trip to Sumalee and Shlomo's wedding, which would be held in Sumalee's family home a few hours outside Bangkok. Hoi and Sumalee weren't in Alex's apartment, having spent the night with Sumalee's family. Seven Israeli men stood crowding the two rooms. Except for Shlomo's brother, who'd come from Israel for the wedding, most were fellow travelers Shlomo had met in Thailand. They looked like Kao San Road types, carelessly dressed travellers out to see the world. Only Shlomo, his brother, Alex, and I looked like we were going to an event. Another sloppy-looking guy was a famous producer for Israeli television who'd heard about the wedding and thought it might be interesting.

"Have you been to a Muslim marriage before?" I asked the producer, a heavy man in his fifties.

He laughed. "No. Jews don't go to many of these."

"I wonder how Shlomo's family feels about it."

He raised his hands, palms out, in an I'm-glad-it's-not-me gesture.

I approached Shlomo's brother and asked him, "Are you the best man?"

"Muslim weddings don't have a best man."

Something in his tone prevented me from asking how he felt about the affair. Besides, I didn't want to suggest I disapproved of his Jewish brother marrying a Thai Muslim prostitute.

"I was in Israel once," I told him. "I volunteered for a kibbutz during the war of '73. With everyone fighting they needed people to pick fruit."

"Are you Jewish?" he asked me.

"Yes." He probably wouldn't approve of a Jewish woman with a Thai Buddhist pimp either.

Our group took three taxis to Sumalee's sister's house, where we were to have breakfast. "Sumalee's sister is a minor wife," Alex told me as we entered her two-story home.

"Is the husband here?" I asked. From the size of the place, I figured he was rich. I wondered how many wives he had to house.

"I think it's that older man over there."

I looked around. "Not that shriveled thing with the wrinkled neck! You're kidding. He must be sixty. Sumalee's sister is so young and pretty."

Alex shrugged. "A Thai woman can't always marry for love. Especially a woman from a relatively rich family. They pick the husband and she can't say no. If Sumalee's family didn't consider Shlomo wealthy, they'd never let her marry him."

I watched the husband wave his arms and send Sumalee's sister on an errand. His face looked tyrannical. What a difference between Sumalee and her sister. With Shlomo, I had no doubt Sumalee could have everything her way. The influence Patpong women had over *farang* men was a heady one—which was why, once they tasted the power and position they had with foreigners, they found relationships with Thai men uncompromising and restrictive.

"I'm glad you're here," Alex said to me. "You'll be the only *farang* woman. It makes it look better. Everyone knows foreign men like Thai women. It doesn't mean much, though, if foreign women don't accept them too."

"I wish I'd brought my Thai boyfriend. Then we'd be really integrated."

"Why didn't you?"

The truth was that Sumalee's family would not have liked Jek any more than they probably liked Hoi. Even I could tell the difference between Jek's speech and that on TV. Jek's was slum talk. My Thai teacher laughed at the words I'd heard Jek use and asked her to translate. They were words I already knew but couldn't recognize because of his pronunciation. Speech habits branded people as members of stigmatized groups. Alex had told me middle-class Thais frowned when Hoi opened her mouth. I was sure they'd do the same for Jek.

"How does Sumalee's family like Hoi?" I asked him.

"They don't like her at all."

"Then believe me, they wouldn't like Jek either."

We *farangs* bunched into one room upstairs while the Thais collected downstairs. We sat on the floor eating cookies and listening to Shlomo recount his marriage requirements.

"To get married, I had to buy things for the bridewealth. It's a Muslim custom. A group of her male relatives arranged it with me formally. First, they wanted fourteen gold chains. My parents sent one as a gift from Israel."

"Your parents know about the marriage? Do they approve?"

"They know. They don't approve." An Israeli made a choking sound, as if choking him were what his parents would do if he married a Muslim woman. "Then I was supposed to buy two buffaloes."

"Buffalo!" someone exclaimed.

"Wait. That's not all. On top of that, I had to furnish a house. A whole house. The house itself was supposed to be a wedding present to me from Sumalee's family, but foreigners can't own property in Thailand. Since we'll be leaving the country anyway, Sumalee's brother will live in it."

"Sounds like a ripoff," someone commented.

"What can I do?" Shlomo answered with a shrug.

"So where's the buffalo?" I asked. "Are we taking them to the wedding with us?"

"I persuaded the family to accept money instead of buffaloes. I've used up all my army savings for this. I even had to borrow from my parents."

After cookies and water, too many of us squeezed into one rented bus for a two-hour ride. Then we boarded a raft to cross a canal. At this point, a Thai man gave Shlomo a black velvet Muslim hat to wear. We landed at a compound of Thai-style wooden houses on stilts that sat along a narrow branch of the canal. Saying "Hello" to lines of people along the way, we were ushered to an unbelievable mound of shoes. Following Thai etiquette, we removed our shoes too and climbed the stairs into the house.

Inside, the *farangs* occupied the floor closest to the end of the carpeted room where the marriage ceremony would be held. The Thais crowded at the other end. The eighty or ninety Thais looked comfortable sitting on the floor; the *farangs* looked awkward, their long legs at funny angles, taking up too much space. Some Thai men wore Muslim skullcaps and had traditional cloths wrapped around their waists in skirts. The Thai women were dressed starchy and prim, but only the older ones had scarves covering their heads. Islam in Thailand was not as strict as in the Middle East. I was glad I'd dressed up, though I sweltered in the unair-conditioned room in long sleeves. Thai propriety never allowed women to expose their shoulders or upper arms. I'd made the effort to look decent.

Cross-legged on one side of Shlomo sat five religious officials in skullcaps or turbans and cloths instead of pants. Sumalee's sister sat on his other side to translate. With everyone seated, Sumalee's sister uncovered the lace from a brass bowl containing the bridewealth. The officials pulled out the gold chains and examined them. Then they pulled out the wad of 500 *baht* notes, which they counted carefully.

Sumalee's Sister and Shlomo

The ceremony began. While Sumalee remained in the bridal room next door, the officials first converted Shlomo to Islam, then married him. The turbaned Imam recited words in Arabic, which the man to his right translated into Thai so that Sumalee's sister could translate them into English for Shlomo, whose native language was Hebrew. Next, the five men chanted, pausing now and then for Shlomo to repeat the words.

"I can't believe he's really doing this," an Israeli whispered. "My mother would kill me."

The Israeli producer held a microphone above Shlomo's head. None of the Thais had cameras, but all of the *farangs* did. They clicked continually.

"I think we're being obnoxious with our cameras," I said as I snapped another picture, causing the wedding party to be bathed again in light. Click-flash, click-flash. The cameras continued to go off obtrusively. I felt we were behaving vulgarly. I needed the pictures, though, so I kept snapping. Click-flash, click-flash. The producer's assistant moved his lens within inches from the Imam's ear. The Thais at the other end of the room sat quietly.

Shlomo stumbled over every Arabic word. We *farangs* suffered with him.

When the ceremony ended, Sumalee entered and sat beside Shlomo. They were now married. I knew women lacked influence in Islam, but it

Officials Counting Bridewealth

astounded me that a wedding could take place without the bride. Sumalee wore a Western-looking white satin and lace dress, white lace gloves, and white flowers in her hair. Around the necks of Shlomo and Sumalee hung *pomalais,* spiritual floral wreaths that Thais not only wore for special occasions, but also draped over shrines and suspended from rearview mirrors for protection. Shlomo gazed at Sumalee as if she were a priceless treasure. He couldn't take his eyes off her. Sumalee gazed around the room at her guests. Food was served—rice with a piece of chicken, followed by pastries. Bowls and dishes filled every space on the carpet not occupied by seated guests. The Thai women who served the food stepped carefully between them in their bare feet. When the Thais started to leave the room, the *farangs* retreated to the bridal bedroom with Shlomo and Sumalee.

Hoi wore a stiff, high-collared, white jacket over a cloth, wrapped Thai-style

into a skirt. For the first time, I noticed she looked chubby. She'd gained more weight in the one month since we'd been to Ubon. "O dress pretty," she said to me.

"Thanks, but these sleeves are stifling me."

Hoi, Alex, and the Israelis planned to stay at the house overnight. I couldn't wait to return to Bangkok to see Jek. The Israeli producer returned with me.

"I'll trade you," I said to him. "You translate your Hebrew interview with Shlomo for me, and I'll take you to Patpong and show you the bar where he met Sumalee."

Sumalee and Shlomo, Now Married

"Okay, but I'm sure you know everything already. Shlomo said it's a love story. He told me he's in love and nothing else matters."

"Have you been to Patpong before?"

"I've heard of it."

"I'll show you around. This is not a simple love story. The women of Patpong are expert at making foreign men go ga-ga over them. They collect marriage proposals. That's their business. The men see beautiful poor girls supporting their families upcountry and, BOOM, they're in love, heroes saving their maidens in distress."

"Shlomo believes this is the real thing."

"They all do. What did he say about converting to Islam?"

"He said he only became Muslim for the ceremony. Actually, to live in Israel, Sumalee will probably have to become Jewish."

"Really?" I laughed. "Not only Sumalee. Now Shlomo will have to convert to Judaism too."

That night I had the producer pick me up earlier than he would have liked. I wanted to see Jek before Patpong became too crowded for me to talk with him. I wouldn't talk long, I just wanted to hear his voice.

"He took someone to massage parlor," the villainous-looking older brother told me as I stopped on the corner with the producer in tow.

Seeing the producer, a tout latched onto us as we moved off. "*Mai jamben* (Don't need)," I said to the tout to get rid of him. He continued following us, ignoring me and describing to the producer the delights he could take him to watch or engage in. "*Mai jamben*," I repeated, annoyed. "I'm taking him, we don't need you. Go away." The producer seemed agog at the trick shows the tout itemized. "That's what I'm taking you to see," I told him. "Ignore this guy." I yelled at the tout, *"PAI KLAI!"* (GO FAR AWAY!—the Thai equivalent of GET LOST!) He'd come with us as far as Patpong 1.

Finally he left. "There. That was Sumalee's bar," I said, pointing to it. "But I'm taking you across the street to Queen's Castle for the shows. Sumalee's bar doesn't have them."

Touts pounced on the producer from all sides. They grabbed his arm and blocked his path, trying to steer him in the direction of a ripoff bar. *"MAI JAM-BEN KHUN. CHAN PAAN KOW."* (DON'T NEED YOU. I'M TAKING HIM.) I yelled and waved my arms. I felt like Zorro defending a stagecoach from bandits.

At last escaping into Queen's Castle, we were shown to a seat by a male hostess. I asked for #24, Nok. Good thing I had her number; I'd forgotten what she looked like. Meeting so many women in so many bars, I couldn't recall faces and weird Thai names. When Nok joined us, though, I remembered the beauty mark on her nose.

I slid next to a pillar and put Nok on the other side of the producer so there wouldn't be room for more girls to sit with us. Otherwise we'd be swamped by women out for business.

Spying the producer's touristy look, five girls tried to join us. One sat by Nok and the rest stood in front of our table saying, "Where you from, baby? You holiday? You buy me drink?" I waved them away.

The producer began the evening calm and dignified but grew friskier and more antsy after each show. We watched a woman mount the stage with an empty Coke bottle and a full bottle of club soda. She removed her bikini and, lying on her back, poured a quarter of the soda into her vagina. She then stood with legs open and emptied the contents into the Coke bottle. The clear liquid that went in now came out the color of Coke. She did this four times, until the Coke bottle was full.

"How does she do that?" I asked Nok.

"Inside, have dye."

In the next show, three girls pulled a string of razor blades out of themselves.

"Ouch!" said the producer.

"How do they do that?" I asked Nok again.

She made a circle of her fingers, indicating they had a protective sack inside. The girls sliced pieces of cardboard with the razors to verify sharpness.

After that, three other girls pulled a long string of needles out of themselves.

"I guess they use that sack a lot," the producer noted.

The girls sat on the stage and stuck their needles into paper flowers, ending with a very long string of paper flowers.

Next, two girls lay on their backs on the revolving center stage. Inside the vagina of one was a horn; in the other's, a squeezy orange noisemaker. They took turns tooting.

Then it was Nok's turn. She did the bottle-opening trick I'd seen at Winner's Bar but more spectacularly. She stood with the top of the bottle inside her. The disk jockey lowered the music and counted one-two-three. A bartender held the bottle and Nok cartwheeled, leaving the bottle open in the bartender's hand.

When Nok returned to our table, the producer clapped for her. "How do you do that one?" he asked.

I translated her answer for him. "She has a bottle opener inside."

By this time I could tell he was aroused. He fidgeted and had the expression of a poodle wagging his tail vigorously—sort of off-balance with neck extended. Though the trick shows were mechanical and unerotic, a room full of gorgeous women in bikinis was titillating enough. When the producer put his arm around my shoulder and grinned in my face, I thought, "Oh no, how did I get myself into this again?"

Why did this man think it was okay to paw me, anyway? I could understand his touching Nok, but did he view every female as molestable?

In the next show, four girls pulled out a long string of bells and then, with one end of the string still inside them, they danced, jingling the bells side to side.

During the Ping-Pong ball show, with his arms around both me and Nok, the producer stated, "What disregard for hygiene!"

Three women stood above sundae glasses into which they dropped Ping-Pong balls squeezed out of their vaginas. Now and then a ball missed and rolled off the stage to be trampled by the busy bartenders. When retrieved, without the wipe of a tissue, the ball was inserted again.

By this time, I was more than ready to leave and find Jek. Nok didn't appear too pleased with the producer either. An older heavy man was probably not what she would have picked for a customer. Perhaps she also felt uneasy with me there.

"I have to go home now," I said.

"I'll take you," the producer offered.

"No, no, I can go alone. Don't worry about me, I'm here every night." To Nok, I said, "Next week, do you want to go to the movies with me? I'll pay the bar."

She nodded, still looking uncertain as to what the two *farangs* wanted from her.

I gave her the money in advance so she'd know for sure I was coming—325 *baht*, cheaper than Winner's. That price was standard for women in Patpong bars. Only the ripoff bars charged more. A Day-Glo sign on the wall listed this price and noted it paid only the bar. It said customers had to arrange their own deals with the girls for sex.

I found Jek on his corner and invited him to the apartment. "Oah, I can only stay one hour."

"That's okay."

"I have something for you," he said going to a vendor's cart piled with mangoes. Reaching underneath he pulled out a dirty-joke book, this one in English. "You can explain for me."

In the apartment, we went to the bedroom first and only later returned to the joke book in the living room. He'd wrapped himself in a towel. Not wanting to be the only one nude, I put on a nightgown. He lay with his head in my lap and I read the jokes, translating them to Thai. He laughed more at my translations, than at the jokes.

"Read this one," he said, pointing to one with a picture of an elephant.

It was about a tiny male bird who begged a large female elephant to let him have sex with her. "Go right ahead," the elephant said. While the bird was going at it, a coconut fell off a tree onto the elephant's head. Hearing the elephant cry out, the bird asks, "Am I hurting you," which I translated as "*Jeb, luh?*" (Hurts, huh?)

Jek thought this was just hysterical, and I realized he'd known the stories all along. He just wanted to hear me tell them in Thai. I pinched him.

"Ow!" he said, still laughing.

"*Jeb, luh?*"(Hurts, huh?) I asked, which made him laugh more. He grabbed me in a hug.

He *hom*med me. Kissing was not a Thai custom. Instead, Thais brushed cheeks and "smelled a nice odor" (*hom*). I wasn't comfortable with the practice. I didn't know how long to hold the cheek contact. Do I close my eyes while I *hom* or stare into space? Was I supposed to make sniffing noises?

When we moved back to the bedroom, he sang me Thai love songs. I encouraged him and he seemed pleased to death. I actually wasn't that thrilled, as his singing went on and on. I was used to getting up early and going to bed early. He was used to working all night. I wanted to sleep, not hear him sing.

Twenty minutes later, he was still singing. I closed my eyes and rested my head on his shoulder, hoping I could doze off.

He didn't let me sleep. He nudged me so I could watch him sing. I wished he would go back to Patpong. He'd said one hour; four hours had already passed.

"Do you dance, too?" I asked, giving up on sleeping.

"No." He got up and began a Kung Fu routine. He did look adorable in my red towel, kicking out his legs.

"Go, go," I shouted encouragingly. He chopped and swung at the air and even danced a bit between martial moves, bobbing his head and wiggling his hips.

Suddenly, a horrible image struck me. He reminded me of the boys at the Apollo Inn. Their bodies were the same—unlike *farang* bodies—thin, with muscles rounded differently. I envisioned Jek having to work in one of those bars and felt a stab in my heart. What compromises did he make to earn a living? Did he feel degraded hawking Thai women to arrogant foreigners who treated him like dirt?

I wanted to hold him and soothe his emotional burden. Was this how the guys felt with their bar girls? He pranced around the room, and my heart broke thinking of what he might have to do for money.

I grabbed his leg as he fashioned a Bruce Lee pose and toppled him onto the bed. I crawled on top of him in defiance of any Thai taboo. His small body felt snug against mine. Another hour went by.

When birds started chirping on the balcony, I said, "I really have to sleep. I usually wake up two hours from now."

"Okay okay, I close my eye," he said. I played dead to convince him I was serious.

Two hours later, I was up at my usual time and unable to go back to sleep. I typed notes and puttered around, checking now and then to see if he was still sleeping. He was. This was going to be a problem. Did he sleep all day?

What should I do with my computer files on him? I couldn't keep writing down things he said. He wasn't a research subject anymore.

I decided to tear up his file and wipe his name off anything I'd written. I wouldn't erase him from floppy disks though. Maybe one day I would need his story.

The maids tried unsuccessfully to get in a few times.

Early afternoon, I attempted to wake him. This time I threw stuffed animals at him, bouncing some on his head. I knew hitting a Thai in the head was a no-no. Thais considered the head the highest and holiest part of the body, and to touch it was offensive. Feet were the opposite, considered base and dirty. Jek didn't twitch. Next, I threw wooden elephants at him. These I bounced off his bum. No response. I threw a rubber bath mat in the shape of a pig at him. This made me giggle but had no effect on him. By the time I gave up, he was completely covered with animals, including a frog oven mitt and three ceramic elephant ashtrays.

I settled down to read some of the articles I'd copied from the Thailand Information Center at Chulalongkorn University. The Center had an excellent collection of articles on prostitution in Thailand, the role of women in Buddhism, plus ancient and modern marriage laws.

At 3:30, Jek still slept. I turned on the radio full-volume. Swimmers in the pool probably heard the music. I hid behind the bedroom door and peeked around it. Jek was sitting up, smiling and looking incredulously at the zoo surrounding him.

"What you do?" he said, laughing.

"I tried to wake you."

"With this?" He held up the oven mitt. I fell on the bed next to him and we laughed together. He tickled me by poking a ceramic elephant in my side.

Then he helped me put everything back where it belonged.

I wondered if I should make him coffee. I didn't want him to think I served men, but he was a guest in my house and courtesy demanded a host offer something.

"Do you want coffee?" I said at last. I would have done the same for a girlfriend.

He nodded. I put the kettle on and said, "Next time, you can make it yourself. Make yourself at home here. In America, women aren't servants."

He checked the refrigerator. "We can eat?" he asked, pulling beef out of the freezer.

"I bought that but don't know how to fix it." I wasn't going to cook him food—that was definite.

"I can cook it."

"Yeah? Great."

"Thai man don't do this. At home I never do, but I know how."

"Thanks." I stepped close and kissed his shoulder. He smiled and gave me a *hom*.

While he fried the beef, I set the table. That was fair.

Near the end of the meal, I said casually, "I think I'm going to write about Patpong."

"You write book?"

"No, just a study. For school." I'd tell him about the research gradually, not all at once. Maybe he wouldn't realize I'd originally lied to him. "It's 4 o'clock!" I exclaimed. "Time for "The Flintstones." We can leave the dishes in the sink for the maids." I knew it was too late for the maids to come, but I didn't want him thinking I washed dishes like a Thai woman.

I turned on the TV and sat on the couch. He lay next to me with his head on my lap, and we watched Fred and Wilma discuss brontosaurus burgers in Thai.

"It's very funny hearing Fred Flintstone speak Thai," I said.

"What job Fred have?" Jek asked.

"He's a construction worker. Remember during the credits, he's digging in a quarry?"

"Construction worker? In America, construction worker live like this? With car and TV and telephone?"

"Sure. They make a lot of money in the States. So do most government employees—postal workers, garbage collectors—a LOT. Maybe sixteen dollars an hour."

"One hour?" A sadness took over his face. "American people very lucky. Here make nothing."

"Plus medical benefits for the whole family. Sick leave. Paid vacations."

Jek shook his head as if he couldn't imagine that possible.

That night we went to Patpong together. On his corner, he kissed me good-bye before I continued to Patpong 1. I waved to the other touts who stood watching. Because of Jek, I was softening toward that creepy bunch.

On my nightly excursions down Patpong, I often passed Pong's husband, Ong, in the doorway of Pussys Collection, trying to tempt, lead, or drag customers up the stairs to the bar. That night, I ran into him on *Soi* Crazy Horse holding up a pussy-tricks card.

"What are you doing here?" I asked.

"Have new job as guide," he answered. "I quit Pussys Collection because problem with murdered manager's wife. She bar manager now."

"What about Pong?"

"She still work there."

An hour later I ran into Ong at Topless, one of the few Patpong bars that catered to Thai men. Though on the ground floor, its dancers were nude,

130

the door locked.

I laughed when I saw him. "Now what are you doing here?"

"I come for Happy Hour."

We sat together and I offered to buy him a drink. All Patpong women except Pong had said they didn't like Thai men, especially Patpong men. Here was one in a longterm relationship. I wanted to keep tabs on him and Pong. I also wanted to talk about Jek.

"My friend works on Patpong 3. He's a guide like you. His name is Jek. Do you know him?"

"No. Patpong have too many guide."

"He's my *fan* (boyfriend)." "I'm not sure about him though. What do you think of *farang* women and Thai men?"

"I know he very happy have *fan* who is *farang*."

"Really?"

On my way home, Jek said, "I can't walk with you home. Haven't made any money yet. I come later. Late. After I finish work."

"Not tonight. I didn't sleep more than an hour last night. Tomorrow."

"Then tomorrow night I come. After work."

13.

Hantrakul (1983: 25-26) notes:

> *Personally, I very much valued the spirit of struggle
> and the relatively independent and defying attitude of
> the prostitutes I know, which I rarely found in women
> who are not of their kind. They are women who have
> the spirit of a fighter—in sexual relations and others.
> While their middle-class sisters are being repressed by
> conservative values and the sexual double standards,
> they seem to have more autonomy in their personal and
> sexual lives. Their frank familiarity with the crudest
> facts of life and male natures is much more enlighten-
> ing to themselves and others than the pretentious
> atmosphere of artificial and conservative thoughts in
> which most "good" women are confined. This trans-
> formation may take months or years but it always hap-
> pens and it is interesting to watch an innocent and obe-
> dient young girl turn into a sophisticated and rebellious
> woman in such a male-dominated society where
> "good" women are all subservient and respectful to
> male superiority beyond question. Having marked
> themselves as whores, they have come out of their
> place—having broken so many repressive rules of good
> women, and developed the spirit of a fighter for sur-
> vival and better living. Most of all, they have outgrown
> the social conditions they were born into.*

The next afternoon, Hoi came to visit me. She looked at the wedding pictures I'd taken. "Can I keep?" she asked, pointing to one of her with Sumalee's three brothers. "Alex angry me that day. He think I make love with this boy. He handsome, no? He sixteen year old."

"Did you make love with him?"

"No," she answered with a laugh, but then she kissed the picture.

"Have you and Alex made up?"

"We always fight. Last night I angry him. He buy food for his friend but not for me. I tell him I go back to work at Rififi. I tele-

Hoi with Sumalee's Three Brothers

phone bar and ask for owner, but he in London."

"Would you really have gone back to work?"

She shook her head but with a look that suggested it wasn't a disagreeable idea.

A few hours after Hoi left, Alex called looking for her. "Did she tell you about the trouble between her, Sumalee, and Shlomo?" he asked.

"No, what happened?"

"Before the wedding, Sumalee had visited an old German boyfriend who also wanted to marry her. Then, just before the wedding, Hoi told Shlomo about their secret meeting. After the wedding, there was an uproar about Sumalee's lying to Shlomo, and Sumalee ran away. She's still missing. Shlomo doesn't know where she is."

"Poor Sumalee."

"I can't blame her for not wanting to come back and see Hoi, with whom she's furious. Sometimes Hoi has a nasty streak."

"She's probably envious of Sumalee. To Hoi, Sumalee has everything."

"Maybe, but she needn't be so vicious."

Alex also told me about the argument he and Hoi had at the wedding. "She was stroking a Thai boy and speaking horrid things to him about me."

I knew the Thai boy was the one whose picture Hoi had just kissed, but I didn't tell Alex.

I didn't go to Patpong that night. Jek had said he'd be over after work, and the next day I had to go to Immigration for a visa extension. I wanted to get some sleep before he came. How would I go to Immigration with Jek in the apartment? Should I leave him alone? I could do the visa in late afternoon, but the more people who got there ahead of me, the longer it would take. Even being the first one in the morning meant three or four hours of waiting. Did I dare leave him in the apartment while I went? He probably couldn't pass the switchboard with a Commodore 64 or a TV under his arm. My bank book I could take with me, and important papers—especially those containing my date of birth—were locked in a drawer.

I'd already taken a chance by letting him into my life; I figured I might as well trust him further. Eventually I would find out one way or another anyhow. With his sleeping late, I'd either have to leave him alone in the apartment or become a prisoner to his sleep habits.

Jek arrived after 2 a.m.

"I'm still asleep," I said with one eye closed but happy to see him.

"We take shower together?" he suggested. "Wake you up."

"Okay."

First we kissed and *homm*ed around the bathroom. He sat on the rim of the tub, and I sat with my legs around him, our cheeks brushing. I was getting used to *homm*ing. He kept his eyes closed, so I did the same. Finally we climbed into the tub and watered each other with the primitive shower hose.

"Thai people very clean," Jek said. "Wash all the time."

We soaped each other and *homm*ed some more, now with slippery, sudsy faces. After rinsing off, I thought we were done. No, he picked up the soap and lathered himself again.

"What are you doing? You're already clean," I told him. "I washed you very well. Everywhere."

"Have to do three time."

"Three times? Why?"

"To be clean."

I watched as he frothed himself. He rinsed and did it again.

"You do this three times every time you shower?" I laughed and grabbed the soap from him. "Thai people are crazy. Let me do this part. This part is mine."

We laughed and made our way to the bed without drying first.

As I was about to fall asleep, he asked, "Do you get jealous easy?"

I wondered what he was thinking. "Yes. Very."

"If we marry and I look at other woman, what you do?"

"You wouldn't live long."

He laughed at the way I said it in Thai—you don't have life a long time—and repeated it a few times.

I pinched him. "Ow."

"*Jeb, luh?*" (Hurts, huh?)

"You don't have life a long time," he said again. "Very cutesy."

"You're cutesy too," I said, putting my arm around his chest.

"What kind of man you like? Strong one?"

"Not with gross bulging muscles, no. Like you. Just like you."

"Oah!" Big smile. Then he asked, "You like rich one? Thai woman only want rich man. I think you find better man than me. You like man with education."

He did have a few points there. He wasn't exactly what I'd take home to Momsy, but I said, "No, no, you're perfect. There's no better man. What kind of woman do you like? Beautiful one?"

"Beautiful not important. Someone with good heart."

"Oh, you like ugly ones. Am I ugly? Is that why you're with me?" I was fishing for a compliment and for reassurance. How did I compare with the gorgeous teenagers in the massage parlor? What a terrible thought—those exquisite beauties, demurely waiting to be picked by a customer. Was that his idea of beautiful?

"Teeth important," he said. "I want woman with good teeth."

"Teeth? How are my teeth? Are they okay?" He didn't answer. Though I'd never thought anything was wrong with my teeth, I suddenly wondered if they met with his approval. Why did he make me so insecure about myself? He wasn't responding the way a *farang* would. He was supposed to say I was the kind of woman he liked, even if he had to lie. I lied for him! I didn't tell him Momsy and my friends back home would die at the thought of me with a Thai pimp from the slums. Maybe he did find my foreign features unattractive and my teeth bad.

135

I set the alarm for 6:30 a.m. I'd be the first one at Immigration and, hopefully, could get through the ordeal as quickly as possible. Jek would probably still be sleeping by the time I returned.

"I'll get my visa extension early in the morning," I told him. "Then, on the way back, I'll pick up lunch. What do you like to eat?"

"Anything. Anything is okay."

We dozed an hour before the alarm rang.

"Sleep," I told him. "I'll be back soon."

He didn't go back to sleep, though. Coming out of the bathroom, I found the bed empty. He was in the living room waiting for me with a cup of coffee.

"You made me coffee? How wonderful you are."

A Thai man making me coffee! I sat next to him on the couch and lay my legs over his while I drank. He put his arm around my shoulder and we sat close. I didn't want to disentangle to get dressed.

He laughed after a while. "You'll be late. You said you wanted to be first one."

"Right. Okay, I'm getting up, here I go."

As I started to rise, he pulled me down for a *hom*.

I put on my Immigration dress—conservative, midcalf length, in a dark, serious color. Jek sat on the bed watching me. I explained, "I have to look like someone they'd want to give an extension." By this time I was rushing. I'd dawdled too long with Jek.

He walked me to the door and we *hom*med goodbye. It was nice to have him there waiting for me. Or had he stayed awake to see me off for another reason? Was he going to rob the place now that he had it to himself? Well, I had to find out about him sooner or later. Here was a test. I was half afraid of what I'd find on my return.

Only one person had reached Immigration before me, and he was Japanese so would go to a different office. I knew the routine. First I had to make copies of my passport at a shop across the street, trotting back and forth over a busy road with no traffic light. Then I had to fill out a form, glue my picture on it, have an official stamp it, stand in line to pay the fee, and go upstairs to wait for someone in the American section to check it over, write my name in a ledger, and ask me questions. Then, after more forms and stamps, the official would lay my passport on his chief's desk. Hopefully, within an hour or so, the chief would sign his name to it and I could go. That day it took under three hours. Images of Jek waiting for me made them enjoyable. It was just as well I wasn't home, I thought. I'd only be waiting for him to wake up.

I wondered if Jek had fastened the bolt after I left. Probably not. Otherwise I wouldn't be able to get in with my key. That meant the maids would have entered. Well, if they'd found someone in the bed, they'd have gone on to another apartment.

What should I buy for lunch? I wanted something that would bring a smile to his face. He probably preferred Thai food, but I didn't know anything about it. Where could I shop? Robinson's department store! The entire fifth floor sold Thai and Chinese food, cafeteria-style and for take-out.

With my passport stamped and signed, I *tuk-tuk*ed to Robinson's on Silom Road. Counters selling a variety of courses covered the spacious area. Everything looked interesting and smelled delicious. I decided to buy a smorgasbord of tasty treats. I would bring Jek a banquet and make him laugh.

I bought a Styrofoam box of meat rolled in dough and another of noodles, one with fried rice, and one with duck. Then I bought fish balls on a stick and spring rolls. He probably liked vegetables, so I bought a bag of stir-fried greens, plus a bag of broiled squid. What else? Dessert. I bought jelly squares in assorted colors and something soaked in honey. For good measure, I picked up eggy-looking things cooked in silver bowls.

I left Robinson's hardly able to carry the bags. Jek would certainly laugh when he saw all this. I couldn't wait to see his expression. He was always needing food; just wait till he saw what I'd bought him.

I entered the apartment building to find a knot of neighbors grouped around the switchboard. I wondered what was up. I couldn't stop to find out, though, loaded as I was with packages. I noticed they turned to look at me, but I didn't think anything of it.

As I entered the elevator, one of them—the handyman—ran after me and squeezed in as the door closed.

He made a hesitant noise and looked at the ceiling. He fidgeted and said, "I'm sorry."

I thought he meant he was sorry for delaying the elevator.

"A problem . . . ," he said. "Thai man . . . "

Thai man? Did he mean Jek? What did he know about Jek?

"Did something happen?" I asked.

"Yes. I'm sorry. Thai man fight with the woman."

Fight? Oh no. Had Jek had a fight with the maids? Did they go in to clean and somehow get in an argument with him? What had he done? Oh no, were all those people in the lobby connected to this story?

Panic flashed through me. What trouble had Jek caused me with the building? Had he hurt the maids?

"Is it over now?" I asked.

"Yes. Finish. He go."

"He left? He's gone?"

"Yes."

There I was with four bags of food and no Jek? The aroma of saucy duck filled the elevator. What had he done? Maybe the maids caught him doing something.

The handyman followed me to the apartment. I opened the door with my key.

"I'm sorry," he said again as I faced a room of total destruction. At my feet lay my camera, the battery door torn off and the batteries lying a few feet away. A chair was turned upside down. Floppy disks were spread across the floor, some looking as if they'd hit a wall first. Also on the floor was the TV antenna and my cassette player with the cassette door smashed and pieces of black plastic strewn near. Deep scratches gouged stripes in the parquet floor, as if something had been dragged across it.

I picked up a fake-leopard-skin headband from the floor. "What's this?" I asked stupidly.

"Must be from woman."

Woman? Not the maids? "What woman?"

"Woman who come fight with him. Thai man have *mia*."

Wife? Jek's wife was here?

"I don't understand."

"He make telephone. She come. They fight. Man downstair think it was you. People worry about you, but the maid say you went out already."

I entered the bedroom. It looked like a hurricane had hit. Every single article of my clothing had been taken out of the closet and thrown on the floor. All three bureau drawers had been pulled out and thrown across the room, their contents falling out on the way. Under the clothes, the floor was covered with ceramic dust. My elephants! My ceramic elephants were shattered. The tall, 30-pound elephant I'd lugged from Vietnam lay on its side in the carnage.

What was that? Blood? Purple splotches covered the bed sheets. As I looked, around I noticed they were all over the floor too.

The two maids entered the apartment shaking their heads. "Woman very angry," one of them said.

"Who was bleeding?" I asked.

"We didn't see them. Only hear shouting. Switchboard operator see. Blood all over. We already clean blood outside. Blood go down the stair, around pool, and out to street."

I wanted to be alone so I could cry. Had Jek called his wife as soon as I'd left? What had the two of them planned to do? I decided to go downstairs so the maids and the handyman would leave the apartment.

I went to the switchboard operator. "I'm sorry," she said. "Woman come ask for you. I think she your friend so I let her up."

"Did he call her?"

"She call first."

"She called here?"

"Yes. She call. Then he call out two time."

"Who was bleeding?"

"Man. Woman crying."

"They left together?"

"Yes." She made a face and said, "Woman not pretty. Have no front teeth."

14.

Hantrakul (1983: 4-5) writes that "Thai society still very much flatters men for their promiscuity and polygamy" and explains:

As far as polygamy is concerned, the Lord Buddha neither condemned nor did he commend it. So it is possible for a Buddhist man to practise polygamy just as it is possible for him not to practise it. However, the Lord Buddha did forbid sexual relationship with wives of other men as one of the Five Precepts for laymen which are generally taken as the minimum moral code of conduct. This teaching leaves to interpret that as long as the woman is not a wife of somebody, it is not a demerit to have sexual relationship with her. A prostitute is ipso facto a wife of no man, thus accessible, and an affair with her could not be considered adulterous.

Back in the apartment, I cried. I let the tears go as I threw the Robinson's food in the garbage. I couldn't stand the sight of it, or the odor. The whole apartment smelled of delicious duck. I'd probably never be able to eat duck again. The image of so much food going to waste increased the hurt.

Unable to stand the smell another second, I put the trash in the hall. Then I pounced on the fake-leopard-skin headband and threw it in the hall too—old, ratty-looking thing. Was that how Jek's wife fashioned her hair? Did she have the long glossy Thai hair *farang* men went bonkers over? How had the headband come off her head?

I faced a room of devastation. Nothing had been left on a table top. The electric mosquito repellent, telephone notepad, emergency candle for when heavy rains blew the lights—everything was on the floor. And nothing looked like it landed there easily. My name-card box was cracked, the name cards scattered all over.

What happened here? The two of them had a fight? The neighbors heard shouting. Had she been angry that he was with me? But how did she get here in the first place if he didn't tell her to come? Why had Jek let her in? He could have seen her through the peep hole. How could he let a woman into my apartment? No reason on earth could excuse that.

The maids had said they'd come clean up, but it was embarrassing having them see what had become of the apartment. I decided to straighten the place to give myself something to do. The neighbors must think me a moron for being with a married man.

I started in the bedroom, picking clothes off the floor and putting the drawers back in the bureau. Then I sat on the bed and held an elephant foot to my cheek. The rest of the elephant lay smashed in a million pieces. How could Jek bring his wife to my apartment? I cried for my elephants.

No use thinking about it. The sooner I got up and fixed things, the less I'd be reminded of what happened. I fetched the broom to sweep the remains of the elephants. What about the big one? Was that destroyed too? I didn't yet have the courage to check him out. I went over and lifted him up. He was fine. My sturdy friend was as good as ever. Well, that was something.

Then I found the iron under the bed. It was covered with blood, the entire length of its cord almost solid red. Had this been a weapon? The pointed end was bloody too.

How could Jek leave after making such a mess? Would he call to explain? What if he didn't call? Should I find him tonight and confront him? No. I had nothing to say to him. It was finished. I had to forget him and stay away.

I didn't have to go to Patpong that night. Tomorrow I was to meet Nok. I'd already paid Queen's Castle to buy her out. I would go on with my life and not think about Jek. Nothing could fix this. There was no excuse for his letting another woman into my apartment. The relationship was finished forever. I should feel lucky I got away with as little loss as I did. The computer hadn't been touched. The floppy disks? I didn't know yet, but they seemed alright despite being flung like frisbees.

The Epson laptop! How fortunate that I'd left it with the building manager! That frenzied woman could have chucked it through a window. This could have been worse.

I took the cassette player to a repair shop. They said they'd try to fix it. I took the camera to a camera shop. They said it was hopeless. They knew me from developing my film, though, and lent me one of theirs until I could buy a new one. Then I waited all day and all night for Jek to call or return. Neither happened.

The phone rang the next day, but by then I was too furious to answer it. Jek demolished my apartment and left me a whole day without explanation—too late now. To escape the phone, I went to Chula University in late afternoon. When I went to meet Nok at 6:15, I entered Patpong from Surawong Road at its other end.

Bright lights exposed the liquor-stained carpet of Queen's Castle as women sat at tables applying make-up. Nok joined me in a ruffly pink dress with puffy sleeves. She handed me a pink, ruffly headband as a present. It reminded me of the ratty leopard-skin one I'd found in my apartment. I didn't put it on.

"I have to wait until 6:30," she said. She held a receipt that said "off" and the amount I'd paid, 325 *baht*. At 6:30, she turned it in at the cashier and we left.

I suggested we go to a movie, she suggested bowling, so we agreed on a place that had both. As we approached Silom Road, I said, "I can't go down Silom. My old boyfriend works there. I don't want to run into him."

"Never mind, we take *tuk-tuk*." She approached the cluster of vehicles that waited there for passengers.

"I hope I don't see him," I said as we climbed into one. "I miss him though. I'm very sad."

"You have broken heart?" Nok asked.

"Yes, I suppose I do."

When the *tuk-tuk* drove off in the direction of Jek's corner, I hid my face.

I couldn't keep myself from looking for him though. "That's his corner," I told her. I didn't see him.

"He guide? Patpong man no good," she said. "You stay away from Thai man. I never go with Thai man. Thai man no good."

"I'm beginning to believe that."

Over and over, Nok repeated that she never went with Thai men. She would never, never have anything to do with Thai men. Ever.

"Did you have a bad experience with a Thai man?"

She recounted the story of her Thai ex-boyfriend who'd had a *farang mia*. Since Thai marriages were often unregistered, when a couple moved in together, they called each other husband and wife. Sometimes, just sleeping with a woman regularly was enough for a man to call her his *mia*.

"His *mia* was *farang*?" I asked.

"Yes." I wanted to know more about the *farang*—a *farang* woman with a Thai man was a rare combination—but she continued. "For two month, he and his *mia* separate. He go with me. Then *farang* return."

"He went back with her?" I asked, and she nodded sadly. "How long ago was that?"

"Three month ago."

"Only three months?" The way she'd expounded on never associating with Thai men had led me to believe that this was an old, established policy. Apparently what Patpong women said about not liking Thai men was not as clear-cut as it seemed. "What does he do?" I asked.

"He work at King's Lounge."

King's Lounge! That was on Patpong. He was a Patpong man! Maybe what the women said about never going with Patpong men was not actually practiced either.

At the alley, Nok bowled with enthusiasm. "I play every week," she said. It turned out she'd been playing only one month, introduced to it by her Japanese boyfriend, who'd also taught her snooker.

I tried to enjoy the game but felt as if I had a bowling

Bowling with Nok

141

ball in my chest. Jek had been wrenched from my life and something inside me felt torn.

Shortly, I had the feeling that Nok couldn't wait to return to Patpong. She behaved the same as Pong had the night I bought Pong out of Winner's Bar. Nok glanced at her watch repeatedly throughout the Thai movie. As soon as it ended, she rushed me back to Patpong—to King's Lounge.

"Japanese boyfriend just come back Bangkok. He meet us 10 o'clock."

"Oh?" I wondered when she'd arranged that. Had she made a date with him, knowing I was buying her out for the night? Annoyed at being hustled, I resigned myself to checking out the guy and observing their relationship. "Is this the man I saw you with two months ago?" I asked her. "Or the one who gave you the gold earrings?"

"No. Other one." Apparently Nok specialized in Japanese men.

King's Lounge, the after-hour "meat market," was empty at that early hour. Seven Patpong men lazed about smoking cigarettes. I found myself considering them differently than I did before my time with Jek. Now they were more like people than research subjects. I saw them as male humans rather than foreign Thai beings.

Nok and I sat at the bar. Nok laughed and joked with the bartenders. "My older brother," she told me, motioning to one of them. Then she whispered, "That one there was Thai boyfriend."

I glanced over. In his bartender outfit, he looked conservative and young. He came by to say hello and showed Nok an invitation he'd received addressed to him "and wife."

"Who's the wife?" I asked her when he went out of hearing.

"*Farang*," she said with a hurt look on her face.

Nok acted sexy and flirted with everyone. When a waiter approached the bar to place an order, she jokingly put her hand inside his jacket and stroked his nipple.

The Japanese boyfriend arrived, tall and dashing; she'd found herself a good one, I thought.

Nok introduced him to me—"Name Yamaguchi." She introduced me to him—"My older sister."

Yamaguchi laughed and noted, "You have many brothers and sisters."

His English had a heavy Japanese accent that Nok barely understood. He spoke no Thai. He and Nok communicated mostly in English, which meant little communication except a few stock phrases. He looked at her adoringly.

I learned that Yamaguchi was thirty-six and worked for a construction company. He'd be based in Thailand another ten months on a one-year contract.

I found it difficult to continue pleasant chatter. I felt too empty. I felt heavy and sluggish, as if I'd lost the spark in life.

I told Nok I had to leave. "So early?" she said.

"I have no energy."

Nok leaned into Yamaguchi and explained, "She have broken heart." To me she said, "You meet me tomorrow? I cheer you up. Ten o'clock a.m. in front of bar."

Now, how could I get home without meeting Jek? I'd been an idiot for involving myself with a man whose culture defined women as collectable items. Only a dummy would have anything more to do with him. Maybe I could just avoid his corner. If I walked on the other side of Silom Road, I wouldn't see him. Silom had three lanes of traffic going in both directions. Through its middle ran a bushy island.

Leaving King's Lounge, I headed down Patpong 1 and crossed Silom.

As I approached the spot opposite Patpong 3, I kept my head down and didn't look across the street. I passed the Philip's store on the corner, where a crowd of people stood watching a boxing match through the store window. I got to the end of the store before I heard running steps.

Jek halted beside me with the saddest expression I'd ever seen. I shook my head and kept walking. I didn't want to look at him.

"We have to talk," he said. "I call you many time but you not home."

"I was home; I didn't answer the phone."

His sad look got sadder.

We walked a bit, then he said, "You wonder what happen to your room."

"I know what happened. You let a woman in."

"She try to kill me. Look what she do." He parted his hair to show me a wound but I wouldn't look. "I have to go hospital. They make many stitch."

"She hurt you—good! You deserve it."

"No you don't understand. We go talk. We can go to A&W."

"There's nothing to talk about. You have a wife. Stay with your wife!"

"No, I don't have wife. We are finish."

"Liar! She doesn't think so."

We came abreast of A&W, another of Silom's fast-food places, and found it closed. I was glad. I kept walking. Next we passed a bar, and he took my hand to lead me in. I hesitated a second, but snatched the hand back and walked on. He followed.

He kept looking at me. My heart cried every time I caught his eye. He looked like a puppy who'd just had his leg run over by a car.

"You phoned her! You let her in my apartment! I hate you."

"No, she phone me. She find your card in my pocket and she phone."

"I thought you said you never saw her."

He looked defeated. "She went to my mother's house. She go through my clothes and find card."

"Where is she now? Is she going to jump out a doorway and try to kill ME this time? Don't walk next to me. I don't want your wife to attack again." I moved as far from him as the sidewalk allowed. "She can have you. HERE HE IS," I yelled into the air. "COME GET HIM. HE'S YOURS."

"No," Jek said and hung his head. We walked on in silence.

We came to the corner of Saladaeng. I wasn't going to let him come to the apartment. I stopped before turning down the street. Since I'd been walking apart from him, he was a few paces ahead and he went around the corner without noticing I'd stopped. I leaned against a building and crossed my arms. He came back and looked at me with that wounded look.

"You're not coming to my place. Forget it."

"I walk you home."

"Absolutely not." I turned my head away from him. Nearby was a bus stop. A line of Thai people waited there, some of them glancing at us.

We didn't speak for many moments but he kept looking at me. His eyes seemed so tragic, I wanted to hug him.

Finally I said, "I'm going home now. Just me. Alone with my broken heart."

"What you say?"

"Broken. Heart." He seemed about to cry. I pointed to myself and then at my block, then pointed at him and made a directional motion toward Patpong— meaning I go this way, you go that way. I walked to the corner. "*Jeb, luh?*" I said before turning down my block. "Yes. *Jeb!*" He didn't follow.

The next day I met Nok at 10 a.m. in front of Queen's Castle. To repay me for taking her out, she planned to take me out, and we would bring along her Japanese boyfriend so he could pay for it. We *tuk-tuk*ed to Yamaguchi's apartment to pick him up, and the three of us went to a shopping mall.

"Is beautiful or not?" Nok asked me pointing to a brooch she wore, a gold shape with red stones.

"Beautiful," I told her.

"He buy for me yesterday," she said smiling at Yamaguchi and cocking her head flirtatiously. He seemed to bask in the pleasure she showed.

We'd planned to see a movie but it had already started. Yamaguchi wanted to see one in English because he didn't understand the Thai ones. He pantomimed that he'd slept through all the movies Nok had taken him to so far.

While Nok was in the toilet, I asked him, "How long have you two been together?"

"One month," he answered. "Since just before her mother died."

I knew her mother hadn't died. I didn't know how to respond. "Oh, uh . . ."

"Very sad. She cry and cry," commented Yamaguchi.

"Yes, very sad."

"Very expensive too. I'm glad I was there to help."

"Ah, yeah. Lucky for Nok. I'm sure she couldn't have gotten through it without you."

Since we'd missed the movie, Nok took us on a tour of the shopping mall, pointing to things she hoped someone would buy her. She didn't press Yamaguchi into gifts, but the way she seeded his brain with the things she wanted was masterly. I could tell by his brow contractions that he took mental notes on what pleased her. Perhaps I could learn how to handle men from these women. I was in the midst of genius, and I seemed to need help in that area.

We went to Yamaguchi's apartment, one little room with no female clothes to be seen anywhere. Nok used her key to let us in, so I asked, "Do you live here?"

"No, only sleep sometime."

We changed into bathing suits and descended to the pool. The two of them frisked around in the water. Nok swam awkwardly, her splashy strokes looking as if this too were a sport someone had recently taught her. Yamaguchi watched her in fascination. I thought it remarkable how Patpong women so completely dazzled foreign men. He kissed her forehead and looked at her lovingly. Once, when he plucked at the neckline of her suit, she grabbed his crotch. A few times she teased him by opening her legs at him.

Another Japanese man sat by the pool. Nok played water games with him almost as much as with Yamaguchi. She tried repeatedly to push him in the water. Yamaguchi appeared displeased when Nok spent a long time at the other end of the pool with him.

Later, Nok told me Yamaguchi had a wife and two children in Japan.

It was easy for her to be with a married man, I thought, because she didn't care about him. I couldn't bear the thought of someone I loved with another woman.

"Next Friday I have party my house," she told me. "After work. Can you come?"

After work? Sounded late for me, but interesting. "I'll see if I can make it. Will Yamaguchi be there?"

"No, only Thai people. You come bar. Then I take you."

When I returned home, the phone rang. I didn't answer. It rang a half hour later and an hour after that. I turned the bell down but could still hear it.

At night it rang again. I ignored it. Then the doorbell rang. Was Jek here? I tiptoed to the peep hole but found only the porter. When I opened the door, he handed me a rose.

"Thai man leave for you," he told me. "He say you home but no answer phone."

I closed the door and pondered Jek's rose. No way would I be added to someone's collection of women! I snapped the stem in half and shoved the flower to the bottom of the garbage can.

15.

To many people in the Thai countryside, prostitution is seen as the means to upgrade one's social standing. Rattanawannatip (1988) reports that in the North:

> *Seeing women who became prostitutes in other parts of the country wearing expensive clothes and accessories when they visit their homes, many young girls in the villages acquire a common dream to make prostitution as a "career." Some young schoolgirls shocked their teachers with their remarks. . . . One girl's compliment to her teacher who dressed beautifully was: "You look as pretty as a whore today."*

Not only does it upgrade one's own social standing but also that of one's family:

> *They show up in beautiful clothes, glistening jewels and gold ornaments, bringing money for their parents to build a new house, to buy a motorbike, refrigerator, furniture and even land (Kanwerayotin, 1988: 31).*

Halloween. It wasn't a Thai holiday, but Patpong knew about it. I wanted to tell Jek about Halloween in New York, trick-or-treating up and down the elevator. I wanted to tell him about jelly apples and pumpkin faces. Would I be able to ignore the phone when it rang today? Or would I be compelled to answer it? What if it didn't ring? Was the rose Jek's way of saying goodbye? Or a way of enticing me to continue an affair with a married man?

What an idiot I was for wondering. I should leave the apartment before he called. Maybe I should leave Bangkok. I wished I had someone's home to visit upcountry. Where else could I go? Pattaya. Good idea. I'd return to Pattaya. Anywhere, just to escape the phone.

In Pattaya, I could see Tom again, the bar owner mentioned in *Foreign Bodies* who'd bellowed at me the last time. So what if I got another rejection; I couldn't feel any worse. Maybe I could even get a copy of the *Foreign Bodies* video. The Thai government had banned it, which meant copies should be plentiful. The movie *The King and I* and the song "One Night in Bangkok" were both banned in Thailand and widely available. I had no doubt *Foreign Bodies* would be too.

The video described prostitution in Thailand so well, I could use it for my dissertation defense in case the professors disbelieved my description of Patpong. Hopefully, in Pattaya I'd be able to recover from Jek.

I hurried to throw things in a bag. As I left the apartment and snapped a combination lock on the front door, I heard the phone ring. Good, I'd missed it.

I arrived in Pattaya early in the evening and checked into a guest house. The breezy Gulf of Thailand air uplifted me. I dined at a Pizza Hut full of old *farang* men with young Thai women. I noticed the women only nibbled at their slices. The tourist *farangs* probably weren't aware that most Thais hated cheese.

After eating, I returned to my room to go early to bed. I looked forward to a night without waiting to hear Jek at the door. I anticipated a full night's sleep.

I didn't get it. Firecrackers soon jolted me awake.

BANG. BANG. NNNNNnnnnnnnneeeeeoooooowww BANG. POP. Rattattatatat. BANG. Was it some kind of Chinese holiday? Did they do this in Pattaya every night? I didn't remember it from my last visit. BANG. NEEEWWWeeeeeyyyut. Every time I woke up, I wondered what Jek was doing. Was he phoning me? BANG. Whistle. POP.

In the morning, I asked the receptionist what the racket had been about.

"Make bad luck go," he answered.

"Was it a holiday?"

"No holiday."

"Why last night?"

He shrugged. Sometimes I felt I didn't know how to ask the right question. As I looked down, trying to rephrase it, I noticed a red spot on my skirt. What was that? Jek's blood! The skirt must have been on the floor when Jek bled all over the apartment. I wondered how many other outfits had this memento of Jek's wife.

I gave up on the firecracker puzzle and went back to the room to change. Then I set out to find *Foreign Bodies*.

I began in the nearest bar and followed leads. The Western men listened to my request with the warmth they'd give a killer wasp. Eventually they'd tell me something useful to get rid of me. "Go see Popeye at the Rolling Stone."

Finally I arrived at a video store with the name of someone to ask for, plus a *farang*'s name to say who sent me.

"No problem," the older Thai woman said. I wondered if she was a retired bar girl. "You come tomorrow, I have copy ready for you in VHS."

Satisfied with that accomplishment, I went to the Wild Elephant Bar to see Tom. He wasn't there yet, so I watched CNN news to find out how the Bush-Dukakis election was going in America.

Late afternoon, Tom entered the bar with friends and sat at a curbside table. I went over. "Hi, remember me?" I said.

He didn't appear jubilant to see me, but he didn't start shouting. "How's it going?" he asked without enthusiasm. Then, since I just stood there, he said, "Have a seat."

"Thanks." When the waitress came, I asked him, "Can I buy you a drink?"

148

After Patpong, that phrase came easily to my tongue. It worked so well getting Patpong people to smile at me, it now popped out automatically when I needed goodwill.

"Sure."

Well, now at least he owed me somewhat. I began small talk and feigned interest in his "hashers" runner's club. He pointed to the Wild Elephant Hashers' T-shirt he wore and said, "For men only. No girls are allowed to wear it."

"Looky here," said one of Tom's friends, lifting his own Wild Elephant shirt to show me what was printed inside—"It is prohibited to give this shirt away or to let a female wear it."

Not knowing what to say I mumbled, "Elephants are my trademark. I love elephants." I remembered my shattered ones.

Tom wasn't as hostile as last time, though, and I even felt him warming to me as he recounted the Halloween celebrations in his bar the night before. "We wore costumes," he said. "Too bad you weren't here."

"I'm sorry I missed it."

"Did you hear the firecrackers all over town?" he asked.

"Yeah, they drove me nuts. Someone said it had something to do with bad luck? What was that about?"

"A Thai fortune teller investigated Halloween and decided it had something to do with a tiger. Anyone that spelled their name using a letter in the word *tiger*, *sua*, had to light firecrackers to prevent bad luck."

"Really? That's hilarious!" We laughed together. "From the sound of it, half of Pattaya was warding off misfortune."

When Tom went to his office to get pictures of his trip to a hilltribe village, I felt I was making progress. I no longer feared being ousted from his bar.

"I saw something interesting on CNN earlier," I told him, hoping to continue the amity we seemed to be having. "They were discussing the presidential election in the States. To see how people reacted to the candidates, they filled an auditorium and showed taped campaign speeches. Each person had a gadget to press when they agreed or disagreed. Then they analyzed the results and discussed the difference between male and female voters. The women reacted strongly on the abortion issue. I guess even in the West, women must still fight for rights. Some old fogies are trying to steal their choice for abortion."

Too late, I realized a women's issue was the wrong topic to discuss with a man who lived in a country where repressed females allowed him to practice old-time values. I quickly said, "What great new gadgets they have. Technology in the West is moving so fast, I can't keep up with what they've invented since I left."

"Technology here isn't moving at all," Tom said. "I always get tourists complaining about the telephone and the sewage system. Then they expect to find a fax machine!"

"Did you vote?" I asked him.

"Nah. I don't even know who's running."

He didn't hanker for any sort of politics as a topic, it seemed. More of Tom's friends showed up—all male resident *farangs*, some in the country since Vietnam. "She's studying Patpong," he told them.

While I was engaged in a conversation with a veteran, I overheard some of them making fun of me and my research.

"Nobody's going to tell her anything," one said.

"How's a broad going to understand?"

"She'll get the ole runaround."

I pretended not to listen.

"She must know what she's doing," I heard Tom say. "She's been here fifteen months and she's gone upcountry."

Tom was defending me! What a surprise. I'd won him over.

Now I didn't want to overstay my welcome, so I paid the bill and got up to leave.

"Why don't you come to the B-52 Bar tomorrow afternoon?" Tom said. "*Soi* 12 near Beach Road. We meet there in the day."

"Great. I will. See you then." Maybe he didn't hate me after all.

Tom

I didn't have Jek, I thought as I walked away, but at least I was making headway in my work.

The next afternoon, I met Tom at the B-52, a beer bar with a swimming pool. The sea in Pattaya was too disgustingly polluted for anyone but a tourist to swim in. Pattaya had built dozens of luxury hotels but had never bothered about disposing of its sewage. It went directly into the, close to shore. What people swam into out there was appalling.

"Can I interview you?" I asked Tom after I bought him a drink and we sat at an umbrella table.

"Uh . . . , okay, but don't take notes. I'm already on the hot seat with the guys because of *Foreign Bodies*."

I learned that Tom was thirty-five years old and had been living in Thailand since 1976. "I saw Pattaya develop from nothing," he said. "The American military base was a few miles from here in Sattahip. When the Americans left the country, they stranded three thousand females. The women never considered themselves prostitutes. They thought they were going to marry the guys they'd been living with. Those women were the cream of the crop." He sighed. "The most beautiful. Not like the ones nowadays." He grimaced. "Pattaya was paradise then. I married one of those first-generation women."

"Yeah? Are you still married to her?"

"Sure am. It's been eight years now."

"Is it a legal marriage?"

"No. I legally married three times—once to a *farang* and twice to Thais. I don't want to do that again."

"What happened to the other marriages?"

"My first Thai wife left me 'cause I wasn't going anywhere. She was right. I'll never succeed at anything. I know that. This is as far as I'll go. I'm not capable of more. I also drink too much. I'm trying to cut down, but it's difficult when you work in a bar."

"Do you think Thai-*farang* marriages can work?" I asked.

"Sexually, I prefer Thais cause they don't have body hair," he said. I noted Tom was covered with hair and silently agreed that Jek's hairless chest was more attractive. "And *farang* women are too big."

I too liked Thais' smaller size. I hated being with someone a head taller and twice as wide. Jek had been perfect.

"But, no, mixed marriages don't work in the long run," Tom continued. "Thais and *farangs* are too different, and the differences get larger over time. The couple grows further and further apart. You take some of these women, refugees from Cambodia. They've spent half their life in refugee camps. There's no way they can relate to Europeans. Many women here have little intelligence or education. They're not interested in current events or the things men are interested in. They talk about make-up and clothes and don't want to hear about politics."

I didn't think Tom was too interested in politics either. "What about Thai men and *farang* women?" I asked.

Tom guffawed at this. "You're joking, right? That doesn't last one week. A Thai man thinks he can slap girls around. First time he hits a *farang*, she's gone. That match is impossible."

I scratched my head, remembering that Jek's wife beat HIM up. "Are there *farang* women living here?" I asked.

"You get tourist couples. Lone *farang* females aren't really welcome."

"I've noticed."

Tom grudgingly admitted, though, that *farang* men liked to speak to *farang* women. "They like to hear a woman's point of view and can't get that from Thai women. There's greater understanding between them. For instance, if I mention the Three Stooges . . . "

I smiled.

"See! A *farang* woman immediately connects with what I'm saying. Then there's the language barrier. The *farangs* I know never learned Thai."

"Can you speak it?"

"A few sentences."

"Then why do *farang* men react so badly to *farang* women going in their bars?"

"They think *farang* women are looking at them with disapproval. *Farang* women make them uncomfortable."

"Will you stay with your present wife forever?"

"Yes."

"Any children?"

"My wife has three children. I don't want one of my own. Her kids are my kids. I lit firecrackers for our daughter the other night. She has a tiger letter in her name."

I laughed. "Do you go with other women?"

"Of course."

"Does your wife go with other men?"

"Of course not. A man can love many women at one time; a woman wants only one. A man needs to sleep with other women. It strengthens his feelings for his wife. He appreciates what he has."

With that attitude, for sure Tom didn't want to hear about women's rights. I had to be careful what I said to *farang* residents.

"You know the American fleet's coming November fourth?" he asked.

"The day after tomorrow? Wow, that should be interesting."

"It's something to see. A carrier and seven escort destroyers from the Persian Gulf. Remember that Irani airliner that got shot down by mistake last year? These are the people who did it. This will be their first shore leave since that incident. Should be a doozy."

"Sounds great. I'll extend my stay."

What great timing. I'd have to miss Nok's party, but that was just as well— I'd probably be expected to pay for the refreshments. I'd heard about fleet-arrival jubilees in Pattaya. Girls from all over Thailand descended on the town. Ten thousand extras had to be brought in. Pattaya needed its regular women for everyday business. Though the Vietnam War had ended long ago, American sailors still came to frolic on Thai shores. Whenever I saw juvenile Americans hollering and staggering through Bangkok, I knew a fleet was in for R&R.

Extending my stay also gave me more breathing space from Jek. My instinct was to rush back to see him or at least be near him and hear the phone ring. I knew those were dangerous urges.

I still had two empty days to wait for the fleet. That night, I decided to look up Sow, the girl Dudley Dapolito had told me about, the one who didn't give him herpes. He had mentioned her bar, the Pit Stop, and it was easy to find. I'd passed it on the corner of Beach Road, next to the B-52.

When I asked for Sow at the outdoor bar facing the sea, I found her there on a stool. She resembled the Oriental dolls given as prizes in amusement parks— long bangs and shoulder-length black hair. She was thrilled that a friend of Dudley's had come to visit her and wouldn't let me buy her a drink.

"How long have you been working here?" I asked her.

"Ten month," she answered, which was exactly what she'd told Dudley four months before. Sow was from Central Thailand. She'd finished school when she was ten and had married at seventeen.

CLEO ODZER

After I promised not to tell Dudley anything she said, she told me about her former husband, a Thai, to whom she'd been married eight years. She had two children—not just the one she'd told Dudley about.

"Marriage very good until I have baby," she said. "Then husband go see other women. Every night I wait for him come home. No sleep. I wait, I wait. He never come."

That was a familiar story. Was that how Jek did it? At the birth of his baby, did he start with other women—me?

"Were you working then?"

"When first marry I work in flashlight factory in Bangkok, make 70 *baht* one day. Husband no work. Later I work construction, 50 *baht* one day."

Fifty *baht* was $2. Many construction workers in Thailand were women. I remembered discussing Fred Flintstone with Jek. I'd told him American construction workers made $16 an hour—quite a difference from $2 a day.

"I leave husband because he owe much money, want me to pay."

"Then you came to Pattaya?"

"I come here with two friend, both now married to *farang*. In Pattaya, can find *farang* husband easy, can make 500 *baht* one day."

"Do you ever see your ex-husband?"

"He have new wife. Two month ago, I see him first time in four year. Me and my girlfriend go find him. I dress beautiful in expensive clothes, all my jewelry. He drive *samlor*."

A *samlor* was a bicycle rickshaw. "Did he ask what work you did?"

"He ask, I no tell. After see him, I feel good. Very happy. He poor man. I rich."

From everything Sow told me, I calculated her age to be at least twenty-nine and not the twenty-two she'd told Dudley.

As Sow and I spoke, two *farang* men passed the bar. "Hey, sexy," she yelled to them. They kept walking, and she turned back to our conversation.

"I have a letter from you for Dudley in my apartment in Bangkok," I told her. "You sent it to my home. He's using my address for mail."

"I pay agent to write for me. Dud-ry write to me from China. He come soon. I wait him."

Letter writing was big business. Pattaya had several shops that did nothing but write or translate letters. Since the girls received mail and money from many men, they needed someone to write answers—thank you, I miss you, I love you, my brother's in the hospital from a motorcycle accident, please send more money.

"I came to Pattaya to run away from my Thai boyfriend," I told Sow, then narrated the tragedy.

"Thai woman sometime very angry. Very danger," she said about Jek's wife.

"Now he calls every day. One night, he left me a flower."

"I think he love you."

"Yeah? You think so?" I paused a second, then waved my hands. "Doesn't matter. He's too much trouble for me."

The next day I faced 24 hours to kill. After mailing the copy of *Foreign Bodies* to my mother in New York, I sat at an outdoor video bar. The owner was an obnoxious Frenchman who couldn't let one of his female employees pass without patting her fanny. He came up behind me and pulled down my shorts.

"Sorry, we made a bet," he said, indicating his male companions, who were falling over themselves with laughter. "I said you had a bathing suit underneath. I won."

In an attempt to save my dignity, I struck up a conversation with a touristy *farang* near me. He was an English painter vacationing in Thailand. When he heard about my research, he grabbed my wrist as if it were a life preserver and he a drowning man.

"Tell me, please, can you catch AIDS from oral sex?" he asked.

"Uh, I'm not an expert on AIDS. I only know what I've heard about safe sex."

"I didn't use a condom," he said in a distraught tone. "I don't know why I was so stupid. I don't know why I ignored everything I'd been told."

"Yeah, well, knowing it and practicing it are two different things." I didn't tell him I knew that first hand. "You've met some of our Thai ladies, I presume."

"Just one. I never meant to sleep with her. She said she needed a place to spend the night."

"Right. She only grew up here and knows half the town."

"No. She was sincere. I believed her."

"Welcome to Thailand."

"So what about AIDS? Do you think I caught AIDS? Is there anything I can do?"

"I wish I knew."

Then I made a mistake. Since I had time to fill, I decided to interview the local police. I went to the Tourist Police Station and started with the policeman at the front desk. All Tourist Police spoke English.

"Hi, I'm a graduate student doing research on prostitution, and I'd like to ask you about the fleet coming in tomorrow. Do you expect trouble?"

The man looked as if he'd swallowed a turtle—eyes bugged, cheeks drawn in. He made wait-wait motions with his hands, said, "One minute, please," and disappeared into the office behind him. He returned in an instant with his boss.

"Please come in," the new man said, holding open his door. I went in and sat. "How can I help you?" he said, sitting opposite.

"I'd like to know what happens when the fleet comes in. Do you get complaints from the sailors about girls robbing them?"

"Just a minute, please." He too disappeared with a strained look, and I realized this line of inquiry was not a good idea. I'd thought Pattaya was far enough from Patpong to be safe to ask questions. Alas, the subject was the same—prostitution, a taboo topic. Since it was illegal, the police probably didn't know how to discuss it as an accepted institution. The man returned only to usher me to another office. At the next attempt, I was handed even further back into the building. Each new person I spoke to had more insignias on his uniform and a larger office. I felt trapped. My questions had caused a stir, and I didn't know how to change my track. As I went up the military-like hierarchy, I felt ever closer to the government officials who'd forbidden me to do research on prostitution. How could I change what I was asking? I couldn't. I was committed.

Finally I arrived at the innermost office, a large carpeted room with bar, TV, stereo, trophies, and a late-twenties Thai man behind a desk loaded with walkie-talkies and telephones. This one wasn't in uniform. Uh-oh, here was the Big Cheese.

He held out his hand and gave me a smile that bespoke more of meeting a woman in skimpy shorts than greeting a visitor. "I'm Lieutenant Colonel Suwat. How may I be of service?"

I decided to follow through with the query and pretend I had authorization. "I'm a graduate student . . . " I began but didn't get far before he cut me off to ask where I lived, with whom, and for how long. He gave me a tourist magazine featuring his picture and went on about what he could do for me.

"Next time you come to my town, I will put you up in a five-star hotel. Everyone knows me and won't charge you. Or maybe you can stay in my friend's villa."

"Oh, ah, thanks."

"Tomorrow, I'll take you on my boat. Tonight, we'll go for dinner and to the Palladium. You like dancing? When you return to Bangkok, you must look up my friend the general."

Not only was he unconcerned about my credentials, he didn't seem to care about my research at all. He hadn't taken my work seriously; he saw me only as a female within reach. Should I be angry or relieved? Or worried—now I had a different problem. How to get out of his clutches? I didn't feel I could protest against someone with so many walkie-talkies. However, I didn't fancy the man one bit. I'd have to handle this carefully.

That night, I returned to the station as ordered. Waiting for him in the hallway, I felt conspicuous as policemen grinned at me as if I were their leader's latest acquisition. After a long time, the lieutenant colonel came to apologize.

"I have to prepare for the Americans tomorrow. Please excuse me for dinner. I will send you with my sergeant."

"No, no, that's okay. I'll go eat alone."

"Very well. Then come back at 10 and we'll go dancing."

At 10, he was still busy and I spent more time in the hallway. Two *katoeys* were brought in—masculine but lipsticked, perfumed, and skirted.

"What did they arrest you for?" one asked me.

"I'm waiting for the lieutenant colonel," I answered, hating to disappoint them that I wasn't a fellow prisoner.

An hour later, the lieutenant colonel was still unable to get away. He sent me ahead with four policemen and three bottles of Johnny Walker. I did feel like a prisoner. The manager of the Palladium welcomed me like royalty when he saw my escort. What had I gotten myself into now?

The Palladium was a wonderment. It equalled any club we had in New York. The computerized, multiscreened video show was magnificent. "Brand new," a policeman told me. "Cost 52 million *baht*." Pattaya business was doing well, it seemed.

As time passed without the lieutenant colonel, I thought I was lucky to have gotten myself into this mess when an aircraft carrier was due.

I wished I could have danced under the rolling colored lights with Jek. I knew Jek had only been to Pattaya once, with a customer from Bangkok. He hadn't been anywhere in Pattaya except a massage parlor. I wished Jek and I could have explored it together. "Oah!" he would have said to the Palladium.

Unfortunately, the lieutenant colonel did show up eventually. Fortunately, when I told him I had to leave a half hour later, he said he too needed a good night's rest for the coming day's event. In a convoy of three police cars, he deposited me at the guest house—alone. Whew! I'd been rehearsing excuses why I couldn't let him into my room if he asked to come up.

"I'll see you tomorrow," he said before driving off.

Next morning, the *Bangkok Post* wrote:

> Pattaya—About 8,000 US servicemen aboard the US nuclear-powered aircraft carrier *Carl Vinson* and its seven support ships will begin five days of shore leave in this resort town this morning, and businesses here expect to reap millions of *baht* during the visit.

Carl Vinson? Wasn't the ship that shot down the Irani airliner named *Vincennes?* The names were close, but was it the same ship? I'd have to ask.

Arrival time was set for 9 a.m. I wore shorts again, hoping to blend in with the women I knew would be on the beach.

I found the sand deluged with beautiful females sitting on a concrete wall,

Waiting for the Fleet

standing under palm trees, and crowding under the thatch umbrellas that lined the beach. Wooden signs staked the spots where liberty boats would land. Each ship had its own Thai fishing boat to ferry the boys back and forth. A cloth strung between trees announced WELCOME U.S. NAVY. At the curb, a Bangkok Bank trailer waited for the Americans so that they could change their dollars right there. Very organized.

One, two, then three hours went

by without action. I met reporters from Thai and English-language newspapers. TV cameras showed up too.

Out on the water, outlines of destroyers dotted the horizon.

"Where's the carrier?" I asked a reporter from the *Post*.

"It's around the point. They anchored last night."

"What's taking them so long to come ashore?"

"Don't worry, they're as anxious to get here as these girls are to see them."

"Is this the carrier that shot down the Irani airliner?"

"What Irani airliner?"

"Never mind."

Suddenly, in a flurry of importance, the lieutenant colonel strode up sur-

Lieutenant Colonel Suwat

rounded by a band of his men. Today he was dressed in medalled uniform complete with dapper beret slanted to the side. Thai TV channel 9 hurried to interview him.

"You go," I heard behind me and found a policeman at my elbow. "You meet lieutenant colonel." He pointed to a parking lot.

I didn't seem to have a choice. I went.

After I waited twenty minutes in the sun, with hot rays reflecting at me off cars, the lieutenant colonel appeared. He said, "Now I'll take you on the boat," as he walked past, expecting me to follow. "Then we'll have lunch."

I followed. "But I want to see the arrival," I protested bravely. "I've been waiting for hours."

"The Americans will be here all week. You won't miss anything."

"No, no, I'll meet you later. Please. I just want to watch them land."

"Very well. Pick me up in one hour." Off he strode with his procession.

I knew I was in over my head with that one. From the tales of police corruption I'd read about in Trink's column, plus my observation of Patpong ripoff bars that operated unharassed, I knew well the extent of police power and protection. Police in Thailand weren't the same as in the West. Though Thailand had changed from the military dictatorship of the previous decade, the power structures of the police and army remained. Authority still lay in uniforms and was often founded on favoritism, graft, and protection. I wasn't interested in the lieutenant colonel's attention, favors, or protection. The other side of protection was what? Not healthy, for sure. I didn't want to make the lieutenant colonel unhappy with me. Neither did I want to make him happy.

I decided to return to Bangkok. I'd send a note to the police station saying I'd been called back to the city on an emergency. He should believe it, since he knew how much I'd wanted to observe the fleet arrive.

I stayed only long enough to see the first liberty boat come ashore, its bow

157

scraping the sand.

I stood with the Thai women and watched the sailors jump to the surf, yelling, "Geronimo." A female chorus of "Ahhh" reverberated around me. Imagining the girls' perspective, I saw the Americans as descending gods. In contrast to most of the customers I'd seen in Pattaya—old, obese men sweating in the heat—these were young, trim, fit, and fresh, possessing an aura of affluence, pockets full of Yankee pay. We didn't see the sailors so much as individuals but as giants, personifying the wealth and might of the war ships behind them. The men beamed our way with excitement and joy. Hundreds of gorgeous women beamed back with the same expression.

As the two groups met, laughter and whoops filled the air. I forgot all about the Irani airliner.

The First Liberty Boat Comes Ashore

16.

In her article on "Women Migrants in Bangkok," Tongudai (1984: 317) shows how the minimum wage law is ineffective, in that 97 percent of workers in enterprises with less than ten workers were found to earn less than the minimum wage. In enterprises with more than ten workers, the percentage under minimum wage was 78 percent. Where factories do adhere to the minimum wage law, women are often hired for the sixty-day probation period allowed (at below minimum wage) and then fired.

With these conditions in mind for the migrant women who come to Bangkok, it is easy to understand that, in terms of necessity only, "other jobs are so poorly remunerated that prostitution represents a rational choice in order to support their rural families" (Ong, 1985: 5).

Back in Bangkok, I faced my scratched-up floor and cracked plastic containers. It was time to recover from the attack of Jek's wife. Maybe brown Magic Marker could cover the scuff marks. What had been dragged across the floor anyway? Did Jek try to push his rampaging wife out the door? Or did his wife try to pull Jek out of my apartment?

I didn't like the thought that she knew where I lived and I didn't know what she looked like. An ugly woman with no front teeth, the switchboard operator had said. I remembered worrying that Jek found my teeth unattractive. In reality, he'd been thinking of women with no teeth at all. Jek and I had been on different wavelengths. No matter what feelings existed between us, our perceptions and experiences would always be eons apart. I couldn't even guess at his idea of a wife or a girlfriend.

Blood stains still covered the cord of my iron; I hesitated to wash them out. I wanted to savor this bit of Jek, plus I delighted in this token of his suffering. He should bleed for the heartache he caused me.

Should I go through my clothes looking for more blood stains? Those had to be washed and not cherished as souvenirs. Maybe I should test the floppy disks his wife had hurled across the room. Had crashing into a wall scrambled the data? Not knowing what to do first, I went downstairs to read the newspaper.

"Hello, kiddles," said the Australian neighbor. "I heard you had a bit of ruckus last week." He chuckled.

"Don't ask," I said and buried my head in the *Bangkok Post*. I wouldn't give him the opportunity to tell me how bad Thai men were and how Thailand was not the same for *farang* women as it was for *farang* men.

"Thai men always have a wife somewhere, kiddo," he said, trying to goad me into entertaining him with details. "At least one. Usually more."

I found an announcement in the paper and commented, "Empower's throwing a party at noon at the Love Boat on Patpong 2." I checked the clock above the switchboard. "I can just make it." Perfect. It would be safer for me to go to Patpong during the day than at night, when I might run into Jek.

"Empower!" My neighbor spit out the word with disgust. "Tight-assed dykes."

Farang men often scoffed at the idea of *farang* women interfering with "their" bar girls. They especially loathed the name *Empower*. They went up the wall at the way Empower spelled its name by using the symbol for *female* in place of the "o." The mere sight of the logo was enough to send a *farang* resident on a lengthy harangue about feminist bitches.

"I'd better hurry so I don't miss the party," I said, getting up and escaping the sarcastic remarks I knew he was bursting to tell me about the relations between the sexes.

On the street in front of the Love Boat, Empower had set up a table to sell Empower postcards and literature. Etaine watched me approach with the frown she'd give a weed in her garden.

"How are you?" I said, being friendly despite her look. She nodded in reply but didn't speak.

Inside, the bar was packed with Patpong women. Some had brought their *farang* boyfriends—only the young, handsome ones, since this was an occasion for showing off. I recognized a couple of *Bangkok Post* reporters from seeing them in the library when I went to read Trink's columns.

For the party, Empower students and their *farang* teachers put on skits. Some skits were funny, others serious. All concerned bar work. One comedy featured a bar scene in which a go-go girl danced wearing a big number 8. Empower's only male *farang* teacher played a customer entering the bar. He asked the bartender for number 8.

"AID no have," says the bartender.

"Yes you do, right over there. I want 8."

"No have AID. Go doctor, check every day."

"Not AIDS, number 8."

"All girl clean. No have AID."

The bar girls in the audience laughed uproariously. The Thai language didn't have a way to make nouns plural the way English did by adding an *s*, and Thai words never ended with an *s* sound. Thais, therefore, found such words difficult to pronounce. Patpong women knew the confusion this caused *farangs*.

The next skit was dramatic. It featured a hotel scene. The Thai said, to her *farang*, "Five hundred *baht*."

He answers angrily, "Five hundred *baht*! No way. I already paid for your drinks. Then I paid 325 to the bar and another 200 *baht* for the hotel room. I'm not putting out more money. Forget it. Get your butt over to this bed."

"Five hundred *baht* is for me. I no get money from bar or from hotel. Money for me."

The women in the audience sat quietly, nodding their heads as if that happened to them often.

"Part-time Lover" by Stevie Wonder played between scenes as theme music.

I had trouble keeping my attention in the room. My eyes kept straying out the door to look down Patpong 2. Jek should have known I'd be at this party. Would he come by hoping to see me? I held my breath when I spotted a Thai man in a shirt with blue stripes. Jek had a shirt like that. With disappointment, I noted he didn't have Jek's walk. Jek took gliding strides with his feet aimed out.

That night, the phone rang. I shouldn't answer it, I told myself as I ran to stand beside it. It rang again. I stood there indecisive. I answered. It was Hoi.

"Father come Bangkok," she said. "My sister Na gone."

"Gone where?"

"Don't know. She fight with someone and have to leave."

That didn't surprise me. "She left her home? What about her things?"

"She take everything and go."

A frantic Alex took the phone from Hoi. "Na vanished with her three children," he said, sounding out of breath and distressed. "We're sure she sold Hoi's niece Ah into prostitution."

"Oh no, not Ah! How do you know?"

"Twelve years old is the right age for those brothels in Chinatown. Remember my friend from the Weekend Market offered to show me one? I feel so bad. Little Ah in a whorehouse. I'd told Hoi before, I wanted to keep Ah when I had enough money. Unfortunately, I have no money left. I just got a letter from my parents saying my bank account is $1,600 overdrawn. I don't know what to do. I have to find a job. I want both Hoi and me to get jobs, and then we can keep Ah with us if she hasn't been sold yet."

"What about Na's other children?"

"The other daughter is only four. That's too young. Besides, Na could live well on the sale of Ah. I don't think I can sleep tonight thinking of Ah in prostitution."

"That's SLAVERY, not prostitution."

"Right."

"That sweet little girl. Isn't there something we can do?"

"I gave money to Hoi's father to hunt for Na."

"What does he say about this? Does he think his daughter could sell her child?"

Alex took a breath. "It's an accepted practice, I guess. Meanwhile, he has no money and expects me to support everybody. He thinks money is the solution to everything. One day I asked him to tell Hoi to go back to school. Hoi loves her father and would do anything he said. I thought he could help me get Hoi to improve herself and learn a skill. If he told her to go to school, she would."

"Did he?"

"No. He wouldn't. They don't see any importance in it."

"So he's gone to look for Ah?"

"He went to find Na."

"I hope Ah is okay."

"I don't think so. Once she's sold, we'll never find her. I'm afraid she's gone." There was a sad pause as we remembered the little girl's trusting face.

"Have you heard from Shlomo and Sumalee?" I asked. "How are the newly-weds?"

"They're at Sumalee's family's country house. I now have mixed feelings about the marriage," he said. "I question Sumalee's motives."

This surprised me. To me, Sumalee's motives were obvious. I thought Alex had interpreted the affair as mercenary from the start. Were his perceptions clouded because he was in the same situation as Shlomo? Did he not see mercenary reasons in Hoi's company?

Alex continued, "I now wonder if Sumalee would have married Shlomo if she'd had two million *baht* in the bank. I talked to Hoi about marriage. I said, I'd want to give her two million *baht* and see if she still wanted to marry me."

"You spoke to Hoi about marriage?"

"Not seriously. Hypothetically. You know."

I knew, but did Hoi know? Perhaps it was Alex who didn't know. I felt Hoi could push him into marriage in a second if she tried.

"Well, let me know if you hear anything about Ah, if there's anything we can do."

After hanging up the phone, I browsed through my upcountry photos with Hoi. I wanted to see Ah. Look how young and cute—a baby. How could anyone think of putting such a child in a brothel? I knew well, though, that it happened. In some impoverished villages of Thailand, it was common practice to sell daughters so that the rest of the family could survive—or so the father could buy a motorcycle; a motorcycle was more desirable than a female child. Sometimes the *Bangkok Post* reported police raids to rescue eleven- and twelve-year-old girls who'd been sold. Once, I read of a fire in Phuket that burned down a brothel. In the ashes, firefighters found charred bodies of young girls who'd been chained to beds, unable to escape.

One of my pictures showed the canoe ride Hoi had taken us on. Ah loomed large before the camera since she sat closest. I remembered how happy she was when I lent her my shoe to bail the boat. Another picture showed Ah and me wearing ponytails on the left sides of our heads. Ah had worn the style original-ly; then, after a day of her following me everywhere I went, I gave myself a pony-tail so we'd look alike. I understood Alex's being upset that Na had sold Ah.

I felt the same.

Alex's predicament with money was a familiar one. *Farang* men who came to Thailand on vacation often became so romantically involved that they stayed until all financial resources back home were exhausted. Some abandoned prestigious careers in order to live in Thailand, where they struggled to earn a living and had to leave every three months for a new visa.

When the phone rang again, I didn't answer it. I wanted to hear Jek's voice, but I suddenly felt aversion for his sex industry, not to mention his wife and his absence of loyalty.

Thinking of ways to go to Patpong during the day rather than at night, when I might see Jek, I decided to meet the owner of the Grand Prix on Patpong 1. Rick, the American owner, was a friend of Trink's, and his bar received special mention every week in Trink's column. Though Trink denied engaging in favoritism, he also listed each sports video to be shown at the Grand Prix on Sunday afternoon, the day after the column was printed.

The Grand Prix had opened in 1969; Rick sounded like someone who could give me the low down on Patpong's history and its connection to U.S. servicemen.

I entered the bar and asked for him. A go-go girl pointed to an office in the back. Sticking my head through its open door, I saw a tubby, fiftyish man at a desk. "Hi," I said, "I'm a graduate student. Can I ask you a few questions about Patpong?"

He was hesitant but not hostile. "What'd you want to know?"

"Do you mind if I take notes?"

"First tell me what you want to know." Now he was hostile.

"Well, what do you think about Patpong?"

"I've been here twenty years, that should tell you something." He was definitely hostile.

"Not necessarily. Are you married?"

"Just recently."

"To a Thai?" I stopped myself from asking, to a bar girl?

"Yes. Listen, I have things to do. I can't be bothered with this. Get the picture? Now, if you don't mind."

He turned his back on me. The interview was over.

I left the bar feeling like a cockroach. Well, consistency counts for something, I thought; if all the *farangs* were nasty to me, it made for good data.

When the phone rang that evening, I answered it.

"How's your broken heart?" Jek asked.

"How's your wife?" I asked back, though I was happy to hear his voice and gratified that he hadn't given up.

"Did you get my rose?"

"I threw it in the garbage." Immediately I felt sorry for saying that.

He paused a second and said, "Meet me tonight. We have coffee and talk."

"No, I'm not going to Patpong anymore."

"I wait for you."

"Don't. I won't be there."

That night I didn't go to Patpong, and the phone didn't ring again.

I couldn't avoid Patpong at night just because I didn't want to pass Jek. That was ridiculous. I had to complete my project. The next night, I decided to go as usual but keep to the other side of the street.

That night, as I neared Patpong 3, I fell into step with a group of Thais so they'd block me from sight. Jek didn't appear.

On Silom Road, just opposite Patpong 1, a brand new McDonald's was having its grand opening. A six-foot Ronald McDonald stood outside, opposite the six-foot Colonel Sanders across the street. The backlit images of hamburgers and hot dogs saddened me. Fast-food places had special significance in my relationship with Jek. We should be celebrating this grand opening together.

First, I went to Nok at Queen's Castle. I wanted to see a familiar person instead of someone new. I needed company and a friendly face.

"I'm sorry I missed your party," I told her. "I was in Pattaya. How was it?"

"Fun. I can show you picture." She went to the dressing room and returned with a packet of them. They featured a small group of Thais around a table. Nok pointed to one and said, "*Fan.*"

Another Thai boyfriend! "That's your *fan*?" I asked to be sure. She nodded. So much for her proclamation of never going with Thais. "How long have you been together?"

"Just meet him."

"What does he do?"

She hesitated. "He student."

"He looks young. How old is he?"

"Sixteen." Nok, I remembered, was twenty-three. Though their customers were older, the women of Patpong seemed to like their Thai boyfriends younger.

"What about Yamaguchi? Do you still see him?"

She nodded. "Yesterday he buy me shoe."

Before I left, I arranged to meet Nok the following week in the afternoon. This was better for me, since I wouldn't have to pay the bar to buy her out.

After Queen's Castle, I had an urge to go to Patpong 3 and visit Chai. If I took the shortcut from Patpong 2, I wouldn't see Jek, I told myself.

That night, I finally arrived at the Apollo Inn late enough to see the show, consisting of all the Apollo Inn boys dancing nude followed by a Fucking Show performed by outsiders. At that late hour, one could hardly see through the accumulation of cigarette smoke. Chai was sick. A host led me upstairs to the fourth floor so that I could visit him. I found him lying on a mat on the floor covered by a blanket. "I have fever two day already," he told me.

I put my hand on his forehead in the caring gesture of the West. Too late, I remembered that in Thai culture you never touched a person's head. Chai didn't react though. Either he felt too sick or he was used to ignorant *farangs*.

His brow was hot. I wondered about AIDS but wouldn't ask about it while he lay there sick. "I hope you feel better soon. I'll come back next week."

Downstairs, I sat at the bar and again noticed I was perceiving the go-go boys differently than before my time with Jek. They'd originally seemed no more than curiosities, half-naked specimens of an alien species. Now I saw them as attractive males. Jek had awakened in me an appreciation of the male Thai form. I was joined by Chai's neighbor from Udon, whom I'd met last time—Number One Off, as Chai had described him.

"*Mee kai kee tua?*" Number One Off said, with a sly smile. (How many chickens [whores] are there?) Did all the boys at the Apollo Inn know about that faux pas of mine? Maybe it was fitting that Thailand remember me by that question.

I tossed my head in a silly-me gesture and asked, "How long have you been working here?"

"Ten month. When I first come, I only sit and watch for three day, very embarrass. I'm not gay. Gay have no future because no have children."

"Do you have a girlfriend?" I asked.

"No. Woman like man who have money."

That night, there were quite a few women in the club, both Thai and *farang*, and a couple of *katoeys*. The show began at 11:45. The go-go boys took turns onstage dancing nude, pulling on their limp penises, none of which grew in response. When the bartender called Number One Off to take his turn, he didn't want to go. "I very embarrass because you here," he told me. "I'm shy."

At that, I did a horrendous thing. He wore only a cloth wrapped around his waist. I tugged at it jokingly and said, "Aw, c'mon."

He giggled but held the cloth so it didn't open. He acted the way the girls did with abusive customers—he put up with my grabbing as he was supposed to.

"I don't want to go," he said, still holding the cloth and looking at the bartender as if hoping for a reprieve. Then, after fussing and stalling as long as he could, he trudged off.

As he left, I realized with horror what I'd done. I'd treated him the way *farang* men treated the girls. Tugging at clothes wasn't playful or a joke. It was a power game between customer and employee, between superior and inferior. I had disrespected his wishes and his privacy. I knew well the attitude of "Aw c'mon." Enough people had used it on me.

Since Number One Off went to the dressing room first, I didn't see him climb onstage. Another go-go boy nudged me and said, "There he go."

"Where?" I couldn't see him.

"Behind." Number One Off had positioned himself behind a pillar. "He hide."

Never once did he move from behind his protective pillar. At the end of his set, he must have jumped from the back side of the stage.

When he returned to sit with me, he asked, "You see me?"

"No."

"Good."

That night there was no Fucking Show. Instead of two men coming to per-
form, only one came. He did the show alone. After an assistant arranged a stool
on center stage, he danced out in a G-string, stroking a greased bottle. Then, plac-
ing the bottle on the stool, he slowly sat on it. He hadn't removed the G-string,
but it was apparent the bottle entered his rectum. After a bit, he pulled out the
bottle, opened the twist cap with his teeth, and poured the liquid contents into his
mouth.

Lounging back on the stool, he next inserted a thick candle up his rectum.
Actually four candles tied together, it had four wicks to light. He lit them. The
rest of the show was masochistic. With the lit candles sticking out of him, he
moved his feet and legs into the flames. Afterward, he removed the candles and,
tilting them at a steep angle, dripped the hot wax on his tongue. It overflowed his
mouth and ran down his chest. He never removed the G-string, leaving me to
wonder what was wrong with what lay beneath.

Leaving the Apollo Inn, I took the shortcut back to Patpong 2, walked to
Patpong 1, up to Silom, across to McDonald's, then back down parallel to where
I'd been ten minutes before. Jek was costing me extra energy.

When the phone rang the next day, I answered it. It was Alex, sounding even more
distressed than the last time. "Hoi's sister Na is here in the apartment," he said.

"What about Ah?"

"She's here and so are the other two children."

"Great! Ah's safe!"

"I don't know how great. Hoi's father found Na in Khon Kaen. He told her
my concern that Ah would be sold into prostitution. He said I wanted to take care
of Ah."

"Oh no!" I laughed. "So now you have her?"

"Now I have all four of them. Last night they turned up at the door. I can't
handle this."

A familiar scenario. *Farangs* didn't just get the Thai girl; sooner or later they
got the girl's entire family.

Alex sighed and continued, "I tried to explain I meant I'd take care of Ah
once Hoi and I both have jobs. Na has no money whatsoever and expects me to
take care of them all and send Ah to school. When I said that was impossible right
now, Hoi accused me of being 'no good.' She said she would go back to Patpong.
Na approved. She advised Hoi to find a new boyfriend with more money. Hoi
agreed. Then Hoi herself suggested they sell Ah. Hoi was going to take Ah out the
door and sell her. I don't know what to do."

The next time the phone rang, it was Dudley Dapolito back in Thailand. He came
later to collect his mail. I handed him a massive bundle of it.

"There's a letter from Sow," I told him. "I met her. I went to Pattaya and stopped at her bar to say hello."

"What did you think?"

"I loved her. She's terrific. I told her my woes with my Thai boyfriend and she was helpful and understanding."

"She's a doll. I couldn't get her out of my mind the two months I spent in China. I'm obsessed with her."

"I think that's how I am with Jek."

"Jek?"

"My Patpong cutie." I described Jek, then asked, "What does Sow say in the letter?"

He opened it and read. It was short; the girls paid the letter writer by the page. "She says she didn't catch my herpes. She thinks I caught it from her little sister."

"Are you going to Pattaya to see her?"

"Day after tomorrow. I'll buy her out and take her traveling around the country."

"If you have luggage to leave in Bangkok, you can store it here," I said. That way I could get an update on his affairs as he passed through town.

"Thanks." Dudley's eyes took on a mischievous glow. "Before I meet Sow, though, I want to butterfly. Tonight I have my sights set on sleeping with a young girl, not more than fifteen. I've never done that before. When in Rome . . . you know what I mean. Do you know where I can find one on Patpong?"

Here was someone who wouldn't think twice about having sex with Ah if he found her in a brothel. I didn't view Dudley as an uncaring person though. He figured it was Thai culture, and he was in Thailand, so why not? I didn't comment; I was supposed to observe, not interfere.

"Patpong doesn't have very young ones," I told him. "Patpong's so commercialized and renowned, they don't dare. The legal age is fifteen, so that's the youngest you'll find in the bars. I know one fifteen-year-old. She's at the Firecat." I checked my database file. "Number 56."

"Are you going to Patpong tonight? We can walk over together."

"Great. You can save me from Jek."

Dudley flinched. "Wait a minute, he's not going to beat me up for being with you, is he?"

I laughed at the thought. "No! He's not a big bad pimp like in the West. He's a little Thai boy. His wife almost killed him in my apartment. We won't see him anyway. I've been walking on the opposite side of the street from where he works. I meant you'll save me from seeking him out. I feel myself weakening in my resolve never to speak to him again. I'm afraid I'll accidentally place myself where I'm sure to run into him."

We set out for Patpong together. Dudley walked curbside to block me from view of Patpong 3. I found it impossible not to peek around him; but Silom was wide, and with six lanes of heavy traffic, the bushy island, and the crowd on the other side, I didn't recognize anyone.

Dudley laughed. "You ARE as obsessed with him as I am with Sow."

Jek must have spotted me, though, for suddenly he was in front of us. He'd dashed across the six lanes without a traffic signal. He must not have noticed I was with a man until too late. Then he must have decided he couldn't turn back, so he pretended he was going somewhere else for some other reason. He slowed his run to a walk only four paces ahead of us, moving in the same direction. He acted like he didn't know me.

I died.

He was so close I could touch him. He wore the blue striped shirt, open over a T-shirt and hanging loose, Thai teenager–style.

I couldn't hear what Dudley was saying because blood was rushing around my head too fast. I pointed to Jek and tried to speak, "Ack . . . tld . . ."

Dudley caught on something was wrong. He stopped talking and looked curiously at my hand movements.

"That's him," I said, finally.

"Him?" He looked at the guy not five feet in front of us. "No, are you sure?"

"Shhh."

With Jek ambling nonchalantly, Dudley didn't seem to believe that was him. Jek probably didn't fit Dudley's image of a "pimp." He did look more like the teenager whose style of dress he wore. "That can't be him," Dudley said. "Did he see you?"

I nodded, then whispered, "He saw me and he saw you. That's why he's pretending not to know me."

"Are you sure that's him?"

"Shhh."

In triangular formation, the three of us walked the distance from Patpong 3 to Patpong 1. For me, each step was agony as I imagined Jek's feelings in this awkward position.

At the steps of the new McDonald's, Jek turned left to climb them. Dudley and I were to go right to cross the street. I could bear it no longer.

"Jek," I called.

I saw him hesitate as if uncertain whether to pretend he didn't hear. He turned. We looked at each other a moment, he at the top of the stairs, Dudley and I at the bottom. His brows rose and drew together. He looked miserable. He started to continue into McDonald's, then stopped. I did the same toward Patpong but couldn't leave.

Finally he came down the steps. I introduced Dudley as "my friend." Jek shook his hand. I introduced Jek as my "ex-boyfriend."

"Ex? What does that mean?" Jek asked.

"OLD boyfriend. Finished. No more," I said with more anger in my voice than I intended.

"No," he said, and shook Dudley's hand again. "Oah, very respectable," he said, to Dudley. To me, he repeated, "Very respectable. Respectable man."

Then we just stood there.

"Dudley came today from China," I said, not knowing what else to say.

"Oah, rich man. Very respectable. Goodbye now." Jek shook Dudley's hand yet again. He walked off to McDonald's. I hated the growing space between us.

"That was him?" Dudley said, apparently still surprised by Jek's appearance. "A nice-looking dude."

"Yeah, I know."

On Patpong 1, Dudley and I split up, he to the Firecat, me to investigate one of the few bars I hadn't yet visited. What had Jek meant when he said that he wasn't my ex-boyfriend? Did he mean he was still my boyfriend? It was probably another one of those cases where Thais and *farangs* miscommunicated.

I contemplated Jek's calling Dudley respectable. Being respectable was of prime importance to Jek, whose line of work was anything but. Coming from the slums and working Patpong, I knew Jek's highest wish was to be respected. Dudley, on the other hand, couldn't have cared less. Being a *farang* in Asia, he had all the respect he needed.

I imagined Jek comparing himself to Dudley. In Jek's eyes, he couldn't compete with a *farang* who had all the advantages. Next to respect, Jek valued money. To Jek, Dudley, as a *farang* traveling around the world and not working, was a millionaire. Next to Dudley, Jek probably felt like nothing. My heart went out to him.

The next day, Alex called to say he'd persuaded Hoi's sister Na and the children to leave for Khon Kaen by giving them all the cash he had left. "Once Hoi and I settle into jobs, we'll bring Ah down and put her in school," he assured me. "I still don't have a job. I can always teach English or French, but I don't think that'd be interesting."

"You plan to stay in Thailand indefinitely?"

"I never planned it, but now I have Hoi. I guess I'll have to do what I can to support us."

"And her family."

Dudley came by to deposit his luggage before going to Pattaya. He recounted the night before on Patpong. "I asked for #56 at the Firecat, but she wasn't there. So I requested a fifteen-year-old but, they only had a seventeen-year-old. It would have cost 325 *baht* for the bar, 500 *baht* for the girl, and 200 *baht* short-time rent for Firecat's back room. Instead I went to the New Key Note, where I'd been before. One time there, I bought a beautiful go-go who was lousy in bed. The pits, you know what I mean? But a dish. Another time, I went with someone else. That one looked like a dog but, woo boy, hot stuff."

"What was wrong with the first one?" I asked.

"She acted like she hated every second. Would you believe I feel guilty when I go with other girls because I'm not giving the money to Sow? I'm really hung up on her. I can't wait to see her."

"That's how I am with Jek. I feel so awful about last night. He seemed so hurt. I was so hurt for him. That was torture."

"He looks like a good man."

"You think so? Should I talk to him?"

"You gotta do what you gotta do."

After he left, a woman called—a Thai woman who spoke choppy English slowly.

"I speak with Jek please," she said. "Is he there?"

My heart pounded. "Are you the one who broke everything in my house?" I asked.

She paused then said, "I am sorry." Silence. "Is Jek there?"

"No. He doesn't come here anymore. I didn't know he had a wife." Then I asked, "Are you two still together?"

"Yes."

My heart fell. "When was the last time you saw him?"

She didn't answer.

"Today?" I asked.

"Yes," she said, but I felt she lied. "I have to see Jek," she said, next. "You can take me to where he work?"

She wanted me to take her to Jek's corner? She didn't know where he worked? Maybe they weren't together after all. "Why?" I asked.

She didn't answer.

"You owe me money for the things you broke. Eight thousand *baht*," I said, guessing at an amount. "Are you going to give me eight thousand *baht*?" I knew she wouldn't.

There was a pause. "I must meet Jek. Please, you take me to him."

"Why?"

She hesitated, then said, "Baby sick."

I remembered Jek telling me his wife had used that excuse once to make his friends think he ignored his baby when it was sick and to make trouble for him.

"I don't believe you. Anyway, I don't see him anymore. What's your name?"

"Toom," she said, using an unaspirated Thai *T*. It sounded more like Doom—a good name for her, I thought.

I wanted to ask more questions, but when she realized I wouldn't help her, she said goodbye.

When I hung up the phone, I felt elated that she and Jek couldn't be together if she didn't know where he worked. Maybe Jek hadn't lied about that. So how much contact existed between them? Had she really found my card in his mother's house? I still didn't know where Jek lived.

Or did Doom want to meet me to throw acid in my face? Maybe she was waiting downstairs.

I decided not to go to Patpong that night. I didn't want to deal with either Jek or his wife. The next morning, I was to meet Nok. The research was advancing enough that I didn't have to go to Patpong every night.

At 11 a.m., I met Nok in front of her bar. We went for lunch at an open-air food place. These cheap stalls, not affiliated with any shop, cluttered Bangkok's sidewalks. They were make-shift affairs with food cooked on fires and dishes washed in one tub of water. The rickety tables and chairs and torn umbrellas were folded and stacked against a building at night. During the day, these "restaurants" took up most of the sidewalk. *Farangs* grew annoyed when they had to step in the gutter to pass them. In general, walking down a Bangkok street irritated *farangs* anyway; they felt Thais walked too slowly.

Nok talked incessantly about her new Thai boyfriend, Moon, whose picture I'd seen a few days before. She couldn't seem to get Moon out of her thoughts. "Yesterday, Moon say . . ." "Last week, Moon go . . ." "Tomorrow, Moon will . . ."

"Are you going to marry Moon?" I asked.

"Yes, but is secret. Next year we marry. Don't tell anybody. Moon think . . ."

After our spicy soup meal, Nok glanced at the other tables and chose an older Thai man. She smiled sweetly at him and pointed to our empty plates. "You can pay?" she called out.

The man seemed eager enough to meet us, but when he preferred to speak English with me rather than Thai with her, Nok huffed and paid the bill herself. Though I knew I'd be expected to pay for the rest of our outing, this pleased me.

We went bowling. I listened to her talk about Moon for another two hours.

"I teach Moon to bowl . . . " "Moon tell me . . . " "Moon can . . . "

"How's Yamaguchi?" I asked her.

"Last night I see him. Then I meet Moon. Moon like . . . "

Were Jek and his wife really separated?

"Moon has . . . " "I hope Moon . . . " "Moon and I . . . "

When I returned home, the phone was ringing.

"I love you," Jek said.

I couldn't say anything.

"Other day, I wait for you."

"I didn't go to Patpong."

"I have to see you one more time in my life."

"But there's no purpose to it," I said, weakly with a whine. I could hear the waffling tone in my voice. Would Jek pick up on it?

He did. "I come over now and we talk."

"Well . . . I don't think so . . . "

"I be there in twenty minute." He hung up without giving me time to object.

I could leave the apartment before he arrived, I thought, or not answer the door. Or should I stay and let him in? He loved me?

17.

Unlike prostitution in the West, the encounter between the Thai bar girl and the farang may not have the outward appearance of a deal. At first the girl establishes rapport, staging attraction and praising the man. Then she offers to spend the night without mentioning a price. She leaves the amount up to him so that the money has the appearance of a gift. When she stays with him for a period of time, the money she asks for is not represented as payment but as reimbursement for the money she's lost from the bar and/or support for her family. The farang can't tell if she's really in love with him or is only after cash. Cohen calls this "open-ended prostitution" because it entails "liaisons which usually involve a complex mixture of sentimental attachment and pecuniary interest on the girl's part" (1986: 115).

The men who fall in love with bar girls are entrenched in the ambiguity of never being sure if the women are girlfriends or whores. Cohen describes the farangs as experiencing "considerable anguish and emotional strain, since the first encounter frequently leads to a quick and intense emotional involvement" (1987: 229).

J ek came in and sat on the couch. I sat at its opposite end so I wouldn't appear too eager. He looked at the cassette player, whose door was noticeably missing, and made a clicking noise with a low, "Oah."

"It works," I said. "They repaired it." I half hoped he'd offer to pay for damages but knew it unlikely. I waited for him to apologize at least, but he didn't.

He picked up a pencil and drew two boxes with arrows leading down. In one box he wrote his name in English; in the other, mine in Thai. "My life. Your life," he said. "Now we have life apart. In future can meet. March 9 is my birthday. I leave Patpong, get job in office. Become respectable."

Was he making long-range plans for us? Though I'd be leaving Thailand in another year, I needed to hear he had deep feelings for me, so this was encouraging. But I also wanted to be convinced he hadn't lied about having a wife.

"What about your wife?" I asked.

"No," he said. "Right now I must work Patpong, make money for new life."

No, what? No, he wasn't married? "Toom called me," I told him. He looked taken aback. "Doom!" I continued. "Doom is a good name for her. Do you know

173

what Doom means?"

"No."

"Ruin! Destruction! Death!" I said, forcefully. I didn't like the emotion I was expressing. I didn't want to seem so vulnerable in my attraction to him.

"What did she say?"

"She wanted me to take her to you. Doesn't she know where you work?"

"What you tell her?" He hadn't answered my question.

"I refused. I told her I didn't see you anymore."

"She want to kill me. She is insane. She always fight with me. When I leave her, I sleep in Stockholm Bar. One day she find me and throw boiling water on me."

Boiling water? I remembered he'd said his shoulder scar was from boiling water falling on him as a child. Had it really come from Doom? "Is she going to attack me?" I asked, concerned over the possibility.

"No. Don't worry about her." Then he added, "She don't know what you look like," which didn't reassure me. I wanted to hear she understood she and Jek were no longer together, not that she didn't know what I looked like.

"What does she do? Does she work?"

"No. Her father is policeman. When I first meet her, she is ideal for me."

"How long were you together?"

"Six year."

"What about that house you drew? Who lives there? Doom?"

He looked embarrassed. "Yes. You too smart. Woman not supposed to be too smart."

I wouldn't debate with him the belief that a female should be inferior to her male mate. I already knew Thailand couldn't relate to the concept of women's equality. The few times I mentioned it to Patpong women, they looked at me as if I were from outer space.

"Where do you live?"

"With Mr. Tam." He drew a picture of an apartment on Silom Road behind a bar.

"Did Doom really find my card at your mother's house?"

"Yes."

"Why was she there?"

He drew more lines. "This my life course. Right now we have different situation."

He was still lying to me. I knew he was. "The baby lives with your mother?"

"Yes," he said, drawing an education box for me and a work box for himself.

"Does Doom know your marriage is finished? I don't think she does."

"I wish she find other man. I very happy if she find new husband."

This sounded true, but he wasn't giving me a straight answer about something. "What about your baby? Bank is his name, right?"

"She also have daughter from husband before me. Daughter is ten year old. I hope she find new husband soon."

With two kids and no front teeth, Doom wouldn't find one easily, I thought.

"Her daughter no like me because I'm not her father. That's why I wanted my own baby. My father never like me. I wanted to have someone who like me."

I wanted to stay angry at him, yet I longed to take him in my arms. I couldn't hug him, though, because I felt a wall of his relatives between us. Feeling defenseless and needing a wall of my own, I told him about my student loans.

"How much you must pay back?" he asked.

"The loans total about seventy thousand."

"*Baht*?"

"I wish! Dollars."

"Oah," he said, softly with the same look he'd given Fred Flintstone. "I have to pay old debt from Mr. Tam but not so much."

"Why did you let Doom in my house?"

"She try to kill me. All my life I have much pain. This year is bad luck for me."

Was he deliberately avoiding answers? I needed to hear encouraging words, so I didn't press him. I said, "This year you met me. Am I bad luck?"

"No. I hope with you it change."

He stayed two hours. All in all, they were friendly. I loved his company in spite of everything. We only kissed once, chastely. Our plan—never clearly stated—was for the future, sometime after his birthday five months away. Perfect for me—maybe by then I'd be over him. I wanted to be with him, but, just as strongly, I didn't want to want that.

I didn't understand, though, the connection between Doom and the waiting period. I wondered if it had anything to do with her father being a policeman. Was that related to Jek's job on Patpong? Or did waiting for his birthday have something to do with age twenty-five being bad luck? Were we supposed to wait for a more auspicious time? Was my confusion due to not understanding Thai culture, or was Jek withholding real explanations? I never seemed to get the right answer out of him, but then I had that problem with all Thais.

After Jek left, I found his wallet. It contained no money, only a few business cards. I copied the names and addresses into a file I had on him. I felt he was still lying to me. If he could be sneaky, so could I. I was no longer writing down what he said, but I saw no reason to ignore good data.

Also in the wallet I found a picture of Bank. It didn't take up the whole photo slot, so I decided to add a picture of myself. It was, in part, a test. If he didn't have a wife or another girlfriend, he'd keep the photo there. Was I setting him up to confront Doom? Or was I setting myself up to get hurt again?

As I included his latest drawings in the file, I noticed he hadn't spelled Mr. Tam's name correctly. I'd seen him write "Tam" before; this time he'd written Mr. Tum. I wondered if he'd slipped up thinking of "Toom." In the Thai alphabet, Toom was spelled with a *u* vowel. Did he really live with Toom and not Mr. Tam? Could the concept of Freudian slips be applied to Asians?

The next day Jek asked for his wallet when I passed him. I handed it over without mentioning my picture.

He held my hand extra tenderly. "Where you go now?"

"To work."

"I see you when you come back."

I kissed his cheek. We had a nice feeling there. I loved this connection to him, and even to the sleazy fellow touts grouped nearby, scanning for tourists.

I decided to visit Pong. When the new doorman at Pussys Collections told me she'd quit, I sought Ong on *Soi* Crazy Horse. He looked distraught.

"Pong leave Bangkok last week," said Ong. "She go to family upcountry. She say she no work Patpong anymore. She go home to work rice field."

Rice field? What did that do to my hypothesis that Patpong was preferable to planting rice?

"Are you from upcountry too?" I asked.

"No, from Bangkok."

While the go-gos came from out of town, it seemed the street people were locals.

Ong handed his trick card to a friend, and the two of us went around the corner to the Topless Bar. "Now I single man," he declared.

At this point, he told a different story from any I'd heard before: he and Pong had been together only one year and had no children together. Pong's two children were from her previous husband. I wondered how I'd ever sort out the truth in what Patpong people told me.

"You don't have children of your own?" I asked.

"Yes," he said, agreeing Thai-style that my statement was correct. I didn't say more; I didn't want him to know Pong had lied to me.

Ong drank a beer. "I have broken heart," he said. "Now I afraid of woman. Afraid feel pain again. I want find someone who understand me." He turned to face me with a penetrating gaze. Uh-oh, what was he thinking? "I need faithful woman."

"I'm back with my Thai boyfriend," I said, but he wasn't listening.

He teetered over on to me and explained, "I drink for my broken heart." He was drunk. He ordered another beer and became maudlin and teary. "I miss Pong very much." He blotted the corners of his eyes with his thumb and forefinger. Then he looked at me lustfully and said, "Can you go with me next week *loi kratong* (float basket)?"

The Loi Kratong holiday was a favorite of Thais—sort of Valentine's Day combined with Yom Kippur. The choice event comprised couples floating baskets on the river. If the baskets stayed together rather than float apart, it meant the couple would stay together. On the full moon night of the twelfth lunar month, it wasn't only couples who floated baskets. Everyone did it to slough off the past year's sins and calamities. Into the baskets went ill health, problems, and misdeeds, which were sailed off with a prayer. I knew from the year before that, on the morning after Loi Kratong, baskets would be clogging canals, ponds, fountains, swimming pools, and whatever else contained liquid.

"I think I'll be with my boyfriend," I said, though I wasn't sure of that. If Jek and I were to postpone sexual relations until a later time, maybe we wouldn't be doing anything together. That was actually fine with me. I felt I had him—but at a safe distance.

When I left Ong, I didn't feel like visiting anyone else; I wanted to hurry and see Jek again.

He came to meet me before I reached his corner. "We go for coffee?" he said. He turned toward Kentucky Fried Chicken, then stopped. "Why don't we go new place?"

"McDonald's! Great. It makes me think of you every time I pass it."

As we crossed the street, the older brother yelled to Jek to bring him back something to eat. I hated crossing that street. Coming from New York, I needed a traffic signal. Thais were like Californians; they stepped in front of oncoming vehicles, confident all would stop.

In the shiny new McDonald's, already crowded with McPatrons, Jek pointed me toward a table and said he would wait in line. I watched him as he waited and thought this was dandy, just as it was. When he came with a tray, I noticed all the Thais watching us. I was the only *farang* there. I'd heard Bangkok *farangs* condemn Thais for not finding Patpong's fast-food places tacky. Resident *farangs* swore they'd never set foot in one. To a Thai, however, 40 *baht* for a hot dog was exorbitant, and that made it elegant.

On the tray was a hamburger for the older brother and something else. "For you," Jek said, handing it to me. It was a large keyring. Inside the clear plastic was a plastic McDonald's french fry bag and separate french fries swimming around. "It's a game," he explained. "You try to get the french fry inside the bag. I buy for you. Five *baht*."

"Thank you." It was heavy and hideous, but I treasured it as a present from Jek. I put my keys on the ring and had a vision of my mother seeing me with a McDonald's french fry keyring—my mother who would insist on nothing less than real gold for her keys. But I loved it anyway.

"I will never forget you," he said.

"Why?"

"Because I have your picture."

"Oh, you found it." He smiled as if he liked finding it.

"I think about your bank loan," he said, next. "You have pen?"

When I gave him one, he scribbled on the paper mat. He'd been thinking about my loan? Maybe he was serious about this long-range plan.

"We both work on something," he said. "You have good education. I have degree in business."

Right, I thought, that imaginary degree from Chula University.

"What job I can get in America?" he asked.

"You're smart and clever, you could make a lot of money there," I lied. I believed he was smart and clever but doubted he could get into America. From dealing with Patpong women, I knew how hard it was for an unwealthy Thai to get a visa—even a tourist visa—for Western countries. You had to prove you had a certain amount of money in the bank. *Farangs* could get on a plane and go anywhere, but this wasn't so for nationals of Third World countries who tried to visit places deluged with immigrants. My heart ached thinking of the differences in advantages between us.

He doodled a plane. He must have really been thinking of me.

"Have you ever flown in a plane?" I asked.

"No." He wrote "JOB?" and underlined it. "In America, I have to speak English very good. I don't want to work sweeping street."

We sat and talked a long time. Sometimes we just looked at each other.

"Oah," he said, suddenly noticing the time. "We sit here two hour." He prodded the hamburger. "Cold. Older brother angry me."

He jumped up, and I hurried to rush after him. Outside he said, "I can't walk with you to your home. Spend too long not working."

I wondered if someone kept track of the hours he worked. I'd tried, once, to find out who organized the touts. Their territory and number seemed fixed. After getting nowhere with the street people, I'd asked the journalist Australian neighbor to inquire for me. At that time, he edited a tourist magazine that carried ads for some of the ripoff bars. He was informed that Patpong's ripoff bars were all connected. Neither of us had learned, though, exactly who divided up the streets and touts.

In the elevator of my building, I fondled my beloved french fry keyring. I chuckled; Momsy would die if she saw it.

Dudley Dapolito and Sow came to the apartment with luggage to store while they went to Chiang Mai.

"What happened to your beard?" I exclaimed, noticing Dudley's shaven face.

He grinned and pulled Sow toward him in an embrace. "She didn't like it so I got rid of it."

"*Mai chaub nuat luh?*" (You don't like mustache?) I asked her.

"*Mai chaub,*" she answered. (Don't like). Thai men had little facial hair, so Thai women weren't used to it.

When I spoke Thai with Sow, Dudley didn't understand. When I spoke English with him, Sow didn't understand.

"I'm back with Jek," I told Dudley in English. I said in Thai to Sow, "Dudley met Jek."

"What about his wife?" Dudley asked.

I shrugged. "I don't know." To Sow I said in Thai, "Jek said he's finished with his wife. Do you think he's lying?"

"I think he love you," she answered.

Dudley said to Sow in English, "I met him last week on the street. A nice-looking dude." Sow didn't understand. "*Lau* (handsome)," he said to her in a louder voice. He knew the word for *handsome*. "*Lau, mach mach*," Sow nodded (very very handsome).

I wondered how we could have such intense relationships with people we couldn't communicate with.

That night when I met Jek, we stood on the bustling street holding hands. Then he said, "I will buy toothbrush to leave in your home. I bring over later."

I was ecstatic. "Oh, yeah? I thought we were going to wait till your birthday."

He smiled but didn't answer. Great. I didn't really want to wait five months. But what about Doom? I still didn't understand his family situation. All I could think about, though, was having him in bed.

I went home early to sleep so I wouldn't be tired the next day. Jek arrived after 4 a.m.

"For you," he said, handing me an English-Thai dictionary. We always had words we didn't know in each other's language. I cherished the gift, even though it had someone else's name written in it.

He brought my radio into the bedroom and turned it to a station with Thai love songs. Oh no, was he going to sing again?

I lowered the volume. "I don't want to disturb the neighbors," I said. I'd noticed how some Thais didn't know how to live in apartments. The Australian neighbor had battled with a Thai woman who moved in above him and pounded chili on the floor like she'd done in her upcountry yard.

"Tell me about your family," I said, as we lay naked in bed. I loved the feel of his skin. I loved having him back.

"Father very bad when I young. He gamble all the time. I have to do everything for myself. Never any money. Father always beat me."

Corporal punishment was the norm for Thai families. Teachers were even allowed to hit students. "What about your mother?"

"Mother big and black. Father is small."

"Do you want to *loi kratong* with me next week?" I asked.

"Alright."

I didn't like his answer. It sounded as if he were agreeing but not enthused. I reminded myself that I didn't understand Thai nuances.

"Then we can visit my mother," he said.

At this, I was thrilled. Not only would we *loi kratong* together, he wanted me to meet his mother. That had to have special meaning for him. This was also comforting, since I'd never dispelled the notion he might rob me one day. If I knew where his mother lived, he couldn't rip me off.

"We are in love," he said. "I won't sleep with other woman." Then he asked, "How you feel about me sleep with prostitute?"

My bones chilled. Then I hesitated remembering it was part of his job when customers offered it in front of massage parlor management. In the pause he said, "Better, right?"

"Better than with another girlfriend, but 'good,' NO!"

He slept through the day. When he finally awoke, in the late afternoon, he made a phone call to check on business cards he'd ordered for Mr. Tam. As I listened to him speak Thai, I noted the pronouns he used. In the lessons at A.U.A., the teacher told us never to use those pronouns or people would laugh. Thais were pickey about status. Thai society was rigidly stratified into classes—the opposite of American ideology, where all people were supposedly equals. Each person had an ascribed position under the royal family.

Jek fetched a packet of instant Thai soup he'd brought with him the night before. "Must eat," he said. "I make for you too. You eat Thai food, become Thai."

I considered telling him about the feast I'd bought for him and threw away; but the memory still hurt, and he'd probably be aghast that anyone could throw away food. He'd think me decadent, not feel sorry for causing me misery.

He prepared the soup and placed it in one bowl to be shared by the two of us, Thai-style.

"Hold it," I said, and added another bowl. "I'm not Thai yet. I need my own bowl. It's too difficult to haul the soup from so far away."

When we watched "The Flintstones", I noticed the appliances Wilma had in her house—washing machine, toaster, lawn mower—and could sense Jek comparing them to his childhood home. Then we watched a Chinese soap opera dubbed in Thai.

While he dressed to leave, he looked sad. He complained about never having a day off.

"Fred Flintstone, he have day off?" he asked.

"Saturdays and Sundays. But when you get an office job, you'll have weekends off too, right?"

He nodded, looking unhappy about having to work, and left.

In reality, I doubted he'd ever have an office job. As a developing country, Thailand didn't have enough jobs for the university graduates it produced each year. To begin with, there weren't enough colleges for all the Thais who wanted to study. Getting into one was supercompetitive and usually possible only for the elite classes, which was why I disbelieved Jek ever went.

Even if Jek had a degree and could get an office job, he'd earn little. Like the women who worked Patpong, men also found it a hard place to leave.

I didn't go out that night. I felt too content and snug to move.

The next morning I was to meet Hoi for a movie date.

I arrived at the apartment to find Hoi and Alex sitting on the floor playing cards. Alex had a job that afternoon teaching English, one hour for 100 *baht*.

"I worked an hour yesterday for the first time," he said. "I HATED it. Today I'll earn 100 *baht* for the day, and I gave Hoi 120 *baht* to spend with you."

Hoi put on Alex's shirt, jeans, and belt. Alex said, "I need the belt." She ignored him. He repeated his need for the belt four times. She didn't acknowledge him once. Then she put on his watch. "I need the watch for work," he said. "How will I know when the hour is up without it?" She ignored him. Again he asked several times.

Alex looked at me and shrugged as if saying, these country girls—what can you expect?

Patpong women relished bending *farang* men to their wills. They used their sexuality and exotic mystique to maneuver them into compromises. *Farang* men weren't really bothered. The situation had them so exalted, petty insults couldn't faze their self-esteems.

Alex pointed to a bookshelf. "I bought Thai books for Hoi. You're reading them, aren't you?" he asked her.

Hoi, at the mirror brushing her hair, didn't say anything, which meant the answer was no. I noted one book was on geography, another math.

"Her English is improving, at least," Alex continued. "She can get a decent job one day—maybe at a travel agency or hotel reception. Speaking English is important in Bangkok."

When Hoi and I left for the movie, she wore both the belt and the watch.

I asked her about getting a job, since Alex made it sound like she was on the verge of joining the legitimate workforce.

She seemed surprised at the question. "Job?" She crinkled her upper lip and shook her head. Then she mumbled about not being able to find a daytime job, and anyway, "Job Alex think okay, no pay money. Only 2,000 *baht* one month. On Patpong, I make 2,000 *baht* one night." With Hoi's fifth-grade level of education, I knew it would be difficult for her to find any job in Bangkok. "Alex want me be sale girl in department store."

"Will you do it?"

She made a skunk-odor face.

"You'd rather go back to Rififi, right?"

She smiled at this. Then she said, "Alex no let me."

I told Hoi about Jek but made an effort not to mention him too much. My urge was to talk about nothing else, but I didn't want to sound like Nok speaking of Moon.

"What are you and Alex doing for Loi Kratong?" I asked.

She frowned and looked down. "You know Alex's friend from the Weekend Market? He took us to Chinatown?"

I nodded, remembering Hoi had been upset when he and his girlfriend snubbed her.

"He have party. He invite Alex but not me. He say he no have room for me. Not true. He don't want me. Don't like me. He don't want Isan-Patpong girl." She looked hurt.

"What will you do?"

"I stay home. Alex go alone."

I felt sad for her, so I said, "Maybe you and Alex and Jek and I can *loi kratong* together."

181

She perked up. "Yes?"

"I'm not sure what we're doing yet. We may just visit his mother. I'll let you know."

"Does Jek take money from you?" she asked.

"No! I wouldn't give a man money." What kind of relationship did she think we had?

Later I pondered the idea of Jek and me and Hoi and Alex celebrating Loi Kratong. Part of me thought the idea great, but I also remembered how vicious Hoi could be. Her jealousy had made her tell Shlomo that Sumalee had secretly met an old boyfriend. It was possible she could do something equally spiteful to me and Jek. I didn't want her asking him if I gave him money. What if he mentioned the 500 *baht* he never paid back? No, I felt too insecure with Jek to tolerate Hoi's tampering with sensitive issues. I wouldn't suggest it to him. I'd have to call Hoi and give her an excuse.

That night, I didn't see Jek on Patpong 3 but found him a few doorways down Silom talking to a skinny man with short legs. Jek introduced him as Mr. Tam; he introduced me as his girlfriend. I noticed they stood where Jek said Mr. Tam lived. That was encouraging. Maybe he hadn't lied.

"We go McDonald?" Jek asked me and Mr. Tam. We agreed. While Jek stood in line to buy our coffees, Mr. Tam and I sat at a table.

Jek had once told me Mr. Tam worked as a bartender on *Soi* Thaniya. Mr. Tam, I remembered, was Japanese, and that street—one over from Patpong 3— was Patpong-like but strictly for Japanese. Its "members-only" policy let in no other nationalities. Another time, I heard about a new business Mr. Tam was organizing, in which Jek would be manager. I was never certain what work Mr. Tam actually engaged in, but the relationship between him and Jek was clearly a "patron-client" one. In the structure of Thai society, "clients" attached themselves to influential "patrons" with ongoing exchanges of favors and labor.

From how Jek had spoken of Mr. Tam, I knew he had to be influential, but from his missing front teeth, I thought he couldn't be very rich. Many Thais had no front teeth because they couldn't afford a dentist. Teeth problems resulted in extractions, not fillings, which I assumed had been the case with Doom. Mr. Tam didn't seem very Japanese either; but, like many *farangs*, I had trouble distinguishing one Asian from another, especially in Bangkok, where the population was so mixed with Chinese.

"I want to invite you and Jek to my *Loi Kratong* party," Mr. Tam said. "I will rent a boat. We travel up the Chao Praya River."

He couldn't be that poor, then, if he intended to rent a boat.

When Jek arrived with a tray, my heart sank as he gave Mr. Tam a french fry keyring. Apparently it lacked sentimental value for him. Jek's face did light up, though, when Mr. Tam told him about the *Loi Kratong* party.

Jek seemed honored to be included in Mr. Tam's classy affair. For myself, I'd rather have spent the time with Jek alone. It would be our first outing.

18.

Upcountry people coming into the city inevitably wind up in the least attractive and least remunerative occupations. Upcountry women are even worse off than men; and uneducated or poorly educated women have a limited and generally depressing range of job opportunities. A recent study established the income ranges of the jobs open to women in the city:

Occupation	*Baht* per month
Housemaid	*150-450*
Waitress	*200-500*
Construction worker	*200-500*
Factory employee	*200-500*
Beauty salon	*400-600*
Clerical	*600-1000*
Services	*800-1500*

(Phongpaichit, 1982: 7-8)

(PROSTITUTES WORKING AS) MASSEUSES' MONTHLY REMITTANCES TO FAMILY

Monthly Remittances to Family (in *baht*)	Number
None	*4*
- 500	*6*
- 1,000	*17*
- 1,500	*3*
- 2,000	*10*
- 2,500	*2*
- 3,000	*4*
- 6,000	*1*
- 10,000	*1*
When needed	*2*

The table shows the maximum amount mentioned ('-2,000' reflects an answer like 'one to two thousand'), and obviously the sums would fluctuate according to the vagaries of supply. Most girls claimed to send around one-third to one-half of their earnings, and the median amount was in the range of 1,000-2,000 baht. Many said they would send additional lump sums on request to cover special outlays like medical fees, school expenses for siblings, or children, and payment for hired labour during the harvest season.

(Phongpaichit, 1982: 23-24)

The next day, when Jek saw me approach, he made a face.

He didn't want to see me? He no longer liked me? What was wrong?

"What's the matter?" I asked anxiously.

"I don't feel good."

"Oh." I was too sensitive about him, I thought. His smallest frown could ruin my day. He didn't say anything more. "I hope you feel better," I said. "I'll see you on my way back."

I went to the Apollo Inn. Chai sat with me. This time there was a Fucking Show. It starred the same man as the week before. On the receiving end, he still didn't remove his G-string but merely pushed aside the back. His partner was nude. As in the male-female shows, the two males had intercourse in every position possible, but with few strokes in each.

Before I left the Apollo Inn, I asked Chai, "I'd like to know your life story. Would you tell me? I'll pay the bar so you don't have to work, and afterward we can go out."

Needing insight on Thai childhood, I hoped to dig cultural mysteries out of him.

He agreed and said he'd come by the next day, a Saturday. On weekend afternoons, he didn't have to work in the restaurant.

I didn't see Jek on the way back, but he appeared at my door shortly after. "I'm sick," he said. "Tonight I take guest to Thai boxing game. I sit many hour, all the time freezing."

He was freezing now too, so I gave him a blue sweatshirt and wool harem pants to wear. He looked like a genie.

"Do you have the flu?" I asked. "Are you sniffly?"

"No."

"What is it then?"

He grimaced. "Maybe malaria. Dengue. I don't know."

"Have you been to a doctor?"

He shook his head. I knew he was thinking of the cost. Poor Thais didn't go to doctors or buy medicine easily. *Farangs* told me stories of dragging their Patpong girlfriends to the clinic when they were sick and then buying their medication. One *farang* visited a girl for months after he had her tuberculosis diagnosed. Though no longer with her, he knew if he didn't buy the medicine, she wouldn't take it.

"Newspapers do report dengue fever in Bangkok lately," I said. "Don't you want to go to the hospital? I'll go with you."

"No."

I hated to see him feeling bad. How awful to be sick and unable to pay for a doctor. Though government hospitals were free, after waiting in line all day, people still had to pay for medication. The access Patpong women had to *farangs* who could take care of their health was an advantage of Patpong I hadn't

184

considered yet. I couldn't pay Jek's doctor bill though. I didn't want it to be that kind of relationship, and I didn't think Jek would accept it anyway. He made it clear when we went for coffee that the man was supposed to pay for the woman.

"Do you want some aspirins at least?" I asked.

He nodded. When I gave him two, he said, "You make good wife."

I considered arguing that a wife shouldn't be equated with a nurse and that men were supposed to be compassionate to the ill too. I didn't think it appropriate for the moment though.

He burned with fever and wanted to lie down and sleep. I told him to get in bed, which he did, still in the genie outfit. I turned off the air conditioner and joined him.

I wondered if he was contagious. Could he have AIDS? I should be more concerned about AIDS, I thought. Since coming to Thailand, it was as if the disease no longer existed. The papers rarely referred to it, and when they did, it was only to say the country didn't have more than the eight cases reported the previous year.

Jek felt hot to touch.

"You feel like an electric blanket," I said, wrapping my arms around him.

"What that?"

"A blanket you plug in to keep warm." I laughed, thinking it must seem funny to someone who knew only the tropics. He looked disbelieving. "Really," I said. "Fred Flintstone probably had one."

He cuddled in my arms. "Maybe I need wet cloth." He tapped his forehead.

He expected a cold compress? This was a little much for me. I was wary of playing that wife-nurse role. "Go to sleep," I said. "That's best."

He woke fairly early the next day. On weekdays, Thai TV didn't begin until 4 p.m., but on weekends it went from early morning. Jek still felt feverish and weak. We moved to the living room, and he lay on my lap as we watched Japanese cartoons dubbed in Thai.

"Look at that! I can't believe it," I yipped when a little girl went behind a bush to urinate. "That's amazing!"

"What?"

"In America, no one in a cartoon goes to the bathroom."

The maids came in and giggled when they saw Jek in my clothes. They knew he was the one from the madwoman incident because I'd mentioned him before. He did look adorable in my clothes. Did they find the situation curious, or were they thrilled for me, thinking, as usual, I must be lonely living alone?

Jek and I lounged around all day. Playing with my fingers, at one point he looked at my nails and said, "Why you have this color?"

"Red? I like it. You don't like it?"

"It's old-fashion. Like for old people."

"Oh." I certainly didn't want to look old. "What's better?" I asked.

"Pink." I made a note to buy new nail polish.

Chai came by in the late afternoon with a letter for me to write. After Jek heard that Chai worked at the Apollo Inn, he barely acknowledged his presence. Was it because he felt sick or because he didn't want to associate with Chai? A tout and a go-go boy were probably not on the same social level. Or was it because of me? Since he had gay clients, Jek often stressed he didn't go that way. Maybe he was demonstrating how negatively he viewed homosexuals.

When Chai heard Jek worked on his corner, he behaved deferentially. Occasionally, while I wrote the letter for Chai, Jek offered a fancy word to show off his English vocabulary. This was offered to me, not Chai. Chai and Jek didn't speak.

After the letter, I decided to leave Jek in the apartment and take Chai to the nearby YWCA restaurant. I couldn't conduct an interview with the tension between them.

"Jek had a fever last night," I said to Chai as we walked over. "I hope he doesn't have AIDS. Do you think he has AIDS?"

Look who I was asking!—someone whose job involved high-risk sex. I remembered Chai had had a fever the week before.

He shrugged as if it weren't important. His attitude reflected that of resident *farangs* who believed what the papers said. AIDS was a disease of the West. Even journalists, who knew the government repressed the subject, allowed themselves to be lulled into complacency. Nobody knew anyone with AIDS, so it wasn't real to them. Though I knew the virus had to be on Patpong, no one had fallen sick yet. When I inquired about it, I found only ignorance, nothing that seemed like a cover up.

Chai asked, "Do you give Jek money?"

"No. Never. I wouldn't." Why did people keep asking me that? Did they think I had to pay a man for his company? Or did Hoi and Chai ask because mercenary relationships were all they knew?

Maybe they saw something else in the relationship. But Hoi had never even met Jek. Stop, I told myself, don't become paranoid from the comments of prostitutes. Worrying over Jek's motives, Doom, and AIDS would drive me crazy if I let it.

In the restaurant, I took out pen and paper and asked, "What was your childhood like?"

"When I five year old, my family rich. Have many horse. When I eleven, poor. Some horse die. One we sell cheap because have bad leg."

"What is poor?"

"No refrigerator, no TV."

"Did you work before you came to Bangkok?"

"When sixteen, I drive *samlor* (bicycle rickshaw)."

"For how long?"

"Only four month. No work when seventeen, eighteen, nineteen. I fail test for air force. I want to join. They say no. At twenty, I come Apollo Inn."

"Did you start having sex with guests right away?"

"First time was day four. Thai man twenty year old. Not handsome. I no like his body. Short-time, I do him with my hand, 200 *baht*. Second man is seventy-year-old *farang*. Again only with hand, only kiss him. Take two minute, 200 *baht*. Third time I make 500 *baht*. *Farang* take five boy. Only one boy fuck with him, other boy help. Then forty-year-old *farang* take five boy, 400 *baht* each."

"What about a boyfriend? Do you have one?"

"Five month ago, I meet boy at a club. We both drunk and go hotel but only sleep. He live with *farang* and no have time see me. Now we just friend."

"One night five months ago and nothing happened—haven't you had a love relationship?"

"No time. I work every day and live in bar."

"There's no one you're attracted to?"

He smiled. "Someone I like, but he work other bar. We never have time to meet."

"Have you ever had a girlfriend?"

"No."

"What is your dream?"

"I want raise pig. Also chicken and fish. I want build house for me, mother, and father."

"What do you plan for your future?"

"Marry."

"Marry! Marry a woman?"

"Thai man must have wife. Children is most important thing. If Thai no have children, he adopt one. Need children for when old."

"You'll marry a woman even though you're gay?"

"Yes. I change, give up boy."

"If you have a boyfriend you love, you would leave him to marry a woman?"

"Yes." He looked at me as if he couldn't understand the question. I looked at him as if I couldn't understand the answer. In his culture, familial obligation came first. In mine, the individual's identity came first. We couldn't understand each other's reasoning.

"You said you'd like to see America. What would you do if you were in America with a rich boyfriend you loved. Would you stay?"

"No." Clearly he didn't understand how I could ask that. "I come back, marry woman."

"What if you can't find one you like?"

At this, he blinked. This was not an issue he could relate to. He opened his mouth but nothing came out. Obviously, a man didn't have to like the woman to marry her. How unfair for the wife. Had that been the case with Jek—did he marry Doom so he could have a child and because she was a policeman's daughter, and therefore respectable?

I asked Chai, "When do you plan to do this?"

"When I have 40,000 *baht* ($1,600) I stop work, give up boy and marry."

"What if you never have 40,000 *baht*?"

"Then I marry when twenty-five."

"What would make you happy?" I asked.

"Money. If I have money, I happy. If have TV, refrigerator, video, car, I happy."

I kept thinking of Jek alone in the apartment. This was the first time I'd left him there since Doom's attack. Though I felt unsure what I'd find on my return, I liked the image of his waiting for me. I had an urge to hurry back. Was he feeling better?

"I'm going home for a while," I told Chai. "I'll meet you tonight and we'll go somewhere. Where would you like to go?"

"Up to you."

"What about the bar where that boy you like works?" I suggested, hoping to see him interact with a potential love interest. "Want to visit him?"

Chai looked pleased with the idea.

Back in the apartment, I found Jek asleep in front of the TV—my sleeping genie. I remembered Chai and Hoi asking if I gave him money and felt a flash of worry that maybe I was being used. Ridiculous, I told myself. I knew Jek liked me—I just didn't know if he was still with his wife. If he was, would that make me a *mia noi*?

Jek stirred when I felt his brow. He smiled up at me.

"What time is it?" he asked.

"Almost seven. Are you going to work? You're still feverish."

"Have to go, sick or no."

I picked up Chai, and we went to a gay bar on Surawong Road around the corner from Patpong.

"Have you been here before?" I asked him.

"No. Too expensive and no time."

Geared for tourists, the bar was ritzier and more expensive than the Apollo Inn but of the same genre. Five boys danced on one stage, five on another, and one more on a stage near the bar. It charged 100 *baht* extra for a *farang* woman's drink and 200 *baht* for a Thai woman's. Chai knew many of the go-gos there—some as ex-employees of the Apollo Inn, others as neighbors in Udon.

He spotted yet another acquaintance, made an exclamatory noise, and said, "I know him too. He live near me in Udon."

"You didn't know he was in Bangkok?"

"Yes," he answered, meaning no.

"Is he gay?"

"No. Only me gay."

For both sexes from Isan, bar work and prostitution seemed the only way to support their families.

Chai's old neighbors came by to say hello. Chai, dressed in spiffy city clothes, seemed lofty sitting there as a customer. For this night, Chai had requested I wear a certain outfit he'd seen me in before—a sexy one, off the shoulder.

"Where's the boy you like?" I asked him.

He looked around and told me, disappointedly, "He's with guest." Chai later pointed him out when he went to dance.

"That's him," he said. "Number 101."

Coming offstage, 101 stopped by Chai to light his cigarette, and they smiled at each other. Then 101 returned to his customer.

Chai made a helpless shrug and said, "There is never time for us."

With my new appreciation of Thai male bodies, I found the dancing boys attractive. One noticed me staring at him and smiled. He had the features of a *luuk krung* ("half child," meaning half Thai, half *farang*). Since most go-go boys weren't gay, I wondered if they viewed me as an available female because I was with Chai. Patpong women and *katoeys* eyed me differently than they did—the former as a customer, the latter not. For sure Number One Off—who'd hid behind a pillar so I wouldn't see him naked—didn't regard me in a financial mode.

I didn't look at the *luuk krung* again for fear he'd come over and expect me to buy him a drink. As it was, I'd told Chai to offer drinks to anyone he wished. I considered it payment for letting me interview him.

Chai and his friends spoke matter-of-factly about their jobs, seeming to take pride in their urban life. Chai appeared to have their respect for being in Bangkok the longest and for having me. They gave me a long look when Chai told them I'd been to his family home.

When Chai asked me, "*Mee kai kee tua?* (How many chickens [whores] are there?)" they laughed.

At 10:30 was a Fucking Show, six men in two groups of three. Stylized and choreographed, the anal sex and fellatio positions on one stage matched those on the other.

The next morning, I faced tax day. Those who stayed in Thailand over 90 days in a year had to undergo this hassle before leaving the country or they weren't allowed to board their plane or cross the border. My visa extension was up that week, and this time I'd have to leave. It would actually expire the day of Loi Kratong, but I wasn't going to miss that. I'd overstay a day or two. When I reached the border, I'd have to pay 100 *baht* for each day over.

The government had implemented the tax rule to make sure working foreigners paid taxes. Since Thailand rarely granted resident permits but needed English teachers, a large number of *farangs* lived there permanently but had to leave the country every three months. A trek to the tax office was an obligatory part of the process. No revenue collector referred to the fact that it was illegal for foreigners to work in Thailand.

Like the Immigration Ordeal, the Tax Ordeal took a minimum of three hours. Foreigners in the country over 90 days who didn't work also had to pay tax, a percentage of the amount they brought in. The government did allow for special circumstances, though, and mine was one. I was exempt from tax if I proved I was a student living on a student loan.

I figured that, in a noncomputerized bureaucracy, one government branch wouldn't know what another did, and so the tax office wouldn't know that the National Research Council had forbade me to do research. The mounds of paper stacked on desks, cabinet tops, and the floor affirmed that I needn't worry about that—but I worried anyway. Did someone know of me? Maybe the student policy no longer applied.

When my turn came, I sat before a woman who pulled out my file, already inches thick. As usual, she made copies of the letters from my school's Financial Aid office, my professor, the Bangkok Bank, etc. Would she charge me an impossible tax fee? Would she ban me from Thailand for doing illegal research? Was I missing a form?

With relief, I received my passport back with the necessary tax stamp and signature.

That evening, I met Nok in front of Queen's Castle at 6 p.m. We were to have dinner before she began work. I recognized the person standing with her from the pictures she'd shown me. It was Moon, her Thai boyfriend, whom by now she'd described as sixteen, seventeen, and once even nineteen.

Moon was fairly tall with a baby face. I wondered what Nok had told him about me.

The three of us went to Robinson's, the department store. It was still early when we passed Jek's corner. I told Nok, "I'm back with my Thai boyfriend. This is where he works, but he's not here yet."

In Robinson's, Nok led me to the floor where I'd bought the food for Jek. The aroma of duck aroused memories; but now that I had Jek back, they didn't bother me—much. Had my situation changed since that day? Or was Doom poised for another strike?

As we settled at a table, Nok told me she was leaving the next day for an island with a Japanese man. Thailand had several resort islands where the girls went with customers.

Since Moon sat beside her listening, he obviously knew about her men, so I asked, "Yamaguchi?"

"No."

"The Japanese man I met in the bar?"

"No." She then asked me to translate an English letter she'd received from yet another Japanese man.

"Okay, sure." I loved reading correspondence from customer-boyfriends.

As Nok opened the envelope, she leaned into Moon and giggled about the Japanese man. She held his letter as if it were a certificate of achievement.

I read and translated. He wrote that he missed her and noted it was a Japanese custom to exchange gifts. What did she want? The letter ended "much love."

Nok grinned at Moon with pride, as if her certificate read "Summa Cum Laude."

"What present will you ask him for?" I asked her.

Her grin widened and she buried her head coquettishly in Moon's shoulder. Then she said, "Bracelet." She laughed. "Gold with emerald."

"Will you send him something in return? He said the custom was to exchange gifts."

She looked at me as if I'd spoken in Greek and didn't bother to answer.

On the way back, we passed Jek. He didn't shake hands with Nok and Moon. Instead, Nok steepled her hands and *wai*ed him, adding a semicurtsy. I wondered if her formality was because of me, because he worked as a guide, or because he was older; age counted for much in Thai status.

"Feel better?" I asked Jek.

"All better." He whispered to me, "I come over after work." I kissed his cheek.

Walking on, I overheard Nok and Moon giggling that Jek had black skin. I noticed they were slightly lighter.

On Patpong 1, I asked Moon, "Where are you going now?"

"I work down there, near *Soi* Crazy Horse."

"Oh? What do you do?"

"I'm guide. Like your *fan*."

Nok's boyfriend was a Patpong man! Surprise, surprise. Was this true for all the girls who claimed they never went with Patpong men?

With so many conflicting statements, it seemed I wouldn't learn Patpong culture from words alone. I'd have to match them with behavior. That applied to Jek too. I'd have to wait and see what he did.

19.

Recounting the history of prostitution in Thai society, Hantrakul (Undated: 117) writes that:

> *Prior to 1905 prostitutes were recruited from the slave market, working under brothel keepers and liable for tax. The abolition of slavery in 1905 resulted in a sudden growth of prostitution as a large number of former freshly-freed slave women became prostitutes. It is also possible that these were joined by slave wives. Slave wives were distinct from slave women in that a slave wife was completely monopolized by her husband whereas a slave woman would have to entertain other men as well if ordered by her master.*

That night, the day before Loi Kratong, Jek came by at 3:30 a.m.

"Oah!" he said, noticing my pink nail polish.

"For you," I said. "And look here." I opened a kitchen cabinet. "Full of Thai food. I don't recognize myself anymore."

"You become Thai," he stated with a grin.

"Almost."

He put the kettle on to make soup. "None for me," I said. "I'm not hungry."

"You should eat more. You too skinny."

"Skinny! Not compared to Thai women."

"No, you same as Thai. *Farang* always fat, too fat. Thai woman only skinny because no have enough food."

"Yeah, I have been losing weight lately." Actually, my weight had dropped to ninety-eight pounds, low for me. Lately I'd felt too anxious to eat. I loved it. Not wanting to stuff my mouth—what a blessing. I didn't like the jitters that accompanied my weight loss though. The ambiguity of the situation with Jek upset my peace of mind—that and the perception of how close to destitution he was. Poverty in Thailand was an abyss unknown in America. No Medicaid, no food stamps, no shelters for the homeless. Through Jek's eyes, I saw the despair behind the hustle. It was a discomforting awareness. In truth, it upset my opinions of Patpong. If this desperation lay beneath the women's job choice, maybe there was no "choice" in prostitution. Would I have to rethink my thesis?

Jek ate, then showered. When he exited the bathroom, I went in. I found the furry carpet completely soaked. Instead of my feet feeling fluff, they squished. I went to take Jek by the hand and lead him back in.

"Listen," I told him, "this is a *farang* bathroom. You must bathe *farang*-style, not Thai. See the tub? You're supposed to keep the water in there. The carpet should stay dry, otherwise it will get moldy and smell."

Thai bathrooms had no special place to bathe. You had a bucket of water and you threw water over yourself, expecting the entire floor to get wet.

"Oah!" he said. "I must become *farang*."

"Right." We giggled and stayed in the bathroom kissing.

"The day after Loi Kratong is Thanksgiving," I told him. "Do you know about it?"

"It's *farang* holiday?"

"No, only American. When the pilgrims first went to America, the Indians gave them turkey and sweet potato, and everyone celebrated."

"American kill Indian. I see on TV."

"Not right away. First they accepted their food and had a party. I'll take you for Thanksgiving dinner. The hotels are having specials. Have you ever eaten turkey?"

"What that?"

"It's like a big chicken. It has a thing under its chin and says gobble-gobble."

"Gobble-gobble?"

We looked up turkey in the dictionary.

"*Kai gnuang*!" he said. "But *kai gnuang* no say gobble-gobble."

I laughed. "Thai animals must have a Thai accent. What does a Thai rooster say? Cocka-doodle-doo?"

He laughed. "No. He say ek-ee-ek-ek. He speak Thai."

"How about bow-wow? American dogs say bow-wow."

"Thai dog no do like that. He bark HEUNG-HEUNG." We held onto each other to keep from falling over with laughter.

"They don't woof?"

"Yes, never."

"Do Thai pigs oink?"

"OOT-OOT."

"That's an owl!"

"Pig!"

When our laughter quieted, Jek said, "You ideal for me."

I loved hearing this. Then I remembered he'd said Doom had been ideal for him. Was this a Thai idiom or did it mean he was going to benefit from the relationship?

The day of Loi Kratong, Jek awoke with severe ulcer pain. He made himself noodle soup and went back to sleep. I wondered about our plans. If we were to visit his mother and join Mr. Tam's party, we'd have to leave early.

I went downstairs to read the papers. The front page reported heavy rain causing a flood in the South. The continuing downpour would only make things worse.

Thailand's monsoon season ended that month in November. That year hadn't seen much rain in Bangkok. I'd found it easy to avoid the periods of heavy torrent and enjoyed the cooler temperature. As usual, November had brought occasional floods to Bangkok, whose drainage system filled to capacity over the monsoon months. My street was notorious for causing pedestrians to wade past their knees in filthy water. Bangkok dwellers were used to it and barely turned their heads when motor boats chugged down avenues.

The flood in Southern Thailand was not commonplace, however, and pictures showed families huddled in the rain on rooftops.

Then I noticed a small article on a back page. It said a Thai woman's group called Friends of Women had gone to Pattaya to picket the arrival of another American fleet, accusing them of bringing AIDS. Bar girls had organized a counter picket with placards proclaiming: *Ben Ets Dee Kwa Ot Taay* (Better AIDS Than Starvation).

Tears welled in my eyes. I restrained them. I didn't want my alcoholic neighbor to ask me what was wrong. He'd been lurching around the lobby looking for someone to talk to, and so far I'd avoided him by seeming engrossed in the paper. I didn't want to explain how intensely I felt the bar girls' plight. Had Jek made me more sensitive to poverty issues? AIDS over starvation was a horrible choice. Maybe my assessment of Patpong and Pattaya had been too simplistic after all.

At 5 p.m., I woke up Jek. "Happy Loi Kratong Day," I said. "It's getting late."

He looked at the clock. "We have time. Meet Mr. Tam at 8."

I wondered when we'd visit his mother. "How's the ulcer?" I asked, but from his face I knew it hurt.

Slowly he got out of bed and dressed. I felt excited about our first evening out but couldn't bubble too much because he was dragging himself around. When we left the apartment, I took his hand. I knew hand holding wasn't a Thai custom and wondered if it embarrassed him. We walked three blocks down an avenue to cross an overpass.

As we mounted the stairs, he said, "When we marry you want a room for yourself?"

Marry? Was he thinking we'd get married? I considered telling him I didn't believe in marriage, that it was good for men but death for women. I knew, though, that marriage in Thailand was not an institution anyone challenged. Like religion, the royal family, and the necessity of having children, it was not questioned. Besides, it felt so nice being with him, I didn't want to spoil the mood.

"I always need my own space," I said.

"I agree. People need to have their own room."

I wondered if he were talking about his living arrangements with Doom. Sometimes the Thai language used the word *room* to mean apartment. Did he and Doom live apart though they were still married, and had he used this argument to arrange it? That way, he could have his freedom, as well as a wife raising his child.

No, I wouldn't take his marriage talk seriously. No need to remind him I'd be returning one day to America. Or was that what he had in mind? Did he imagine he could get to America as my husband? Over Momsy's dead body, I thought.

Jek grimaced and held his side as we climbed into a *tuk-tuk*. I asked, "Isn't there medicine you can take?"

He nodded hesitantly, which I figured meant yes but no, he wouldn't give up the money to buy it.

I couldn't bear Jek's suffering, so I said, "We must stop at a pharmacy and I'll buy the medicine for you." He seemed to agree but then let stores go by. "There's one," I said, after passing half a dozen. He let that one go too, but when he saw how determined I was, he finally stopped the *tuk-tuk* and got out and bought it for himself. I felt he regretted spending the money, so I decided to insist on paying for some things that night.

After he took a few sips of the white liquid, I asked, "When are we going to your mother's?"

"I tell you later."

At this I felt something was wrong. Had he lied about going? Or had he decided against it? Was Doom there? Maybe his son Bank wasn't there, and if he took me I'd know he'd lied. Worrying that he was keeping something from me, I insisted, "Tell me now. I need to know now."

I could see he didn't want to answer but eventually he said, "I have no money to bring my mother. I haven't seen her in long time."

"Oh." At first I felt bad for him. How sad not to visit your family because you didn't have money to bring them. I wondered if he'd spent the money for his mother on me. Then I thought, it couldn't have been that long since he'd seen his mother because he'd said Doom had found my card in his mother's house. Where was the lie?

I hated feeling manipulated. It seemed there was always something off kilter in what he told me, enough to make me feel lied to.

Not wanting to ruin the night, I dismissed suspicions from my mind.

Our destination was Wat Arun, an exquisite temple on the bank of the Chao Praya River. Jek refused to let me pay the *tuk-tuk* fare but then accepted half.

Inside the temple grounds, festivity charged the air. A mob of revelers made progress slow. Everywhere, vendors sold *kratongs* made of paper, plastic, or banana leaves.

"Are we going to buy *kratongs*?" I asked, jubilantly looking at the variety. Historically, Thais had made *kratongs* with banana leaves painstakingly folded in pointy designs. My class the year before at A.U.A. had learned how. It took us hours to cut up banana leaves and fold fifty or sixty of them just so, sticking them in place with splinters of bamboo. Inside the baskets we'd placed incense sticks and candles fancied-up with colored paper. The modern era, though, had done away with old-fashioned do-it-yourself *kratongs* and supplied ready-made plastic ones in glaring colors.

"Not yet. We wait for Mr. Tam."

Fireworks exploded left and right but mostly made noise only. The rare one rose into the sky with a pop of color. From loudspeakers, Thai music crackled. In a corner, women danced in traditional dress—glittery cloth wrapped tightly around their hips. They made stylized movements: one wrist bent this way, the other bent back, foot out, head cocked. Gold crowns held their hair pulled into buns. To a tinkle of bell music, their wrists flipped over and their heads cocked the other way.

Jek and I strolled the grounds. As far as I could tell I was the only *farang*.

Jek held his side and said, "I need to eat. You feel hunger?"

"I should. I haven't eaten all day."

We sat at a food stall, and he bought me something that looked like an omelette but puffier and orange. "I teach you Thai food. You know already?"

"Uh-un, I never saw anything like this in my life. What is it?"

"Wait, I get more." He left and returned with pastry-like things filled with creamy stuff in different colors. "What's that?" I asked him.

"Taste first."

"What is it? What are you feeding me? Beetles?"

Laughing, he aimed a spoonful at my mouth. I tasted. "What you think?" he asked.

"Mmmm, sweet. *Arroy*." (Delicious.) I felt so content, I'd probably find beetles delicious too. "What's that green goo?"

"Coconut."

We pushed through to the pier. Lightbulbs dotted rice barges and long-tailed boats cruising the river. Ferries came and went, docking a moment to pick up celebrants and then sailing off. Flowery *kratongs,* carrying lit candles and incense sticks, bobbed on the waves they left. For twenty feet out from the bank, *kratongs* covered the river. Their twinkly candles speckled the water. Some turned upside down in the wake of docking craft.

On the pier, families pushed to the water's edge and crouched to set their *kratongs* adrift. An old man solemnly *wai*ed his as it floated off.

"Does water have religious meaning?" I asked Jek.

"Buddha leave footprint on shore of river."

"This river? Buddha was here?"

"Not this river."

We waited over an hour but never spotted Mr. Tam.

"That's okay," I told Jek. "It's better just the two of us. Let's go *loi*."

He seemed disappointed he'd miss Mr. Tam's fancy affair but quickly cheered up. "I take you good place. We go to zoo."

We boarded a ferry to cross the river, then walked past the Grand Palace. As we approached the royal park, Jek said, "My father read fortune here." He looked around but didn't find him. "You see those women?" he said, pointing to lines of them standing by the park railing, by trees, and at the bus stop. "Eighty *baht*."

"They're prostitutes?"

He nodded. "Cheap."

"You sure they're not waiting for a bus?"

"You see corner? I used to sell pornograph magazine there. Sometime have to run from police. One time they catch me."

"Did you go to jail?"

"No. They keep me few hour, then let me go."

"Have you ever been in jail?"

"No." He had a faraway look. "In my life, I do many thing for money. My family poor. I always work."

"How did you pay for college?" I asked, still disbelieving he went.

"I sell food, corn. Have cart. Push all day. Go everywhere, sell food."

"The U.S. government paid for my undergraduate education. We have government grants to pay tuition and provide extra money to live on."

He looked sad. "Not in Thailand. Here must pay everything yourself. American people very lucky." After a pause, he said, "I hope I can get job in America. Your loan is how much? Seven thousand? What if we can't pay back?"

"SevenTY thousand," I said. Was he really thinking we were going to America as husband and wife? Should I be flattered? Or insulted he never bothered to ask me? Was he that sure of my affection? Or was this a Thai man's take-charge attitude?

"In America," I said, "if you can't pay back a loan, you declare bankruptcy and that's the end of it."

"Oah!" he said, looking stricken. "You can't do that in Thailand. A debt goes to children and their children and will stay forever."

As we waited at a red light, a Thai teenaged girl stared at us. Jek and I giggled.

"She thinks you're *narak* (cute)," I said.

"No, she don't look at me. She look at you."

"Me?"

"She never see Thai man with *farang* before. *Farang* man with Thai woman, yes."

We giggled some more. "No, I think she's looking at your cute face."

We bussed to the zoo. Only once had I ridden in a Thai bus. Crowded and hot, with people hanging out the door, they weren't for me. Riding with Jek, though, made it wonderfully exciting. At that hour we could sit, and the curious glances from other passengers delighted us.

We found another mob in front of the zoo and dozens of *kratong* vendors.

"Look at those," I said. "They're beautiful. Can we buy some now?"

He stopped to ask the price. "Oah! Too expensive."

As we made our way into the park, Jek stopped to ask the price at every stall. He shook his head and looked more dejected after each one. I wanted to offer to pay but felt he might be insulted. Today he was treating me to a Thai holiday; tomorrow was my turn with Thanksgiving.

Finally he bought two small crepe paper *kratongs*, inexpensive and ugly.

The zoo was as jammed as the *wat* had been. Jek found us space by the lake.

The entire surface of the water teemed with floating baskets wafting the scent of incense. Jek lit our candles and incense sticks, then closed his eyes pensively for several minutes. Points of tiny flames blinked around us, from the lake and from the shore.

I wondered if he were wishing about me but had to admit he was probably wishing away his ulcer. I had no wish to make for myself. Everything was perfect the way it was. I loved being with Jek but didn't want to marry him, or anybody. No, just like this was fine with me. Except . . . I would have liked to be more sure about Doom.

When Jek was ready, we placed our *kratongs* on the water and pushed them out. I wanted to stay and see if they floated together—according to folklore, that meant the couple would stay together—but Jek itched to move on. He couldn't have been wishing about me, I thought, if he didn't care to watch our *kratongs*. As we walked away, I turned back to see how they were floating. They stayed abreast close to the bank. We walked on and I turned again. I saw someone push them with a stick to steer them to the center of the lake. The force pushed them apart.

Jek didn't see it. He seemed to be quietly contemplating whatever he'd prayed for. I wanted to ask him what it was, but I suspected it didn't concern me and didn't want my feelings hurt.

We *tuk-tuk*ed back to Patpong, where he had to resume work.

"Will you come by tonight?" I asked.

"No. Tomorrow we go for Thanksgiving, right?"

I nodded, wondering if he would *loi kratong* with Doom later that night.

I dropped him off and made a tour of Patpongs 1 and 2. The bars had tubs of water on the street for people to float *kratongs*.

A drunken *farang*, with his arm around a bar girl, placed a paper boat made from a bar bill in a tub and flicked it with his finger.

"Very good, honey," said the woman. "Now you are Thai man."

Inside the bars, hostesses wore traditional costumes. The go-gos in bikinis danced with crowns on their heads. Patpong had its own way of celebrating Loi Kratong.

20.

For many poor country families, there is no choice about whether or not family members should migrate. Whether adult or still child-age, there often comes a point when either the migrant or the family decides that extra income is a necessity. "Peasant and rural families now routinely send their daughters, some as young as 9 or 10, to work as child laborers or prostitutes in Bangkok establishments" (Ong, 1985: 5). Inbaraj (1988: 31) describes the huge number of migrants arriving at Bangkok's train station, where a study revealed that "about 31 percent of the people migrating to Bangkok were children between the ages of 5 and 14 years and the majority of them were from the poor provinces in the Northeast." Private employment agencies are at the station waiting for them.

After traveling around Thailand for two weeks with Sow, Dudley Dapolito came for his luggage and mail while Sow went to visit friends.

"Happy Thanksgiving," I said to him. "Are you taking Sow for turkey dinner?"

"Nah, I eat turkey every year at home. Here's your article back," he said, handing me a paper by Eric Cohen I'd given him to read. Cohen had written several articles about *farang* men falling in love with Thai bar girls engaged in "open-ended prostitution." He discussed the torment they suffered never knowing whether the women were with them for love or money.

"What did you think of it?" I asked.

"He wrote many things that fit Sow to a tee."

"Like what?"

"Like writing letters to guys who send her money and come back to see her. She has lots of these 'boyfriends,' as she calls them."

"Who are they?"

"One is a fifty-year-old American with a wife and children. He's returning for a week on December 8th, so I won't be with Sow during that time. Then she has a fat German who wants to marry her. Sow doesn't want to go to Germany though. He too will be arriving soon. The German offered to pay for English lessons. I told her to accept. I'd like to teach her the English alphabet myself so she can sound out words. Sow also writes to a thirty-three-year-old Belgian who'll be back in Thailand for two weeks in February."

"It must be complicated answering mail and keeping track of who's coming and when."

"She complained that the German's letters are too long. She has to pay 60 *baht* to translate them."

"What did you think of Cohen's analysis of *farangs*? Did it describe your situation with Sow?"

"Yes and no. Sow doesn't treat me like the others. Real feelings are involved with me." Dudley stopped and laughed. "That's what everyone says, right?"

"It's difficult, isn't it, to be involved with people who have nothing when we have everything? I wonder if it makes them angry and hate us."

"Jek doesn't hate you, that's for sure. I could tell how emotional he was over you."

"Yeah? But how do we know if they see us as individuals or as relatives of Uncle Sam?"

"I'm really working on a relationship with Sow. For one thing, I tell her we must have honesty between us. Truth will keep us pure. Without sincerity and trust, I'd be just another trick."

"Thais don't see honesty the way we do. Revealing your inner feelings and being The Real You are Western concepts. The idea of being true to one's self and expecting everyone to accept us as we are—that's foreign to Thai culture. We consider ourselves individuals; Buddhists see themselves as family members linked with past and future incarnations. Besides, your 'honesty' is contrary to their concept of 'face.' Ever try asking someone for directions?"

He slapped his leg. "I've been sent far out of my way. Has that happened to you too?"

"Thais won't admit they don't know or don't understand. If they did, they'd 'lose face.'"

"So they tell you any old direction? That doesn't make sense."

"It does to them. Behavior we call dishonest, they think is polite."

"I told Sow she has to tell me the truth about her customers. Anything is okay as long as she tells me about it."

"I don't think we can demand honesty and expect them to go against ingrained reflexes. Do you think she really believes you'd accept everything she does in her line of work?"

"I do! Sort of. I understand why she works as a prostitute."

"How serious are you about Sow? Do you plan to stay here forever?"

"I have to leave at the end of December but I'm coming back to be with her. My parents sent me a round-trip ticket. I was due to go home ages ago. My father wants me back. They're getting bills from my credit cards. The only way they could get me to leave Thailand was to send me the ticket."

"Round-trip, of course."

"I wouldn't go if it were one-way."

"What will Sow do while you're gone? Continue working?"

He shrugged. "My impulse is to give her all my savings so she can escape prostitution."

Travelers who fell in love with Thai bar girls always faced this problem. If they left the country, should they leave their beloved to continue in the business?

"Have you given her extra money?"

"Heaps of it. She has debts. What I give her only pays the interest."

"How's your herpes?" I asked with a smile.

"Bummer. It's creating sexual problems. I worry that too much sex will incite an outbreak. If I feel a herpes tingle, I'm careful to go gently and use a condom to reduce friction."

"Otherwise you don't use condoms? What happened to safe sex?"

He hesitated with half a grin. "I hate those things, you know what I mean?"

"Aren't you afraid of AIDS?"

"I am. I took an AIDS test in Hong Kong. They promised to send the result here, but it hasn't come yet. I've cut down on sex because of the herpes. Sometimes I abstain completely if I feel a tingle. A full outbreak can last seven to ten days. Now Sow and I have sex only once a day and sometimes even skip a day."

That night I was to meet Jek at 8:30. I watched TV news before I left.

The flood in Southern Thailand had become a national disaster. The rain still hadn't stopped, and newsreels showed crying children sitting in mud under umbrellas. Families carried their injured on make-shift stretchers but had no place to take them. The streets of Hat Yai, a large town, lay eight feet underwater. Hospitals were submerged and nobody had electricity. An aerial shot of a hillside revealed a mud slide caused by a flash flood. Over three hundred people were believed buried underneath.

The Minister of Transportation came on the air to report that the flood had submerged all roads in the two-hundred-mile isthmus connecting Thailand to Malaysia. A hundred miles of railway track had been destroyed, which he said would take six weeks to repair.

Oh no! My train to Penang! How would I get a new visa? I was already two days over. I was supposed to take that train tomorrow.

I hurried to call the airport, but as I feared, all flights to Malaysia and even Singapore were booked for the next two months. What to do?

Half an hour later, I met Jek on his corner. "You ready?" I asked.

"Yes. Where we go?"

"I made reservations at the Sheraton Royal Orchid."

"Oah!" he exclaimed. The Sheraton was one of the best hotels in Bangkok. I knew he'd be impressed.

We crossed Silom to take a *tuk-tuk* going in the right direction. Without meters, fares had to be bargained in advance. I didn't think it would have cost one *baht* more to hail the *tuk-tuk* from the original side, but I didn't say anything. I knew we'd never agree on the value of time and effort. In this, money made my situation different from that of *farang* men and Thai women. A Thai woman adjusted up to the *farang*'s level. A *farang* woman had to adjust down to the Thai's—unless she wanted to assume the entire financial burden. I wouldn't have minded doing that with a *farang*. I couldn't do that with a Thai, though, who invested social meaning in the man paying. If I paid for everything, it would change the relationship.

Jek looked uncomfortable as the Sheraton doorman let us in the spacious lobby.

"Everyone look at me," he declared.

"So what?"

He shook his head and glanced around like a thief in a jewelry store.

I'd made a reservation for the coffee shop's Thanksgiving dinner. At 350 *baht* a person, I knew the price would floor Jek. The price of a dinner in the hotel's fancier restaurant would have really shaken him.

The maitre d'hotel showed us to a table where starchy napkins rose from the plates. Jek sat before the tower with marvel in his eyes. He squirmed as he looked around at the diners.

"Have you been here before?" I asked.

"I bring girl to hotel room but never come in here."

Dinner was a buffet with a separate table holding the Thanksgiving fare.

"Take some cranberry sauce," I told him as we stood before the turkey.

"What this?" he asked, pointing to something the tuxedoed server had deposited on his plate.

"Stuffing. You'll probably hate it. It's made with bread."

The server added a slice of corn loaf. I giggled. "You'll hate that too."

When we returned to the table, I said, "Momsy gives me a chocolate turkey on Thanksgiving morning. Do you like chocolate?"

He grimaced. "I like but can't eat. My teeth hurt."

"You have cavities? You should see a dentist." Jek looked down. "Don't you go to the dentist?"

"Cost money."

"But you should go regularly to get your teeth cleaned."

At this he looked confused. He had probably never heard of a Cavitron machine. He said, "I must go soon get tooth taken out."

"Why?"

"Tooth bad."

"Can't they repair it?"

He shrugged. I thought of the years of orthodontics I had as a child. The cost of those braces could have supported a Thai's whole life.

"How's the turkey?" I asked.

"Alright."

"*Jut,* huh?" (Tasteless.) I laughed. "You can go back and take something spicy if you want."

"No, delicious," he said, but when he emptied his plate, he went back for Thai food.

Over pumpkin pie, I told him, "I'm stranded here. The flood wiped out the railroad to Malaysia."

"Good, you can't leave."

"Not good if they put me in jail." They did jail people who overstayed their visas and couldn't pay the fine. Kao San Road had notices requesting people to visit foreigners in jail and bring them books. Most had been arrested on drug charges, but visa detention was not unheard of.

"Flash flood very bad," Jek said.

"What?"

"Flash flood," he repeated with a smile, seeing my laughter. "I no say right?"

"You said frash frod. Very funny." In Thailand, *l* and *r* were interchangeable to all but the most educated. Before coming to Thailand, I couldn't understand how anyone could confuse the two sounds, but after doing it myself once, I no longer doubted it. When you knew *l* and *r* were interchangeable, you never knew which to use, even though the written language made a clear distinction. An *f* with an *l* was even more difficult because it wasn't a Thai formation.

"Fratch frod," he tried again.

"Not even close."

I thought his eyes would fall out when he saw the bill.

I paid it with my American Express card.

"Oah!" he said, seeing the card. "One time I have American Express too, but I lose when have debt."

I found this hard to believe. When I'd first arrived in Thailand, the bank rebuffed my request to open a checking account. Apparently, your average Thai couldn't have one, only big businesses could. Everyone else paid bills with cash. Remembering this, I was sure credit cards were even harder to get.

"One day we go to Malaysia together," Jek said. "I must pay debt first. Until I do, I can't get passport. I want to travel with you."

Walking back to Patpong, he appeared frisky and happy. He spoke about the American Express card he'd had and how he'd entertained his friends, running up a bill. That was why he had to work Patpong now, to get his credit back and to pay Mr. Tam. I didn't believe a word.

"I saw Dudley Dapolito today," I told him. "He's trying to make a meaningful relationship with a bar girl from Pattaya. I told you I met her, didn't I? And that she lied to Dudley about how many children she had?" I laughed.

"Sometime they lie to save their life," Jek said, seriously, staring into the distance.

I looked closer at him. He suddenly seemed miles away.

I'd mentioned Dudley's situation to make Jek an ally in my research. Instead, I felt like I'd created a Thai-*farang* barrier with Jek on the other side.

A block from Patpong, he let go of my hand. It felt deliberate, though he disguised it by turning to say something. Was he afraid of Doom catching us together? Was she here somewhere?

When I left him at his corner, I had mixed feelings. We'd had a wonderful dinner but walked two blocks through Patpong without holding hands. I felt rejected.

He came over that night, which, as usual, made me happy enough to forget my qualms.

"Why you have this?" he asked when he saw the bottle of ulcer medicine on the dresser.

"For you. So your pain goes away," I answered. I'd bought it because I hated to see him suffer, and he obviously wouldn't buy it for himself. He seemed touched by the gesture. He took a sip.

"Why you love me?" he asked next.

I wasn't ready to acknowledge that, but I answered, "I don't know."

"Then it's really love. If you don't know why, then it's love."

Did he not think he was loveable, or did he mean it was love when no ulterior motive was involved?

The next morning, I hurried to the newspapers to find out about the flood.

The rain in the South continued. The centerfold held more disaster photos: hungry homeless people clustering under loose palm branches, and monks lugging Buddha statues to higher ground. An aerial view portrayed curlicued Thai roofs protruding from flood water like glaciers. Another picture showed trucks submerged to their windshield wipers.

How could I leave for my visa? I wondered if Immigration would accept the flood as reason for overstaying. I doubted it. Those Immigration officials loved giving foreigners a hard time.

Alex called in anguish. "Hoi ran away from me," he wailed.

"Oh, no." I wondered guiltily if my canceling Loi Kratong had anything to do with it. "Did you go to your friend's party without her?"

"No. You're supposed to spend that day with your girlfriend. I couldn't go to the party alone."

"Then did you two have an argument?"

"No, nothing like that. She just said she was going to Pattaya for the day, but that was two days ago and I haven't heard from her."

"Oh, that's nothing. Don't worry. She'll be back. Remember how long she stayed in Ubon? It's called Thai time."

"I think she's gone for good."

Despite my reassurances, Alex sounded so distraught I invited him for lunch. He accepted thankfully, as if he were desperate for a *farang* to talk to.

He arrived looking pale. "I'm very depressed," he said. "I haven't been able to eat for a month. And now Hoi's left me!"

"Sounds familiar. I haven't been able to eat either. Here, have some Camembert."

For lunch, I'd bought French bread at the Dusit Thani pastry shop and imported cheese from Robinson's supermarket.

Alex's eyes shined as he looked at the spread. "I haven't had real food in a long time," he said.

"Where did Hoi say she was going?"

"She went to a friend's house in Pattaya. She told me there was no phone, but I heard her tell a neighbor there was one. Though I can't speak Thai, I've picked up some words, and I know when Hoi lies."

"Do you tell her?"

"No, I let the lies pass without comment."

"That's what happens with Jek. I KNOW he's lying, but I can't really catch him at it. Also, because I see how advantaged I am being a *farang*, I don't feel I have the right to challenge petty issues when all the cards are stacked in my favor. Other times I wonder if I'm being overly suspicious because his job involves tricking tourists. I worry that I mistrust him unfairly."

"I'm so sad Hoi left because it was my dream to get her out of this."

"Out of what?"

"Prostitution. Poverty."

"That poverty is a killer. They can't even go to the dentist."

"It's giving me a nerve crisis. It's not enough to help Hoi; there's Hoi's niece Ah and Hoi's father. I feel bad for them all."

"It's tough being privileged, isn't it? Did Hoi get a job?" I asked, remembering how negatively she viewed that idea.

"I found her a job as a waitress. She needed pink clothes to wear. I bought her pink clothes. But the day she was supposed to start, she refused to go."

"I guess waitressing can't compare with Patpong."

"I try so hard to give her a better future. Nothing works. I wanted to sign her up for typing lessons, but she wasn't interested. I bought her an atlas and books on Thai history. She no more than glanced at them. I tried to teach her the alphabet. She said I think too much."

I laughed. "People have said that to me too."

"She's rough. Once, she punched a policeman in the stomach. The policeman came to the door. I *wai*ed him politely and Hoi punched him. I don't think she did it deliberately. It just happened."

"You can't be too dainty growing up in Isan."

"When Hoi grabs me and kisses me, she's ungraceful. It's embarrassing when she does it in front of people. When she dances, she's clumsy. She loves to go Thai dancing. Have you been to those dance halls?"

I shook my head.

"Men buy flowers to give the women who work there as payment to dance with them. They dance Isan-style to Isan music, which Bangkok people consider base. I think Hoi likes it because she's higher-class than the other women. Hoi, herself, puts flowers on the girls and dances with them."

"That was mean of your friend to exclude her from his party."

"Everyone speaks badly of her and tells me to leave her. Thai men hate Patpong women—call them lazy and independent and complain they like money too much. My Thai students say dark skin is dirty. I could never let Hoi come to my job."

"I think she's great."

"You do?" Alex had gratitude in his eyes. He seemed to long to hear a nice word about the woman he had invested himself in.

"She has her own charm. She's beautiful and funny. I have a good time with her."

"Sometimes she's a lot of fun. But she's trouble too. I think she sells things from the apartment. My penknife is missing. The neighbor's Walkman disappeared. When we first met, we trekked in the North with a German man. One day, the German told me he was missing 500 *baht* and he thought Hoi had stolen it. I was indignant. I denied it and was convinced she didn't do it. Last month, she confessed!"

"Are you working full-time now?"

"I'm not making nearly enough money." He paused and glanced at me with a weird smile. "To get through the next month or so, I've been thinking of selling myself to rich older women."

"You want to sleep with them for money?"

"Many of my older students have shown an interest in me. Maybe I can find a Thai man to be my pimp. Or I could work for the Yakuza. You've heard of them?"

"Japanese organized crime. You do NOT want to get involved with them. Why don't you go to an escort agency and let them find you customers?"

"I'm not interested in homosexuals."

"They might couple men with women. But I thought you wanted to set a good example for Hoi."

"Maybe working as a prostitute will bring me closer to her."

"Well, forget the Yakuza." I looked through my collection of escort-agency advertisements and found one for Playboy Entertainment. "Here, listen to this." I read: "For travellers and businessmen, we have beautiful, charming, and friendly guides. Ladies of all ages for any occasion. Escorts from Europe, America, Spain, and Philippines. Male escorts for both men and women. Special! Thai models, film stars. Sightseeing and shopping. Car rent service." I showed him the page. "See, male escorts for women."

Alex copied their phone number.

Very interesting, I thought after he left. Who was changing whom?

208

21.

That evening, as I prepared myself for Patpong, I worried about my visa. The tax certificate was valid for only two weeks, and if I didn't leave Thailand by then, I'd have to return to the tax office. I didn't know how they'd treat, me seeing that I'd overstayed. I didn't have enough money to fly farther than Malaysia or Singapore. Cambodia, Laos, and Burma adjoined Thailand but wouldn't admit tourists. Hong Kong was the next-closest noncommunist country, but it was beyond my budget. Fall's student loan check hadn't arrived yet, and I didn't want to charge more to American Express than I could pay.

I waited for TV news. The rain had finally stopped, it reported, and relief efforts were underway. I saw the prime minister climb out of a helicopter to inspect the damage, which turned out to be greater than thought. Whole villages had been swept away. Crops, livestock, shrimp farms—gone. Military personnel unloaded rice sacks for tens of thousands of people who'd lost everything. The newscaster beseeched viewers to take donations to their local schools. Blankets, clothes, utensils—everything was urgently needed. The entire country was called upon to help their compatriots in the South. A reporter noted that one highway, detouring through back streets, was open to Malaysia.

I could leave! Now I had to find something to take me down that highway. A public bus? For sure they'd have no seats left. Kao San Road! It had dozens of low-budget travel agencies that organized buses. That's where I had to look.

I hurried out of the house.

At 8 p.m., Kao San Road bustled as always with young travellers—guys with long hair, blue-jeaned women with rucksacks, and guitars aplenty. The sounds of a video in an open-air restaurant competed with another video across the street. Souvenir stores of hilltribe crafts did business till midnight. All travel agents were open.

"Do you have a bus to Penang?" I asked in one.

"Sure do."

"Tomorrow? My visa's over."

"You're not the only one. How's tomorrow morning?"

"Oh, thank you, thank you."

As he wrote a receipt, I wondered about taking a bus full of Kao San Road people with overstayed visas. Thailand was fussy over what it considered hippy types and even hung notices at the border declaring that hippies weren't welcome. They described what hippies looked liked: long dirty hair, bare feet, ragged clothes. Many Kao San Road patrons fit that description.

Map of Thailand with Isan Highlighted

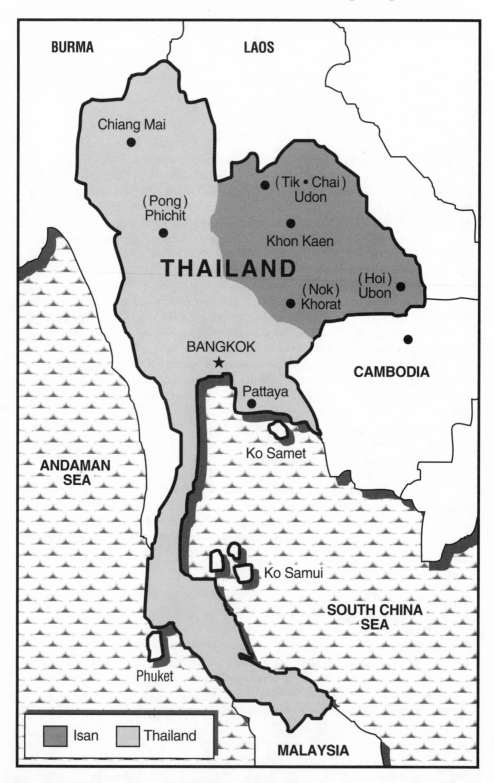

BURMA

LAOS

Chiang Mai

(Tik • Chai)
Udon

(Pong)
Phichit

Khon Kaen

THAILAND

(Hoi)
Ubon

(Nok)
Khorat

BANGKOK

CAMBODIA

Pattaya

ANDAMAN
SEA

Ko Samet

Ko Samui

SOUTH CHINA
SEA

Phuket

Isan   Thailand

MALAYSIA

I hoped none of my fellow travellers would be carrying drugs. Malaysia had the death penalty for small quantities. Maybe this wasn't such a good idea after all. But I had no choice.

I didn't go to Patpong that night and Jek didn't come by. I awoke to sunlight instead of Jek ringing the doorbell. The bed felt empty.

Just as well, I thought next. What would I have done with Jek asleep and me ready to leave Thailand? I certainly didn't trust him in the apartment for three or four days. I wanted to leave a combination lock on the door during my time away. How could I have done that without insulting Jek? What if he asked to use the apartment while I was gone?

That morning, Trink's column announced that a Patpong bar was having a flood concert. Proceeds would be given to the South. Other bars were acting as collection stations for donated goods. The rest of the newspaper carried pictures of the catastrophe.

A half hour before I had to leave, Jek called.

"I'm leaving for Malaysia," I told him.

"I can bring over lunch before you go," he said. "I want to say goodbye."

"No time."

"I will miss you. You don't see other man in Malaysia, okay?"

"No! I only want to be with you. And you won't go with other women, right?"

"Yes. For sure."

His voice sounded definite. I was very happy. "Not Doom either," I said, jokingly.

"Yes. I wait for you come home. Don't forget me. I love you."

I rushed to catch my bus on Kao San Road. Its seats were filled with scraggly types, low-budget travellers, and army-completion Israelis. Oh no, I thought, as I saw two long-haired guys with patches and musical instruments climb onboard. Here come the people who'll get us all into a Malaysian prison. I felt relieved hearing them speak Swedish as they came down the aisle. Swedes liked to drink. Maybe they weren't carrying a pound of heroin each.

As we pulled out of Bangkok, the driver's assistant distributed box lunches, and I met the person sitting next to me, a late-twenties American male. With a degree in sociology, he worked as guidance counselor in a Chicago public school.

"How long have you been in Thailand?" I asked him.

"Ten days."

"Did you go to Patpong?"

"I don't think so. Is that a Thai city?"

I loved Kao San Road people; many of them had never heard of Patpong. How refreshing to meet people who didn't buy women. I told him about my research.

Our cardboard boxes contained pieces of chicken and Chinese pastry.

"I'm starving," I said, munching the dessert, which was indented with

Chinese characters. "I haven't been able to eat lately. This research has taken me too close to destitution and deprivation. Especially with my Thai boyfriend. I'm living his poverty and his cultural dilemmas. My stomach's always in a knot."

"Do you meet with other graduate students?"

"No. Wish I did. I'd love to be able to discuss ideas and feelings with someone."

"How about close friends?"

"Only *farang* men who tell me their problems with bar girls."

"You need peers to relate to. You're too involved with your subject. You'll lose your perspective if you don't take a break now and then."

"I lost my perspective long ago. I'm living their perspective. Sometimes I forget I'm not poor and hopeless, that I'm not the one who's going to lose teeth because I can't afford the dentist."

The bus hours dragged by, cramped and uncomfortable. I wished for my sleeper bed on the train. Called the Visa Express by resident *farangs*, the train brought the same people together every three months for trips to Malaysia. I knew the waiters, the conductors, and the kitchen director.

As we entered Southern Thailand, everyone leaned to look at the flood. Despite being built on stilts, houses were submerged past their windows. Of the outhouses, only roofs could be seen, and I wondered about the stuff that had to be floating out of toilet holes.

People occupied the houses where the water had receded below porch level. Muddy mattresses and clothing hung from tree branches. The inhabitants looked defeated.

It turned out our bus was going to Hat Yai, where we would divide into separate vans to Penang, Kuala Lumpur, and Singapore. The flood had drained from the town, but a black water line could be seen on buildings as we drove through. The streets were piled with ruined possessions—books, clothes, bedding, pictures.

I was glad to see the Swedes weren't on my van, but we had three long-haired guys; and the one other person with an overstayed visa, an Englishman, looked shabby. I hoped the border guards wouldn't think he and I were together.

"They won't make us pay," he said, naively. "I was supposed to leave five days ago but couldn't because of the flood. I don't have money for a fine, so they can't charge me."

The stop at the border wasn't too bad. I made sure my shabby van-mate and I went to separate windows, and the whole process took under an hour. The government officials did get a good laugh, though, when I tried to use the flood as an excuse not to pay the fine.

"One hundred *baht* a day for every day over visa," they told me. "You owe 500 *baht*. You no pay, you no leave."

I paid. Back in the van, I learned that the shabby guy had paid too. "Bloody unfair, it is," he said. "Now I don't have enough for the freighter to Sumatra."

Ten minutes into Malaysia, we were pulled over by a police car. Actually it looked more military than police. Nearby was something like a tank. Heavily armored but with wheels, it had gun turrets protruding from the roof. Its uniformed men looked merciless. Alongside was a barred bus for transporting prisoners.

They ordered us out and demanded our passports and luggage. Here comes the drug bust, I thought. The paddy wagon was a discouraging sight. If they found drugs, would they take us all?

A half hour later, they let us go. Apparently they found nothing. Kao San Road must have primed its people well.

In Penang, I checked into my usual hotel and told the desk clerk to call Mr. Moto. Penang dealt expertly with Thailand's immigration policy. Since each day deluged the town with Bangkok residents, systems had developed for processing them quickly. Mr. Moto was the one I used. Hotels notified him, and he made room calls to collect passports and photos and to help fill out applications. The next day, he took armloads of passports to the Thai embassy and returned that night with everyone's new visa. I thought the fee he charged well worth it.

Penang was a charming, formerly British colonial island. Tourists were pedaled leisurely through town on seats built in front of bicycles. As I rode to a restaurant, I wished Jek was with me. I would have loved to show him Penang.

Though adjoining Thailand, Malaysia was completely different. One sensed this immediately crossing the border. For one thing, it seemed more affluent. The highway on the Malaysian side was twice as wide, with neater signs and more traffic signals. The houses were bigger; contained glass windows, which most Thai houses lacked; and had more TV antennas. The Malaysian people were darker-skinned than Thais, and being Muslim, many women had their heads covered. Penang had quaint cobblestone streets and pastel colonial mansions.

Passing souvenir stalls, I had an urge to buy Jek something. I pictured him in a "Welcome to Penang" T-shirt but stopped myself from opening my wallet. Money was a troublesome ingredient in our relationship. I couldn't encourage him to view me as a financial boon.

I bought him a pack of cheap Malaysian cigarettes instead, just to prove I'd been thinking of him. Then I bought myself a camera. Malaysia's tax-free policy made them less expensive than in Thailand.

The return trip to Bangkok gave me another problem. Finding a van to Hat Yai was easy enough, but from there I couldn't get a decent bus. After waiting in line at the public bus station for over two hours, I was appalled at the bus I finally boarded. It seated *seven* across, and the aisle was packed with standing people.

"There's no room," I said to the only other *farang*, a nondescript bearded man with a backpack. We'd met on the ticket line. "How do they expect to fit four people on that bench? This is for animals, not people. I can't survive nineteen hours in a seat with no headrest or reclining back!"

I stormed off the bus, and the *farang* followed. We hunted down a private company, and though their seats were more civilized, the only two vacant seats together (they thought the *farang* and I were a couple) were squeezed in the back row. I didn't feel like spending the night riding like that either. As we got off that bus too, the line manager decided he wanted to keep our fares, so he reshuffled the other passengers. Only we two *farangs* and a Chinese man had the whole back seat to ourselves. The displaced Thais gave me a dour but wistful look as I sprawled out to sleep my way home.

Smiling to myself in a comfortable position, I concluded that the sojourn in Penang had restored my *farang* senses. Had I been with Jek, I wouldn't have thought twice about suffering for nearly a day on the public bus.

22.

In many cultures, prostitution is the only way women feel power over men. Nestle (1987: 144) points out: "The earliest Biblical descriptions of the prostitute say that she is brazen, full of arrogance and rebellion."

In Sex Work *(1987), Delacoste and Alexander present writings by women in the sex industry. The women divulge their feelings concerning the unequal relationship between males and females in today's Western society and make comparisons between their lives as prostitutes and their lives as nonprostitutes. "Many women told me that the first time they felt powerful was the first time they turned a trick" (Ibid.: 15). Rewards came in positive and recognizable changes within oneself. Leigh declares that "prostitution is a crash course in assertiveness training" (Ibid.: 33).*

"When you're making money yourself," said one prostitute, "there's an immediate value on you, you're selling yourself, your person, your charms, your appearance, your ability to persuade, your ability to sell. It takes skill, definite skill, and a lot of strength. I've come to appreciate those qualities in myself" (Alexander, 1987: 54).

I arrived in Bangkok in time to meet Nok and Moon for dinner before they began work. We'd made this date to celebrate Moon's birthday, but I doubted it was really his birthday. By now, I could tell when Nok had invented something to suit her purpose. I remembered her dead-mother story with Yamaguchi. The last time I'd seen her, she seemed so enthralled with Moon that she needed to impress him with her roguish prowess. By inventing a birthday for him, she'd be tricking me into giving him a present. To shower favors on the one they loved, Patpong women used their wiles with others.

Though annoyed at being considered a mark, I wanted to watch the development of their romance. I wrapped a wooden elephant for Moon and instructed myself not to look sarcastic when I wished him "Happy Birthday."

The three of us went to Robinson's department store again. When I gave Moon the present, Nok seemed disappointed it wasn't a stereo or a gold chain but nonetheless shot Moon a prideful glance, as if acknowledging her ruse had worked.

"How was your trip to the island?" I asked her, remembering a customer had planned to take her. "Did you have fun?"

She hesitated, made a face, then reluctantly agreed to a little. I guessed it had been a chore.

When we met Jek on the way back, I let Nok and Moon go off while I stayed.

"I brought you a souvenir from Malaysia," I said, giving him the pack of cigarettes. Noticing a scab on his forearm, I asked, "What happened?"

"Last night I bring guest to bar but bar no have show. I don't want to return man's money, so I run away. I cut myself on electric wire."

I felt sorrier for Jek in his perilous profession than for the customer without a refund. I wondered how often Jek had frightening encounters. I knew he didn't enjoy ripping people off and would have preferred an honest and "respectable" job.

"I'm going home early tonight," I told him. "I'm exhausted from the trip."

"I come later."

"Great."

Before going up, I stopped to read the paper. The front page of the *Bangkok Post* showed a photo of women in strapless gowns with the caption: Masseuses Raise Cash for South. The article said:

> Women from five New Petchaburi Road massage parlors have raised over 200,000 *baht* to help southern flood victims.
>
> Under the half-month programme, more than four-hundred service girls will donate ten *baht* from each of their ninety-minute "precious" sessions to the victims of the flood.
>
> "We decided to donate our earnings to help them, even though most of us are from poor families and have hungry parents and children to care for."
>
> The masseuse said she knew what it felt like to be hungry because she had been through that experience herself.

Everyone in Thailand understood *masseuses* to mean prostitutes and had no doubt what "precious sessions" were. I felt anger that, on one hand, Thailand praised prostitutes for compassion and, on the other, condemned them (but not their clients) as dregs of society.

Jek's ringing woke me at 3 a.m. "I smoke your cigarette," he said. "Taste like Marlboro."

I doubted the cheap Malaysian brand tasted like Marlboro. Marlboro—banned in Thailand but available bootlegged on the street—was expensive and a status symbol; it was the brand Jek finagled customers to buy him. A foreign brand transported by one's *farang* girlfriend probably had the same flavor of prestige. I was pleased that he appreciated the gift.

I told him, "I read in the paper that masseuses are donating money to help victims of the 'fratch frod'."

"I can say now. I practice. Frash fraud. Is good?"

I laughed. "Nope. Have you been practicing that with your customers?"

"Yes, but they don't understand me."

"FLASH FLOOD."

"Frash fraud."

"Gobble-gobble."

"OOT-OOT."

"That's an owl!"

"No. Pig!"

We made love and taught each other words and had a wonderful time, but I wanted to sleep before the sun came up.

"I have to do things in the morning," I said. "Let's go to sleep."

"We stay up a little longer," he said, maneuvering the clock so it faced us. "I have to leave at 6 to wake Mr. Tam."

"You're leaving?"

"Not yet. At 6 o'clock."

We lay together hugging, but I soon grew disturbed as I realized, yet again, something didn't make sense.

"Why do you have to wake Mr. Tam?"

"If I no go, he no wake up."

"Why doesn't he use an alarm clock?"

"No have."

I felt he was lying. "I don't believe you. What's going on?"

He looked trapped.

"Tell me why you want to leave. If it's just to wake Mr. Tam, you can go and come back. You can even take my alarm clock."

He moved around the room and combed his hair and looked like he wanted to concoct something brilliant.

"You have to explain this to me. I have to know," I persisted. My doubts about everything rose to the surface. This was the one-too-many I couldn't let pass. "You can't tell me any old lie and expect me to believe it."

Finally he said, "Okay, I tell you truth." He made a few starts but retracted each time and changed the subject.

"I don't want to hear about Mr. Tam's business! Tell me why you have to leave at 6 a.m."

"I want to tell you," he said convincingly, but as he started to speak, he looked worried and skipped again into describing his life.

"ANSWER THE QUESTION!"

"Okay." He sat beside me with his hand on my leg. "Sometime Toom come see me. I have to be there."

Doom! He was meeting his wife! I felt mistreated and jealous and furious. I crossed my arms and sat against the wall, away from him. "Go then. Go. You have a wife. Stay with your wife. Don't come back."

He looked stricken. "I don't have a wife."

"Yes, you do. Go meet her. Go. Go."

217

He didn't move. He looked sad.

"Go already. I can't live with this Doom business. I won't be with someone who's married. In America, you can't have many wives. Women won't allow it. Get out of here. Go to Doom."

"She mean nothing to me. I want her to find someone else."

"She won't; she has a husband."

"I'm not together with her."

"Yes, you are."

"She will find another man."

"No, she won't. Why should she? She has you."

"No, she don't have me. I tell her to go away and she goes."

Was this supposed to make me feel better? That he could order around his wife?

He repeated that everything would be solved in six months. He doodled more boxes and wrote '6 month'. "I need time to fix my life," he said.

"Fine. Go fix it. Just don't come back here."

He wouldn't leave as long as I was angry.

"Who has your son Bank?"

Jek's eyes shifted as if I'd trapped him again. Then he faced me and said, "Toom has him."

Did this mean he was finally telling me the truth? Was I supposed to take his side now that he was opening up to me? He was sitting on one end of the bed and I on the other. We looked at each other mournfully.

"It's after 6. Why aren't you leaving? You'll be late for Doom."

"I can't go when you like this."

I took a deep breath. What should I do? He did tell me before that the time for us was a few months away. That was not new. Was I supposed to be understanding during this tough period of his life? Was I acting like a spoiled brat, demanding he relinquish his family life when I had no intention of considering marriage? Did I have a right to be angry with him for lying when I'd been lying too?

What if he did give up everything to be with me? I didn't want that either.

I didn't know what I wanted except to hold him and wipe the miserable expression off his face. I crawled over and put my arms around his neck.

We hugged for a time without speaking. Then he left.

As he went out the door, I was filled again with doubt and foreboding and confusion. I didn't like feeling part of a harem. Was this how Thai women felt? Was this how Doom felt?

I had to absorb myself in my project. What should I do? Go to Chula University? The *Bangkok Post* library? I had to do something dazzling with my work so I could feel in control of that at least. I needed success to balance my failings with Jek.

Maybe I could interview someone at the *Post*. How about Trink? Maybe it's time to meet Trink. If I could develop a rapport with a *farang*, perhaps my insecurities with Jek wouldn't be so devastating.

This time, when I approached the sign-in desk at the *Post*, I asked for Bernard Trink. They phoned and found him in. Instead of heading left for the library, I went right, into a partitioned area with many desks. Trink's was in the far right corner.

A balding man in his fifties, he had a pipe dangling from his mouth and seemed willing to talk to me. Apparently everybody wanting information on Patpong or prostitution looked him up.

"I'm from New York too," he said after I told him about myself. "I first came to Thailand in 1962, settled in Bangkok in 1965."

"You married a Thai?" I already knew this from his column, where the only reference to his wife concerned her cooking.

"Yes. We have three children."

"Do you speak Thai?"

"No."

"How do you interview bar girls?"

"I have someone translate."

"Could I see your files on Patpong bars and Patpong women?"

"I don't keep files. I just write the column and that's it."

Though our conversation began pleasantly, it degenerated when I thought I could engage him in an exchange of ideas. I forgot that, as a man living a long time in Thailand, he probably didn't view women as people to have discussions with; that, being far from the West, he would have no concept of feminist theory; and that, as a male living with a Thai, he had to protect his own concept of man's place and woman's place.

He didn't like it when I suggested that "Patpong offers an arena for spunky women who have no chance to achieve anything otherwise. If the women stay within the format of Thai society, they have no opportunity for effectiveness or power."

"Power! Thai women are very powerful," he argued. "Men hand over their money to their wives and then live on an allowance. The wives control the money."

"But the wives can't do anything with it except buy rice and pay the butcher," I argued back. "Men use their 'allowance,' as you call it, to go out, meet the guys, have affairs, do things. Who cares if women hold the money if all they do with it is stock the house with detergent and chili!"

"Prostitution only makes it worse for them."

"Worse? With no education, no financial cushion, no emotional support to take initiatives males take—what else exists for strong women who don't want to be one wife out of many?"

"No," he said. "There's nothing for them on Patpong. The women are ruined there. They throw their lives away. They're ruined as women. They're ruined as human beings. They get greedy."

"You mean they're ruined as virgins and ruined as pliable little women who'll make docile wives."

"You don't know what you're talking about."

By now, I knew *farang* men cherished the image of helpless females tossed by fate into a despicable job. They felt superior as they decried the women's deceitful ways and felt like princes when they handed them a *baht* or two. I knew the attitude I should adopt with Trink, but in the tumult over Jek, I didn't apply it. What an idiot I was.

"The notion that nonvirgins are ruined is sexist," I went on like captain of a freshman debating team. "Your column is also elitist and even racist, whereby you judge destitute Thais by values appropriate for privileged middle-class *farangs*. Sometimes, honesty and fairness in business are luxuries, impossible for those on subsistence levels."

How could I let that escape my mouth? Jek truly had me nuts. "And you're too hard on the Patpong men," I went on regardless.

"What Patpong men? You don't mean the *chicos,* do you? They're despicable. They flim flam everyone in sight."

"They're doing the same as the women. Why do you pity the women but scorn the men?"

"Nobody has a good word to say about those repulsive *chicos*. Except you. The Patpong girls won't have anything to do with them. Every one I've spoken to says she hates Patpong men."

"They tell me that too, but I don't think that's how it really is. I know they resent certain attitudes the men have, but in the end the men and women of Patpong have a lot in common. It's them against *farangs* and *farang* culture."

"Listen, there's nothing more I can tell you," he said. "You'll never see it my way and I'll never see it your way. You don't have a clue to what's going on in this country. I'm considered an expert here, even by Thais. I think you'd better leave."

There was nothing more I could say to Trink. I'd blown that one.

At least I scored points for consistency, I thought, as I walked back to the apartment. I knew, though, that the failure with Trink could have been avoided. If I'd kept my mouth shut, I could have collected his opinions. They reflected the *farang* residents' view, whether or not I agreed. Jek had muddled my capacity to plan. My immersion in Patpong had created a need for intellectual communication, but I should have known I couldn't find that with a male resident *farang* any more than with a young Thai lover.

Jek called at around 2. Early for him, I thought. He wanted to come over for lunch.

He brought noodles in a plastic bag.

"Why you don't eat? You don't like?" he asked.

My stomach had been telling me not to send it the stuff on my fork. "I'm not hungry. I can't eat because I'm upset. Because of you. I can't sleep either. I'm a wreck. Why are you up at this hour?"

220

"Me too. I'm not *sabai jai* (at ease)." "I can't sleep. I must come be with you."

I told him about the disaster with Trink. "I should have planned in advance what I was going to say to Trink instead of thinking about you."

He acknowledged that he was the reason I wasn't working well.

"Did Doom come see you this morning?"

"No, she didn't come." Then he said, "This problem with Toom is my problem. I don't want you get upset. You must not think about her anymore. I want to be with you. We will travel. We go Penang. To Phuket."

I loved hearing we would travel together, though I didn't know how I'd prevent him seeing the birth date on my passport. Since he didn't even have a passport yet, I didn't have to worry about that right away.

"You agree?" he asked. "You won't think about her anymore?" He offered his hand so we could shake on it.

He seemed as distraught as I was about our situation and, truthfully, I was crazy about him, so I said, "Okay."

He let out a big "Okaaaay" himself and looked relieved.

We had a nice afternoon, but then he fell asleep watching TV. Why was he always the one lying down with his head in my lap, so that I had to sit? He woke up for the news, then left for work.

As soon as he was out of sight, my head filled with conflicting statements again. How could he ask me not to think about his wife? Was that some kind of manipulation? Now that I'd shaken hands on it, I wouldn't be able to mention the subject. I resented being cornered like that.

I decided to get rid of the McDonald's french fry keyring. Heavy ugly thing! I was exaggerating the importance of Jek's giving it to me. He'd given one to Mr. Tam too. If it didn't mean anything to Jek, I wouldn't let it mean anything to me. How dare he leave me to meet Doom! I threw the keyring under the sink. Good riddance.

The next morning, I called Alex to see if Hoi had returned. Hoi answered the phone. "Hello, O."

"You're back!" I exclaimed. "Alex thought you'd left him. He was very depressed."

She giggled as if expecting *farang* men to be depressed over her. "Sister Na here too," she said. "You want speak to her?"

"No, no. I'll speak to Alex."

When Alex came on, I said, "See. I told you she'd be back."

He sighed. "Yes, but Na and her daughter Ah are here too," he said, sounding as down as he'd been the week before. "Na is rude to me. She demands I give her money and won't apologize for the things she took last time she was here."

"How's Ah?"

He moaned. "I try to get her to study, but it's impossible. She follows Hoi's example. She's become lazy and only cares about eating. Now I have two lazy girls with their legs in the air, reading cartoons and eating."

"What happened with the escort agency? Did you call them?"

"Nobody answered. They must have moved. I've given up that idea. I joined a model agency, but I don't think I'll get work. I'm not good-looking."

The conviction in Alex's tone surprised me. Alex was very good looking. I wondered if his low opinion of himself had anything to do with his involvement with Hoi.

That night, I didn't go to Patpong. Jek called at 3 a.m. As usual, I was so glad to hear his voice, I put aside bad feelings.

"Where are you?" I asked.

"At Mr. Tam's. I come see you now. In forty minutes I be there, because traffic."

I was elated. Then I thought, forty minutes? It didn't take forty minutes from Patpong. And since he walked, traffic had nothing to do with it. Where was he? At Doom's? Since I'd promised not to think about her, I couldn't ask. I burned with anger that he made me agree to that.

When he came, though, I was so happy to see him I kept suspicions to myself. He corrected my Thai homework and tried out, "Frash fraud."

"FLASH FLOOD!"

We laughed. "When you take Thai language exam?" he asked.

"In May. It's given only twice a year. If I don't pass it, I'll have to pay for another eight months of lessons."

The Thai government gave a *bau hok* (sixth-grade) equivalency test for foreigners. It consisted of four parts: a dictation, a letter written in formal Thai style, a thirty-line composition on a given topic, and a one-on-one reading and speaking session with a Thai official. I wanted the *bau hok* certificate to prove to my professors that I'd learned the language. A.U.A. had been preparing me for the exam with Thai grade-school books where Pitee, Manee, and a monkey named Jao Jaw were the counterparts of Dick, Jane, and Spot.

"Your school books are terrible, you know," I told Jek. "The boy Pitee is daring and creative and logical, while Manee the girl is afraid of bugs and caves and doesn't want to climb things and is stupid. Those books teach Thai women to be wimpy and retarded."

Jek looked confused, the same as the Thai teacher when I'd mentioned it to her.

"In the book," I continued, "Pitee's class had an assignment to plant something. The boys planted vegetables and bamboo and discussed the utility of their project. The girls planted flowers. That's teaching boys to think and plan and girls to be frivolous and useless."

"Man must be smarter than woman," Jek said. "Otherwise no good."

Right, I thought; if women were too smart, they would know when men lied to them. I wondered if Jek considered that the problem with me.

We played tic-tac-toe, and I won every time. Then we played a game where we wrote down numbers and had to figure out each other's number. I won that too. Then we played Thai Monopoly, and he raked in the money and property.

"Business," he explained. "This game is my profession."

He also cheated heavily, I noted. He was lively, and the time went on and on. It was getting near sunrise and the birds were chirping. I wanted to sleep but couldn't interrupt the game now that he was winning.

"Hey, you gave yourself too much money! Put that back. No fair!"

"Sorry," he said. "I make mistake."

Finally I lost. Hallelujah. I thought I finally could sleep, but no. He found a puzzle game and arranged the clock so we could race to see who did the puzzle faster.

"I'm tired. I want to sleep."

He seemed intent on the game, so I got in bed and let him play on his own. Soon he lay beside me and said he had to leave early to go to the dentist.

"I get tooth pulled today. One day I have no tooth left."

This broke my heart. I remembered what he'd said about disliking women with bad teeth. The thought of his having no front teeth and ruining his beautiful face hurt me like a physical pain.

He said he'd feel terrible after the dentist and would come back to my place to sleep. Since I planned to go out and he didn't know how long he'd have to wait, I offered him my extra key. I couldn't believe what I was doing as I saw the key dangling at the end of my extended arm. This was one thing I'd sworn never to do. I still wasn't sure he wouldn't rob me one day.

He hesitated, then said, "Not yet. I can't accept key until I fix my life."

I'd meant to give it to him only for the afternoon, not forever. I felt immense relief that he didn't take it. Then I felt rejected.

As soon as he left for the dentist, I felt suspicious about his leaving in the morning. Was I being conned again? Was he really leaving to meet Doom?

He phoned in the afternoon to make sure I was home and said he'd bring lunch.

"Lunch" turned out to be three tiny pastries like I'd had on Loi Kratong, barely a snack.

I felt something had changed from the time he called to when he arrived with the measly fare. Had he met Doom, given her his money, and so had none left for lunch?

He did have a bloody hole in his mouth, though, and his cheek was swollen. He swal-

Jek Sleeping

lowed a painkiller and a sip of ulcer medicine and fell asleep. Why did I spend most of this relationship watching him sleep?

When he woke up, he held his mouth. We watched TV, again him lying and me sitting. I wouldn't put up with this one-sidedness forever, I told myself, but

223

couldn't complain while he lay there in pain.

He didn't go to work until 11 p.m. He dragged himself to the door, pointed to his mouth, then to his stomach and shook his head. "Everything no good."

23.

While money may be the primary reason for engaging in prostitution, money is not the only gain. Also important is what money represents and buys—adventure, independence, security, opportunity, power, respect from their families, and glamor. In a weeklong newspaper exposé on hilltribe prostitutes, Boonsong mentions the problem of "rescued" girls who are sent home to their tribe but many of whom return to Bangkok. "Some find the city life much more colourful and prefer to remain here instead of going back to their villages" (Jan. 23, 1985: 5). In one case, 15 girls were rescued from a Bangkok brothel and sent home. "But a few months later, they slipped back into Bangkok and Yala where they again engaged in prostitution. 'They told us that they couldn't stand the harsh village life'" (Ibid.).

J ek didn't return that night. The next night, I didn't see him on Patpong. I visited a new bar on Patpong 2, called Sexy Stars, which had just opened. Twelve bikini-clad women danced on stage in the crowded club. Bar openings attracted *farang* regulars who liked to keep updated on Patpong happenings.

Suddenly, someone rushed over and threw her arms around me. It was Pong. With her hair coiffed differently, I almost didn't recognize her. Originally kinky, it had been cut and straightened. She looked good. This brand-new, downstairs, bikini-dancing bar was a step up from a ripoff bar like Pussys Collection. She radiated contentment.

"What happened with Ong?" I asked. "He said you'd left Bangkok forever. That you were working in a rice field."

She laughed. "Rice boring. I see family and come again Bangkok."

"You prefer working with *farangs* to working the land?" I prompted.

"Make love take three minute. Make rice take eleven hour in sun. Skin turn black; body have pain." She turned her lip down as if imagining something awful.

"Are you back with Ong? He was lonely for you."

She nodded and seemed glad to hear this.

When the manager of Sexy Stars stopped by to introduce himself, Pong left to sit with two *farangs*, one of whom she engaged in a French kiss. Pong had a habit of depositing me with the manager. When we'd first met, she'd done that with the soon-to-be-murdered one. I felt like a coat left in coat-check as the manager sat down beside me.

Jek didn't come by that night either. I awoke to sunlight and indignation. Where had he been? With Doom?

I was angry and unhappy. This relationship was not good for me. All I did was watch him sleep and suspect I was lied to and that he left me to be with his wife.

He called late afternoon.

"I can't take this anymore," I told him. "I want to end this. You have a wife. I don't want to deal with your marital situation. Don't come over."

"What happen to you?" he asked.

"You happened! You're making me miserable. I don't trust you. I can't believe anything you say."

"I come to you now."

"No. I have nothing else to say to you."

"I'm coming," he said and hung up.

He arrived shortly. I crossed my arms angrily and sat on the couch. Jek wore a baby-blue-and-white striped knit top with shoulder pads. He looked adorable. I'd never seen that top before and wondered if some woman had lent it to him.

"You breathe hard," he said.

I noticed I was breathing with difficulty. "I'm upset. You didn't come yesterday."

"Yesterday I sick. I go hospital." He showed me a needle hole in his inner arm where they'd taken blood. "I afraid have malaria or AIDS."

I flushed with panic. "AIDS? Did they test you for AIDS?"

"I don't have AIDS."

The wave of relief tempered when I remembered what I'd heard about testing in Bangkok. "Did they test you?" I asked. "It takes days to get the result back."

He hesitated as if I'd caught him in a lie. "They don't know what I have."

I was sure he hadn't been tested for AIDS. Could he have it? It sounded like he mentioned it and malaria just to convince me how sick he'd been. He didn't believe he might have it. He hardly knew what AIDS was. I didn't think he had it either. Bangkok hosted lots of strange fevers.

Maybe the government's suppression of AIDS as a topic had done its job, convincing both of us that the disease wasn't a problem in Thailand.

"You're sick because you lie," I said. "Dishonesty hurts your mental health."

He looked confused again, and I remembered he'd never had a psychology class.

I did feel sorry, though. I'd been angry and anxious that he was neglecting me, and, in truth, he'd been in the emergency room. I melted.

"Why didn't you call and tell me you were in the hospital?"

"I can't do that," he answered with tragic eyes. "I have no money and don't want you to pay."

I looked at him deeply. "I never know when to believe you. I hate this. I hate always distrusting you. You tell me something different every day. You tell me it's forty minutes through traffic from Patpong. We were supposed to visit your mother and never did. I can't trust you. I can't live like this."

"You want meet my mother? Okay, tomorrow we go."

"Really?" I wanted so much to believe him and be with him. "I'm supposed to see Chai tomorrow night. I already paid the bar."

"Ten o'clock. Is good for you?"

"Isn't that late for your mother?"

"Any time is alright."

I remembered that visiting in Thailand was never an imposition. You dropped in on people unannounced any hour of the day or night.

Early the next night, I met Chai at the Apollo Inn. We went to another gay go-go bar, a block past Patpong 1. Since it was early, we were the only customers. Again I told Chai to order drinks for anyone he wished.

A TV in the corner showed gay porno films. The sex acts onscreen allowed me to ask questions that would otherwise be awkward. Do you like to do that? Have you ever tried that position? Doesn't that hurt? Only one Patpong heterosexual bar had porn movies, and I'd found them useful with the women too. Answers normally difficult could be communicated with yes, no, must pay extra, or disgusted grunts.

"Do you know anyone that works here?" I asked Chai.

"Yes, but no see him. I don't know his number."

Unlike at the Apollo Inn, the go-go boys weren't sitting in the room. Instead, the bar had albums with nude photos of their employees. Customers were to browse them and order by number.

Chai and I looked through the pictures, and Chai pointed out friends.

"This one," he said. "He win Most Handsome Go-Go contest at the Sheraton."

"Yeah? Should we call for him?"

"Up to you."

I motioned for the waiter and asked for #57, who showed up dressed in shorts and a T-shirt. He seemed pleased to see Chai, and the two of them discussed old friends and the advantages of their respective bars.

Meanwhile, I couldn't wait to meet Jek. Counting the seconds until 9:30, I finally left Chai in the company of 57 and gave him money for the bill.

When Jek arrived at my door, he looked as excited about our plans as I was.

"This afternoon I work for Plaza massage parlor," he said. "Make extra money to take to my mother."

Plaza was on Patpong 2. "You worked on the street?" I asked.

"Yes. I find man to bring into parlor."

"I went to Patpong early today, to Foodland; I didn't see you."

"Before I become guide, I work there. Now, if I need extra money, I go to Plaza massage in the day."

That didn't explain why I hadn't seen him. Was he trying to change the subject? Or didn't my statement about not seeing him call for explanation? Every time he lassoed a customer, he'd have to escort the man inside. I could have missed him. Why would he lie about it? Was I becoming neurotic? I had to stop doubting every word he said.

We *tuk-tuk*ed to a slum in a distant part of town. Down an alley, we approached a shrine of Buddha figures. Jek stopped and *wai*ed. We continued along dark, winding paths.

"This is not good place," he said. "Are you afraid?"

"Not at all. I'm with you, I'm happy."

After several turns we came to his parents' house, an unhealthy-looking thing made of wooden planks and corrugated tin. An outhouse sat in front of it, three feet from the open front door. The door led to his parents' room, hardly bigger than the double mattress that occupied the floor space. Jek *wai*ed his mother and father, bending deeply. The couple lay in front of a color TV, watching a beauty contest. After taking off my shoes, I sat on the edge of the mattress while Jek was left sitting in the doorway. His parents looked at me curiously but not too surprised. I wondered if Jek had told them about me.

Jek's father was lively and cute. He looked like Jek. He moved close to me and sat crosslegged. The mother was heavy with one deformed-looking eye partially closed. "Old ugly woman," the father said, pointing to his wife. Her face had no reaction to this, as if she heard it often. Though she didn't say anything, she smiled at me warmly.

Jek pointed to what looked like a closet on the far wall, as long as his parent's room but only three feet wide. "My room," he said. A half-door led into it. It had no light. "I grow up in there."

How horrible. He'd have to climb over his parents' mattress to get in and would hear every word they spoke. I didn't want to ask if his brothers slept there too.

"I make your fortune," the father said to me. "What you year of birth?"

"Nineteen sixty-one," I said easily, having calculated that when I first decided to lower my age. He wrote a list of numbers and recounted my past and predicted my future.

"This year no good for you," he said. "Next year good, year after good. This year no *sabai jai* (peace of mind)." He nodded toward Jek. "You love him?"

I had to say yes. It made Jek look proud, but clearly he didn't like his father's train of thought.

"No good for you. You have troubled heart this year."

Though I didn't take his predictions seriously—because I didn't believe in fortune telling, and because he was eleven years off my birth year—he did know his son. Hence, the implications were not comforting.

"No *sabai jai*," he said again. "Is true?"

"Exactly," I answered strongly. Jek looked uncomfortable.

His father mentioned—more than once—"When Jek little, he get beating all

CLEO ODZER

the time. Always naughty boy. You no *sabai jai* with him." He laughed. Jek's smile went crooked.

I'd hoped to dig up information about Jek's life from his parents, but now I didn't want to embarrass him any more than his father seemed to be doing.

Maybe I could see photos of him and Doom and find clues to their relationship.

"Do you have baby pictures of you?" I asked Jek. The family photos came out. I saw a few shots of his mother when she was married to the Dane—and when she was younger and richer, which gave the father another opportunity to say how old and ugly she was now.

"Old woman," he said. "Too ugly." He insulted his wife continually and never addressed her except in an offhand way. He rarely looked at her. She acted as if this were normal.

Though there were many pictures of Jek's stepsiblings, there were few of him as a child. Jek brought out an album with teenage pictures of himself taken at the zoo.

"You keep," he told me.

"Really? Thanks."

He'd moved near me to display the pictures and now stayed next to me, our legs touching. It was sweet. He also seemed to need reassurance that his father hadn't turned me against him.

There were no shots of Jek as an adult. Did they hide pictures of Doom from me? I didn't get the impression they were concealing photos, though. They'd pulled out the whole shelf.

The legion of mosquitoes in the room devoured me. Zillions of them flew in and out of the glassless window and the open door. I refrained from slapping at them for fear of being rude, the way I wouldn't have called attention to a cockroach in someone's apartment. But I couldn't stop from scratching the bite bumps now covering my arms and legs.

Jek's mother noticed and sent Jek for a mosquito coil, which he lit and placed at my feet. Too late, I thought; I didn't have a virgin spot of skin left for them to eat. I appreciated the mother's gesture, though, and smiled at her. I thought I detected a puzzled wrinkle in her brow, as if she couldn't understand why I'd want to associate with a man from this place.

Jek's father asked me, "How much money you spend one month?"

This was a typical Thai question, not considered impolite the way it would be in the West. "Oh, I don't know . . . "

"Maybe fifteen hundred?"

"Oh, more than that."

Jek chuckled and said, "At least ten time that."

His father's eyes glowed with astonishment and his mouth hung loose.

"We're going to America," Jek told his parents.

The father looked at his son as if he'd won the lottery. The mother looked at me as if I must be crazy.

229

For the first time I thought it might be fun to show Jek New York. I could take him up the elevator of the World Trade Center, ride with him on the subway, teach him about ear muffs and snow.

Jek's ulcer bothered him and, grimacing, he held his stomach. His mother commented, "Still?" and shook her head sadly.

Jek looked thoughtfully into space and murmured, "Why?"

I'd heard him say that before when he seemed cursed by fate. No one answered.

As we prepared to leave, Jek insisted I *wai* his parents to show respect, though *farangs* in general were not expected to do this.

I stopped in the outhouse, a tiny nook with no light, no toilet paper, and no water, though it was difficult to see for sure in the dark. The door had no lock and wouldn't stay closed. I decided I could wait till I got home.

Before we left, Jek handed his mother a wad of money. As we were leaving, Jek's father looked at me as if I were a goose that laid golden eggs. His mother's look said, "Poor thing."

Out on the street, young slum residents now congregated. They seemed to know Jek but evinced no friendship. At most there were nods, no greetings.

"Are they your friends?" I asked him.

"I know everybody but no live here anymore. I make myself better."

In the *tuk-tuk* back to Patpong, Jek spoke acidly of his father. "He never let my mother speak." This was true. Jek's mother had hardly entered the conversation, but then none of us had had the opportunity to say much since his father never stopped talking. He often repeated what he'd said moments before.

"When I child, father very bad," Jek continued. "He gamble and then complain there's no money. He very bad to my mother, always taking her last *baht*. One time he break her sewing machine. Sewing machine was only thing she have in the world. He break it on purpose. My mother cry. He never pay me attention. I have to do everything for myself. Never any money. Never have food for lunch."

On the other hand, Jek clearly admired his father's good looks and peppy personality. "He handsome man, you think so?" he asked me.

"Very cute, just like you."

Jek got out of the *tuk-tuk* at my door but then left to go back to work.

Upstairs, I found a job application and a resume hidden behind a picture in the photo album he'd given me. It had no mention of Chulalongkorn University. Instead, it listed a ninth-grade certificate followed by three years of vocational education at a Bangkok commercial college. Hah!

Then I noticed the date on the letter, 1986, and the marital status, "single." Single? Not only was 1986 the time Jek admitted being married to Doom, it was also the time their son Bank was being born. Yet Jek had called himself single. Obviously, this was something he'd been lying about a long time.

24.

In modern Thailand, it is accepted—and even expected—that men have major and minor wives. A 1988 interview with a woman who writes an advice column for a Thai woman's magazine reveals the common attitude:

Q: What does the modern Thai woman think about this polygamy business?

A: It doesn't matter if she is modern or not. As a Thai woman she is more or less forced to accept it. . . . It is in male nature and as long as she is treated justly, I suppose the reasonable woman can take it (Schalbruch: 1988).

Jek did come by later that night, which pleased me enormously. He seemed roused by my meeting his parents and we were closer than ever, as if a bond had been forged.

The next morning he woke early—surprise—and suggested we go to a movie at Maboon Krong, the shopping mall adored by Thai teenagers. As we rode in the *tuk-tuk*, he put his feet on the metal barrier between us and the driver. I noticed his beautifully polished shoes were coming apart at the sole. They were probably cheap, and my heart broke at how he tried so hard to be snazzy but just didn't have the means.

At the mall we lunched where I'd once eaten with Nok and Yamaguchi. Jek had a bowl of Chinese soup. He aimed a spoonful of something across the table, "Try this."

"What is it?" I asked, eyeing a grey oval with a hole through its center. "Meat?"

"Yes, meat. You try."

Noticing amusement on his face, I only nibbled. It tasted like rubbery matzo ball. "Okay, what is it?"

He continued eating and answered nonchalantly. "Penis. Chinese man like to eat this. Good for sex. You want more?" He glanced at me with laughter in his eyes.

"No, thanks. What animal does it come from?"

"Beef."

"It's too small! Looks more like pig."

"Yes, pig."

He still had humor on his face, and I wondered if he'd fabricated the penis story. I felt uncomfortable thinking he enjoyed fooling me. Why did he always make me feel victimized?

After lunch, we strolled around the mall, waiting for show time; he stopped to look at clothes, I stopped to browse the computer wares. When we wandered into a furniture store, Jek marveled at the chintzy, mass-produced stuff. He fondled a plastic table as if it were Chippendale. A wooden bed with a trashy yellow canopy caught his fancy. He asked its price and gazed at it longingly, as if fantasizing about owning it. Why did I feel excluded from the fantasy? He didn't look at me and the bed as if imagining us both in the same dream. His yearning seemed only for the bed.

Near the theater, we came to a stand selling eyeglasses. He tried on a pair.

"Soon, I start work in office," he said. "I change my life after my birthday. Eyesight no good. I'll have to wear eyeglass." He turned to me in tortoise–shell frames. "I look respectable?"

"Uh . . . yes."

The movie we saw was *Poltergeist 3*, in English with Thai subtitles. The theater was air conditioned to North Pole temperature, and goose bumps soon covered Jek's arms. We snuggled to keep him warm. Every now and then he made a comment without lowering his voice. Other viewers turned to look at him in annoyance. I wondered if movie-going was something he wasn't accustomed to.

Jek thought the little blond girl in the film was adorable. "You look like that when little?" he asked me.

"Yup."

"I want baby that look like that," he said, sounding like he considered it a possibility. I wondered if he thought he'd have a little blond with me. The image of having a baby with Thai eyes did appeal to me, though it probably wouldn't be blond.

When we returned to the apartment, I felt satisfied.

That night I went back to Sexy Stars to visit Pong, as I'd promised. I ran into Ong outside the door at the club's beer bar. He came in and sat with me.

We spoke awhile before Pong came offstage.

"I very happy Pong come back to me," Ong said. He told me about a French woman who'd wanted to sleep with him but whom he refused because he was with Pong and in love with her. "I no go with other woman," he stated. "I'm not playboy."

"Are you working?" I asked him.

"No. Pong work. I take care of children."

Now he claimed to have been with Pong five years, not the one year he'd told me the last time. Since he appeared too sloshed to remember our former conversation, I asked, "You and Pong have two children, right?'

"Three-year-old girl belong to me and Pong, but boy is mine from other wife."

232

So! First Pong had told me the children came from both of them, then he'd said they were both Pong's from another man, and now here was yet another version. Actually, this one sounded truest. Ong was Muslim, so it was possible he'd brought the boy with him from a previous marriage.

When Pong finished dancing, she joined us, and the two of them joked around. "I hate him," she said, but they looked at each other lovingly. Later, when she danced again, she smiled at him from the stage and danced special.

When I left the bar, Ong walked me to the door. "Tomorrow is my birthday," he said. "You come celebrate with me?"

"Um . . . I don't think I can." Somehow, this birthday sounded legitimate, but he could be inviting me to a real event in order for me to buy him something or to pay for the outing. In either case, I wasn't up to it. I felt too insecure in my role with Jek to go along with another possible deception, even if it might be good for research.

Jek didn't come that night but appeared the next afternoon at four. He told me he'd arranged to meet a Thai business man that night on Patpong. "Important man," Jek said, all hyper. "I take him for drink. I have to leave soon to hurry make money."

As it turned out, Jek didn't leave till late. It made me feel good when he couldn't seem to detach himself from me. "I see you later," he said finally at the door. "You come with us for drink."

That night, on the way home, I spotted Jek on Silom attempting to engage a *farang* in conversation. The *farang* wasn't interested and walked off as I approached.

"Oah," Jek said, seeing me. He took my hand to lead me to his corner. "Man here. We wait for you."

I felt honored. Since Jek had met him hours before, they must have been waiting a long time.

A Thai in his late forties sat on an overturned box by a papaya vendor. Jek introduced me as his *fan* (girlfriend). Another tout said by now I was his *mia* (wife).

"We go your house for beer," Jek said to me. "You still have beer right?"

"Yeah." Part of me liked the idea of entertaining Jek's friends in my home, the other part wondered if Jek's motivation stemmed from the free access he had to my beer. Had he been unable to make money that night and was using me as a last resort?

When we passed the pool in my building, Jek suggested we go swimming the next day. Since he'd never shown interest in the activity before, I suspected he was only showing off.

Jek's friend was openly impressed with the apartment. Jek turned on the air conditioner, which was another thing he usually ignored. Then he turned on the TV and put his head on my lap as the two of them talked. He held my arm around

233

his chest. I liked that he was more affectionate than usual but questioned the purpose of it.

"I teach Jek many things," the man said to me. "But he go far beyond my teaching."

I didn't like that. Jek had mentioned the man's occupation involved organizing construction projects with cheap, illegal labor and high profits. Did he mean that by being with me Jek surpassed his training in how to be a successful hustler? I didn't appreciate his viewing me as an achievement along those lines.

They finished the beer, which I didn't mind since it had been sitting there since a party I'd had the year before; but the hours dragged past my bedtime, and I grew sleepy and annoyed.

When they were ready to leave, Jek kissed me goodbye and said, "Maybe I see you later."

I knew immediately that meant he wouldn't be back. Anger exploded in me and I said, "LIAR!" He came only for free beer and showed affection to prove a point! I told him, "If you don't come back tonight, tomorrow I won't be here."

The man was halfway out the door with Jek behind him. Jek heard my tone and turned back. The man heard it too and said he'd wait outside.

Jek said soothingly, "I want to come back." He slid his arms around my waist. "I want to be with you."

I felt better as he kissed me goodbye again, but then he left, and seconds after the door closed, my anger returned.

I had trouble sleeping and tossed around, frequently glancing at the clock. He didn't come at 3. He didn't come at 4. Was I being unreasonable? Were my uncertainties making me a shrew? I remembered the paper by Eric Cohen I'd given Dudley Dapolito to read. It spoke of the torture *farang* men underwent in never knowing if their Thai girlfriends loved them or were with them only for advantage. Had I fallen into the same quandary?

Jek didn't come back that night. I was furious.

When I awoke to an empty apartment the next day, I fumed with outrage. He knew I'd been upset and hadn't cared enough to return. I decided once again that the relationship had to end. Since I'd told him I wouldn't be there that day if he didn't come back, I had to go somewhere. Where? Kao San Road. I'd go watch a video. I could feel anxiety coursing through my body. I had to get my mind off Jek.

I should occupy myself with work, I thought. I decided to post more notices asking for stories about Patpong women.

After printing a pile of them, I went to Kao San Road with Scotch tape. I began at one end of the street and stopped in every guest house, coffee shop, and ice cream parlor. In the lobby of P.B. Guest House, I spotted a friend—Choo Choo Charlie, the former Firecat doorman. He sat at a desk in front of a typewriter surrounded by traveler-type *farangs*.

"Charlie! What are you doing here?"

"Hey man, what's cookin? I work here. I make press cards and student IDs.

234

Take a look. Dynamite quality. Exactly like the real thing. You get cool discounts with the student ID, and the press card can get you into things—rock concerts, maybe even communist countries. Will you be around later? I'm busy now."

Since Charlie knew Jek, I seized this opportunity to talk about him. I needed advice and reassurance. "I can come back. I'll go see a video."

"Pick me up at 6, man. We'll go for a bite."

Since the places that showed free videos were restaurants, I ate before I returned to P. B. Guest House. Just as well—Charlie wasn't hungry. He took me to a roof where, beneath hanging laundry, floor mattresses made it a hippy-type lounge in the open air.

"Wanna smoke some weed?" he asked me.

"No, I gave that up long ago."

"How 'bout a hit of coke?"

"That too."

"Heroin? I have a taste. Someone left for Penang and gave me his stash. Can't take anything into Malaysia, you know. They have the death penalty there. Better be careful when you go for your visa."

"I'm not worried about the death penalty. I don't do anything illegal. Well," I laughed, "except illegal research. Why did you leave Patpong?"

"Can't make no money there. They only pay 3,000 *baht* a month for a doorman, and they dock you if you come late. At the end of the month I ended up owing THEM. I make a decent living here. I do about fifty ID cards a day, 250 *baht* each. I meet groovy people. Did I tell you I used to get high with John Belushi and Cathy?"

"Yeah. You know Jek, don't you? He told me once he met you."

"Jek! A big bullshitter, man. I lent him money and he never returned it. I tried to get it back a few times, but he always ran me a line. Once, he tried to borrow more!"

I tensed up. This was not what I wanted to hear.

"Didn't he have a problem with you over money too?" Charlie asked. "He borrowed some and never paid it back?"

"Uh, yeah, 500 *baht*."

"You ever get it back?"

"Uh, no."

"See man, he's a bullshit artist." Charlie lit a joint and passed it to a young Japanese sitting near.

Since Jek always paid when we went out, the 500 *baht* had ceased to bother me. Now, put this way, my misgivings about it came back.

"Jek was real hung up on you," Charlie said next, which warmed me to my toes. He continued, "We spent a night together sleeping in a truck outside the Royal Orchid Hotel waiting for a German dude. He spoke about you the whole night. He told me about his wife finding him in your apartment and sending him to the hospital. I thought you returned to the States because of that incident."

"No. I didn't speak to him for two weeks but eventually gave in and went back with him. We're still together."

"You went back with him!" Charlie seemed incensed at this, mostly as if he regretted not being the one to accomplish it. "That smart motherfucker."

I didn't like the insinuation that being with me was "smart." It seemed that, through me, Jek was scoring points with all his friends. "He said he's not with his wife anymore," I stated.

"Don't you believe it. He's a clever cookie. He told me his wife gets jealous and beats him if she sees him on the street with another woman."

The wife issue again. I'd never escape it. The only way to end the torment was to end the relationship. "Well, I think I'm finished with Jek anyway," I said. "Maybe I'll stay on Kao San Road a few days to get away from him."

"I can book you a room here, man. I'll go down and get you a key."

"No, wait. I have to go home first for things. It does sound like a good idea, though. I can't think straight when I'm in his company." I surveyed the friendly atmosphere. The Japanese had closed his eyes. A blond woman in camouflage shorts was writing an aerogram. Others lay on their backs pointing to constellations in the sky. "I'll do it," I said. "I'll be back around midnight."

I rushed home and packed. When everything was ready, Jek phoned. "I call you all night," he said. "You no home."

"I told you I wouldn't be here today if you didn't come back last night. It's over between us. I can't go on like this."

"I come right over," he said and hung up.

I hid the bag in a closet and in minutes he was there.

"You always lie to me," I yelled as soon as I saw him. "You said maybe you'd be back when you had no intention of returning."

"I don't lie. When we first meet, you say to me all the time: 'Maybe next week'."

"I didn't mean that. I didn't know you then."

"I meet *farang* on street and he say, 'Maybe later,' but he never come again."

"Those phrases are just quick ways to get out of a conversation."

"At beginning, you tell me you have roommate."

I groaned. "THAT WAS AGES AGO!"

"What you want?" he asked. "You want me move in here?"

We looked at each other. I didn't want that. And I did want that. Before I could answer, he said, "I'm not ready to live here. I can't pay rent. I don't want to live off your money. I must pay half."

I sighed and made a face because that had nothing to do with the fact that I felt lied to and manipulated because he was married.

He picked up pen and paper and scribbled as he went into a dialogue about his deprived childhood. He wrote, "Born in slump, my parents don't like me. I never have everything. I do everything myself. My personality. My ambition." When he wrote, "I come to America for my self and my money," it disturbed me. He hadn't written anything about love or going to America to be with me, only about himself and his money.

I grabbed the pen from him and said, "I'm talking about one thing and you always talk about something else. That's why I feel tricked, that you're treating me like a stupid female."

He smiled. "I don't answer question."

"Right. You change the subject and think I don't notice. I saw Choo Choo Charlie. He said you're still married."

"No."

"Charlie said you spoke about Doom as your wife, not your EX-wife."

Jek didn't say anything. He had that look when I caught him at something.

"What do you need?" he asked me after a pause.

"That you're not married."

"Okay, I'm not married. What else?"

"Nothing else."

At this he became sprightly. "Then you have what you want. Definitely. For sure, I'm not married."

"What about Doom?"

"That is finished. I don't see her anymore."

"Do you give her money?"

He hesitated, then said, "Yes."

I sighed.

He looked at me sincerely. "My responsibility. What kind of person am I if I don't give money for my son?"

I couldn't argue with that. "How do you give her money? Does she come get it?"

Another pause. "No, I send it through post office."

I didn't believe him. If she'd been coming before so he had to be at Mr. Tam's in the morning, why would he send her money all of a sudden?

He did seem to be trying hard to please me though. I began to soften. I wanted things to be right between us. I wanted to take him in my arms. I couldn't, though, because he wasn't saying anything new or acceptable. I was dying to touch him and put aside temper.

"I wish you could be more *sabai jai* (at ease)," he said looking forlornly at the ceiling. "I can't stay here every night because I can't pay half the rent."

Oh, no, not that argument again.

Then he said, "What if I sleep at my mother's house instead of Mr. Tam's? How is that?"

Would he really do that for me? He would spend an hour traveling late at night just to make me happy? I put my head against his chest.

Finally we curled up together on the bed.

"What are you afraid of?" he asked. "Broken heart?"

"Yes."

"I'm not afraid of broken heart. In my life I suffer everything." He pointed to the scars on his shoulder and arms. "I have everything bad happen already."

Sometimes I thought I'd drown in how much I loved him. I felt it at that moment. Was there something in his miserable life stories that made me love him more? Pity? Was this how *farang* men became nuts over Patpong women?

I snuck my hands under his shirt and we kissed passionately.

Just before I fell asleep, I realized he never said he WOULD stay every night at his mother's. He only asked if I'd accept that. Since I hadn't insisted on it, I knew he wouldn't do it. I felt tricked again.

25.

Phongpaichit (1982) reveals that migrant prostitution is only a temporary occupation. Due to the rural-urban financial gap, within a few years the women are able to buy houses back home for both themselves and their families as well as to amass the capital necessary to begin their own small businesses. The following table shows the future plans of the 1,020 masseuses in Muangman and Nanta's study (1980: 68).

FUTURE PLANS OF (PROSTITUTES WORKING AS) MASSEUSES

ITEM	NUMBER	PERCENT
Small business	416	40.78
Tailor making	159	15.59
Agriculture	120	11.76
Service shop	1	0.10
Farm	10	0.98
Housewife	20	1.96
Go home	30	2.94
Gov. officer	7	0.69
Don't know	104	10.20
Others	33	3.24
*No response**	47	
TOTAL	1,020	100.00

**Not included in total*

The next day, Jek woke up early again—early enough for the maids to come in and clean. He discussed plans for the life he'd begin in March after his birthday. "I must buy good clothes for when I work in office. I need new shoe, new watch. One time, I have guest who wear beautiful watch. Very expensive. He want to make love with me. I say okay if you give me watch." Jek laughed. "He no agree."

I knew the gay men Jek accosted on the street were often interested in Jek himself. Jek had always insisted he'd never have sex with a man. He found the notion repulsive. But I also knew how much he liked money. My heart ached thinking he might actually consider doing something he abhorred. Then I wondered if he'd actually do it. Or had done it. A shiver went through me as I imagined Jek sleeping with men—gay *farang* men, the group with AIDS. Oh shit.

I quickly asked, "Would you have done it?"

"No, never! I never sleep with man. I only wanted to know what he say."

"All gay *farang*s must want you."

"One man offer me much money just to kiss him." Jek made a face. "I refuse. Sometime, man want to hold my hand when we walk. I hate it."

"Does that happen often?

He frowned. "Too much. Other night, I bring guest to gay bar. He pick four boy to take upstair. He want me join. I say no. But he insist I watch. I have to say okay. I sit on chair in the room for many hour. I watch five of them make love. Guest call me to come over. Very bad. Very boring."

Again I felt moved by the anguish of Jek's existence and loved him more than ever. Was it love? That's what *farang*s with Patpong girlfriends called it too. Maybe these mighty emotions weren't love but something else. Maybe I had indeed fallen into the same trap as the Western men I studied.

Not long after he left, Dudley Dapolito called. He'd just returned from Chiang Mai in Northern Thailand and wanted to pick up his luggage and mail.

"How was your trip with Sow?" I asked when he arrived.

"I spent $2,000 in six weeks."

"Where's Sow now?"

"She went back to Pattaya ten days ago to meet her fifty-year-old American. She'll join me in Bangkok tomorrow. Then she has to return to Pattaya to meet her German. No emotions are involved with these men," Dudley assured me, "just big money."

"Are you still in love with her?"

He sighed. "Yes, but it's giving me grief. This time we were together twenty-eight days. I got gonorrhea on the twenty-fifth day."

"Oh, no!"

"Gonorrhea has only a three-day incubation period, you know."

"So how was that possible?"

"Sow said it was a recurrence of a bad case she's had before. Originally she told me she'd never had VD."

"She lied."

"Yeah. I told her many times, I don't care what you do as long as you tell me the truth. We have to have honesty or we have nothing. That's the one thing that really bugs me—if she lies. When I complained of her lying about the gonorrhea, she got angry."

"So you think it was her old gonorrhea that resurfaced?"

"I don't know. There's a possibility she had a short-time customer one night."

"You're kidding. Why?"

"One day we had a fight. Sow became savagely angry for a reason I never understood. Maybe I didn't pay enough attention to her; maybe I spoke English too quickly; maybe I didn't find her a toilet fast enough. I don't know. She was in a rage and I couldn't calm her. She disappeared for a few hours. My friends told me to send her back to Pattaya, since I couldn't talk to her and she was bumming me out."

"You think that's when she took a customer?"

Dudley shrugged. "The next day I went to the bank to change money to pay her off and send her back. I gave her more than we'd agreed on. But then she cried so much, I relented. She blamed her tantrum on her birth-control injection. She hadn't had one in three months and her next shot was overdue. Have you heard of that stuff?"

"Depo Provera. Most bar girls who practice birth control get those injections. One shot four times a year. I never heard it could make you cranky though. So you and Sow made up?"

"Yeah, we stayed together till she left to meet the American. I paid her an extra 500 *baht*."

"After that, you were in Chiang Mai alone?"

"Alone? Hell, no. This is still Thailand. Once I slept with a woman for 80 *baht* short-time. A cheapie. I gave her a 20 *baht* tip. Another woman cost me 3,000 *baht* for the night. Most of the time, though, the sex was no fun. One woman wanted me to finish quickly. I told her to slow down but she refused. There wasn't much I could do short of throwing her off. Sometimes I think Thai women are too small inside. I seem to hurt them. Is it true that Thai men are teeny-weeny?"

I thought of Jek. "Not that much smaller than *farang*s. A bit, and narrower. Will you be looking for women in Bangkok before Sow arrives?"

"I got in from Chiang Mai yesterday afternoon. Last night I went to *Soi* Cowboy. I bought two women out of a bar. I never slept with two women at the same time before. It's something I always wanted to do. But it didn't work. While I had sex with one, the other ran around the room. Then, as soon as I came, they said they had to go back to the bar because three new girls were in from Isan. I'd already paid them 400 *baht* each. I didn't think that was right, but they promised to return with me later."

"So you went back to the bar?"

"Till closing time. They ran up a monstrous bill. Then the one who hadn't slept with me didn't want to come back to my room. She wouldn't talk to me and slapped my hand. She wouldn't give me back my 400 *baht*. Eventually, the other girl found me someone else. I gave the new girl 500 *baht* and slept with her, but the original one wouldn't have sex with me again. She left after getting another 100 *baht*. The new girl stayed till morning and wanted me to meet her family. When I refused, she asked for 300 *baht* for her mother. No, I said. Then 200 *baht* for a taxi. No way José, but I let her have 30 *baht* for a *tuk-tuk*."

"Safe sex?"

"Nah. And because of all the activity, I broke out with herpes. Meanwhile, the gonorrhea hasn't responded to medication, so now I have both gonorrhea and herpes. Bummer."

I laughed. "What about tonight?"

"What do you think? Hey, I'm in Thailand, you know what I mean?"

"Will you miss Sow when you're in the States?"

"I miss her now. I hate the idea of her working while I'm away. I don't want to send her money, though, since she has so many guys doing that. If I could send her $100 a month and know she wasn't whoring, I would."

The ringing doorbell surprised me. It was Jek. I was glad to see him but didn't want to end the talk with Dudley.

"You two already met once, remember?" To Jek, I said, "Dudley's telling me about his girlfriend, Sow," hoping that would make him realize I was "working."

After they shook hands, I continued the interview with Jek next to me. He remained quiet for two minutes, then jumped in. I didn't mind much because I'd started to feel uncomfortable asking Dudley about sleeping with prostitutes in front of him. I didn't want Jek to think this was what all *farang* men did naturally. Though it was expected of Thai men, I'd tried to explain to Jek that in America men would never admit sleeping with prostitutes because that meant no regular female would touch them. I'd said both men and women were free to have sex in the West, so only old, fat, ugly men needed to pay for it. Now here was sex-buying Dudley, whom Jek already believed to be "respectable," and there went my argument.

Jek asked Dudley, "You plan do business in Thailand?"

"Uh, no, not really."

"I can help you. I can show you where buy good sapphire. You see Thai sapphire? Very beautiful."

Oh, no, Jek was going into his sales pitch.

"Yeah?" said Dudley, unenthused. "Gems are a profitable industry here, I know. You must be a rich man."

Jek took this as a go-ahead to embark on a spiel. "I'll take you to factory. Get you good deal. Cheap price."

"I'm leaving the country soon. Maybe when I come back. I promise if I ever enter the gem business, you'll be the first person I contact."

I was embarrassed that Jek was trying to scam Dudley and that Dudley was treating Jek like an infant.

Since it was already evening, I decided to go to Patpong. The three of us prepared to leave the apartment together.

As Dudley hopped on one foot by the door to put on his shoes, Jek continued running his line.

"You give me your card," Jek said. "I can write you and tell you about business deal. I send you souvenir, you sell in America."

Dudley gave him his card—just to shut him up, I was sure.

With the three of us bunched by the open front door, I stood by Jek's shoulder as he opened his wallet to slip in Dudley's card. I saw the photo of his son Bank.

And the empty slot where my photo used to be.

I froze. I felt dead.

Then I pounced. "WHERE'S MY PICTURE?"

Jek knew immediately he was in trouble. I saw panic in his eyes.

Dudley, however, was unaware that anything had happened and went out the door, still condescending to how he might go into the import-export business with Jek.

Jek and I followed him out and down the stairs, which were quicker to take than the elevator. In Thai and with acid in my voice, I asked Jek, "*Roop pai nai?*" (Picture, went where?)

Jek's eyes looked begging as he said in Thai, "No good," which I knew meant no good if Doom saw it.

In cheery ignorance, Dudley, who was a few paces ahead of us, stopped and said with dramatic resonance, "What's that? Looks like someone was slaughtered here." He pointed to an invisible line going down the stairs.

"What? What is it?" asked Jek, probably hoping to escape the dispute with me.

Dudley held out his arm like he was playing Hamlet. "I see blood. A trail of blood going down the stairs."

I knew what he meant. I'd told him about Doom attacking Jek in my apartment and leaving a trail of Jek's blood down to the street. Descending the stairs with Jek had made Dudley remember that, and he was making a joke. He had an expectant grin on his face as if waiting for us to laugh. What bad timing.

Jek didn't understand the gag. I had to explain. "I told him about Doom coming here." I glared at him and added with ice in my tone, "Your WIFE!" Then I brushed past him and said in Thai, "You threw away my picture. Not smart."

In fury, I hurried past the pool and out to the street. Dudley still had no idea what was going on.

"Which way are you going?" I asked him. "Maybe we can share a *tuk-tuk*." I ignored Jek.

"Down Sathorn Road."

"I'm going the other way."

I flagged a *tuk-tuk* and jumped in, leaving Dudley to head in the opposite direction. I wanted to get away fast. Jek jumped in too.

"I come with you," he said, sounding scared.

"I'll let you off on Silom."

"Where you go?"

"Kao San Road."

"I go too."

"NO." I had venom in my voice.

"I stay with you," he said.

"You got rid of my picture. You don't care about my feelings. You only think

243

about Doom."

"You don't understand. I already tell you my situation."

"I understand—Doom is the one you worry about most. Fine. She can have you."

"She don't have me. I'm with you."

"Hah! My picture's not with you."

As we approached the place opposite his corner, I made the *tuk-tuk* stop. Jek told the driver to keep going, which he did.

"STOP," I yelled to the driver. He stopped abruptly. "GET OUT," I yelled to Jek. Jek didn't move. He looked wretched. I said convincingly, "If you don't get out, I will. I'll take another *tuk-tuk*."

He stepped to the street with a dreadful expression. I didn't wave or say goodbye.

26.

Discussing prostitution as a part of Thai society, Hantrakul (1983: 30) stresses that:

> *It is a historical fact to recognize that prostitution had existed and was institutionalized before the arrivals of the Chinese, the G.I., and lately the tourist. What had happened was not, in my opinion, the simple corruption of innocent native maidens into sinful prostitutes by the vicious foreign man. All he did was introduce an additional demand into the existing situation, whereupon the internal economic pressure and the laws of supply and demand took over.*

I didn't go straight to Kao San Road. Halfway down Silom, I told the driver to take me back to where I'd flagged him down.

I'd had enough. I couldn't let myself continue one more day in the relationship with Jek. I was a skinny, anxious, raving, paranoid wreck. For sure, I'd never be *sabai jai* with him. Even my project was suffering. I should have joined Ong's birthday celebration, no matter what I had to pay for. Anything to bond me to an informant was desirable. Jek had sapped my ego strength to the point of making me oversensitive to personal assaults. I had to end it, and to do that I had to prevent myself from seeing his lovely face and hearing his pitiful stories.

I had to go away, clear my brain, and exorcise my lust.

I returned home, packed a bag again, and put the combination lock on the door so Jek would know not to bother ringing. Then I left for Kao San Road.

Kao San Road was great for seeking travel deals, meeting people, and watching uncensored videos (Thai theaters fuzzed nudity and deleted racy dialogue). But it wasn't the most comfortable place to stay.

I avoided Choo Choo Charlie's hotel because I didn't want Jek to find me easily. The area had forty or fifty guest houses, so even if Jek did guess where I'd gone, he would have trouble tracking me down. I checked into a place on a side street and was shown to a decrepit cubicle down the hall from communal toilets and showers. No sheets covered the stained mattress, and, if one could stand the tornado made by the ceiling fan in that tiny space, hot air was all one got. The flimsy walls made every footstep and whisper next door perfectly audible.

I grew instantly depressed. Not only did my soul ache from missing Jek, look at this squalid place I now had as an abode! How ridiculous. From a luxury apartment with maid service and swimming pool, I'd been reduced to this.

But I knew I couldn't go home. There was no way I could resist Jek if he was in my presence.

I sat on the filthy bed and cried.

Late in the afternoon, I went to a café and watched *Good Morning, Vietnam*. It succeeded in distracting me. In the early evening, I watched another video, then another. I met an aged hippy from Oregon who told me about his pot plantation and how the police had raided it and burned his plants.

Later that night, I joined him and a group of others on the roof. Rooftops were havens on Kao San Road. Mattresses carpeted this one too, and we listened to an Israeli with ringlets sing "Blowin' in the Wind." I felt reconnected to my youth. The familiarity of the scene lulled me. This environment suited me better than Patpong, prostitution, and Thai touts.

Though I felt wonderfully homey, it was difficult to ignore the pain of missing Jek.

And I didn't really fit into that scene either. I'd given it up long ago, and in-depth discussions about the Grateful Dead no longer entranced me.

My Oregon friend lent me his sleeping bag to cover my foul mattress. I cried myself to sleep, sweating in the heat and regretting I hadn't had the foresight to bring the electric mosquito repellent.

I wondered if Jek would make the effort to find me.

I loved Kao San Road but hated living there. Since shoes were left downstairs in the lobby, one had to walk barefoot into the disgusting squat toilet. My feet seemed forever wet with something, and I dearly missed my air conditioner and TV, not to mention my refrigerator, telephone, computer, and daily laundry service.

There was a limit to how much hanging-out talk I could put up with, and no place showed videos until 4 p.m.

The one intriguing aspect of Kao San Road was the Western women. Kao San Road was the only place in Bangkok with as many foreign women as men. I so rarely saw them, they fascinated me. They were much rounder than the bony Thai women I was accustomed to, and they wore skimpy midriff blouses and cutoff jeans with a freer sexuality than even naked Thai bar girls. Blond hair especially captivated me, and I stared at blond ponytails gleaming in the sunlight. They were striking. Did I look like that?

I met a few of the women, two Swedes and a Canadian. The Swedes had just graduated from Stockholm University and were off to see the world.

"We just spent four months in Bali," said one. "After Thailand, we go to Peking."

The Canadian woman, in her late thirties with hennaed hair, had recently arrived from Nepal with Tibetan jewelry she hoped to sell.

"I should be able to make enough money from this to get me to Japan," she told me and the others sitting at the table. "I heard it's easy to get a job there as a hostess. I'll do that for a while and then head to Mullumbimby in Australia."

"I'm going to Japan too," said a man with shoulder-length gray hair who leaned over from the next table. "You can make a lot of bread selling cards there on the street. I have a phone number to call."

"If not, you can always teach English. Tokyo pays well for English teachers."

By day three, I had a collection of aged hippy pals and had even met a few people who knew people who knew friends of mine from India. I was bored to death and dying of heartbreak. There were almost no Thai boys around, except for a few cassette vendors with their wares laid out on the sidewalk.

What was I doing here? Ridiculous.

I called Dudley Dapolito at his guest house in another part of town.

"I'm just leaving for the States," he said. "Did I get any more mail at your house?"

"No."

"I never got the results of that AIDS test I took in Hong Kong."

"I'll forward it as soon as it arrives. Did you develop those pictures you took of me and Jek?"

"Yeah. Come get them. Sow is here to see me off. I'll leave them with her."

That evening I went to Sow for the pictures. It hurt to see Jek and me laughing into Dudley's camera.

"So, Dudley's gone back to America," I said. "Will you miss him?"

"Yes," she answered. "But woman must hold on to her heart. I never give away more than half of it."

The next day, before returning to my neighborhood for a Thai lesson, I decided to go home first. Jek would never show up in the morning. I could collect my mail and change clothes. I would be safe there until at least 2 p.m.

My front door held no note, flower, or sign of Jek. My misery deepened.

The apartment with its elephants, though, was a welcome sight. I wished I could move back home but knew Jek would appear sooner or later and that I'd give in to him the moment I saw his face. My only salvation was to avoid that; but how long could I live in a flea-bag hotel? I couldn't hide forever. How would I continue my work?

I decided to go to Patpong that night, via an alternate route, and then taxi back to Kao San Road from there.

I spent the late afternoon in the coffee shop of the Dusit Thani Hotel and then went to Patpong by detouring around Surawong Road.

I visited Sexy Stars with a ring for Pong, since she'd given me one the last time. I also gave her a pocket video game for Ong as a late birthday present. She appeared more thrilled to receive the present for him than the one for herself.

"When do you want to go upcountry with me to visit your family?" I asked her. Maybe now was the ideal time to leave Bangkok and meet families. "I could be ready tomorrow. We'll take Ong too."

"We go for Songkran. Is good for you?"

The Songkran holiday, Thai New Year, was in April—four months away. There went that idea.

After another day in the Kao San Road dump, I knew I had to find a better hide-out. Slummy living worsened my depression. Where could I go? What about one of the islands the girls went to with customers? I could do research there.

"Try *Ko* Samui," suggested my latest café mate. "It's a happening place."

"Does it have bar girls?"

"No. Mostly foreign travelers. You see only a few Thai girls with old European men. Go to Phuket if you want bars."

"Phuket's too far south."

"Samui's far too. *Ko* Samet's the closest island. Only three hours from Bangkok."

"Then that's the one. How do I get there?"

27.

Music: "Part-time Lover"

Come in, come in, come in. Don't wait too long. Come and
get to know our kind of love

(Refrain)
No matter whether you're old or young
    The aim is to succeed
    Come in and meet love

Dream, dream, dream as far away as possible
    It's necessary to look to the horizon
    To hope and not to lose heart
    And make it a challenge for all to see

But for me, who will understand
    that need to reach for the horizon
    Just to dream as far away as possible
    When in the end there's no one there

*Narrator: Who is it who says that people are of equal worth?
If it's so, the son of the field should not have to struggle, to
take a chance, to escape from hardship and head for the city;
the daughter of the land, who has not even the minimum com-
pulsory education, has to sell her labor from a young age, risk-
ing being raped and bullied, just for so little in return. Many
lost children with little education here are just like her, disappointed with love and ruined in relationship. They are also
mothers who sacrifice their bodies so their children would
have a better chance in this society.*

    *Yes, this is the life that has to struggle and hang on to the
hopes and dreams, that things will be better . . . just like everyone else.**

    * From the Patpong musical presented by Empower, 1987

Descending from the bus near a port, I was bombarded by Thais hawking
ferry tickets to the *ko* (island). Accustomed to shooing away Patpong touts, I told
them, "*Mai ow* (Don't want)," and followed the other passengers.

    A ferry consisted of a small fishing boat with a wooden bench along the rails
and an empty center for luggage, baskets of fruit, and burlap bags of ice.

    "How do I get on board?" I shouted to one of the Thais sitting in the boat, which was eight feet down from the pier and two feet out in the water, with no gangplank in sight.

"Jump," someone answered.

A woman pointed to a wooden pillar tilting from the pier. Did she think I would step out on that? Its top wasn't flat across, but jagged, like a broken broom handle.

As I looked around for the gangplank I refused to believe didn't exist, an ancient Thai woman with two armloads of shopping approached the edge of the pier, stepped on the pillar, and lunged down to the two-inch hand rail of the boat. From there she ducked under the boat's roof and lowered herself to the bench. They had to be joking!

I looked around for inspiration or a savior but found neither. I had no choice. I threw my bag to the deck, crawled out on the pillar, leapt, and landed in the boat on hands and knees. Only the *farang*s awarded my ungraceful entrance with a sympathetic smile.

Filled with backpacking tourists, as well as *Ko* Samet residents toting produce from the mainland market, the little boat chugged us across this bit of the Gulf of Thailand. In the half hour it took for the crossing, I noticed the foreigners seated opposite me became drenched with spray. When I returned from *Ko* Samet, I'd have to remember to sit again on the side with the Thais.

The island's dock looked as treacherous as the mainland's. As the boat slammed into hanging tires, I hefted my bag to my shoulder and climbed on the railing. With a handhold on the boat's roof, and without looking at the water below me, I flung a foot to a pillar and hauled myself to the dock on one knee. I didn't know how *Ko* Samet could attract tourists with such a transportation system.

Ordeal over, I followed the Thai passengers as they mounted the back of an open truck. During the jolting ride over craters carved into the unpaved road by the rainy season, I managed to avoid being decapitated by the branches that scraped across the open roof.

Arriving at a beach, I looked around before deciding which way to go. To my right, the shoreline curved around a bay to a rocky point five miles away. Colorful sails of windsurfing boards dotted the sun-speckled water. Thatch-roofed buildings, open to the beach, could be seen under the seaside palm trees, but nothing was visible behind them through the greenery that stretched up the hill to the island's middle. I turned right and walked along the shore, passing outdoor restaurants.

The beach was sparsely populated by sunbathers. How refreshing to see that many of them were Western women. Though they seemed mammoth next to the tiny Thai women I was accustomed to, they looked as luscious as ripe tomatoes, their tanned skins glistening with coconut oil. Compared to Thai women's bony angles, the female flesh before me seemed barely able to contain its healthily plump potency.

The Western women I'd met on Kao San Road had raved about *Ko* Samet.

Maybe this place—without go-go bars or prostitutes—was the right spot for me after all. Maybe I needed to be around Western women. They did look alien to me. Was I that out of touch with myself?

I picked a bungalow lodge that had rattan tables and chairs and a long-haired Thai waiter carrying a tray of food barefoot through the sand. I was shown to bungalow A2, which cost $6 a night.

A2 was up on stilts, made of wood, and topped with a palm-frond roof. With the hammock on its porch, it looked like a beachcomber's fantasy hut. The inside held a double bed and a fan. The attached shower contained a toilet hole to squat over. Brown and gritty water filled a tiled vat to be scooped for flushing. The mass of mosquitoes that lived in the toilet flew up as I approached. I thought of the malaria pills I refused to take, because I didn't want to seem like a tourist, and consoled myself that only eight to twelve people a year caught malaria on *Ko* Samet.

That evening, at an outdoor seaside restaurant, I wolfed down a Thai version of a hamburger and saw a "Star Trek" video. Then I went to another restaurant for durian ice cream and another video.

When I returned to A2 after watching *RoboCop*, I felt too sad and empty to appreciate my tropical setting. I missed Jek terribly. I wished we could have come here together. He'd never visited his country's tourist paradises. He knew of them only by secondhand report from customers. I would have loved to experience the quiet stillness of *Ko* Samet with him. Only the bright lights of fishing boats on the horizon could be seen under the stars. Peace and shadow surrounded me, the pointy outline of palms darker than the night sky.

By the end of my first week, two things had attracted my attention—windsurfing and *Ko* Samet boys. I decided to try out the former, still too heart sick to consider the latter.

Not far from my bungalow was a pile of windsurfing boards with their sails parked against trees like giant butterflies. Stacked inner tubes formed a twelve-foot pyramid near deck chairs, beach umbrellas, kites, Frisbees—rentable toys for vacationers. A Thai woman and her son worked there from early morning to sunset. I told her I wanted to rent a board and learn to windsurf. A sign noted this cost 100 *baht* ($4) an hour.

The woman was fully dressed except for bare feet, her head and arms also cloaked in cloth. Since Thai people viewed light skin as the ideal, few of them had Westerners' urge to bask in the sun or spend long hours on a windsurfing board. Except for *Ko* Samet boys. From my observation of those magnificent males, it seemed windsurfing was their goal in life and their reason for being on Samet Island; that and the foreign women. Most of the boys worked in the island's restaurants and discotheques or as drivers for the trucks that took people around the island on the single road. A few ran their own businesses, a bungalow lodge or a beach equipment shed, sometimes co-owned with a Western wife. *Ko* Samet boys had a more relaxed rapport with Western culture than Jek or other Patpong males—perhaps because their contact with it included being admired by Western women, instead of disdained by Western men. *Ko* Samet boys were beautiful male specimens, many with very long hair and perhaps an earring or two, the perfect look to attract a Californian, Israeli, or Swedish girl. Any nationality would do, as long as she had blond hair. *Ko* Samet boys loved blond hair.

It turned out the woman had only the barest knowledge of windsurfing—as sports in Thailand were deemed suitable for men only—and her son had gone down the beach after an inner tube a tourist had let float away. Not wanting to risk losing my courage, I nonetheless followed her and a board into the water.

It didn't matter that she couldn't give me champion advice because I spent the next hour crashing into the sea after repeated attempts to balance on the board and lift the sail. Once, I managed to stay upright long enough to move four feet and for a moment forgot my broken heart.

After dragging the cumbersome board and sail back to the beach, I felt exhausted but exhilarated—and sore. My back ached from the hundred times I pulled up the sail only to lose control and tumble into the surf.

Since I wanted to try again the next day and feared a sprained muscle, I decided to get a Thai massage—the real thing, taught at temples and not related to prostitution. I'd never had one before, but I'd been accosted daily by elderly Thai women who roamed the beach offering an hour's massage for 100 *baht* ($4).

Suddenly famished, I bought squid on a stick from a huckster lugging an iron burner that dangled from a pole across his shoulders. Delicious.

After the snack, I hailed a passing masseuse, and she spread a sheet on the sand under a tree and told me to lie on my stomach. The next hour could only be described as bliss as I lay in the warm air and listened to the call of sea birds as she maneuvered my body into ecstasy.

Ah, this was life. Learning a new sport. Indulging myself with massages, videos, exotic food. I felt like a *farang* again. This was my heritage—decadence and self-indulgence. How wonderful to be a Westerner!

Christmas on *Ko* Samet held nothing denoting the holiday except a glittery green and red streamer in my bungalow lodge, which, from the dust, seemed to have been hanging there for years. Had Jek bought me a Christmas present? Did he miss me?

When a group of Swedes invited me to join them for dinner, I jumped at the offer. Christmas dinner was macaroni—Thai-style. Since Thais didn't eat pasta, it resembled macaroni by sight alone.

The only hint of celebration in the restaurant was the single "Merry Christmas" toast among the Swedes. Since they spoke to each other in Swedish, they weren't the best company for holiday cheer, but I felt so deprived without Jek that nothing could have made me less mopey. I was glad *Ko* Samet was ignorant of Western festivities and that hot weather and sand didn't inspire a holiday memory in this New Yorker. Had Jek given up on me yet? I'd be so happy to see him walking down the path with an anxious face, as if he were searching the country to find me. Not likely to happen, I had to admit, but I watched the path anyway.

Ko Samet turned out to be perfect therapy. Three videos a day, an hour of wind-surfing, a massage, sun, and swimming—a *farang*'s legacy; rehabilitation to bring me back to my *farang* senses.

On *Ko* Samet, I didn't have to concern myself with poverty and hunger or women's rights. *Ko* Samet parted me from those inequalities of life. I no longer suffered their injustices because the island reminded me I was on the side that had it all. Money wasn't a problem, and I had all the rights I wanted. There was nothing a *farang* man could do that I couldn't, and I possessed what ordinary Thais didn't—easy access to a passport, visas, and bank loans; freedom from financial responsibility for all my relatives; welfare nets so I needn't worry about starvation or unpayable medical emergencies.

From *Ko* Samet, my Bangkok woes looked petty. Why did I care if Jek had a wife? As a *farang* woman, I had the right to collect lovers, and my culture would never consider me his minor wife, no matter how Thais viewed it.

Ko Samet also brought me a revelation about my work. After a year and a half in Thailand, I had more than enough material to put an end to the Patpong research. I had visited all forty-seven go-go bars and had more prostitutes in my database than I could ever write up. Somewhere along the way, I'd forgotten this project had an end. Now I realized I could terminate the on-the-street portion of it. I could start the dissertation. I could continue following primary informants, while writing the literary review and background analysis. By this time next year, the dissertation could be finished and ready for my professors.

I could stay on *Ko* Samet and not have to expose myself to Jek. Why not work here on my portable laptop computer? I'd return periodically to Bangkok to pick up money and mail.

Nice plan. I had to go home for a night to get the computer and more clothes.

I could live without Jek. I'd write the dissertation, become expert at wind-surfing, and indulge myself in the luxuries that were my *farang* prerogative.

I left the next morning. Sitting at a table in the bus station, I looked up to see a Thai with short hair and a sexy body. "Hello you, how you do?" he said.

I recognized him as a waiter from the bungalow lodge next to mine, where I'd gone once for a video.

"Oh, hi. Are you going to Bangkok too?"

"No, they need me work every day in restaurant. I'm here for shopping."

"What's your name?"

"Toom."

Bungalow A2

253

wife. Well, that certainly didn't ingratiate him to me. I didn't tell him about his namesake.

In Bangkok, the pile of mail contained no letter or note from Jek. No flower awaited me at the door.

The result of Dudley Dapolito's AIDS test had arrived from Hong Kong. It was negative.

When the phone rang, I didn't answer it but felt better thinking Jek might still be calling. I didn't want to see him, but I wanted to know he still cared.

After retrieving the laptop from storage, with bags packed and letters answered, I was ready for an early-morning departure.

That night, as I shut the lights, I saw images of Jek everywhere I looked. The kitchen light dimmed over his bottles of *krajiep*, a pink fruit drink. In the living room, the notepad by the phone held numbers scribbled in his handwriting. His ulcer medicine sat on the bedroom dresser. Why didn't I throw it away? I couldn't, yet.

Turning the air conditioner on low before getting into bed reminded me of how he'd wake up shivering and turn it off.

No, I wasn't nearly over him. Maybe I'd have to stay away from the apartment a long time. *Ko* Samet wasn't a bad exile, though. How lucky to be a *farang* and have that option.

From a deep sleep I heard the phone ring. I panicked. Only Jek would call at that hour. I ran to the living room but didn't answer it.

I reached for the light switch and froze. Maybe he was calling from downstairs. I had to pretend I wasn't here. I ran to the curtain and peeked down at the phone in the lobby by the pool.

Jek was there. With the receiver to his ear, an intent expression covered his face as he waited for me to pick up.

I stepped back from the window. He hadn't been looking up, but I wondered if he'd notice the curtain move. I stood in the dark like a statue until the ringing stopped. Had he called earlier and found out from the switchboard I was back? Was he gone now?

I sat on the edge of the bed, then rose to go to the kitchen for a drink but realized I couldn't open the refrigerator or its light would go on. I returned to the bedroom.

The doorbell rang. I flew to the bathroom, the furthest point from the door, and sat on the tub.

Jek had to know I was in because the lock was off the door.

Two instructions fought each other throughout my body: answer the door, don't answer the door.

Could I resist him? Not if I saw him. Did I want to see him? Yes, desperately. Did I want to return to the negative feelings he aroused in me? Absolutely not.

A few minutes after the bell stopped, I tiptoed to look through the peephole.

Nobody there. I returned to the bedroom, torn anew by how much I wanted him.

Then I rushed to open the door to see if he'd left a note. Nothing. Why didn't he do something sweet to win me back?

During the bus ride to the *Ko* Samet ferry, I worried about the computer. Boarding the ferry with it would be more harrowing than usual. I couldn't throw it ahead of me, and I couldn't risk falling into the harbor with it. At the dock, I clambered successfully onboard, then worried about disembarking. Worrying was good for me; it took my mind off regretting I hadn't answered the door for Jek.

Two weeks later, I knew I'd made the right decision. I spent mornings at a rattan table under a palm tree typing. Writing the history of women's status in Thailand put Patpong in perspective for me.

Prostitution in Thailand was directly connected to the position of women in society. Thai society created prostitutes and minor wives because they were a man's right and male status symbols. The right to sexual expression belonged to men alone. Women were to be chaste and available for sex to one man only. Thailand's 1805 Law of the Three Seals had spelled out three categories of wives: the major wife, the minor wife, and the slave wife. Slavery in Thailand was abolished in 1905, which led to the flourishing of the prostitution industry for Thai men. In modern Thailand, it was accepted and expected for them to have major and minor wives and to frequent prostitutes.

The story of Patpong women was related to the worldwide struggle for women's rights, especially the right to promiscuous sex. The morality of repressed female sexuality plus ideas of maleness created prostitutes. The fact that only men had the right to be sexual made sex a recreation for them, a reward, expected behavior, required proof of virility, a need. Assembly-line blow jobs were a quick way to affirm the latitude of masculinity. On Patpong, sexual release wasn't the sole objective. Market sex was a symbol of privilege.

For *farang* men caught in intense emotional relationships with Thai prostitutes, another factor was at work—an Eliza Doolittle syndrome. The *farang* become obsessed with "saving" a woman and turning her into a lady. He wanted to protect her from the vagaries of life. He tried to implant in her the values of his culture, like the work ethic and the quest for knowledge. He helped her in her self-sacrificing commitment to help her family. Western storybooks and video games emphasize the hero saving a maiden in distress. Patpong and Thailand presented Western men with the ingredients to play out that scenario. As rich Westerners, they were viewed as something special. Then, believing their culture to be superior, they used Western ideology as a tool for rescue. Beyond feelings of love, and long after romance died, men felt compelled to live out ideals they may or may not have practiced back home. Honesty, trustworthiness, and notions of Christian charity guaranteed that Western men continued to send money and support for long periods of time. They lived out the role of hero.

Was some of that involved in my relationship with Jek? I'd played those same video games. I'd dreamed of saving a handsome man in distress. I'd had the urge to rescue Jek from his difficult existence, only I'd been prevented from doing so by cultural attitudes that limited how much a woman could spend on a man.

Prostitution in Thailand was the result of a skewed male-female relationship and its unequal power and resource structure. Patpong prostitution involved racism and classism as much as sexism. While the younger, newly arrived *farangs* lived out Eliza Doolittle fantasies, the long-term residents—expectations of grateful adoration dashed—underwent a change. Jaded old-timers displayed overt sexist and racist leanings, seeing themselves as demigods being serviced by inferiors. They adopted Thai men's right to have major and minor involvements with various women.

Then there were the *farang* men who came to Thailand specifically to find a wife. Bangkok marriage agencies advertised the submissiveness of Thai women to attract them, the same way cheap and passive laborers in the Third World were used to attract capitalist investors. The Friends of Women organization warned Thai women about such marriages, where brides were taken to foreign countries to be housekeepers and childbearers. Sometimes their "husbands" prevented them from learning the language in order to keep them housebound and dependent.

Ultimately, the issue was dominance—sexual, social, and economic.

Finished with the morning's work, I went next door for lunch and a chat with Toom. Because he had Jek's wife's name, I felt connected to Jek as well as unfaithful to him. It felt avenging to have a Toom of my own.

Noon's breeze rustled palm leaves, announcing it was my time for windsurfing. In late afternoon, the stronger wind flapped a white flag that alerted *Ko* Samet boys of their time. They preferred hurricanes but settled for the winds of sunset.

I changed into a bathing suit and left for the equipment shack. The Thai woman who worked there knew me now and charged me a discounted price, $3 an hour. I helped her drag a board to the water's edge and steadied it as she hammered in the sail with a fallen coconut.

With the board bobbing over waves, I climbed on and seized the sail's rope. Before pulling up the mast, I gazed the length of the beach. What a paradise. Only a few open-air restaurants could be seen along the coastline. All else appeared to be pure, untouched nature. *Ko* Samet was a small island. That hateful ferry could cruise right around it in under two hours. Though the island had many tourists, they were spread out, leaving the shoreline relatively empty. On weekends this changed, with hundreds of vacationing Thais pouring in and staking orange and blue plastic tents back to back on the sand.

My sail caught the wind and I leaned back, countering the force, as the board took off in the direction of Cambodia. Water sloshed my feet, and I could feel my ponytail flutter behind me. Still a novice, I knew that when I reached the rocky point and wanted to turn, I'd end up face down in the sea; but rushing out from shore was pure exhilaration.

This racy delight was payment for Jek. I'd made a bargain with myself: I'd give up Jek in exchange for windsurfing. It was a good deal. My body felt alive and alert as muscles strained with new firmness and tone. I felt joy as I sped with the wind. Next time I returned to Bangkok, I'd throw away the bottle of ulcer medicine.

Writing the Dissertation on *Ko* Samet

28.

* The land of Isan is cracking
     and our hearts are breaking

Is this our sin or karma . . .
     Is this our sin or karma . . .

That Isan should suffer so . . . Oh

Brothers and sisters have to turn their backs
     Brothers and sisters have to turn their backs
     Leaving their homes and the paddy fields heading for the city

To the city to sell their labor
     With little education not even Primary Four

Hopeless for a good job
     Hopeless for a good job
     Fighting and kicking just to be a coolie

It hurts the more you think
     Of father and mother, brothers and sisters left behind
     Of what have become of them, what have become of them
     But we can only keep on wondering . . .

Narrator: Young men and women, from Isan, North and South, have escaped the heartbreaking poverty and come to find refuge in the city. Many of them are brought by fate to the street of Patpong, the so-called sin strip. These people become Patpong people, with happiness to sell, even if only to be a part-time lover.

Music: "Part-time Lover"
From the Patpong musical presented by Empower, 1987

On a trip to Bangkok, I decided to invite Hoi for a weekend on Samet Island.

Alex answered the phone, and I discussed it with him first. "See if you can find her a job there," he said. "There's no work in Bangkok she'll agree to. Maybe she'll like it on the island. She can be a waitress and work with foreigners. Her English is really good now."

"I'll see if anything's available."

When Alex asked Hoi if she wanted to go, I heard excitement in her reply.

The next morning, Hoi picked me up and we *tuk-tuk*ed to the bus station. She appeared thrilled about the trip and said, "I hope I find boyfriend on *Ko* Samet."

I noticed her cheeks glow with the possibility and wondered how to ask her about Alex, the boyfriend she already had. Then I decided not to say anything that might seem judgmental. I'd leave her to follow her instincts and watch where they took her.

When we passed the Australian Embassy, she remarked, "I sleep there one night with man."

Her brows lowered, so I guessed it was an encounter without pleasant memories—except that it took place in the Australian Embassy, a beautiful, burnt-yellow structure.

"I meet him when work at Rififi."

"Alex asked me to see if I could find you a job on Samet, " I said.

Hoi turned her head to the passing street. It was clear she hadn't the least interest in this. She even seemed offended that Alex would seriously want her to work. She changed the subject by showing me recent pictures of her niece Ah.

I noticed Ah wasn't smiling and didn't look happy, a change from the pictures I had of her in Ubon. I asked, "Why does she look so glum? Where is she?"

"She now in Bangkok. My sister Na cook food at factory that make jewelry."

"Where do they live?"

"In factory. Ah work there too. She baby sit for 600 *baht* one month." Hoi made a disgusted face. "Toilet smell bad."

Hoi's nose must have become Westernized, I thought, remembering Ubon.

"How's it going with Alex?" I asked, figuring enough time had passed since her comment about finding a boyfriend.

"Last week we have fight. I pack bag and stay overnight with Na. Next day I go back, Alex say he cry all night for me." Hoi looked pleased.

At the bus station, we stopped for reading material. I noticed Hoi fuss with the shopping bag she used as a suitcase. She looked like she was stealing comics. She'd put them in her bag, then take them out when she caught me watching.

When we arrived at the dock, I approached the ferry with trepidation. I seemed to dread it more each time I boarded. Hoi took it in stride, though, as if hazards without safety precautions were a normal way of life.

Clambering to the boat with pounding heart, I felt vindicated for my fear when I saw a tourist drop her Gucci bag as she extended her leg to board. Splash. The ferry had no crew except the pilot, and he shrugged when she beseeched him to do something about her fallen property. If she wanted it back, she'd have to go after it herself.

While she argued with him, the pilot smiled. Thais responded that way to angry foreigners. It was their reaction to the embarrassment of someone yelling, which Thais never did. Foreigners didn't understand and mistook the smile as insensitivity or mockery. As the tourist's ranting grew louder, we watched her bag sink from sight. Finally the woman climbed off the boat, and we left without her. None of the other passengers believed she'd ever see her Gucci again.

I thought of the lawsuits the ferry could have generated in the West. In

Thailand, you couldn't sue for liability.

It turned out to be a university holiday, and young Thai people swarmed the beaches of *Ko* Samet. When Hoi and I got off the truck and spotted them, Hoi complained, "Too many Thai people. I don't like Thai people."

How could she not like her compatriots? Here was a mystery for me to unravel.

As we approached the bungalow lodge, Hoi saw a couple she knew, a *farang* man and a Thai woman, sitting in the restaurant. Hoi didn't want them to notice her and pulled me behind plants to avoid them.

"Who are they?" I whispered as we crouched in the foliage.

"Man named Bob. His girlfriend is Fun. I know Fun from Rififi. We worked together."

I had no idea why she didn't want to meet them. The weekend might prove informative if I could figure it all out.

The lodge was filled with Thais on holiday. After establishing ourselves in a bungalow, we changed for the beach. Hoi wore a peach bathing suit. She'd lost weight and looked perfect.

"Alex make me diet," she explained. "He call me fat."

"I've gained seven pounds since I've been here," I told her.

"You still skinny."

I couldn't wait to windsurf. I'd been telling Hoi how much I loved it, and now, as she helped me drag a board to the water, she said she wanted to try. I'd never seen a Thai woman windsurf before.

I made two short runs to show her how it was done and then cruised back. Fearlessly, she climbed

With Hoi on *Ko* Samet

on and sailed off. I was shocked. I wondered if this daring was related to working Patpong. Did some poor women not become prostitutes because they lacked the courage? Hoi's audacity was also remarkable in view of the fact that she couldn't swim. She didn't go far, though, since she was headed toward the beach.

I heard her call out, "Bob!" She'd windsurfed into the couple she'd tried to avoid.

I swam after her, and she introduced me to Bob and Fun. The word *fun* meant "rain" in Thai and, with its rising tone, sounded like "Fun?" The three of them were chatting amiably as I put the sail in gear and left them.

In the late afternoon, I took Hoi for a fruit drink so that I could visit Toom. When he had a lull in orders, he sat with us. I noticed he wasn't initiating conversation with Hoi and answered her questions minimally.

"How long you work on *Ko* Samet?" she asked him.

"Two year," he answered and looked away.

261

Toom knew the subject of my research, and I guessed he assumed Hoi was a Patpong woman. He, like many Thai men, had displayed repugnance toward prostitutes—toward socializing with them, that is. His father had taken him to a brothel to introduce him to sex when he was a teenager. Apparently, sleeping with them was okay but being civil to them was not. I knew Thai men went out of their way to show their disapproval of prostitutes, but I couldn't believe Toom would insult someone who was in my company.

The strain between them grew, and I worried that one would say something offensive to the other.

After Toom left to fetch someone a papaya shake, Bob and Fun happened by and joined us. Fun and Hoi spoke in Thai, and Bob and I became acquainted.

"Have you and Fun been together long?" I asked him.

"I just returned to Thailand last week after being away a year. Before that, I lived in Bangkok eighteen months."

"You were working there?"

"A friend and I opened a lounge near Patpong. It didn't have bar girls, though, and never got off the ground. We had to sell it."

"Then what did you do?"

"Before Thailand, I was an engineer with a helicopter company based in the Falkland Islands. When the bar failed, I went back to that. I'm only here now on

a two-week vacation. It's taken me this long to save the money to see Fun again."

At sunset, Hoi and I took a walk, and she complained again about the numerous Thai people and how she didn't like Thais. She seemed angry that they were there and maybe afraid of them. Was she worried that they'd snub her the way Toom had?

That night we joined Bob and Fun for dinner. Hoi and Fun gossiped about Patpong.

Fun, Bob, and Hoi

Hoi told Fun about Alex. "He handsome and have good body." She turned to me for confirmation. "Is true, right?" When I nodded, she described the fight they'd had recently and how Alex didn't go to work because he was so upset.

Hoi asked Fun if she'd ever been out of the country.

"Yes, once to Hong Kong."

I wondered if she went there with a man or to work in a brothel.

"I never leave Thailand yet," Hoi said, "but I fly on airplane two time when man take me to Phuket."

Hoi and Fun spoke about not wearing make-up anymore. Fun, who no longer worked Patpong, hadn't worn any in five months.

On Saturday morning, Hoi, Fun, and I went to the beach. Bob had sun poisoning from the day before and stayed in bed. Fun spread a towel and lay on her stomach in the sun.

Hoi dragged her chair under an umbrella and said, "I hate black skin." Both Fun and Hoi covered themselves with sun block.

"When did you meet Bob?" I asked Fun.

"Three year ago. I was fifteen, working at Rififi. I stopped work to live with Bob. He sent me for English lesson and to hairdressing school."

"How old is Bob?"

"Thirty now."

Fun looked great in her black bikini, and her English was pretty good. I wondered if Bob was satisfied with how his Eliza Doolittle had turned out. I thought she carried herself well; I'd give him a gold star.

After a dip in the sea, Hoi and I noticed the name "Hoi" written in the sand in Thai letters. We shrugged it off, thinking someone else had the name.

Later, when we returned to our bungalow for a nap, we heard the name "Hoi" called repeatedly and again assumed someone else had the name. But then "Hoi-Hoi" sounded near our window. A head popped up. It belonged to a young Thai about sixteen.

"Have you been calling me?" Hoi asked him.

"Yes," he admitted.

"Did you write her name in the sand?" I asked.

He admitted that too. He appeared intrigued by Hoi. "I ask Fun for your name."

Hoi seemed to swell with pleasure. Not long after he left, an older Thai man came to the window. Hoi didn't discourage him either. She didn't mention hating these Thai people, I noticed.

That evening, I dressed in an off-the-shoulder playsuit with scalloped shorts. Hoi looked at me wistfully and said, "Alex make me throw away my sexy clothes. I miss those clothes."

We joined Fun and Bob in the restaurant. An Israeli woman recognized me from Kao San Road and sat with us. Hoi and Fun stared at her shapely biceps.

"Did you just get out of the army?" I asked her.

"Army?" exclaimed Fun. "Woman in Israel are in the army?"

"Of course. It is our duty to our country. Now I want to relax for a year. I want to travel."

"Where are you going after Thailand?" I asked her.

"The Philippines."

"Israel people like Philippine," Hoi remarked, probably remembering Shlomo had gone there with Sumalee.

"Not many countries give visas to Israeli citizens. Countries with ties to Arabs don't recognize Israel and don't have Israeli embassies. Thailand and the Philippines do. That's why there's so many of us here. I wanted to go to India, but my application was rejected."

Fun nodded her head. "Is difficult with Thai passport too. Two time, they wouldn't let me in Hong Kong. First time, okay. Other time, they send me back to Bangkok."

"Were you traveling alone?" I asked.

"Yes."

I remembered the estimated number of Thai women working overseas in brothels—200,000 in Europe, 50,000 in Japan. For that reason, countries were suspicious of lone Thai women as travellers.

By the cashier we noticed a dark-skinned Thai.

"Who is more black?" Hoi asked us. "That girl or me?"

Bob said, "It's close, but she's darker." I didn't think Hoi was anywhere near as dark and knew she'd dislike his reply. I didn't find her dark at all. With my tan I was darker than Hoi.

At 10:30 p.m., Hoi and I went to meet Toom. In the past, Toom had told me he went to the discotheque after work and asked if I wanted to go. I'd never joined him because I went to bed early to wake early and write. Now, with Hoi, I decided to accept his offer. I knew I'd be up late anyway.

While we waited for him to finish filling sugar jars and bottles of imitation ketchup, we sat at a table. Suddenly Hoi declared, "I hate my black skin. I hate myself." She balled her hands into fists and said with deep hard feeling, "I HAAAATE IT!"

Her passion moved me almost to tears. I couldn't believe she'd been dwelling on that.

"I'm ugly," she said, staring at nothing, seemingly absorbed in self-hatred.

"You're beautiful."

"No, I'm horrible. And fat."

"You're not!"

She didn't believe me. "I like your white face," she said in a whisper. "I want your face."

Since arriving on *Ko* Samet, she'd frequently pointed to any blond woman, no matter how old or ugly, and said, "Beautiful." Had coming to Samet confronted her with the lifestyle of *farang*s and her reality as a Patpong woman from Isan?

I felt bad for her and didn't know how to convince her she was ravishing.

When Toom came for us, we set out for the disco along the beach.

Hoi asked him, "Who go there—Thai people or *farang*?"

"Thai."

She didn't like hearing that. "I hate Thai people," she told him and seemed about to stop walking. Maybe going with Toom wasn't such a good idea. In truth, I'd been thinking of myself. I'd wanted to spend time with him. Maybe I should have considered Hoi's feelings first.

We walked on. Hoi seemed expectant of something unpleasant.

The seaside disco was outdoors with Western music blasting a dancing beat.

We sat at a table in the sand.

When Hoi went to the toilet, Toom asked me, "Is she from Patpong?" I nodded, and he said, "I know right away." He shook his head in contempt. "I couldn't take a woman like that to my family."

"Where are you from?"

"Just outside Bangkok on the sea. My father is fisherman. My family not rich, but honorable."

Toom didn't dance but liked to drink. He bought himself a small bottle of the Thai liquor Mekong. Hoi and I danced, and when we returned to the table, I made sure I sat between Hoi and Toom. I liked it that way anyway. My arm touched Toom's across our armrests. I felt a sexual surge from the contact.

"How old are you?" Hoi asked him.

"Twenty-three."

I wondered if she'd asked him that to put him in his place. Age meant status in Thailand, and making him admit being younger than my "twenty-seven" lost him points.

Back at the bungalow, Hoi complained that Toom didn't speak to her. I denied it by saying he'd been drunk but knew it was true. I also knew that I hadn't thought of Jek once the whole time with Toom.

On Sunday morning, Hoi slept late. I left to hide and write notes and returned to find the hut packed with Thai males sitting on the bed, standing by the doorway, and hanging in the windows. Hoi held court in the center, painting my red nail polish on one boy's finger. She didn't seem to hate these Thais either. Maybe she only hated the ones she feared would disapprove of her. Her face radiated as she said, "O, come in, sit."

Hoi joked with one young Thai, named Bom, who looked twelve but was fourteen. She paid constant attention to Bom and touched him often.

When her entourage heard Hoi and I were going to the beach, they decided to go too.

Settling on the sand, I asked Hoi, "Want to try windsurfing again?" She was so involved with her admirers that she didn't answer. "I'd like to take a picture of you windsurfing," I said, brushing across two Thais to tap her elbow. From her quick glance at me, I knew she was no longer interested in the sport. "Let me just take the picture, okay?"

She followed me but offered no help with the board. Five Thai boys formed a circle around her.

"Get on," I said to her. "I'll go get the camera."

By the time I came back, Hoi sat perched on the board while the boys held it like royal servants with a portable throne.

"I'm ready," I said. Hoi seemed reluctant to budge, and I figured she didn't want to fall and wet her hair.

Finally she stood, but this time there was no quick sailing away. She couldn't even pull up the mast.

I yelled to the boys, "Let go! Let go! The board can't move if you hold onto it. Step back."

They refused to let go; they didn't want their Hoi to sail away. With two of them in front, two in back, and one grasping Hoi's legs, she'd have no windsurfing that day.

I consoled myself with pictures of Hoi and her fan club and then sailed off myself.

When I returned, Hoi and her followers were nowhere in sight. I

Hoi on Windsurfing Board

found them in the restaurant. Fun had joined them. Hoi looked the happiest I'd ever seen her.

Hoi Next to Bom

She took hold of Bom's wrist and told me, "He no act like fourteen, right? Look at him smoke cigarette." He smiled at her adoringly.

Since we were due to return to Bangkok that afternoon, we soon had to go pack. Bom accompanied us.

I left them a moment to say goodbye to Toom. I waited till he served a trayful of banana pancakes. Then I told him, "I'm leaving for Bangkok."

"I'm going to Bangkok too, on Wednesday. I make interview for army."

"You're enlisting?"

"No! All Thai man must report. My family pay money and is finished."

"They'll bribe someone to get you out?"

"All my friend do like that."

"Well, come see me in Bangkok, if you want. Here's my card."

He took it and gave me a long look. "I think I have to telephone you," he said.

I ran back to Hoi, energized by the possibility of Toom's visit.

During the three-hour bus ride to Bangkok, Hoi spoke continually about Bom.

"Bom is from Ayuthaya, north of Bangkok," she told me. She speculated on what he might be doing at that moment and told me what he planned to do that night. "I'm in love," she declared. "I'm in love with Bom."

Then she said, "Fun no want me leave *Ko* Samet. She ask me to stay with her and Bob. But I say no. I say I have responsibility to go back with you."

Hoi appeared proud to display this example of correct behavior. I remembered how she'd abandoned me in Ubon, and I imagined the lessons in etiquette Alex had given her.

Across the aisle sat a Thai couple. Hoi, sitting by the window, leaned over to point them out and declare the woman beautiful. After the couple went to sleep in each other's arms, Hoi repeatedly leaned over to watch them sleep. She stared openly, and I felt her longing for that kind of communion. Living with a foreigner, she must have hungered for a closeness she couldn't have.

For the first time, I realized how locked-out she was from her culture. Though her beauty attracted admirers aplenty, she didn't have the means to involve herself with a Thai man like the girl across the aisle could. Hoi supported herself and her father by living with *farang*s. She also knew most Thai men wouldn't associate with a prostitute. Her only salvation came from convincing herself that she hated Thais, therefore it was she who was rejecting them.

Before reaching Bangkok, Hoi decided not to return immediately to Alex. She wanted to stay overnight with her sister.

The next morning, Alex called me distraught. "Where's Hoi?" He was devastated that she hadn't returned the night before.

That day he had nine hours of teaching. He asked if Hoi had mentioned plans for her future, such as a job.

"No."

"Did she mention going to school?"

"No."

He sighed.

Hoi called. She told me her niece Ah and her sister Na had loved the shell souvenirs I'd bought for them on Samet. "Na say thank you."

I was positive Na would never have thought to send thanks and that this was another example of Alex's training.

29.

Brown (1977: 1) from the U.S. organization Black Women for Wages for Housework wrote:

> *Part of the job of being a prostitute is to be used as a sign to other women of where the bottom is—to be labeled a whore and an unfit mother, . . . a loose woman. So that part of the work of being a prostitute is to be made an example of what it costs us to refuse the poverty, . . . to be the whip against other women to make sure that they strive always to be "respectable" though poor. And this means that part of the work of being a prostitute must also be living with not only the contempt but the envy of other women for having the little bit of money, the little bit of independence, that they don't have.*

Two and a half months after my first trip to *Ko* Samet, the self-indulgent fare of windsurfing, massages, pseudo-European food, and videos brought me back to my decadent American self. That and the *Ko* Samet boys. There's nothing like the attention of a little cutie to induce revival.

Returning from another weekend in Bangkok, I lunged again onto the ferry. After two days away from the island, I grew excited at the prospect of seeing my new boyfriend, Toom. Toom and I had been together three weeks now, since the time he'd come to Bangkok to bribe himself out of army duty. I hoped no Norwegian beauty had taken possession of him in my absence. Friendly Toom joked with all the girls as he served them *saté*, octopus, or tea. He was a *Ko* Samet boy.

When I arrived at the beach, I eagerly anticipated the first glimpse of him. There he was. He deposited a plate of soup in front of a blond in a metallic-green bikini. He said something I couldn't hear and made his "Hae-ae-ae" laugh. Drunk as always, I surmised as I looked over the blond. Then I noticed the mustachioed guy next to her who tasted a spoonful of her soup. Good, she wasn't a rival.

Toom grinned in delight when he saw me. "Hello, my honey," he said.

"Here I am," I announced. "Still alive after that miserable excuse of a ferry. How are you?"

"I have happiness now my girlfriend come."

Toom wore typical *Ko* Samet boy attire—colorful knee-length shorts imprint-

269

ed with the word *AWESOME*, a T-shirt with the Canadian maple leaf, and no shoes.

"Can you get off work for a while?" I asked.

"Four o'clock I make break. You come for me?"

I glanced at the white flag and noted, "Wind looks good. I'll pick you up at four and we'll windsurf."

"See you soon, my dearest honey."

As I moved off, I leaned into him and pushed him slightly with my shoulder. Though Thais felt uncomfortable showing affection in public, Toom was used to it—much more than Jek had been; he was a *Ko* Samet boy.

Since the journey from Bangkok had eaten up much of the day, I had just enough time to check into A2 before changing into a bathing suit and leaving for the equipment shack.

I'd become fairly adept at windsurfing, though when the wind blew hard I was down more than up. I knew to head for shore if I saw the *Ko* Samet boys leave their jobs and run for their boards. Their arrival forecasted fierce winds. During those times, it was impossible to get service on the island. All the waiters, truck drivers, and souvenir vendors were out at sea.

After a short ride across the bay, I whisked by the umbrella-dotted area of Toom's restaurant and recognized a speck on the beach as Toom. I pointed the mast down, flipped the sail over, and headed inland.

Toom was in the water when I steered near. I slid off and moved to the front of the board. Toom jumped on. He always piloted when we rode together. As I sat cross-legged on the nose of the board, he pulled up the sail and swept us into motion.

Through the wind, I heard him laugh, "Hae-ae-ae" and declare, *"Mao! Mao pai!"* (I'm drunk, I'm too drunk!) However, Toom, like all *Ko* Samet boys, was an excellent windsurfer, and I never feared that the mast would clunk on my head. Had it been the reverse, with me standing and Toom sitting, he'd have had a concussion before long.

I loved when we windsurfed together. Since my research dealt with Western men who paraded their Thai girlfriends as prizes of womanhood—women who knew the real way to treat a man—being with Toom afforded me revenge. I knew the Western guys on the beach watching us wouldn't approve. *Ko* Samet was loaded with Western women with Thai boyfriends. I loved it. What a switch!

On the other hand, sitting at the front of the board was not the best way to experience the sport, with waves slamming me in the face.

When we were far from shore, beyond where that wretched ferry passed, we stopped and sat on the board, looking at the wondrous view. I put my arms around Toom's neck. We kissed.

"Who are yooooooou?" he asked when we broke apart. He often said that at intimate moments, and I wondered who'd taught it to him and what was its original context.

"Who are yooooooou?" I answered back, having never figured out a more

270

appropriate response.

The sun burned hot on our skins, and he splashed water over my shoulders, cooing, "My sweetie pie honey."

Too soon, we started back; Toom had to return to work. He began at seven in the morning and served food till eleven at night. For this he received a basic salary of 1,800 *baht* ($72) a month. But *Ko* Samet boys loved their lives there. Work was a small part of it. Water sports and Western women were the rest.

"I stay away too long. My boss will angry me," said Toom as we glided to a stop before the restaurant. "You come tonight at eleven, okay my honey?"

"For sure." We gave each other a parting kiss. He phoned me nightly when I was in Bangkok and knew how to keep me happy and fulfilled. "See you later," I said.

"Not if I see you first," Toom answered as he swam away. "Hae-ae-ae. We play hard to get." *Ko* Samet boys frequently uttered snappy sayings they'd picked up from tourists without having a clue as to what they meant.

That night, when I met him, Toom led me to a table occupied by a tanned guy with curly hair. "Here, keep your company with my buddy system, my pal Beer," Toom told me.

"Beer?"

"Pierre," said the *farang* with a tolerant smile.

"Beer come from Belgium. He make vacation in Thailand. This is my girl-friend Creo, my honey bunches."

Toom didn't sit with me at Pierre's table, but he drank from a glass there. Toom always found himself a pal among the restaurant's clientele. When one pal's vacation ended, he never had trouble finding a new one. Toom's quick laugh attracted immediate friendship from visiting tourists. Of all the waiters, he was the jolliest and most outgoing—helped, I'm sure, by the Mekong his pals bought him, which he swigged at continually. Toom would show them the island, and the foreigners would pay for the Mekong that Toom's small salary couldn't cover. These pals and benefactors were always male. *Ko* Samet boys adhered to the belief that a man should pay for a woman. When we'd first gotten together, the time he'd come to Bangkok, I couldn't persuade Toom to ride in the taxi I'd pay for instead of the bus he'd pay for, and I'd dined on rice when I hankered for steak. *Ko* Samet boys did accept gifts from women, though, which left them dripping with jewelry and trinkets, wearing T-shirts advertising the Heineken brewery in Amsterdam or a Road Runner's Bagel Run, and possessing colossal assortments of stuffed animals.

One by one, the restaurant's lights extinguished, and by the time Toom came for us, Pierre and I sat in the dark. I'd have preferred to be with Toom alone. But after a whole day of Mekong, Toom was now at his friendliest. He also needed a pal along to pick up the tab.

The three of us walked by the sea to the discotheque. I loved to dance. Toom loved to drink. Going to the disco was perfect for me—while Toom drank, I danced under stars, fishy breeze in my hair, sea stretched before me, a blessed existence.

271

Unfortunately, Toom didn't like me dancing by myself or with the occasional guy who joined me.

So I hadn't been on the dance floor longer than a Pink Floyd song and a Michael Jackson song before Toom had me and Pierre back on the beach on our way to another seaside bar, this one packed with *Ko* Samet boys and their foreign girlfriends, all blond and looking gigantic next to the small-boned Thais. *Ko* Samet boys seemed to prefer their girlfriends big and tall. Two inches shorter than Toom and about five pounds lighter, I almost felt out of place.

Toom greeted everyone and pulled Pierre and me to a table where a bunch of *Ko* Samet boys knotted around a sad-looking one. "Beer, Creo, meet my pal Lek. He just back from Sweden."

Lek gave us a watery-eyed nod and continued his talk with the *Ko* Samet boys who surrounded him protectively. I could understand what he said, but Toom translated Lek's Thai into English for Pierre. A year ago, Toom explained, Lek had had a Swedish girlfriend. After she returned home, they'd kept in touch by mail, and Lek learned that she was pregnant. He sold his windsurfing board and borrowed money to join her and the twins she gave birth to in Sweden. Now here he was back in *Ko* Samet, having just arrived that morning.

"By the time I arrived in Sweden," Lek told his listeners, "she had a new boyfriend." The *Ko* Samet boys shook their heads and mumbled about the fickleness of foreign women. I noticed that they didn't call them "bad," though, the way they would have called a Thai woman. They accepted the fact that foreign women were as likely to play around as Thai men. The *Ko* Samet boys offered Lek consoling words. Their blond girlfriends, not understanding, looked from one to the other with a raised eyebrow or half a smile.

"She and her mother were not interested in a Thai boy," Lek continued. "They let me see my two daughters only once. Beautiful babies—half Thai, half Swedish."

Toom poured himself some of the Mekong Pierre had ordered and told Pierre, "Girl have new boyfriend already. Very butterfly."

"I found a job cleaning apartments," Lek said. "So much money! I thought I was rich for sure. But Sweden too expensive. The money was not enough to live."

A *Ko* Samet boy—with a gold pendant around his neck from the Tivoli Gardens in Copenhagen—banged his Singha beer on his armrest. His blond girlfriend looked at him questioningly, patted his hand, and said something in Danish to her friend across the table.

"He no can make money there," Toom translated. "Europe not for Thai boy. Only job cleaning floor."

"One day you go high up," Lek said. "Next day, fall very hard."

Toom nodded agreement and stared out to sea.

"I know a Thai who went to live abroad," I told Toom. "A Muslim named Sumalee. She married an Israeli." I laughed and said, "I wonder what religion she is now."

Toom looked depressed as he commented, "I think Thai people can only live in Thailand. Other country no want us."

Pierre poured more Mekong into Toom's glass. The two Danish girls went off to the toilet hut. Somebody yelled to the bartender to play a Bob Marley tape. *Ko* Samet boys loved Bob Marley.

When I pried Toom loose from the Mekong, he came to stay with me in A2.

Toom left early in the morning to prepare the restaurant for breakfast, and I went to work on my next chapter. I was just finishing my analysis of prostitution in Thailand.

Prostitution is never an ideal profession. But given the male-female situation in Thailand and the state of its economy, prostitute women did gain more power, independence, and chances for a better life than their parents had or than many women of their same background had. They faced opposition and supported families in the countryside; these Thai women were the front legs of the elephant.

I realized, though, that the prostitutes themselves didn't necessarily agree. Looking at prostitution as providing the women with independence and power was looking at something Thais didn't see or didn't value. Independence, for instance, had no role in the structure of their society. Living alone was usually something to be avoided.

So, while Patpong prostitution offered benefits to the women, it may have benefitted me more than them. Their breaking from traditional behavior helped the cause of women in general but not the specific women who had to deal with society's condemnation of them and the possibility of contracting AIDS. Though Hoi received admiration from her neighbors in Ubon and respect from her father for supporting him, she felt Thailand as a whole rejected her. Dudley Dapolito's girlfriend, Sow, had flaunted her rich clothes and jewelry to her ex-husband but couldn't tell him how she'd made the money.

The fact remained that Thai women lacked the right to possess their sexuality the way Thai men (or foreign women) did. Promiscuity marked them as ruined, spoiled, or just plain bad.

They also suffered the isolation of living with foreigners. Though the goal of some was to marry a *farang* and move to a rich country, they often returned to Thailand after a few years. They hated being in strange places and feeling they didn't belong there either.

I remembered Lek from the night before. A relationship with a Thai, male or female, was exotic and adventuresome in a foreign land. Having the Thai in one's home country was a different matter altogether.

Each day at sunset, I went to Toom's restaurant for a snack and to practice for the *bau hok* language exam. My teacher had given me essay questions from past years, and I answered one a day. When Toom had time, he sat with me and corrected my grammar.

"What year is this in Thailand?" I asked him as I wrote an essay on Songkran, the Thai New Year festival. "I forgot."

"Buddhist year two thousand, five hundred, and thirty-two," he answered.

At the end of the week, I packed for Bangkok. Though Toom wasn't supposed to leave work during busy lunch hours, he always accompanied me to the dock. We walked there, of course. I knew Toom would be unhappy if I talked him into letting me pay the fare for the truck.

At the ferry, Toom held my bag as I crawled on a pillar, leapt, and landed in the boat on one knee. Toom boarded effortlessly. Behind him, a *Ko* Samet woman with a cloth-wrapped bundle of fish in one arm and a baby in the other stepped in the boat with no more concern than someone getting off an escalator.

Come to think of it, in Bangkok I'd witnessed country Thais approach the escalator in Siam Center with undisguised terror. That was fair, I thought—they couldn't master the escalator, and I couldn't master their ferry.

Seeing the boatman hadn't arrived yet, Toom sat with me. "My heart is missing you already, honey my dearest tootsie."

"I'll be back soon." I didn't grab him and hug him as I wanted to. I knew the Thais at the pier were friends of Toom's boss, and no matter how accustomed they were to foreigners' behavior, it was still not deemed proper for males and females to touch in public.

Toom looked silently at the wooden slats in the boat's floor. Then he presented me with a mango that he pulled from his pocket. He knew I loved mangoes. I knew the mango was his lunch. That and a plate of rice was all the waiters got for the noon meal.

In a sudden movement, Toom grabbed me and wrapped me in his arms. "I will have sadness until I see your face again," he said.

He always knew the right thing to say. He'd probably taken many foreign girlfriends to the ferry for a goodbye. He knew us well. He was a *Ko* Samet boy.

30.

Oftentimes, prostitution is the only alternative to starvation; in particular societies, it may be the only alternative to an oppressive marriage. Rosen (1982) says prostitution, as described by the women themselves, is easier and more lucrative than other jobs available to them. To Beirut prostitutes, it represents sutrah, *protection and shelter (Khalaf, 1965), while to many child prostitutes it is the only escape from an abusive home life (Sereny, 1985).*

Writing about prostitution in Asia over fifty years ago, de Leeuw (1934) cites examples from various countries where families sold their daughters into the trade when faced with deprivation and starvation. In Yokohama after every natural disaster, he reports, agents went looking to buy new "JuJu" for cheap prices. In 1933 Hong Kong during a season of famine, the Relief Commission estimated that two million people were likely to die and that the "price of girls is now $1 per year of age" (Ibid.: 85). It was later reported that 25,443 females were sold from one small district alone.

In Bangkok, I went to Patpong, still taking the long way to avoid Jek. I wasn't up to seeing him yet. Even with Toom and windsurfing, I didn't trust myself in his bewitching presence.

Though I'd been away less than three months, Patpong had changed. New bars had opened, a new drugstore, another disco, and a 7-11 on the corner of Surawong and Patpong 1. A new beer bar had female boxers. All the ripoff bars had changed names, and I remembered Jek telling me that when his ripoff bar became too well-known it gave itself a clean new name.

I visited Nok at Queen's Castle.

"I have baby," she said, patting her stomach and seeming ecstatic about it.

"How many months?" I asked.

She held up one finger.

"Have you been to a doctor?"

She shook her head.

I didn't know what more to say about the doctor without sounding skeptical of her pregnancy or critical of her lack of medical care; and I stopped myself from mentioning the fortune teller who'd told her she couldn't have a baby. Instead, I asked, "Will you have to quit your job?"

"No, when grow too big I work reception."

I also didn't know how to ask who the father was. How could she know? I said, "Is Moon happy about it?"

"Yes. Next year we marry."

When I met Nok often, she treated me like a friend, inviting me out with her customers so I wouldn't have to pay. But whenever I didn't see her for a few weeks, she'd return to her hustle mode when next we met. Now her con was in full force. When I offered to take her to *Ko* Samet, she insisted two nights were not enough.

"You pay bar for three night," she said. "Or I no have time to get ready for work."

"Yes, you will. We'll be back early afternoon."

"I too tired to work when come back."

"You can sleep on the bus."

She tried several tactics before dropping the idea. Then she said, "Moon come too."

"No way! I can't pay for another person. We'd need another bungalow. I can't, really. Just the two of us."

"Moon won't like me go alone."

I found this hard to believe. He'd prefer she worked with other men than be with me? I knew Nok was trying to scam me into giving them a vacation together.

I said positively NO.

The soonest she could get away was the weekend, so I spent the next few days in one-on-one lessons with my Thai teacher. At night, I talked on the phone with Toom.

"I miss you, my honey bunches," he'd say.

"I miss you too."

I also visited Chai at the Apollo Inn. I found him in pants and a checkered shirt.

"I have promotion to waiter," he said with pride.

"No more go-go?"

"No."

"Do you like it better?" He nodded. "More money?"

"My salary now 1,400 *baht* one month plus 10 *baht* for each guest I fix with boy."

"How many do you set up a month?"

"Maybe sixty or seventy. In future, I hope to have promotion to Captain of Apollo Inn."

"Do you still go with customers?"

"Sometime."

"How's Number One Off?" I asked, looking around for him.

"He gone. Guest take him four time. Then give him 200,000 *baht* ($8,000) ."

"Wow! That's some tip!"

"He stop work and go home."

"What about the friend you brought to my apartment? Is he still here?"

"He quit. He lazy. No want to go all night with guest."

I guessed that short-time wasn't too bad, but "all night" meant the customer had to be serviced an additional two or three times.

Chai added, "He no mind all night if guest was woman."

"Have you heard from the guy I helped you write to? The man in New York?"

Chai went upstairs to bring me the New Yorker's latest letter. I read more about AIDS. The man wrote that he always practiced safe sex but that he didn't go out much. New York didn't have nice, gentle boys like in Thailand. If he lived in Thailand, he said, he'd be in love all the time.

That sounded similar to how heterosexual *farang*s viewed Thai women— nice and gentle, docile and manageable. Was that supposed to be a compliment?

Chai asked for a lesson in what to say in his new job as waiter.

We wrote phrases for him to practice: "Hello, how are you?" "Which boy do you like?" "If you want to take a boy out, you must pay 200 *baht* to the bar. Then you pay him what you think is fair."

Chai asked how to explain that customers couldn't be the aggressor in anal intercourse with some of the boys. Some allowed it; some didn't.

We wrote: "These boys will do everything, but you cannot fuck them, they will fuck you."

"In my job, I also take boy to airport hotel," Chai told me. "If someone ask hotel for boy, hotel call Apollo Inn. I bring."

The higher position had given Chai new poise. Now that he was officially in charge of the go-gos, he had the keys to the third-floor rooms. The added responsibilities seemed to make him more confident.

"I'm staying on *Ko* Samet now," I told him. "Have you ever been there?"

"I never go anywhere except Udon and Bangkok."

"I'll take you one day." Then I thought of Toom. Toom wouldn't like me to share a bungalow with another man. So I said, "How about Pattaya? We could go for a weekend in Pattaya."

Chai loved the idea.

When I rendezvoused with Nok Friday morning in front of her bar, Moon was with her, suitcase in hand, ready for the trip. My "Positively no" had had no effect.

What could I do? I didn't want to make a scene, so I took a breath and told myself *mai ben rai* (never mind). I consoled my ego by thinking of the self-restraint I was learning.

When the bus stopped halfway to the pier, Nok and I went to the Ladies' Room. Nok urinated on the floor instead of in the squat toilet. I'd previously noted, both by observation and by evidence left, that some Patpong bar girls preferred the floor to the toilet, with which they must have been unfamiliar. Perhaps I shouldn't let Toom meet this Patpong woman, I thought.

On the bus, Moon wanted to practice English with me, since his new job as a Patpong tout involved speaking to foreigners. He asked me questions concerning the correct terminology for persuading people to enter a bar. I taught him "no obligation," which he practiced over and over.

"How long have you been working Patpong now?" I asked him.

"Four month. I meet Nok one night and start work next day."

"How many hours do you work?"

"I work Patpong from 7 p.m. to 3 a.m. From 8 a.m. to 2 p.m., I help my mother sell noodle. I live part-time with Nok, part-time with mother."

It was drizzling when we arrived at the pier, and, to my horror, my sandal slipped on the wood and my right leg went through the wide-spaced boards of the dock. The boatload of people who'd already boarded had a good laugh as one whole leg—up to the crotch—appeared beneath the dock. Nok and Moon giggled at each other. I HATED that ferry.

In the boat, scratched and bleeding, I asked Moon, "Have you been to *Ko Samet* before?"

"No, only once to Pattaya."

Nok said she'd been to Samet twice with Yamaguchi.

I rented one bungalow for Nok and Moon and another for me and Toom. Nok said she had many friends at the bungalow lodge, but I didn't get the impression they considered Nok a friend. After checking in and cleaning my leg, I took Nok and Moon to the restaurant. I could see the family members, who owned and ran the lodge, restraining themselves when Nok yelled for service. She did this often and loudly, shrieking across the room, unconcerned that people were watching a video.

"NAM PRICK! NAM PRICK!" (HOT SAUCE! HOT SAUCE!)

The waiter gave her hot sauce without looking any of us in the eye.

On the island, Nok and Moon were like honeymooners. They played in the surf, giggled, pushed each other around, brushed noses Eskimo-style, and touched each other constantly.

I found out Nok came from Khorat, and not from Bangkok, as she'd previously told me. "Baby will be Lao," she said. She invited me upcountry to visit her family.

Nok spoke often about the baby, wrapping her arms protectively around her stomach and smiling at Moon. They both acted thrilled about it.

Moon told me, "Look." He raised Nok's hand and his own to show me the rings they wore. "We are engaged."

"When did you get those?"

"Two day ago," Nok answered with a sweet look at Moon.

At 11, I left Nok and Moon by themselves and went alone to meet Toom. I'd decided against the four of us ever being together. Patpong and Toom didn't mix well. He had conditioned reactions to prostitutes, and I didn't want them directed at Nok. I didn't want Moon affected by them either. How long could a man, in love with someone he was supposed to despise, resist public opinion? I was sure Nok and Moon wouldn't miss me. They paid little attention to anything outside themselves.

I wouldn't spend much time with Toom this trip, but it was okay. I didn't need to be with him twenty-four hours a day the way I'd wanted to be with Jek. Knowing Jek lived by scamming tourists, I'd been forever mistrustful and off-balance, needing a reassurance that never came.

An hour a day with Toom was enough for me. Perhaps more than enough. When it came right down to it, I didn't have much in common with these Thai cuties after all.

On Saturday morning, Nok, Moon, and I played with a beach ball; one of us in the middle tried to snatch the ball from the other two. I could have been invisible. Nok and Moon were so enthralled with each other, they shut out everything else. We'd begin each game in formation, but soon Nok and Moon threw the ball only to each other; then they'd end up wrestling in the sand, with me and the ball somewhere on the side.

Nok must have noticed my exclusion because, when I rented an inner tube, she and I went out with it while Moon stayed on the beach guarding our belongings.

A group of Thai men noticed us. They called out, *"Pai nai?"* (Where are you going?)

Nok beamed a dazzling smile at them and shouted back a joking response.

The men paddled in. They too were on inner tubes. They held onto ours, forming a ring around us starfish-like. They gazed at Nok as if she were a treasure. For one thing, she wore a bathing suit. Most Thai women who came with family or friends for a weekend on Samet swam in full dress. Moon himself never went into the sea in less than sweat pants.

Nok absorbed the men's admiration like a cotton ball, laughing at maximum volume and heedless of her fiancé on the beach. Though I didn't doubt she was utterly in love with Moon, she seemed to have forgotten him in the glory of being the center of attention.

She cackled, squealed, and splashed water in everyone's face. Two of the men wrapped their legs around Nok's as an anchor.

Like Hoi, she seemed to thrive on male awareness, as if being worshipped was her calling in life.

One man whispered to me with a disapproving face, "She's too loud."

Eventually Moon approached the edge of the beach and waved us in. He was obviously distressed.

I went windsurfing, and each time I sailed passed their spot I saw Nok and Moon arguing in the surf. By the time I came out, they were sitting apart and Nok showed me her naked hand.

"What happened to your engagement ring?" I asked.

"We throw them in the sea."

But they soon made up. Within the hour, they were wrestling and cuddling and smooching again.

That evening, a new problem occurred: Nok had started to bleed. I thought that meant she was having a late menstruation and had never been pregnant after all. Nok speculated she was miscarrying.

Nok and Moon on *Ko* Samet

Oh, no. Was she going to invent a fortune's worth of doctor bills and say they were my fault? I felt concerned about her condition but afraid of the dollar signs I saw in her eyes when she looked at me.

The next day, we were scheduled to return to Bangkok. When we boarded the ferry, Moon and I sat in back but Nok went up front to join a group of *farang*s.

She latched onto a blond Dutchman, a gorgeous prize with blue eyes. "You want appen?" she asked him, aiming an apple at his mouth. He took a bite and she held out her hand and said, "Fifty *baht*." The boatload of thirty people laughed uproariously.

The only Thai woman present, Nok was very cute and tiny next to the Westerners, but she was also very loud. The way she had zoomed in on the man, touching him and hitting him playfully, marked her a bar girl, despite the fact that she wore no make-up and that her shoulders and upper arms were covered, as is considered proper for Thai women. Everyone laughed at her attempts to speak English. They laughed when she leaned against the man to listen to his Walkman. They laughed when she searched his pockets.

"What you have inside?" she asked, poking a finger in his shirt. "You have food for me?" The *farang*s guffawed.

Nok seemed intoxicated by the attention of the crowd and the smile of the attractive man, who openly responded to her. Moon was not laughing. Neither was the man's Dutch wife, sitting beside him.

At the bus station, we went to the restaurant to wait for the bus. The Dutchman and his group of six sat at the next table. Nok stared at, gestured, and motioned to each man in the group. One of them came over to give her a stuffed penguin doll.

With this encouragement, she called out, first to one, then to another, "Come sit here. Come pay bill."

She continued this until the Dutchman became visibly annoyed. He'd told her once he was with his wife. When the facial expressions of both the man and his wife revealed they'd lost patience with her antics, Nok raised her middle finger at them. Now the couple became really irked and eyed the three of us menacingly.

I was embarrassed to death but also surprisingly jealous. From the way the

Dutchman had originally looked at Nok, I knew that, if it weren't for his wife, Nok would have him. He hadn't noticed me at all.

By this time, though, Nok had squandered any allure she'd had. Apparently she couldn't judge when she'd gone too far. The Dutchman was clearly repulsed by her advances, which were now abusive rather than fetching. Moon, meanwhile, maintained the sick smile he'd had frozen on his face since leaving Samet.

On the bus, Nok and I sat in the front seat, with me by the window. Moon sat across the aisle by the other window, looking out with a pout. As it turned out, the Dutchman and his wife had to sit separately, and he had the seat between Nok and Moon. Right away Nok touched him and slapped at him sensuously.

He grew angry at constantly being hit and warned her, "If you do that again, I'll give you a black eye. No, TWO black eyes."

Nok did calm down for a while but then swatted him again, at which point he grabbed her arm and twisted her wrist.

Relinquishing the Dutchman, she spotted a Japanese two seats behind us in the aisle. After leaning over and joking with him, she asked me, "You write for me, Nok, Number 24, Queen's Castle, Patpong 1."

I did, and she passed the message to him. She'd scored after all.

31.

"*From her own observation,*" one adult Pattaya prostitute says, "*most child prostitutes go to Pattaya of their own choice*" (Jaroonpanth, 1988: 34). A Bangkok newspaper reports:

> *Nart is 12 years old. Her friend, Lek, is the same age. Tonight they are sharing the same customer, a big American sailor.*
>
> *They hang on to his arms, one on each side of him, laughing constantly and teasing one another as they make their way along Beach Road.*
>
> "*I'm so happy tonight,*" *says Nart, a tiny girl with a ready smile.* "*I don't often get a customer. They usually say I'm too small, and they prefer older girls*" (Ibid.: 31).

A few days after the trip, I brought Nok the pictures I'd taken on *Ko* Samet. "This one's my favorite. You and Moon hugging on the rocks. Isn't it great?"

She nodded but didn't seem happy or lively. She looked depressed.

"How's Moon?" I asked.

"Fine," she answered without feeling.

"Are we going upcountry next month to visit your family?"

"Okay." She didn't rejoice.

"The three of us," I added.

She nodded again but looked away. On *Ko* Samet she'd made the point of saying it would be the three of us going. She wanted Moon to meet her family. Though I wasn't looking forward to paying for his ticket, I thought it would be worthwhile to see how the family responded to the in-law to be.

I couldn't bring myself to ask about her pregnancy. Was she acting miserable to make me feel guilty for taking her on a trip where she miscarried? Yamaguchi had paid for a dead mother she'd invented; I wouldn't pay for a phantom dead baby.

Following my recent routine, I *tuk-tuk*ed home to avoid Jek's corner. Today was his birthday, March 9th. Was he thinking of me? This day was supposed to be the turning point of his life. Now he'd start a career, working a respectable job in an office. Maybe I no longer had to detour Patpong 3. Did that mean I'd never run into him again? I felt saddened over losing all contact with him.

Chai and I went to Pattaya—or rather Jomtien Beach, next to Pattaya. I'd heard they had windsurfing there. We checked into a guest house and headed for the sea.

Jomtien Beach, like Pattaya, was a tourist playground; but while Pattaya had the bars, Jomtien specialized in seaside amusements. Everywhere I looked, I saw toys for foreigners. The shoreline was jammed with scooters and catamarans. Signs advertised water-skiing, and a *farang* was being lifted into the air on a parachute tied to a motor boat.

"You ever try this stuff?" I asked Chai.

"No," he said with wide eyes as he watched the parachute rise. "For *farang*."

"I heard they have glider planes here too."

The beach was loaded with equipment huts, each with its own pile of windsurfing boards, inner tubes, and assorted tourist playthings.

We walked to the right, and I looked for a board with a small sail. By the time I found one, we were near the end of the beach, where the rocky point turned into the bay of Pattaya.

We sat on lounge chairs under a twenty-five-foot palm-frond umbrella and discovered we were in the gay beach. Chai looked pleased as we found ourselves surrounded by middle-aged European men and Thai teenaged boys, with not a female in sight.

There was no wind, not even the little breeze I usually settled for windsurfing in.

Minutes after we sat down, Chai met an old friend from the Apollo Inn. They chatted in an Isan dialect before the friend moved on.

"What's he doing here?" I asked Chai.

"He work here in gay bar for eight month. But bar is closed to make change. Now he have no money. He hungry. He try to find guest on beach."

"Can I see that?" I asked Chai, pointing to the tourist magazine he'd brought with him from our room. Like Bangkok, Pattaya had its own weekly tourist magazine that advertised bars, restaurants, massage parlors, and special events.

"I find another friend inside," Chai told me, opening to a page with an ad for Adam and Eve, a gay bar, which proclaimed in English and German:

We are pleased to welcome you, our friends,
and our 70 masseurs and go-go dancers
will receive you with a warm welcome.
Come to enjoy your unique lifestyle and dance in our discotheque.
Private rooms available.

"We can go there tonight, if you want," I said. "We'll visit him."

Chai smiled.

"Pattaya's incredible," I said, thumbing through the magazine. "Horseback riding, scuba diving, elephant shows. Look at this—even go-cart racing. Amusements galore. Let's go in the water."

"I can't. I don't know how to swim."

"We'll take an inner tube. You just hold on. C'mon, it's fun."

Chai wouldn't get out of his chair, and I remembered that he'd never been to the sea before.

I decided not to get wet right away either. So much was going on, it was a treat to simply sit and look around. Scooters buzzed by, parachutes took off, Frisbees sliced the air, and fascinating sights occurred nearby.

The beach abounded in *farang* men in their forties and fifties with young Thais. *Farang*-Thai male couples formed as we watched. A fiftyish Frenchman carried a thirteen-year-old into the sea, where they caressed each other's genitals.

Chai recognized at least ten *farang*s he'd seen at the Apollo Inn and knew many of the Thai boys too. A group of Thais joined us when Chai called out to ask where they worked. They began a lively comparison of business in Bangkok and Pattaya. A passing boy, known to the Pattaya Thais, announced that he now worked on Patpong. He said it in such a way as could only be described as bragging. However, his bar was not, in fact, on one of the three Patpong streets, but was situated two blocks away.

I could sense Chai's pride at working in the desired area.

Chai's Thai acquaintances didn't sit with us, but moved off to other umbrellas. It seemed that each thatch umbrella had a territory that included five rows of lounge chairs with ten chairs across, plus a few small striped umbrellas leading to the water. These territories had their own sets of Thai boys, the same way Patpong streets had touts assigned to specific areas.

Though most of the Thais were in their teens or early twenties,

Chai on Jomtien Beach

I noticed a few children too. Two deck chairs over from Chai and me sat a sixtyish *farang* with a boy who looked eleven. At first, I couldn't believe theirs was a sexual liaison, but when the *farang* leaned over to brush sand off the child's chest slowly and sensuously, I had no doubt.

"What do you think about old men with little boys?" I asked Chai.

He was silent.

"Does the Apollo Inn have customers who ask for children?"

"Many man need boy twelve year old," he said.

"Does the Apollo Inn supply them?"

He hesitated, then answered, "Sex with children is illegal."

I decided not to mention that prostitution itself was illegal in Thailand.

285

Without staring, I kept watch over the strange duo. The boy listened to music on a Walkman and played with an electronic video game. At one point, the *farang* took the boy's shirt and, after turning it right-side-out, placed it over his head to dress him in a fatherly manner; his hands lingered over the child's body in an unfatherly manner.

On a previous trip to Pattaya, I'd seen many street-kid beggars panhandling from tourists. Compared to them, I had to admit that this one looked healthy and relaxed.

Shortly after, two same-aged *farang*s came by to make plans with the man for lunch. They spoke in accented English. Behind them trailed two more Thai children, another about eleven years old and one no more than eight. The six of them left together.

Apparently no one there found anything amiss in the three couples. Chai and I looked at each other and shrugged.

We saw his friend from the Apollo Inn make another pass down the beach, looking for a customer. He never did find one. The regulars stationed in territories had the market sewn up. Eventually Chai gave him 20 *baht* so he could eat.

Chai told me, "In Bangkok, I give away many 10 *baht* every day to friend who stop work and are hungry."

I thought of the precariousness of these people's lives, surviving day to day and meal to meal.

I noticed Chai watch some of the Thais with interest. He focused on one particularly beautiful one, about eighteen years old, wearing a long T-shirt over his bathing suit.

"You like him?" I asked Chai.

His eyes sparkled. "Very handsome. You think so?"

"A beauty."

We watched the teenager joke with the others there. He seemed to belong to our umbrella.

Eventually he noticed us watching him and nodded.

"Go talk to him," I said to Chai. "He's smiling at you."

"No, he smile at you."

"Me! No, no. He's for you."

Chai shook his head. "I think he not gay. He like you."

Chai called out to him, and the beauty came over.

He and Chai discussed life in Pattaya.

"Where do you work?" Chai asked him.

"I used to work at Adam and Eve but no more."

Chai told him we were going there that night and asked if he knew his friend who was pictured in the ad.

"No, I only work there one week."

"What's your name?" I asked him.

"Em," he told me with a penetrating look.

"You two go swim," Chai suggested. "Take tube."

Em thought that was a great idea.

"No, no," I said. I didn't want Em for me!

Chai pressed us and Em jumped up. He went and fetched us a tube.

"I don't want to," I insisted to Chai.

Chai pulled me up, and Em waved me over as he hefted the tube to the water.

"He's for you," I said to Chai, "not me."

Chai grinned and pushed me. I went.

At first Em and I held onto the tube as we treaded water. Then Em moved next to me so our shoulders touched. To get away from him, I suggested we sit on the tube. We did, one on either side. Well, at least he was opposite me, but now he arranged it so our legs intertwined. I had no place to move without losing my balance.

I didn't really know what to say to the guy, especially since he kept looking at me as if he'd never been close to a *farang* female before, or perhaps any female, given his line of work. I told him, "I've had enough water for today."

Back at the umbrella, Em sat next to me and stared at my face.

"Where does your family live?" I asked him.

"No have family. I live in Pattaya."

I wondered if he was one of the Pattaya orphans who survived by sleeping with foreign men, like the little boys I'd seen earlier probably were. He could have been one of them, now grown.

Em slid his chair closer and played with a strand of my hair.

He was absolutely beautiful, but I wanted to get away from him. I didn't want to be bothered struggling with conversation. I'd brought Chai to Pattaya to study Chai's behavior. I didn't need new people, and Pattaya male prostitutes weren't my field anyway.

"I'm going back to the room," I told Chai. "I need to rest before we go out."

Chai grinned and turned to Em. "Want to come out with us tonight?"

Em sure did.

Oh, no! I didn't want to pay for another person. Since Chai wasn't a date but an informant I bought out of a bar, I expected to pay for him. I didn't want my role as benefactor to get out of hand though. And I didn't want Em crawling all over me. I knew Chai was trying to please me. How could I get out of it?

"I come meet you," Em said. "What hotel you stay?"

"No, no," I said. "Anyway, I have to go to Pattaya first to look up a friend. Her bar's on Beach Road."

"We meet there," Chai said.

It was arranged. The three of us would meet at *Soi* 12 and Beach Road at 8 p.m.

That evening, I went to the Pit Stop to visit Sow, the bar girl Dudley Dapolito was in love with. I wanted to see how

With Em and Chai

she was and if she'd heard from him.

"Sow no here," the mamasan told me.

"Will she come tomorrow?"

"Maybe she back next week."

I wondered which customer she was traveling with this time. "I'll leave a note for her," I said and took out pen and paper.

As I sat on a bar stool to write, a bar girl noticed I was writing in Thai.

"Aow!" she exclaimed. Soon the other women gathered to watch.

I couldn't remember how to spell *Thursday*, which had a complicated, unphonetic construction.

"How do you spell Thursday?" I asked my audience.

The women looked at each other blankly. One turned and shouted the question to the mamasan. They didn't know how to spell *Thursday*? I was shocked at their lack of basic skills. No wonder they were so impressed with my writing! It was something they couldn't do themselves.

One woman took the pen and went to the other side of the bar to inquire for me. The others debated the spelling among themselves. I'd been aware that the *bau hok*, sixth-grade exam was a landmark in Thai education for country people. Many of the women I'd befriended had never come close to taking it. It was comparable to how people in the States viewed the high school diploma, only it required six years less work. To me, passing the *bau hok* was like a hobby. I did it as a challenge and to prove to my professors that I'd learned the language, but it wasn't necessary for the degree.

I left the note for Sow and went to meet Chai and Em.

Em arrived before Chai and stood close to me—too close.

"Have you passed the *bau hok*?" I asked him.

"No. Only finish grade one."

Chai came, and we boarded a *song-tow* to *Soi* 2, one of the streets filled with gay bars and massage parlors. When we jumped off, Em took my hand and continued to hold it as we walked to Adam and Eve. "Oh well," I thought as I looked at my beautiful escort, "maybe this wasn't so terrible—kind of fun actually."

Adam and Eve was elegantly decorated with floral-cushioned rattan couches. The go-go boys weren't in bikinis, like at the Apollo Inn, but were fully dressed with pinned number badges. Some danced on the center stage and others on circular platforms around the room. The rest of the go-gos sat in chairs on the dance floor.

I was the only female there except for the large transsexual proprietor, who stood at the bar surrounded by admirers.

We found Chai's friend still working there, and when we requested him he joined our table.

"How's work here?" Chai asked him.

"They don't pay salary like at Apollo. I only get money from guest."

Em also had a friend there, and he joined us too. I could see my bill growing proportionately.

"Is your friend gay?" I asked Em.

"No. Me too. I'm not gay."

I felt Em was exhibiting me like a trophy he'd won. He kept hold of my hand and kissed me now and then, which I was beginning to enjoy.

Around his wrist, he wore a beaded band of the type made by hilltribes. He took it off by chewing the string and tied it to mine.

"For me?"

"Yes, for you," he said and kissed me again, this time on the mouth.

My body responded down to my toes. Every part of me tingled. Now I stared back at him as he stared at me. We remained leaning into each other, scrunched in the cushions.

Chai grinned as if pleased he'd finally paid me back for all the good times I'd shown him.

Suddenly I loved the Adam and Eve—luxurious and comfortable, with so many perfect men dancing in front of me. I felt right at home, even though I was female. Because I was a *farang* female, these places were open to me. With the history of the women's movement and the history of my rich country behind me, these delights were as much mine as any other tourist's.

When we left Adam and Eve, I felt electrified with pep, though it was past my usual bedtime. "Where should we go now?" I asked.

"Up to you," said Chai.

"You like disco?" asked Em.

"Yeah, let's dance. How about the Palladium? I went there once with Lieutenant Colonel Suwat of the Tourist Police."

Em cringed at the word police, so I dropped the topic quickly.

Em flagged us down a *song-tow*, and as I climbed in, the thought of the expensive entrance fees didn't bother me a bit. I was having a wonderful time with my new darling.

The Palladium's flashing colored lights and throbbing music peaked the rapture in me. I remembered how I'd pined for Jek the last time I'd been there. How silly I'd been. What did Jek matter when the world was full of dashing beauties like the one who now had both arms around my waist?

Em and I danced to all the slow tunes. Our bodies crushed together and we barely moved our feet. Under purple lights we held deep kisses for whole songs.

At closing time, they held a lottery according to the numbers on our entrance tickets. We won a bottle of champagne. I could have guessed we'd win something. Everything was running at maximum intensity for me. As Em went to collect our prize, I felt like a *farang* with the entire world as my inherited right.

Of course, Em wanted to come back to the hotel.

"Not tonight," I told him. "I'm sharing a room with Chai."

"I sleep there too," he said.

"No! There's only two very narrow beds. Next time. I'll come back next week. Alone."

"You promise?"

"Yes. Positively."

Our heads closed the two-inch space between us, to kiss again.

"What about champagne?" he asked when the kiss ended, long minutes later.

"Tomorrow. On the beach. You'll be there?"

"Yes, I come see you."

The three of us took a *song-tow* in the same direction. Em and I kissed and caressed until he stopped the *song-tow* in another part of Pattaya.

"Are you sure I can't come with you tonight?" he said before getting off.

"Next week. I promise."

He stepped down to a street filled with bars and loud music. I wondered if he were going to work now.

Next morning, seeing the palm trees bending in the wind, I got to the umbrella early so I could windsurf. I asked the attendant to put the champagne in his ice box for me. Each umbrella also served beers and colas.

With the sail in my hands, I felt connected to the wind as it pushed me swiftly along. I felt glorious slashing across the water.

After that, I had an urge to parasail.

"Want to try it?" I asked Chai, knowing he'd refuse.

He made a fearful face and declined the offer.

Strapped in a harness as three Thais held the parachute behind me, I was told to run after the motorboat that they signalled to start. Within seconds, I soared to the sky and hovered high over the bay. I could see for miles and had the urge to sing: "This land is my land, this land is your land, from the Gulf of Thailand, to New York Island . . . "

After the parachuting, I had a massage.

"This is life," I said to Chai as an old woman kneaded my back. "I could live like this forever."

When Em arrived, we hugged in the sun, ran splashing into the sea, and groped each other's body in the water. Then we opened the champagne.

"You no drink some?" Chai asked me.

"No, it's for you two. I think I'll treat myself to a scooter ride. I want to do everything this fabulous place has to offer. You ever drive a scooter?" I asked Em.

He shook his head and said, "I go with you."

I'd never driven one before, but after windsurfing, parasailing, and Em, I felt capable of anything.

The umbrella attendant fetched me a scooter, and I waded into the water to board it.

"I just turn the handle to go faster, right?" I asked, not wanting to admit my complete ignorance. "What happens if the engine stops?"

"You pull cord," the man said.

Though I wasn't positive I could handle it, I was eager to go. Em climbed on behind me and wrapped his arms around my hips.

With a twist of my wrist, I zoomed away. Faster and noisier than the wind, the scooter shot me into space. I bounced over waves and roared around buoys.

This had to be the best feeling in the world, I thought—speeding over a tropical sea with a delicious doll behind me.

If I'd been with a *farang* male, he'd probably want to be the driver and put me on the back.

32.

Ekachai (1988: 31) reported there were "1.7 million children forced to leave the countryside to find work in the city." Child labor (aside from prostitution) is more prevalent among girls, who are considered less troublesome than boys and more suited for domestic work and light manufacturing. The boys who do migrate are absorbed in male-dominated fields, such as crafts, where they acquire skills that will earn them more money.

In Bangkok, child prostitutes are mostly found in Yaowarat (Chinatown) and are usually kept under guard, having been sold by their parents. In his article "Inside the Teahouses of Yaowarat" for the Bangkok Post *(1984: 6), Ekachai quotes the prices at which children are initially sold: the best looking (mostly from the North) 5,000B to 20,000B ($200-800); dark girls from the Northeast, 2,000B to 3,000B ($80-$120). One girl reported that her parents received 18,000B ($720) for her. For her Virginity Breaking Rite she was paid 7,000B ($280); then 3,000B ($120) for her second time and 500B ($20) for the third. Now, after four months, she receives 80B ($3.20) each from her average of ten customers a day. Her parents came once to borrow more money.*

Back in Bangkok, I found an article in the *Bangkok Post*:

Pattaya—Tourist Police chief Lt-Col Suwat Chindavanij has been suspended from duty pending disciplinary and legal investigations into allegations of power abuse.

Hah! I could have told them that six months before.

I went to Sexy Stars to see Pong and confirm our visit to her family for Songkran.

"She no work here now," the hostess told me. "She pregnant. She go home."

I tried to track down her husband, Ong, at Topless and on *Soi* Crazy Horse but with no success. They were both gone from Patpong.

Next, I went to Queen's Castle with a train schedule to fix a date for visiting Nok's family. Nok didn't seem glad to see me or excited by the prospect. When we'd first planned the trip, she'd been eager for her family to meet Moon. Now she made me feel that I was annoying her.

Finally she said, "Not this month. We go next month for Songkran."

Well, since Pong was gone, I was free to spend Songkran with Nok.

Then I went to the Rose Bar to see Dang. It had been eight months since I'd last braved the blow-job bar. Would Dang be hurt that I'd neglected her? Was she still working there?

I entered the bar to find a much heavier Dang dancing on the stage. She rushed down to smother me in an embrace.

"I just come Bangkok last week. I spend three month in Udon," she said, which eased my guilt for staying away so long.

"What were you doing there?" I asked.

"I have baby. I have baby boy."

"Congratulations! What's his name?"

"Bed."

"Bed? Is that a Thai name?"

She laughed. "No, I name him after English word *bed*."

I knew Thais chose nicknames that had significance for them. Jek had named his son Bank based on his love of money. But Bed? I remembered Dang telling me she slept on the floor of the bar. Maybe she was so used to sleeping on the floor and servicing her customers on her knees that a bed did hold symbolic promise.

"Where is Bed now?" I asked.

"He stay with my mother. I have to work."

"Were you working until the time you left Bangkok to give birth?"

"Sure, get good money. Man like make love with pregnant woman."

Across from us, a man sprawled spread-eagle on the couch. A woman on the floor was fellating him. To his left, a woman looked at the room with a bored expression while he sucked her nipple. I suddenly realized I'd always seen the Rose Bar women on the left side of the man. I remembered the lesson on Thai culture at A.U.A. that said a wife was to sleep or sit on the left side of her husband as suited her subordinate position.

I smiled, thinking how that practice had been carried over to the Rose Bar and used with *farangs* who were unaware of the geopolitical honor.

"Is the baby *farang*?" I asked Dang.

She nodded. *"Luuk krung."* (Half-child.)

If it were possible to know who the father was, I'd have enjoyed telling the *farang* he had a son named Bed from Dang at the Rose Bar.

At home, I called Hoi. She and Alex had now been together one year.

"My dream has come true," she said. "My whole life I wish I no have to work and can do nothing all day. Now I have my dream."

"I'm so glad for you. You're happy then?"

"Yes. I'm very happy." She sounded happy—relaxed and satisfied.

"Alex is working full-time?"

"He work every day. He teach English and weekend he model. Last week he on TV; newspaper show his picture as TV actor. He rich. He can give money for my father."

I was pleased Hoi had gotten what she wanted. Thai stories usually centered on upper-class families where the "major wife" appeared to do nothing but reign over the estate and boss the servants. That image probably formed the basis of Hoi's dream, the highest achievement for a female in her society. She could never attain that in the traditional way, but with a foreigner she'd succeeded. As much as she was able, she'd made her dream come true. She'd achieved what she wanted.

I knew it wasn't what Alex wanted though. Alex wanted to give Hoi an education, to instill in her a desire for knowledge and advancement. He wanted her to learn a craft so that she could support herself and her family in a legitimate way. He'd have loved to make Hoi a yuppie. All Hoi wanted was the freedom to do nothing. In that, her dream had come true.

I received a call from Fun, the woman I had met with Hoi on *Ko* Samet.

"Will you go with me to Australian Embassy?" she asked. "I need help to get visa."

Bob had asked her to join him for a month in Brisbane, where he was working.

"I'll come with you, but getting a visa won't be easy. They'll want to see you have money in the bank."

"If they need money, Bob send me."

She came to the apartment first so we could plan her strategy. Fun had two passports and sought my advice on which to use.

"I don't want embassy to know I go three time to Hong Kong but only go in once."

I noticed she listed her occupation as hairdresser.

I tried to prep her on an approach to take and discovered she had little guile in her. It seemed Bob had rescued Fun from Patpong before she learned the ruses that would have helped her here.

We walked to the embassy and they accepted her application, telling her to return Monday for an interview. From there, she rode in my taxi to Patpong. Though she no longer worked there, she visited friends who did.

"Where do you live?" I asked her.

"With girlfriend. Lesbian."

"Are you lovers?"

"Yes."

"Does Bob know?"

She shook her head.

I'd heard that many Patpong women had lesbian relationships, but I'd never found out if it was sexual preference or spiritual comfort.

"Does your girlfriend mind you going to meet Bob?" I asked.

"She understand."

On Monday morning, I met Fun at the embassy, but they wouldn't allow me in the interview. Apparently Fun didn't do well on her own. She left the office with an armload of immigration forms, including one for Bob to fill out as sponsor of the new immigrant.

"Immigration forms!" I exclaimed, flipping through forty pages I feared she'd expect me to help her fill out. "But you only asked for a tourist visa! You didn't want to immigrate—just visit! What happened?"

"Australian woman speak to me. Ask me if I want to marry Bob."

"Oh, no—did you say yes?"

She nodded glumly.

I thought it unfortunate that Fun lacked longer exposure to bar work, where she could have honed manipulative skills. She'd never be approved as an immigrant, even if Bob sponsored her, which he couldn't do since he wasn't Australian. Nok, Hoi, Pong, or Tik would have breezed through that interview.

At the beginning of April, I went again to Queen's Castle to make plans for going upcountry with Nok and Moon for Songkran. When they called her out of the dressing room, she didn't appear pleased and barely acknowledged me. She avoided looking at me.

"So, are we going to visit your family?"

"No. Not for Songkran," she said. "I go to Pattaya three day with guest. Maybe next month. You come again two week and I tell you."

Though most of the time I liked Nok, her friendliness and charm winning me over, sometimes I didn't like her at all. When her connivances slipped from cute and understandable to hostile and insulting, she could be offensive. At this meeting, I became exasperated as well as hurt by Nok's attitude, which I interpreted as a personal rejection. Since she seemed so distressed by my presence, I didn't arrange to see her again.

I spent Songkran with Toom on *Ko* Samet, then went to visit Em in Pattaya.

Three months later, I decided to investigate a new VD clinic above King's Lounge by passing myself off as a patient wanting a routine checkup. The clinic had recently opened to service the employees of the King's Group, which owned several Patpong bars. Trink's column had reported, with approval, that the King's Group had instituted a new policy: All their women would go for a check-up after every tryst with a customer, instead of the weekly or bimonthly visits of the past.

I went in the early evening, since the office opened in the afternoon and closed late at night. I was ready to act like a dumb tourist if anyone challenged my presence in a clinic for Patpong Thais.

I entered to find merriment and gaiety in the waiting room as friends came in and met each other. Clearly, they were on their way to work. Beautiful women in fancy miniskirts appeared with VD books in hand. A *katoey* applied mascara with fluttery fingers sporting long, orange nails.

Being the only *farang*, I felt conspicuous until I ran into three women I knew from Queen's Castle. They guffawed when they saw me.

"You have AIDS?" one asked with a peal of laughter.

Then I found out Nok and Moon had split up.

"Why?" I asked.

"Don't know. Many month now, he no come bar see Nok."

I felt terrible. I knew the depth of feeling Nok had for Moon. I had the way she looked at him recorded in a myriad of photographs. If something had happened to break them up, I knew she'd be devastated. No wonder she hadn't wanted to go upcountry with me if Moon wouldn't be going with her to meet her family!

I felt awful for not putting aside feelings and keeping in touch with her.

At that moment, the receptionist called my name for my turn with the gynecologist. I suddenly had doubts about this medical exploration into the workings of Patpong. Perhaps this act of Participant Observation was going too far. Did I really need to research the technique of Patpong doctors? I hoped they sterilized utensils between patients.

I was led to a cubicle and told to remove my underpants and spread myself on the table. I would have fled were it not for the three Queen's Castle women I'd have to run past. This was definitely a bad idea, I told myself when the doctor picked a clamp out of a jar of liquid. Was that disinfectant? Did all the women get the same clamp? What about the *katoey*?

The nurse shined a bright light on my lower parts, and I wondered what the girls considered worse: a romp with a customer or an internal exam.

My "checkup" was wholly attuned to its setting. I didn't know how successfully the doctor cured VD, but he fit masterfully as a cog in the prostitution industry. A clean-out was what he was geared for—flushing traces of one customer to prepare for the new. I left the clinic feeling like my insides had been through a car wash.

In the elevator, I ran into an old friend from India, an American from Florida with dark blond hair.

We gave each other a huggy greeting. "I knew you were in Thailand," I said, "but I had no idea where to find you. What are you doing in this building?"

It had been eleven years since we last met. Though I no longer lived in India, I received occasional gossip. I'd heard that a few of us could be found in this part of the world, but so far the Floridian was the only one I'd run into.

"My office is upstairs," he told me. "I have a computer publishing firm on the fourth floor. I bank in Hong Kong and make buying trips to computer conventions in Europe. Thailand's a laid-back place with easy living. What are you doing here?"

I told him about my research and the visit to the clinic.

"Don't tell me you let one of those doctors touch you," he said jokingly, sure I hadn't done that.

Appalled at what I'd just subjected myself to, I couldn't admit it.

"Do you still go to India?" I asked.

"No. I left that scene long ago. I've lived here ever since. Meet me tonight and I'll take you around Patpong. I know all about it."

"I've been studying Patpong over a year. I know it too," I answered, a bit vexed at his assumption that I needed it explained to me. "I have to go to Queen's Castle later to find out something, but otherwise I'm finished with the streets and bars. Outside of the handful of Thais and *farangs* I'm following, the research is over."

"You should meet my partner," the Floridian said next. "When he wants to get rid of his latest Thai bunny, he sends her to boarding school in Switzerland."

"I'm not interviewing *farangs* anymore. I have enough information on them."

"I'll take you to some of the better bars. Have you seen the Fucking Show at Supergirl? It's done on a motorbike."

"Uh, no. Supergirl just opened last week. I haven't kept up with new openings. I've been writing my dissertation on *Ko* Samet for the past seven months. Every time I return to Bangkok, something's new. If I kept track of each change, I'd never be finished."

"I can tell you stories about Patpong you wouldn't believe."

"I'll come by tonight after my meeting," I said, happy to see my old friend but offended by Western men's possessiveness of Patpong, as if it were theirs alone.

And I didn't want to hear more stories about their sexual exploits with Thai women. I'd heard them all. Now that I spent less time with Patpong people and more time in tourist havens, I met a barrage of *farangs* overeager to recount their escapades with prostitutes and nonprostitutes. Whether I was interested or not, I became the one to tell about Thai-*farang* romances, especially those mismatched in income, education, or cultural level, with the *farang* preeminent. Whenever a *farang* male heard about my topic, he automatically expounded on his latest encounter with crosscultural sex. *Farang* men relished describing how Thailand was a paradise for them. I'd had more than enough of that.

This time at Queen's Castle, Nok did seem happy to see me and immediately invited me for bowling. Once again she was smiley and spunky.

"I heard you and Moon broke up," I told her. "What happened?"

"He's a Patpong man," she said forcefully and bitterly. "Patpong man are NO GOOD. I have new boyfriend."

"A Thai?" I asked, wondering if she'd returned to her doctrine of never going with Thais.

"Thai," she affirmed. "He work in bowling alley. He never come Patpong. Man on Patpong very bad."

I couldn't get more out of her about what happened with Moon. Since Moon had started working Patpong the day after they met, I wondered how much her behavior had contributed to the change in him.

I went to meet my old friend at his office. "I'm ready," I said, appraising the up-to-date Western technology. Macintosh computers, with CD-ROMs and color printers, lined the walls. "Let's go to Supergirl."

"I'll introduce you to an ex-girlfriend of mine who works there," he said.

"We met years ago, when she first arrived in Bangkok. Sixteen and didn't know a thing. I gave her money to build her family a well . . ."

On the street, Patpong touts greeted me. When I stopped to speak with them, the Floridian kept walking. It always astonished me how Western men could be so oblivious of the Thai men of Patpong. They completely negated their existence. If you didn't know otherwise, you'd get the impression Patpong contained Thai women only.

In front of Supergirl, five Supergirls stood in costume; each wore a big *S*, a satin cape, and a microminiskirt. Inside, every seat had a person in it and the aisles were packed.

At 10:30, the go-gos left the stage and the lights dimmed. The ceiling opened and a motorcycle descended. Lying across it was a naked Thai couple who performed the Fucking Show using the bike as support in creative ways.

Supergirl also had a lesbian show. One of the "lesbians," however, had not yet made the full transition to female. He never removed his male underpants, which contained a noticeable male bulge. He had breasts, though, and a female haircut. For the show, he strapped a dildo to his groin. After applying a coating of jelly, he performed.

The Floridian introduced me to the ex-girlfriend with the well and whispered how he regretted she'd lost her giggly shyness. Then he told me, "I know the exact person you should meet. He's upcountry at the moment, a real expert on Patpong . . ."

"Thanks anyway, but I'm finished with the research."

"He's been with girls from every ethnic group in Thailand . . ."

"Truly, I do not need one more piece of information about anything."

"He knows a girl in every bar here . . ."

"Have you been to Chiang Mai?" I asked, hoping to steer the conversation to a topic I wasn't overdosed on.

"It's the best," he said with feeling. "The best place in Thailand."

"Better than *Ko* Samet?" I exclaimed, thinking of the heaven I'd found there.

"No comparison. I have a beach house on the mainland opposite *Ko* Samet. I go down for weekends. I also have a cottage in Chiang Mai. Believe me, that's the place."

"I can't imagine anywhere better than *Ko* Samet. Have you trekked in the mountains near Chiang Mai? I've been thinking of doing that."

"I did a three-day trek into hilltribe country. The first day we hiked to a Karen village untouched by civilization. We spent one night in a Karen hut. The next day we rode elephants, clumping through the forest. We came down the mountain on a six-hour raft ride over rapids. It was the most sensational experience of my life."

"Yeah? I'm going! I'll buy a train ticket tomorrow."

"My friend's there now doing business with one of the hilltribes, selling their handicrafts. He plans to marry a hilltribe girl, a fourteen-year-old virgin . . ."

November 1989

*From the Patpong musical presented by Empower, 1987

I want someone to listen to my heart
To hear the whisper of my mind

It's not that I don't have a dream
Even if it's only a shadow
That envelopes me in darkness

But it gives me strength to go on with life
To walk into the future
And never give it up

I want someone to listen to my heart
To hear the whisper of my mind

I have hurt many times before
With hopes that came to nothing
that perhaps I should die to end it all
Yet it cannot be a life that's losing all the time

I have been alone and drained
And my soul mate parted
So desperate in the dark nadir
So lonely in my misery
But something dawned and I saw a light
It's the dream shining ahead
Alone but strong . . .
This is us

Let's build a new hope
Let's neither be afraid nor despair
However tired and drawn, let's fight on
This is us

Narrator: If life can be chosen, who would want to stand here. But since we are here, all we ask for is understanding . . . and a chance to live the hope that one day we can walk away. We are life, we are part of society. We have to struggle for a better life. There are many roads leading to it and the one we are walking on is called Patpong.

Music: "Part-time Lover"

One week before I was to return to America, on the way home from a travel agent on Surawong Road, I decided to cut to Silom by way of Patpong 1. On the sidewalk in front of Queen's Castle, I found Nok. It had been four months since I'd seen her. I hadn't met any of my Patpong people since then, having spent the time writing and moving from one tourist wonderland to another. It suddenly seemed an effort to put myself in a Patpong frame of mind and I wished I'd walked down a different street.

Nok's stomach formed a suspicious bulge in her tight skirt.

"Are you pregnant?" I asked, noticing that my Thai was rusty. I'd hardly spoken a word of it since passing the *bau hok* exam.

"Four month."

"Who's the father?" I said and immediately realized how estranged I'd become from Patpong issues.

She looked at me in confusion, then answered, "My boyfriend is man from bowling alley."

I didn't chat long. I no longer had to let myself be conned into paying for things; and with the dissertation written, I didn't need new data.

I said goodbye without telling her I was leaving the country. I didn't want her to know this was the last opportunity she'd have to milk me for her retirement fund.

I did have things I wanted to tell her but, having tried in the past, I knew she wouldn't understand. I'd have loved to tell her my conclusions about Patpong prostitution.

I believed Patpong prostitutes had advantages over nonprostitute Thai women who didn't belong to the rich upper class. They had more independence and opportunities. They were more worldly. They met and maintained contact with people from around the globe. They had experiences they'd otherwise never be exposed to, such as flying in planes and being taken abroad or going abroad to work. People taught them to swim, bowl, play snooker, drive motorbikes. They learned English and other languages.

They became daring. Having broken one of society's taboos, they dared to break more. They went out alone at night and traveled on their own. They met people easily.

They developed skills to obtain what they wanted. Becoming deft at hustling, they recognized their ability to influence their environment. They stepped into ventures confident that they'd find someone along the way to pay.

Most importantly, they had money. Money allowed them to fulfill familial obligations while providing freedom of movement. They felt pride in seeing their parents' new houses, built with their earnings. They returned to their villages as superstars distributing alms. With money, they bought the symbols of success: clothes, accessories, and electronics. It gave them the base to lay plans for the future. Money also gave them leeway to escape bad relationships, unpleasant situations, and the harshness of village life. It provided the wherewithal to do nothing if that's what they wanted.

Patpong itself offered the comfort and stability of an esoteric community. The girls had their own friends, VD doctor, moneylender. They had a favorite after-hours club. They knew the Patpong taxi and motorbike drivers who took them home. They knew the staffs of short-time hotels.

Nok and Pong couldn't wait to return to Patpong the nights I bought them out of their bars. They felt at home there and safe. Months after she stopped working, Hoi kept in touch with her bar to update herself on news and keep connections open. Tik, too, after six years away from it, felt an attachment and attraction to the street, and Fun returned there to visit friends.

Working Patpong offered adventure, excitement, and romance. It was an alternative to low-paid, long-hour factory work or other nonskilled labor. It was easier than planting rice. It was a place one could return to in time of need. It was a place where women could express their anger at the way society fashioned Thai men—an outlet for revenge where women could reject them, at least verbally. Within Patpong itself, their occupation was not only accepted but glamorized. They had the organization Empower, which offered free English and Thai lessons plus a bimonthly newsletter where their pictures were published and activities praised. In Patpong, they had support systems, benefits, and potential rewards. It was an easy place to find a *farang* husband, whether for love, money, security, or, as Trink said, to be bought a bar of their own, at which time they divorced. It was a place to find someone to give them a chunk of money so that they could leave Patpong, the way Number One Off had.

On the other hand, life on Patpong carried the stigma of prostitution. While granting the right of sexuality to men, Thai society forbade it to women outside of marriage. Men were praised for having lovers, but women who did the same were considered "bad women," "no good," and "dirty." A Thai's outspoken disapproval of Patpong women was automatic and uttered litany-like, as if required for his or her own personal stature. "Bad women!" "No good!" "Dirty!"

Ultimately, working Patpong was—as Jek would say—"not respectable." I knew if I made any reference to prostitution or Patpong to Nok, she would take it as an insult. Patpong women saw themselves in a familial perspective, tied to generations above and below, and to incarnations behind and before them. As women in the here and now, they still believed themselves to be the *hind* legs of the elephant. As prostitutes, they knew Thai society viewed them as "ruined." They wouldn't believe a foreign woman thought otherwise.

Thai politicians and journalists frequently posed the question, How to solve the problem of prostitution? The two most cited solutions were 1) enforcing the laws, closing brothels; and arresting prostitutes; and 2) legalizing prostitution in order to license and thereby control prostitutes and their diseases. But since prostitution in Thailand was directly related to the position of women in Thai society, enforcing existing laws or legalizing the profession would do little to change the fact of prostitution itself. Until women had the same recognized rights as men, including the right to sexuality, this form of commercial sex would continue to exist as a perquisite of manhood.

The day before I was to board the plane home, I decided to see if Jek was still on Patpong 3. I put on his favorite outfit and walked over. With adrenaline rushing, I wondered if he'd still be there. If he was, would he be glad to see me?

From down the block, I saw him standing on the same corner, as if he belonged to it. The corner had changed, though. It had been renamed Silom 4.

"Oah," he said spotting me.

He shook my hand. The formality disheartened me, though I knew it didn't have the same meaning for him as it did me. Or maybe it did; maybe I was just a *farang*, and *farangs* got a *farang* greeting, a handshake.

"I'm leaving Thailand tomorrow," I told him. "I wanted to say goodbye. I didn't think you'd still be here. I thought you'd be working in an office by now."

He looked embarrassed and explained, "No, I stay here. I make more money as pimp."

That was the first time I'd heard him use that word. It sounded wrong. It disturbed my sense of balance. Had he become hardened in his occupation, accepting his role as trafficker in bodies?

Or had I changed? Maybe the open mind I'd had as a researcher had closed, leaving me with the emotionally charged stereotypes of my culture.

"Oh. So how's business?" I asked.

"Very busy. Have many *farang*. Other day I made 20,000 *baht*. See, I buy 5,000 *baht* gold chain." He pointed to it around his neck.

I hated it. I hated the thick flashy thing. It emphasized my conditioned image of "pimp." It erected a barrier I didn't want to cross.

"I have new name," he told me next.

"What is it?"

"Jeff. Now my name is Jeff. *Farang* can remember."

I hated that too. Jek was gone from me.

That night I received a phone call from Hoi.

"Where are you?" I asked, hearing a loudspeaker voice in the background.

"Bus station. I'm going to Phuket."

"With Alex?"

"No. I don't see Alex many month already."

"What happened?" I asked, astounded to hear they'd broken up.

"We move to new house. Alex share house with his friend. Friend no like me. Then I have fight with owner of house. Nasty woman, she hate me. I cannot stay near her. She speak bad to me every day, call me bad name. She speak in Thai. Alex no understand. I have to leave. Go back to Ubon."

"It's finished with Alex? Are you sure?"

"Finish. He said he send me money. He bullshit me. Money no come. He

304

want me get job, work as servant in hotel."

I grieved for her and didn't know what to say. "Are you going to Phuket alone?" I asked.

"Father with me. I go work in bar. Make money *kai hee* (sell cunt)."

The next day, as the porters dragged my luggage out the door, I wasn't thinking too much about Hoi. Or Nok, Pong, Tik, Chai, and the other Patpong prostitutes. Instead, I thought of the Thai men I'd known—Jek, Toom, Em, and the Chiang Mai trail guide I'd spent a memorable night with on a mountain top.

With six other people in my group, I'd trekked for two days into the territory of an indigenous mountain tribe. Wearing ancient dress with beaded headgear; the tribal people welcomed us and taught us folk dances. In an interlaced ring of natives and tourists, we stomped and clapped round a fire.

When the guide distributed blankets for us to bed down on the ground, my trailmates went off to sleep. I stayed at the dying fire, chatting with the guide as the camp sounds grew quiet. We lowered our voices and drew closer together. When only the night creatures could be heard hooting and gnawing, the guide and I went to his personal hut made of bamboo and thatch by that mysterious tribe in that exotic jungle on a mountain somewhere near Burma.

At dawn the next day, we raced down the mountain on rapids. As the guide poled our raft around perilous turns and protruding rocks, he threw me flirty looks. He'd promised to take me on a free tour of Chiang Mai on his motorbike that night.

Thailand was a paradise for Western women too.

Afterword
1991, New York

When I presented my dissertation back in New York, no one complained about the graphic description of the Fucking Show at Supergirl or the diagram of the Rose Bar with X's marking the three blow jobs in progress. The professors accepted the thesis entirely, except for one thing.

"You proceeded with the research after the Thai government denied you permission!" exclaimed the only male on the dissertation committee.

Oh, dear. I'd forgotten about that.

"Didn't you think of future graduate students who now may be mistrusted by the countries they want to study?" he continued. "You were in Thailand as a representative of your school! Your fellow anthropologists! The United States!"

Oh my god. S.O.S. hormones flooded my bloodstream as I realized that calamity was upon me. Why had I never connected the Thai government, the research, and my school? Too much distance in time and space, maybe.

"We have enough trouble as it is, getting foreign nations to grant research visas," the professor declared with an ominous squeeze of his eyebrows. "It's imperative that we be regarded as possessing the social conscience of scientists."

Feeling like an embarrassment to the entire discipline of anthropology, I imagined my three years of work flushing down the drain. I wanted to burrow into the carpet. What would I do if the committee rejected the dissertation?

Through a fog of despair that my life was over, I heard him advise me to ask the American Anthropological Association to send me their Principles of Professional Responsibility. He suggested I read their guidelines on ethical behavior and add five pages to the appendix, justifying my defiance of the Thai government's wishes.

My life wasn't over? All I had to do was justify my motives? Was that it?

In a surge of relief, I knew that would be easy.

I would center my defense on AIDS in Thailand. Besides prostitution, AIDS was a topic the Thai government wished to repress. Thailand kept secret its true rate of HIV infection in order to preserve its tourist trade. If I could show how the policy of secrecy served financial interests but caused disservice to the people, my actions would be vindicated. To defer to an information blackout was to support the status quo, whether it be Thailand's mistreatment of women or the unchecked spread of AIDS. A true social conscience would challenge a distorted system, not support it.

So I wrote the additional five pages, outlining the American Anthropological Association's guidelines concerning responsibility to the people under study, the scholarly community, and the host government. Then I documented what happened in September 1989, when word leaked out that three prostitutes, diagnosed HIV positive, were found working in the Southern Thai town of Hat Yai. It was Malaysia that broke the story, and a newspaper debate between Thailand and Malaysia continued for several weeks. A headline article for the *Bangkok Post* reported:

Hat Yai—Malaysia's campaign against the danger of AIDS in Thailand is seriously affecting tourism in this Southern border town, tourism officials and hotel operators say.

Malaysia has stepped up a campaign against AIDS at its border checkpoint, warning its citizens headed for Hat Yai about the deadly disease . . .The more than 60 hotels in Hat Yai are losing one to three million *baht* a month.

The lull in business, though, lasted a short time, and eventually Hat Yai's tourism returned to normal. Meanwhile, during the same week when the above article appeared, another *Bangkok Post* front page showed a picture of people dressed as condoms holding a sign proclaiming "Thailand Responds to AIDS." The caption read "'Condom Night with Mechai' a big hit on Patpong." Because of the publicity about the infected prostitutes, over 10,000 condoms had been distributed to Patpong bar girls and customers. Mechai, the spokesman for the Population and Community Development Association, was quoted as saying that bar owners had previously refused to listen to his warnings, but "Now they understand that we are campaigning for a good cause and know that if AIDS is not stopped there will be no customers."

Breaking Thailand's silence about AIDS had had a positive result.

I received no further objections to my disobedience of the National Research Council of Thailand.

A year later, in May 1991, I presented a paper for the Gender and Industrialization in Asia conference at the State University of New York. The conference included a Korean woman who discussed the plight of female factory workers in her country's textile industry. Under the influence of Confucian patriarchy, females were exploited as cheap, nonunionized, docile workers who couldn't earn enough for subsistence without double shifts.

An Indian woman reported how her government had slowed the fad of bride burning. In some parts of India, families had been arranging marriages for their sons to women with dowries. Then they'd set fire to the women and keep the booty. The Indian professor noted that, though progress had been made on the issue of bride burning, female infants were dying due to systematic neglect. To rid themselves of valueless female children, people allowed infant girls to waste away.

Another participant revealed that, in China, some families aborted female fetuses to ensure a son under the rule of one child per family. Someone raised the question: What happens to the Indian and Chinese men who remain spouseless due to a shortage of women? The answer came during a presentation by the representative from Vietnam. He described the abduction of young girls from Northern Vietnam, taken from the country to serve as wives or be forced into brothels.

When my turn came, I traced the history of prostitution in Thailand and tied it to the low status of women. The two Thai participants at the conference, professional women from the elite class, objected. They accused me of being ethnocentric for advocating sexual liberation for Thai women. One was particularly incensed by the report I gave on Hoi. In a private discussion, she told me I should have used another example of a bar girl to show that not all were bad like Hoi. To her, Hoi was no good because she became attracted to men while with Alex, the idea being that, even as a prostitute, a woman is supposed to be faithful to her man. A woman must repress her own desires, whether she's a wife or a paid companion.

It is not my intention to glorify Patpong prostitution. To do so would be to exalt the institutions that give rise to it—the poverty of much of the Thai populace and the inequality between Thai males and females. Nonetheless, to me the prostitutes are pioneers in advancing women's autonomy by breaking from the mold of suppressed and passive females. In the same way that soldiers striding into battle are called brave and patriotic regardless of whether they enlisted or were drafted by the government, Thai prostitutes can be called pioneers in defying women's subjugation. They allow themselves this little bit of selfishness and self-indulgence, which Thai culture otherwise denies them.

I can understand how advocating equal rights to sexuality may be viewed as ethnocentric to women who are fighting for the more basic right of allowing female babies to live. However, for the Korean factory workers, the fried brides, the aborted female fetuses, and the women stolen from Vietnam, the issue is, in fact, the same—the devaluation of the female gender.

As for me, I miss Thailand terribly. I miss the scents, the *tuk-tuks*, and the singing sound of the language. I miss tasting strange fruit and standing still twice a day while the king's anthem blasts from public places. I miss seeing life through a double perspective, mine and someone else's, therefore seeing the illusions of both. Living in a foreign culture makes one's own seem less absolute.

BIBLIOGRAPHY

Boonsong, Chamlong. "Ordeals of Hilltribe Girl Prostitutes." *The Nation* (Bangkok newspaper), Jan. 20, 1985, pp. 1 & 2; Jan. 21, p. 5; Jan. 22, p. 5; Jan. 23, p. 5.

Boontawee, Kampoon. *A Child of the Northeast.* D. K. Books, Bangkok: 1988.

Brown, Wilmette. "Money for Prostitutes Is Money for Black Women." *Black Women for Wages for Housework*, New York: Feb. 1977.

Chulachart, Vipa. Introduction to Aspects of Thai Women Today. Presented for the World Conference of the U.N. Decade for Women by the Thailand National Commission on Women's Affairs, Copenhagen: 1980.

Cohen, Eric. "Lovelorn Farangs: The Correspondence Between Foreign Men and Thai Girls." *Anthropological Quarterly*, 59 (3), pp. 114-127: 1986.

———. "Sensuality and Venality in Bangkok: The Dynamics of Cross Cultural Mapping of Prostitution." *Deviant Behavior* 8, pp. 223-234: 1987.

Delacoste, Frederique, and Priscilla Alexander, eds. *Sex Work: Writings by Women in the Sex Industry.* Cleis Press, U.S.A.: 1987.

De Leeuw, Hendrik. *Cities of Sin.* Henderson and Spalding, G.B.: 1934.

Dharmasakti, Sanya, and Wimolsiri Jamnarnwej. "The Status of Women in Thailand: A Working Paper for the United Nations Seminar on the Status of Women in Family Law." Tokyo: May 8-21, 1962.

Ekachai, Sanitsuda. "Inside the Teahouses of Yaowarat." *Bangkok Post*, Mar. 8, 1984, p. 6.

———. "Helping Child Workers Cope with City Life." *Bangkok Post*, Oct. 4, 1988, p. 31.

Empower. "This Is Us." The Patpong musical, written and directed by Aurapin Dararatana, Bangkok: 1987.

En Route: Tourism Business Newsletter, Vol. 1, No. 16, J 1989.

Fawcett, James, Siew-Ean Khoo, and Peter Smith, eds. *Women in the Cities of Asia: Migration and Urban Adaptation.* Westview Press: 1984.

Hantrakul, Sukanya. "Prostitution in Thailand." Paper presented to the Women in Asia workshop, Monash Univ., Melbourne: July 22-24, 1983.

————. "Prostitution in Thailand." In *Development and Displacement: Women in Southeast Asia.* Glen Chandler, Norma Sullivan, Jan Branson, eds. *Monash Papers on Southeast Asia* #18 for S.E.A. Studies, Australia (date not available).

Inbaraj, Sonny. "Great Expectations That End in Misery." *The Nation* (newspaper), June 21, 1988, p. 31.

Jaroonpanth, Kanokrat. "Where Prostitution Is a Way of Life." *Bangkok Post,* Nov. 16, 1988, pp. 31, 34.

Kanwerayotin, Supapohn. "More New Faces in the World's Oldest Profession." *Bangkok Post,* Oct. 28, 1988, p. 31.

Karnjanauksorn, Teeranat. "Gender Relations, Sex-Related Services and the Development of the Thai Economy." Paper presented at the Association for Asian Studies annual meeting, Boston, April 11, 1987.

Keyes, Charles. "Isan." Regionalism in Northeastern Thailand Data Paper #65. Cornell Univ.: 1967.

Khalaf, Samir. *Prostitution in a Changing Society: A Sociological Survey of Legal Prostitution in Beirut.* Khayats, Beirut: 1965.

Leigh, Carol. "The Continuing Saga of Scarlot Harlot." *Sex Work: Writings by Women in the Sex Industry.* Delacoste and Alexander, eds. Cleis Press, U.S.A.: 1987.

Muangman, Debhanom, and Somsak Nanta. "Report on A.K.A.P. Study of 1,000 Thai Masseuses Concerning Family Planning, Pregnancy and Abortion, Venereal Disease Infections, and Narcotics Addiction." UNFPA Project No. THA/76/PO5/E22-011. Mahidol Univ., Bangkok: 1980.

Nash, June, and Maria Fernandez-Kelly, eds. *Women and Men and the International Division of Labor.* SUNY Press, Albany: 1983.

The Nation (newspaper). "Officials Mum over Child Prostitution Rise Report." Jan. 17, 1989, p. 1.

Nestle, Joan. "Lesbians and Prostitutes: A Historical Sisterhood." *Good Girls Bad Girls: Feminist and Sex Trade Workers Face to Face.* Seal Press, Toronto: 1987.

Ong, Aihwa. "Industrialization and Prostitution in Southeast Asia." *Southeast Asia Chronicle,* Jan. 1985, p. 96.

Phongpaichit, Pasuk. *From Peasant Girls to Bangkok Masseuses.* International Labour Office, Geneva: 1982.

Rattanawannatip, Mayuree. "Prostitution Plays on Rural Ignorance." *The Nation* (newspaper), Feb. 18, 1988: p. 16.

Rosen, Ruth. *The Lost Sisterhood: Prostitution in America, 1900-1918.* Johns Hopkins Univ. Press: 1982.

Schalbruch, Martin. "The Hind Legs of the Elephant." *Bangkok Post*, Aug. 14, 1988, p. 25.

Sereewat, Sudarat. "Sex for Sale." Pamphlet for the Women's Information Center, Bangkok: 1983.

Sereny, Gitta. *The Invisible Children: Child Prostitution in America, West Germany and Great Britain.* Alfred A. Knopf: 1985.

Thai Development Newsletter, Fourth Quarter, Vol. 2, No. 3 (Issue 4) 2: 1984.

———. Second Quarter, Vol. 4, No. 1: 1986.

Tongudai, Pawadee. "Women Migrants in Bangkok: An Economic Analysis of Their Employment and Earnings." In *Women in the Urban and Industrial Workforce Southeast and East Asia.* Ed Gavin Jones, ed. The Australian National University: 1984.

Usher, Ann. "The Dangerous Truth of 'Foreign Bodies'." *The Nation* (newspaper), Aug. 19, 1988, p. 31.

Ward, Barbara, ed. *Women in the New Asia: The Changing Social Roles of Men and Women in South and South-East Asia.* UNESCO, Amsterdam: 1963.

Wongpanich, Malinee. "Health Development of Women in Thailand." Aspects of Thai Women Today, presented for The World Conference of the U.N. Decade for Women by the Thailand National Commission on Women's Affairs, Copenhagen: 1980.